They had to get out of the burning house or a lack of oxygen would suffocate them.

Two kicks and the barrier fell outward. Rowan turned to Jo and swung her into his arms. With her clasped against his chest, he ducked his head and stepped sideways through the gap and into the sunlight.

God, life was great!

He made it to the lawn. With his lungs heaving, he halted and watched the fire swallow up the room they'd fled from with less than a second to spare.

Rowan threw back his head as relief ripped a huge bellow of glad-to-be-alive laughter from his throat. Then he turned his attention to Jo.

Perspiration beaded her forehead, and smoky trails of tears painted her cheeks. She'd never looked more beautiful. She was alive. *They* were alive.

"Rowan…" Her lips seemed to tremble on his name. Her beautiful mouth filled his vision. His head dipped to take her lips with his own. Just one kiss. A hero's kiss. He was entitled, and this time he would claim it.

Dear Reader,

It's August, and our books are as hot as the weather, so if it's romantic excitement you crave, look no further. Merline Lovelace is back with the newest CODE NAME: DANGER title, *Texas Hero*. Reunion romances are always compelling, because emotions run high. Add the spice of danger and you've got the perfection of the relationship between Omega agent Jack Carstairs and heroine-in-danger Ellie Alazar.

ROMANCING THE CROWN continues with Carla Cassidy's *Secrets of a Pregnant Princess*, a marriage-of-convenience story featuring Tamiri princess Samira Kamal and her mysterious bodyguard bridegroom. Marie Ferrarella brings us another of THE BACHELORS OF BLAIR MEMORIAL in *M.D. Most Wanted*, giving the phrase "doctor-patient confidentiality" a whole new meaning. Award-winning New Zealander Frances Housden makes her second appearance in the line with *Love Under Fire*, and her fellow Kiwi Laurey Bright checks in with *Shadowing Shahna*. Finally, wrap up the month with Jenna Mills and her latest, *When Night Falls*.

Next month, return to Intimate Moments for more fabulous reading—including the newest from bestselling author Sharon Sala, *The Way to Yesterday*. Until then...enjoy!

Yours,

Leslie J. Wainger
Executive Senior Editor

Please address questions and book requests to:
Silhouette Reader Service
U.S.: 3010 Walden Ave., P.O. Box 1325, Buffalo, NY 14269
Canadian: P.O. Box 609, Fort Erie, Ont. L2A 5X3

Love Under Fire
FRANCES HOUSDEN

Silhouette®

INTIMATE MOMENTS™

Published by Silhouette Books

America's Publisher of Contemporary Romance

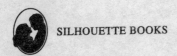

SILHOUETTE BOOKS

ISBN 0-373-27238-3

LOVE UNDER FIRE

This edition published by arrangement with Harlequin Books S.A.

® and TM are trademarks of Harlequin Books S.A., used under license. Trademarks indicated with ® are registered in the United States Patent and Trademark Office, the Canadian Trade Marks Office and in other countries.

Visit Silhouette at www.eHarlequin.com

Printed in U.S.A.

Books by Frances Housden

Silhouette Intimate Moments

The Man for Maggie #1056
Love Under Fire #1168

FRANCES HOUSDEN

has always been a voracious reader, but she never thought of being a writer until a teacher gave her the encouragement she needed to put pen to paper. As a result, Frances was a finalist for the 1998 Clendon Award and won the award in 1999, which led to the sale of her first book for Silhouette, *The Man for Maggie*. Frances also teaches a continuing education course in romance writing at the University of Auckland.

Frances's marriage to a Navy man took her from her birthplace in Scotland to New Zealand. Now he's a land-lubber and most of the traveling they do is together. They live on a ten-acre bush block in the heart of Auckland's Wine District. She has two large sons, two tiny grandsons and a wheaten terrier named Siobhan. Thanks to one teacher's dedication, Frances now gets to write about the kinds of men a woman would travel to the ends of the earth for.

This one is for family. My darling husband, Keith, for all his encouragement, my sister-in-law, Susan Church, for her courage to read my first draft, and in memory of my mother-in-law, Yvonne, who introduced me to the delights of reading romance. Also, my thanks to Graham Pelham for teaching this perennially bad sailor to drive a boat without ever having to leave solid ground.

Prologue

Life as Jo Jellic knew it had become increasingly filled with little quirks. Okay, so she was being facetious, yet less than an hour and a half ago, she'd anticipated spending the evening in the local pub with her colleagues. After letting out a collective sigh, they'd have let off a little steam, celebrating the successful conclusion of a case which had tied them up 24/7 for four months.

Instead, she was up to her elbows in dirt, listening to an ultimatum—"I'll give you five minutes to back off or I'll shoot the girl"—with the *whaump, whaump, whaump* of the helicopter they'd arrived in still hanging in the air.

Every breath was filled with dust, its bitter tang coating her tongue, no matter how hard she swallowed.

Her meager cover was a scrubby pittosporum bush and twenty yards away, on the other side, Maggie, the best friend she'd ever had, was being held hostage.

Jo squinted, eyes straining to cut through the darkness. "Where the hell is Max?" She shred the words between teeth clamped as tight as her jaw. No need for anyone but her to know her boss had gone walkabout. Only a minute ago, Detective Sergeant Max Strachan had been positioned not less than five yards away. His disappearance wasn't part of the plan, though understanding his desperation, she couldn't give him away. Just this afternoon, Max had asked Maggie to marry him.

This was the man she'd actually imagined herself in love with for years, but naturally it had been one-sided. Max didn't find her all that lovable and who could blame him? She was a product of the job she did, made by the career she loved. A person couldn't work the homicide cases she had and remain the same naive girl she'd been when she joined the force.

It was as if she'd locked all her finer feelings inside and thrown away the key. The truth about love had struck her that afternoon when she'd watched Max and Maggie together. If she ever found a man who could bring out her softer side, she'd know the love was real.

What a time to start bleating, Jellic. She had more immediate problems, like what could she do about Max?

Senior Sergeant Rowan McQuaid on her other side was in no doubt of her feelings for Max. Hell, they'd been making book on it at Auckland Central, betting on the outcome, but their money hadn't been on her. Soon they'd be able to collect. She'd a notion if she started fussing over Max, Rowan would think she'd given in to her own brand of paranoia.

Jo huffed out air to release her tension. It didn't work. Her heartbeat raced on a full head of steam, her grip tightening on the 9mm Glock held against her cheek. Metal that had once been cool to the touch now burned in her hand.

She stared into the growing darkness on her left. This shouldn't be happening now, not in the middle of a hostage drama. Max was in charge. He'd no right to leave. They'd departed Auckland on what seemed a whim, unprepared for an armed siege.

Sure, the Armed Offenders Squad were on their way, but for now, they had to make do with two detectives, including herself, a senior sergeant and the helicopter jockey who had ferried them to the vineyard. Add to that four local cops, country cops, nervous as hell and excited to boot, who'd probably be about as much use as her Glock when it came to hitting a target in the gloomy light.

"Ooh." Darned if there wasn't a bug crawling up her arm on the inside of her sleeve. She shuddered. Man, she hated bugs. She hated dirt, too, yet her fingernails had clawed grooves in the ground. Pushing up on the ball of her palm, she paid for her view with the fetid stench of wormy earth on a defrost cycle.

Give her the city any day. She breathed easier with asphalt underfoot and streetlights overhead. This country stuff was a whole other world.

She pushed up higher. Well, the view was better, but Max wasn't part of it. Drat the man. She hoped he wasn't doing something stupid.

Glancing over her shoulder she watched Rowan. At least *he* was still in position, though facing toward the youngest of the cops they'd brought in to help. Knowing Rowan, he'd be doing his level best to calm the kid's nerves. Something about his size was reassuring; the sergeant had muscles to die for, and didn't have a nervous bone in his body. Always in control, that was Rowan.

Turning back, she caught a glimpse of movement, a glimpse of black hair slashed with silver darting through the trees. Max.

Anger and fear clutched at her chest, followed by guilt. She might have missed him by letting her attention wander. The urge to haul Max back screamed up her arm. As if *he* gave a snap of the fingers for her wants. Maggie, the woman Max loved, was inside the house. Nothing, absolutely nothing, she or anyone else said was going stop him acting the fool for love.

"Is Max all right?" Rowan whispered as a movement at the window caught her eye. A glimmer of light slid down the dull-gray barrel of the rifle following Max's trail like a heat-seeking missile.

Everything she'd ever been taught about safety sloughed right off. *Distract the gunman or Max's as good as dead.* "He's gone!" she shouted to warn Rowan as she leaped to her feet. The rifle in the window swung, taking a bead on her position. She couldn't move as fast.

"Damn and blast!" yelled Rowan.

A thud of feet and snap of twigs raced time, raced the swing of the barrel. No time to yell, "Stay down!" Although time appeared to stop, she didn't have any. Then his hand gripped her shoulder.

An inane thought that this was the first time he'd ever laid hands on her, struck at the same moment a shot cracked and the air beside them opened in a rush.

Rowan lunged, his legs straddling hers. His large body barreling into hers dragged her down. She tasted dirt. The scent of dead leaves, grave-cold earth and the coppery tang of blood filled every breath.

Blood? Who was bleeding?

Though Rowan's weight crushed her, she felt no pain.

As the truth hit, she wanted to scream, "Noooooo!" And she did. "No, no, no," she repeated the word, repeated the prayer.

She squeezed out from under his lax body and struggled to her knees as if daring the gunman to try again. Blood and some other stuff she didn't want to put a name to covered her shoes. "God, don't let him be dead." Groaning, she rolled him over.

There was no need to feel for his carotid pulse. Proof of life pulsed in the fountain of blood gushing from a hole the size of a fist in his thigh. "You fool, McQuaid. What you want to go and do that for?" She dragged the sleeves of her jacket down her arms and flung it aside.

"I don't want you to die for me." There were no other sounds in the world except her beating heart and Velcro ripping as she pulled at the straps of her Kevlar vest. Peeling the vest off, she started in on her shirt buttons. "I don't need a stand-in. I'm quite capable of dying by myself."

"Is Sergeant McQuaid all right?"

She'd forgotten that anyone but Rowan and her existed. Her shirt was off, and the kid Rowan had helped was staring at her underwear. "No, he's not all right. We need an ambulance."

"I already called the paramedics."

He hunkered down at Rowan's head and continued to stare. She knew he was waiting for orders, but her mind raced faster than her lips could frame the words. And no wonder. She was kneeling in the dirt, her hands fighting to staunch the flow of blood with her second-best shirt, while all she wanted to do was howl, to let her feminine side have its way and cry her damn eyes out. But there was no time. She didn't know where Max had gone but Rowan was down and that made her in charge.

"Press down on this, kid. Let's hope the ambulance doesn't take too long," she told him and shrugged back into her vest, then jacket while he complied. She nudged his hand aside, replacing it with hers. "Now give me your shirt and your belt," she ordered, digging her other fist into Rowan's groin in search of the pressure point.

Too busy now for tears, she'd save them for another day, praying that it wouldn't be at his funeral.

Chapter 1

A little over two years later

"**B**abe alert."

The shout jarred Jo out of a daydream. Her head jerked around in time to see the fierce concentration on Ginny's face as a piercing, two-note twist of air whistled through the gap in her front teeth. Then awe threaded a breathless gasp. "Cooool."

Good grief, had she ever been so young?

Thank heavens the air-conditioning god insisted on tightly closed windows; she'd hate anyone to think the wolf whistle came from her.

Jo had been quite content to layer her own thoughts over her passenger's prattle—*prisoner* was too harsh a word. Ginny sure could talk, and had started the moment she entered the car taking her to the station house. The constant stream of words laced with a mixture of nerves and relief, had settled into a comfortable drone in her ears when Ginny's shout brought her out of her reverie.

By rights, it should have been the owner of the Two Dollar Shop on the receiving end of all her youthful fervor. The suggestion to let Ginny off with a warning for shoplifting had come from him. Yet from the moment Jo had explained the conditions she'd been promoted to saint...well, let's say knighthood.

It was kind of nice, really.

Half an hour later she was redundant. Ginny had found someone new to worship. Replaced by a babe no less.

"Where? I can't see him." She might be twice Ginny's age, and then some, but she wasn't immune to an attractive male, so she let her gaze follow the direction of Ginny's pointing finger. No use. The glare of late-October spring sunshine against the windshield blinded her. All she got for her effort was the impression of an elongated black shadow sliding across the white weatherboards cladding the Nicks Landing station house.

Wasn't that always the way? One bright spot in a mediocre day, and she'd missed it. Win some, lose some, usually the latter.

A designated parking space was one of the perks of being a detective, and Jo automatically swung into hers.

"Look out!"

Heart pumping, Jo slammed the brake pedal to the floor, skinning a week's worth of rubber off the tires in the process.

"Darn," she spat, ever mindful of her fourteen-year-old passenger, the ineffectual curse bearing no resemblance to her true feelings. "I don't believe this."

She blinked and shook her head but the Jaguar S-type, squatting between the white lines of her parking space, was still there. Two vacant spaces, yet again, someone stole hers. Some people simply failed to comprehend the meaning of the word *reserved*.

Jo spun her car back into the road. Chances were she'd find a spot in the small, crowded visitor's parking lot on the far side of the station house.

Two years she'd worked out of this station house, and still

was no wiser why, out of the three spaces assigned to detectives, no one ever pinched the other two?

"Now that's what I call a car," said Ginny.

About to agree, she caught the tail end of Ginny's expression. So her car wasn't top of the line. She liked it. Tongue in cheek, Jo responded, "Pretty good huh? Maybe they'll deliver mine next week." Ginny's jaw dropped. Jo's smile said, "tit for tat."

"So...did you recognize *the babe,* Ginny?"

The girl's smile was dreamy. "I wish."

"What do you think, should I give him a ticket?" Jo joked.

"Noooo!" Ginny squealed. "The guy wouldn't know any better. He's not from Nicks Landing. *Him* I would have remembered."

Same goes. Of course it was that Jag, Jo had in mind.

Who was she kidding? Since arriving in Nicks Landing, there had been a dearth of any male who could draw a wolf whistle from her lips, or she suspected, even Ginny's.

She wasn't sure why, but she felt drawn to the girl. Perhaps she found an echo of her own patchy youth in Ginny's overbright chatter.

Rounding the side of the station house, her car began to whine. Envious of the leashed power nestling under the Jag's hood, no doubt. Well, her mind had been on other matters, too. Male matters. Changing down a notch fixed her car's complaint, but didn't stop her wondering what kind of man it took to handle such lethal-looking power.

Slotting her car into the only available space, she imagined her palms wrapped round the walnut steering wheel of the Jag, and took vicarious pleasure in imagining the money-flavored newness of the leather. She resisted an envious sigh and instead, unfolded her six-foot length from the driver's seat.

Once, she'd been secure in the knowledge of her own personal worth, her own capabilities. Not anymore. Living in Nicks Landing had done a number on her ego. A few more friends might have sweetened her stay, made her feel less of an outsider. Maybe...

With Ginny skipping to keep up with her longer stride, Jo glanced at the white station house. Two years on and she still hadn't gotten over her first impression. That down-home, country look didn't quite gel with what went on inside. Friday and Saturday nights were the worst. That's when the drunks came out to play. The local innkeeper couldn't seem to tell when they'd had enough. Oh, he'd excuses aplenty. Personally, Jo figured it had more to do with getting back at them for still being cops while he'd been made redundant, though no one else saw it that way. Hell, maybe her prejudice *was* showing.

Since it was closer, she shepherded Ginny to the back entrance.

"Coming through."

The warning left barely enough time to pull Ginny to the side of the ramp as Seth McAllister, the cop who manned the reception, ran past. "Where's the fire?" she called to his back view.

"Personal emergency."

Jo could have said, "Again?" but kept her own counsel. Seemed Seth had one of those emergencies at least once a month. The fact that he and his wife were desperately trying to conceive a child couldn't have anything to do with it. And pigs could fly!

The air in the station house rang blue with curses. Someone was putting the boot into one of the metal cell doors. The lockup was pretty rowdy considering it was only two in the afternoon. She noticed Ginny wince and hardened her heart against an urge to erase the fear she could see in her young eyes. Fist clenched close to her thigh, Jo's emotions warred between duty and empathy. There was a lesson for Ginny to learn here. A lesson that would do the girl more good than harm. Jo swallowed the tightness clogging her throat as she guided the teenager to a bench on the wall. Jo remembered the first time she'd visited the cells. Yeah, she knew what it felt like.

"Sit." She squeezed out the command, aware of how

brusque she sounded. And when Ginny bobbed up again, hovering nervously a few inches above the seat, added, "Stay." Ginny's blue eyes paled against the whites as they widened. Blood drained from her face and promoted her carrot-colored frizz from unusual to startling.

The color of that hair was one reason Jo had known the kid couldn't seriously have intended to steal. The idea of pink barrettes holding back such riotous brilliance put the mind on hold. Though she allowed there was something about pink that tempted with its sheer femininity. That was something else she'd remembered since picking up the girl.

Gently, she pressed Ginny down to the bench. "You're okay here. No one will hurt you." Jo nodded toward the desk. "See the sergeant over there? He'll look out for you."

As always, Jo's first glimpse of Senior Sergeant Harry Jackson reminded her of her father. Maybe it was the silver buttons sparkling against the navy uniform, or an echo in the mannerisms. After all this time, the subject was still up for discussion.

Her first memories of her father had to be of those buttons. She'd sit on his knee, feel the scratchy wool under her skinny little legs, and play with the shiny baubles while he told her about the events of his day. Of course he'd always been the knight in shining armor, rescuing fair maidens, locking the bad guys up.

Even after he'd made detective, she'd waited for his stories, sometimes falling asleep before he got home. Two weeks into the job she'd realized he'd always given her the abridged edition.

The day he died had felt like they'd amputated her soul.

Four sons and one daughter he'd had, and out of them all, she was the only one following in his footsteps. Maybe being the youngest, she'd been the only one not taken in with their lies about him.

Jo caught her bottom lip in her teeth, stifling a grin at the way Harry ignored the clamor around him. He looked up as she approached, putting down his pen.

"Busy day, Sergeant?"

"Just a couple of local bad guys Bull and Jake caught growing cannabis in a house they'd rented. A right pair of smartasses! They lined the walls with foil and grew the weed under lights."

Jo's hearing pricked up at the mention of drugs. Features bland, she prevented her longings from showing. Those kinds of cases seldom came her way now, and though her homicide training might have given her an edge in that area, no one had been murdered in Nicks County since the day she'd arrived.

Her immediate superiors seemed to be under the impression shoplifting and breaking-and-entering were more her speed. It wasn't as if she'd never protested. She had, long and loud. Which was one reason why *the boys* had handed over the one case they hadn't known she wanted. The one they'd decided would never be solved. An assault on Rocky Skelton, local innkeeper, purportedly by satanists who'd torched his house with him inside.

It was the kind of tale that made her eyes roll. Satanists in Nicks Landing...it sounded like a play on words, but when she'd mentioned "Old Nicks Landing," no one had laughed.

She'd had her eyes on Skelton from the moment she'd hit town. Finding her father's ex-partner running a bar in Nicks Landing had been like striking gold. And landing the case had been finding the mother lode, as if some power was at work, nudging her on, helping her to resolve the past. So what if her means of getting to Nicks Landing had come through a sideways demotion? They'd blamed her for what happened to Rowan. But in comparison, none of that mattered now. She'd been in the right place at the right time. Her father had been innocent and this might be her chance to prove it.

Harry's expression grew paternal, a ridiculous state of affairs as barely eight years separated them. "Nothing to worry your head about, little lady," he said in reference to the drug bust.

Maybe it was just Harry's protective instincts, and if so the disease was endemic. Where once she'd found it amusing, slightly endearing, now she felt smothered by living in male-chauvinist territory. If anyone in Nicks County had ever heard of equal rights for women, they'd quickly forgotten it.

Nicks Landing was about two hundred and fifty miles from Auckland where she'd worked before, and about fifty years backward in time. Located on New Zealand's East Coast, it was the sort of place needing a detour—and a damn good reason—to visit. It certainly wasn't on anyone's way to anywhere else.

The reasons she'd been transferred there were solid, nothing to be proud of, and she'd taken her licks, no sense in making excuses. She hadn't expected to be the only woman working out of the station house, or that she'd still be the only one today.

"Who have we got here?" Harry asked, nodding toward Ginny.

Jo's mind shifted gear and she told Harry. "Ginny Wilks. The owner of the Two Dollar Shop caught her slipping some plastic barrettes into her pocket. He didn't want to press charges, though, just give her a warning. Can you call this number and get her mother to come pick her up? She should be all right sitting here with you. I'll be upstairs if you need me. Call me when her mother arrives."

Jo had just turned away when she remembered. "Someone stole my space again."

"I keep telling you, take one of the other guys'."

Shaking her head, she didn't pursue it. Harry didn't realize she couldn't do the very thing she was complaining of to someone else. She couldn't be that hypocritical, or dishonest. Twelve years' service and she still felt the need to mind her p's and q's.

"I just wondered who owned the S-type Jag."

Harry's smile deepened, becoming more knowing than friendly. "Go on upstairs and find out for yourself. He's in your office."

The words *your office* were a misnomer. Harry knew it and so did she. Jo shared with two other detectives, including Detective Senior Sergeant Bull Cowan. Since his section took up half the space, the likelihood of the car's owner actually waiting to see her, in *her* office, wasn't something she contemplated.

Logic told her the driver and the stranger Ginny had admired earlier were one and the same. It could prove interesting to discover if he lived up to his car's image, and Ginny's high approbation.

In less than a minute she would know.

The stairs disappeared behind her two at a time. She stopped her momentum by grasping the door handle, her palm sweating lightly in anticipation of *the babe* being inside. She heard a rumble of male voices through the gaps where the door didn't fit the frame, too indistinct to decipher, and behind the gold-leaf lettering and frosted glass panel, their images blurred grotesquely.

Silently, she eased the door open, keeping hold of the handle so it wouldn't spring back and give her presence away. She indulged her curiosity by watching through the six-inch gap. *Disappointment,* she decided, wasn't a word she would use in the same breath as this man, not even from behind.

He had legs a mile high slicked in black denim. The supple, wash-softened fabric gloved his muscled thighs and calves in a way that set her mouth watering.

She knew her weaknesses.

His butt wasn't half-bad, either. At least nine on a scale of ten. Just looking at those firm glutes made Jo's hormones twitchy—a sensation she'd almost forgotten existed. And as if anything more was needed, he drove a Jag, her favorite car. Together they made one very attractive combination.

Sunshine caressed his tawny hair, the way a woman might to determine if the waves were real. It tipped the collar of his black cotton Polo shirt, which told her he wasn't a cop, another point in his favor. To date, her association with the male members of her fraternity had been doomed to failure. She'd found that breed never let a lie stand in the way of a good story.

As a child, she'd grown up glorifying the force and its aims. Seeing it through her father's eyes. But her father's death had shattered her rose-colored glasses and she'd mourned the loss of her ideal almost as much as she'd mourned her father.

Jo's mouth twisted as she puzzled over his presence. Could be the guy was undercover. In that case, why Nicks Landing? Nothing here ever warranted that kind of scenario. The biggest excitement to hit the sleepy little burg occurred two and a half months ago, and was the case they'd handed her on a platter. Because of its black-magic aspects, the media, TV and newspapers, had given the story a whirl at first, but that had died a natural death. Hence her male colleagues' unconditional generosity toward her.

She'd never believed Rocky Skelton's story. Satanists lurking in small-town New Zealand? Give her a break. Besides, she'd known for most of her life that the man was a liar.

Why should this time be any different?

Jo's gaze slid up the tall stranger's spine. It was a long, long spine, supporting a broad back and wide shoulders that hid the man he was talking to. Although, Bull Cowan's flat country twang was more distinct now that the door was open.

It wasn't every day of the week a woman got to see shoulders that broad. The fine knit of his shirt clung to them like a lover's caress. Jo sighed. She should be so lucky.

As she continued to watch, the palm of his large hand fanned over the back of his neck. His muscles flexed under the sheen of taut, golden skin, stretching the ribbed band on his sleeve. He had the kind of lean strength she liked, powerful without being bulky or obvious, hardly an ounce of fat on his body. As she speculated about the amount of work it took to look that good, Jo felt something curl deep in her belly, then expand as heat, sending a bloom of warmth across her skin.

With a twitch of her nose, she delivered a small personal chastisement. Too much fantasizing, that was it. Why, she still hadn't seen his face. Knowing her luck, he would be dog ugly, though likely he'd have more in common with a Doberman than a Saint Bernard, seeing as he was so lean.

Mind made up, she swung open the door and went to find out for herself. Both men turned as the door banged shut behind her, and Bull came into view at last. Now here was a man who lived up to his name. He had the kind of body that owed more to lifting a handle of beer than working out at the gym. Heaven only knew how he ever passed a physical.

Jo kept her eyes lowered slightly, her gaze hitting the stranger about midchest. It lingered over the glint of gold-edged sunglasses casually hooked in his shirt pocket, as a quick, indrawn breath tightened the fit of his shirt.

The view was everything she'd imagined.

Pretending disinterest, she didn't raise her eyes until she drew level and Bull was saying, "This is the *little lady* you want to talk to. Detective Jo Jellic."

Bull's *too* precious diminutive put a hex on the smile she'd been holding back to blind the stranger with. Deliberately, she thrust out her hand, getting in first.

At chin level she got her first surprise. Not at the few days growth of dark gold beard that covered his skin, but the several weeks older sun-tinted moustache. Her eyes held on it as if counting each hair, each sun-lightened strand above his full, firm mouth. If he'd been smiling, his teeth would have made a dazzling contrast to all that gold. But he wasn't.

Tilting her head—for the man topped her by at least five inches—Jo added another point to his total. It took a couple of seconds for the penny to drop, then her breath caught in her throat, and her greeting stuttered to a halt.

Shocked, her hand clutched air while she doubted her own eyes.

"Jo, meet Rowan…er…McQuaid," said Bull with a quick look at the business card in his hand.

"Rowan McQuaid," she wheezed as her oxygen ran out.

God, he'd changed!

Time froze as he looked down his long nose at her, nostrils flaring slightly, with eyes the opaque green of glass that has been battered by rough waves. Cold as ice, his hand enveloped hers. A shiver she badly wanted to hide slowly crept up her spine, never missing a notch. Jo let out another breath she hadn't realized she'd been holding as his eyes lightened and hazel flecks patterned the green, the way she remembered.

"As they say, long time no see," he drawled, a dry sound, lacking warmth.

And where was the surprise in that? The changes she perceived in this man, who had once been her friend, had all been her doing. All her fault.

"You…you look well. I hardly recognized you, Rowan."

"Well, it's been two years, and you know what they say about time." *It healed all wounds.*

But what about their friendship, could it even come close to fixing that? Jo let her hand drop, and took the opportunity to ease her tense body through the narrow space between him and her desk, wary of brushing against him.

She'd once prided herself on nerves of steel, yet they quivered now, like a plucked bowstring. It puzzled her mightily when the dull, leaden feeling of guilt she'd expected was superseded by feelings of uncertainty. As if she was indeed that *little lady* her colleagues kept calling her.

Sitting down, she took advantage of the distance the width of the desktop allowed, and sheltered behind it.

A frown shaped her brows in a V of futility. What couldn't be mended would have to be endured, for she'd demolished everything that had held them together the night Rowan had busted his leg taking a bullet meant for her.

Oh, she had paid. Paid well. Lost touch with most of her friends while she frittered away her homicide experience on jobs any beat cop could handle. But at least *she* still had her career.

She wanted to give him a great big hug to show she knew his pain, that she cared, but she was afraid any expression of empathy from her would go over like a lead balloon. Instead she asked, "How are you really doing, Rowan?"

Jo was the last person Rowan had expected to meet in Nicks Landing. Clutching tight to control, he chivvied her to prevent betraying himself. "Lighten up, Jo. Don't take it so seriously."

Don't do as I do, do as I say.

He'd outgrown the habit of enclosing his senses in a protective coating when Jo was near. He'd even ousted her from his dreams. Deliberately, he hadn't kept up with her whereabouts. Seeing her today had come as a shock. But he would be damned if he'd let her know why, or pity him for it. Feigning a grin, he put his weight on his injured leg and lifted his arms. "Look, no hands."

Jo's smile didn't reach her eyes. Their dark brown irises melted like chocolate. A look that Rowan wanted to reach out and smooth away. And therein lay the danger.

Now he knew why the hairs on the back of his neck had lifted, as if a ghostly hand ruffled them, filling his palm with an urge to brush them down. Now he knew it was a ghost from his past.

"So, Rowan, what brings you to Nicks Landing?"

"McQuaid's here about that case you're working on. Wants it cleared up fast," Bull answered for him, rushing the gate like the animal he was named for. Unlike most other things in Nicks Landing, Bull hadn't changed. He still acted the way he had when they were both boys, running wild during summer vacation.

"I thought you'd left the force...."

Her words dwindled away softly, but Rowan noticed she hadn't said "had to." Or "you were unfit." No, he'd give her that. She'd finally learned discretion. The art of not running off at the mouth and saying exactly what she was thinking.

"Take a look at this." Bull handed over Rowan's business card. "Insurance Investigator."

Rowan watched Jo's eyes linger over the card. He'd had a few of them made under two or three different headings, today's one for Allied Insurance. Few knew that even his name was misleading, only people like Bull and Harry Jackson who remembered him from the old days. He'd counted on their friendship not to give him away, using it to oil the wheels with this Skelton business.

"And what's that to do with me or my case?" Jo gasped, her mouth quivering as if disturbed by the turn of events.

Bull answered, "Allied has been taking a lot of crap from Rocky and his wife, and they want this puppy put to bed."

"Just like that. I can't just call it quits to suit your employer." Her chair bumped the wall as she stood leaning forward, fists clenched. "This case is important to me."

"C'mon now, girlie. You know that case is going nowhere."

Jo blinked, and under her lashes her eyes flashed a warning in Bull's direction before turning back in his.

She was good and mad now. He preferred her spitting fire than looking all soft and sad, tempting him to do something about it.

"I've only been on this case two weeks. That's not enough time. I need more. I deserve more."

Bull came round the side of her desk, mouth open to speak. She cut him off. "I know what you're going to say, Sergeant. You only gave me the case so I could tidy it up and stick it away in a file, but that's not the way I work."

"Don't worry, Bull. I know what Jo's like. Once she gets her teeth into something it's hard to prise them apart."

Bull looked from one to the other. Rowan could almost see his mind working. His brow furrowed and black eyebrows twitched. His mouth twisted to one side, then the other, as if making a decision his divided loyalties found difficult to spit out. "Just to be fair, I'll give you a week."

"A week!" blurted Jo.

Drawing himself up to full height, Bull sucked in air, pushing his gut up to his chest. "One week. Take it or leave it."

"I'll take it."

Regretfully, Bull wasn't done. He eyed Rowan with a lift of one brow. "McQuaid here can help you. Two heads are better than one, and maybe that way you'll both be satisfied."

Satisfied? Rowan would never dare to be satisfied when it

came to Jo. He'd spent years avoiding that kind of satisfaction. He'd recognized the danger the first moment he saw her. Like reading an old map that warned, *here be dragons*.

Although he still counted meeting Jo as the point in time when his life started going downhill, the image had fixed in his mind. A memory, which the unlikely scent of locker rooms could trigger off.

That's where he'd been, Auckland Central locker room, reading a long boring letter from his brother, Scott, after a hard night keeping his friend Max Strachan company. When your best friend's first marriage breaks up, what else can you do but help him tie one on over a bottle of whiskey?

Someone barging through the door of the shower room had jarred him from a miasma of facts and figures he really couldn't be bothered sorting, but Scott insisted on relaying. Downing a cup of coffee at his desk had suddenly seemed like a much better deal. Prepared to slip by with a quick wave and a "Hi," he'd stopped dead in his tracks, adrenaline pumping through his veins.

Wild animals took notice of the time-honored signal and ran for their lives. *He* hadn't been able to drag his gaze away.

He'd yet to see a woman who could match her. Smooth, honey-colored skin all the way down to her toes; lush, rounded hips and long, long legs that were stepping into a pair of scarlet, silky French knickers. God knows how long he stood there caught in a trap by his hormones like a pubescent schoolboy. It seemed like forever. He'd *wanted* it to be forever, even while he recognized the danger as the elastic snapped on a scrap of red silk that would color his fantasies for the rest of his life, he'd known he should leave—get out of there quick. Instead he'd taken a step back, and watched her turn to snag a matching bra from the locker.

Instant arousal!

Her long tangle of black curls swung back, revealing the face behind their curtain. Strong features, straight nose, high Slavic cheekbones and lips that even memory couldn't improve upon. All that before he'd seen her breasts. Once that

happened, his hands itched to cup them and his mouth went
dry at the thought of suckling their treacle-dark nipples.

Honey and treacle.

Poison where he was concerned.

The last thing he'd wanted from life was to meet a woman
who could tempt him to fall in love.

So, he'd worked alongside her, knowing the pain he endured was nothing compared to the hurt that loving and losing
her could bring. And he'd based his security in the knowledge
that Jo couldn't see him for Max, his best friend, and the man
Jo loved.

How was he going to get through this week and still maintain that distance? He'd shaken the dust of Nicks Landing off
his boots once before and all he could think of now was how
soon could he do it again?

A week. Seven days. A hundred and sixty-eight hours, give
or take a few if she wanted to sleep. It was going to be difficult
working alongside Rowan. She'd never felt so unsure of herself in her life. Never felt as if her life was balanced on a
knife's edge with Rowan responsible for which way she'd fall.
Never in all the years she'd known Rowan had she felt the
mouth-gaping, heart-stopping attraction he had for her now.

She and Ginny had more in common than she had realized,
for when she looked at Rowan she didn't feel any older than
the kid she'd left downstairs with Sergeant Jackson.

Why did it have to happen now, when she was on the most
important case of her life, and the prize her father's reputation?

She took a deep breath and settled the squirmy feeling in
her gut. "Okay. Here's where we start. I'll give you all I've
got to look over...."

Rowan's eyes narrowed slightly, their cool, flecked green
at odds with the slight curl of his lips. "Generous of you, Jo,
but don't you think the work on hand should be our first consideration?"

Well, she'd left herself wide open to that one and blushed.

Rowan was sharp, too sharp, but maybe she could turn it to her advantage.

"Exactly what do you think we're investigating here, Rowan? Attempted murder, attempted suicide, or just plain old fraud?"

Bull went first. "Jeez, Jo. This is Rocky Skelton you're talking about. One of us."

Jo swung around. She could see everything slipping away from her, from her father. She wanted to shut up, hold her tongue and not get into trouble, but she couldn't. "Great, well why don't we ask Rocky to help out? It's already turning into *Old Boys' Week* around here."

She lifted one hand, not to swipe at the tears frustration had brought to her eyes, but to disguise them by brushing back her hair, and found her wrist enclosed in a firm grip. Rowan's.

His fingers burned where they touched her skin. She looked up, ready to tell him not to manhandle her, and couldn't. One look at his face whitening under his tan and she was distracted. He didn't look well. Maybe the tan was simply camouflage he'd gotten up in the islands where he'd gone for some much-needed R and R.

Her mind drifted as his grip softened, warmed.

"Okay, Jo, we'll do it your way. Where do we start?"

Chapter 2

Get over it, McQuaid.

The warning in Rowan's mind didn't go unheeded. It was simply impossible to implement while Jo's scent filled his head with every breath. It was torture. Sheer bloody torture. And he was no masochist. Neither was he a coward, but what he wanted now was to exit her office without making an ass of himself, and take a few hours to get his act together. He was positive that's all it would take. Just a little time to get his head on straight.

The words on the papers he was supposedly reading merged into one, making nonsense of the evidence. The utilitarian clock on the wall behind Jo made it plain only an hour had passed since her arrival had caught him off guard. Eyes closed, his gaze turned inwards as if his parole lay in the dark behind his lids. Damn, this had to be the longest afternoon of his life.

The hairs on his arms prickled each time she passed a piece of evidence, or pointed out a particularly interesting photograph. It was as if his body reiterated what his mind denied. He wanted to touch her. To hell with the weight of regrets lying in the pit of his stomach since he'd grasped her wrist and felt her heartbeat race under his thumb. Felt it pulse, tinting her soft skin blue, and still it hadn't been enough. Not when he'd wanted the whole of her under him, naked and writhing as they joined for the first time right there on top of the desk.

A wry grimace crossed his mind at the thought of Bull's face if he'd actually given in to his urges under his old mate's nose, so to speak. Out of the three there, he'd be hard put to say who'd be the most shocked. And with Bull out of the office, Rowan knew even that small hindrance to temptation was lost to him.

Jo's attention switched from the papers in her hand to her watch. "Hey, why don't I just bundle this lot up and let you take it away to work on? I presume Bull won't have any beef with that." The pun lit a small smile in her features, the first to brighten them since they'd begun sifting through information which neither confirmed nor denied Jo's theory of Rocky conning them.

Shoulder level and palm out she raised her hand as if to say pax or peace. If only she knew. Peace could never exist between them while this primitive tempo surged through his veins.

Then, very un-Jo-like, she giggled. "Don't give me away. The one-liner was straight off the cuff, not a jibe at my boss. I can see how he got the name though, Bill Cowan. Bull. Perfect."

Rowan nodded. Old nicknames stuck, Bull's and his, McQuaid, his middle name and mother's maiden one. Back then he'd been a real pain in the ass about being half-Scottish, and he'd put it to good use when he'd decided to join the force because he answered to it naturally, and made the powers-that-be less inclined to nix his application. Sure, McQuaid didn't have the same ring of power as Stanhope, but it wasn't as tempting to the lowlifes he'd dealt with as Stanhope spelled R-A-N-S-O-M.

Jo turned her back on him and stepped over to a gray,

chipped metal stationery cupboard. She didn't have the kind of walk that shouted, "Hey, guys, look at me." She didn't need it. The way her black linen pants curved into her waist, and fit snugly across womanly hips and thighs was enough publicity, a tall woman, neat without being skinny. But, hey, he hated skinny, and life would have been a lot easier if she'd been built like a plank.

Jo returned with a large yellow envelope and passed it to him. "None of these are originals, so I'm sure Bull won't mind you taking them home to study."

Though her hands worked quickly, collating photos and statements, she kept rearranging the order, as if changing her mind about more than the papers. "By the way, where *are* you staying?" she asked, as if she'd just that moment thought of it.

Bloody hell! Was she about to offer him a bed? Petrified that he might be tempted to accept, he rushed out with, "I borrowed a boat from a friend. It's at the marina. The Landings."

It was a lie, but a white one, or maybe gray. His brother, Scott, used the boat most of the time, though the craft belonged to the family, two brothers and himself, all that was left.

"Good. I was about to warn you against the local motel, an experience I never want to repeat, but a boat at the Landings, how lucky are *you*? It's lovely along the harbor. I often go walking there. I might even know the boat. What's it called?"

"*Stanhope's Fancy Two*."

"So, what happened to number one?"

Trust Jo to pick up on a subject he wanted to avoid. "It sank," he said, shrugging, as if the tragedy had absolutely nothing to do with him. Hadn't changed his life at a time when his emotions still bled from the earlier blow. His feelings on the disaster were nobody's business but his.

It had been seventeen years since the boat went to the bottom. Everyone said Scott was tempting fate when he named the new boat after the first. But Scott didn't give a damn. If it made anyone squirm to know their parents had drowned on the original *Fancy,* let them stay home.

"You be careful."

"Didn't know you were superstitious. Doubt it'll come to much harm tied alongside."

"I guess not."

With everything in a pile, she squared the papers, bumping the bottom edges against the desk like playing cards. Her eyelids tilted at the corners as she watched him through long, thick lashes. "Hold the envelope while I slip these inside."

"Sure thing," he said, suiting action to words, trying not to acknowledge certain parts of her anatomy might get too close for comfort, trying not to imagine touching them during the exchange. And knowing he'd be a darn sight better off setting his thoughts on leaving as soon as he had the evidence in his hands.

"I take it you've heard of the Stanhopes? After all, they're lending you their boat."

"You could say that, considering they have a substantial holding in Allied Insurance."

His answer achieved a lift of Jo's dark winged eyebrows. Under them, stars twinkled naughtily in the dark brown depths. Rowan knew that look. Knew from experience the pull that teasing warmth had on his libido, and braced himself.

"Then you'll know they're what passes for nobility round here. World famous in Nicks Landing."

Jo's words hit a nerve. Luckily, he knew it was just her quirky sense of humor, she didn't mean anything by it. She'd no way of knowing it applied personally. And no need to for the few days he'd be in town.

"I suppose that's one way of putting it."

"Guess my city origins are showing. No offence to the Stanhopes but it makes me laugh to hear the locals hold them in such awe when Auckland is swimming in millionaires. I heard they're pretty lavish spenders though, so the boat must be out of this world. Maybe I could come down and let you show me around?"

Not if I can help it! The *Fancy* was fairly large as boats went in these waters, but the thought of being in its confined quarters with Jo made him break out in a cold sweat. As far as he was concerned, this office was as up close and personal as he dared get with her.

As if it had never come up, he deftly changed the subject, hoping he'd heard the last of the idea. Gauging the envelope's contents with his hands, he remarked, "Not much here for two and a half months' work." His plan worked.

"Got it in one. I always knew you were more than just a pretty face, McQuaid. Surely if they were satanists, we'd have found a lot more than this? Eyewitnesses at least. But no, we're supposed to assume said satanists have the power of invisibility. Get real. And Bull doesn't want to know. Far be it from me to cast aspersions...."

She halted midflight as if waiting for a comment about glass houses and stones. He didn't oblige. "You know Rocky used to be Bull's sergeant, huh? Skelton could still have set the fire himself," she continued.

"Why? Why would he torch the place?"

She looked surprised, as if suddenly finding him wanting. "Money, of course."

"How do you explain the cuts on his back?" He riffled the tops of the pages with a thumbnail. "Satan's initials it said here."

"Self-inflicted." Her tone said, "I ain't taking any crap." "You have to agree, they're indecipherable. On the other hand, diving through the glass door could go a long way to explaining them."

"You really don't like the guy, do you?"

His question merited a minimal lift of her shoulders and a pout. "That's neither here nor there. In all my time in Nicks Landing, I've never heard one whisper about satanists or black-magic cults. And Rocky can't come up with a good reason why, if one existed, they'd want to roast him. Come on! The man's lying. He pulled the story out of thin air, and now he's stuck with it."

As if there had been a wind shift, she changed tack.

Experience had taught him to be wary of that glint in her eyes. It meant she wanted something. "Getting back to the subject of money, does Skelton's insurance policy have a clause setting aside his right to privacy once he makes a claim?"

The glint brightened when he confirmed her supposition. "Most of them do these days."

"That's it then. I think we've got him. *You* can look into his finances, banking and etceteras, where I can't. The bar at the Hard Luck Inn couldn't possibly cover all his expenses. Losing his shirt would be a helluva incentive for torching his house."

"Then why didn't he simply sell the house?"

"Molly, his wife. It was her pride and joy. I'll take you to Rocky's tonight and let you get the feel of the Hard Luck Inn. That should give you enough time to go over what you've got there." She nodded toward the envelope. "Personally, I don't think Rocky had any notion how prophetic the name of his bar would be. He named it that because he was made redundant."

Now that his afternoon and evening had been arranged to Jo's satisfaction, all he wanted was out of there. It simplified matters to go along with her plans. "What time?"

She picked up his business card and glanced over it. "I'll call your cell phone when I'm done, and arrange a time."

From under her desk she produced a sturdy leather bag, too large to be called a purse, quickly slipping his card into a front pocket. Her next move set his heart racing. Slinging her bag over one shoulder, she slid her fingers through the long black silkiness of her hair before loosing it to fall in a flurry of waves and curls onto her shoulders.

The movement lifted her pink shirt's miniscule tail above her waistband, allowing a glimpse of smooth satin skin. Her pants slipped lower on her hips, and the shadowy hollow that was her navel, broke up the curve of her honey-colored belly.

How would it feel to cradle his head on its softness and simply lie there breathing her in?

Bad move.

Rowan lifted his stunned gaze and swallowed hard.

Their eyes caught as she tucked her shirt in, patted the side of her leather bag and started to walk round the desk. "Ready?"

If he were any more ready he'd be lethal. He'd been half-hard for the past hour, and now he had an ache pressing against his zipper that had to be noticeable. Who'd have thought he'd ever be grateful for the protection of a yellow envelope.

Waving his free hand in the direction of the door, he said, "After you." Following the convention of ladies first, with heartfelt thanks.

Jeez, she couldn't believe she'd actually done that. Jo stood at the top of the stairs feeling ashamed of testing the waters the way she had, lifting her arms above her head, knowing it would emphasize her breasts.

She'd watched him swallow the knot in his throat, an involuntary action that only confirmed he was human.

Knowingly, she'd set out on this provocative path, hating to think the buzz zapping her nerves every time he glanced her way was one-sided. That all these hot, bothered and bewildered feelings affected Rowan not one iota. Honestly. Some people read auras, whereas she could sense Rowan's presence even without hearing his tread on the stairs behind her.

Where had it sprung from, this awareness? When?

Was it really new, or simply something she'd chosen to ignore? With each glance she'd cast his way, hoping he wouldn't catch her, the hum in her temples increased and the blood in her head bubbled and fizzed as if she had the bends. She couldn't remember getting this worked up over any man, not even Max Strachan, the last man she'd imagined she loved.

Imagined being the operative word. God, he would have the

last laugh now. Max, the one man who'd been honest with her, even if only to tell her she'd no shot of him ever returning her affections.

And Rowan? She'd always thought of him as slightly up-tight, at least in her company. First and foremost a by-the-rules guy. Never a step out of place until the last night they had worked together.

On the only occasions they'd met since, he'd acted pretty cagey, accepting her apology for darn near getting him killed with his usual stony face. As if nothing touched him, not even death.

So who had changed, her or him?

Jo stopped at the foot of the stairs, turned, waiting till Rowan drew level. "I have business with Sergeant Jackson. I'll call you this evening."

"No problem. I'll walk with you. I want to tell the sergeant I'm leaving and thank him for his help. I expect to be in and out of the station house quite a bit. Might as well stay on the guy's good side."

Jo rolled her eyes and shrugged, a small piece of body language she'd inherited from her Dalmatian grandmother along with her cheekbones and black curls. "Suit yourself."

What was he really after? It was unlike Rowan to be ingra-tiating. And how could he bear to watch Harry doing the work he'd had to give up? If she'd lost her job, the way Rowan had, she'd never enter another police station.

Spinning on her heel, she marched along the corridor, her steps brisk, concealing her doleful thoughts. But soon her true nature won through. She had a comic mental flash of what might have been, if Rowan had still been there when she'd arrived with Ginny. She broke into a grin as she pictured Rowan's face.

All teenagers morphed into an alien life-form these days. What was the betting Ginny would have gone off the planet? Jo was grateful Rowan hadn't heard the wolf whistle of ap-proval coming from her car. With a sigh, she acknowledged she'd made a few hormone-driven moves herself in the last hour, as if her body had been taken over. The green light had gone on the moment he teased her about her offer to show him everything she had.

Then later…her feeble attempt to get a reaction from him, well that memory was plain embarrassing. Rowan would never really be attracted to her. She'd known him too long. In future it would pay to keep her eyes to herself and off Rowan. The problem being, the new Rowan was just *so* easy on the eye.

Dear heavens, now there was a thought to jump-start her brain. She was responsible for the new and improved model. Responsible for all the pain he'd gone through while they'd fought to piece his shattered leg together. She forgot how many times he'd gone under the surgeon's knife.

Rowan's strength of mind showed in taut, sleek muscles that couldn't be bought. She ought to be thankful he hadn't lost himself in the pain her foolish actions had inflicted.

How would she fare if she lost *her* career?

Would she even know herself anymore?

She burst through the door, mind made up. All thoughts of Rowan as a living, breathing babe were banned. All her priorities were in a straight line. She needed his help to prove her father's ex-partner had burned down his house, not to discover how it felt to kiss a man with a moustache.

Of greater importance was a chance to prove to her superiors that she'd always known Rocky Skelton was a liar. Maybe then they would take a fresh look at the black marks on her father's record. She simply *had* to place that doubt in their minds, and make them realize Milo Jellic had been done wrong.

Rowan had barely passed through the doors when Harry Jackson asked, "How's it going, McQuaid? Was Jo able to set your mind at rest?"

Rest wasn't exactly the way Rowan would phrase it. Set fire to his libido? Yeah. Tightened the thumbscrews on his hormones? You bet! After this, he'd be lucky to get a good night's sleep for dreaming of Jo. *Being over her, under her, inside her.*

Damage control! He pulled a lead curtain across his thoughts.

Harry's grin didn't attempt to hide that he'd been conniving as he looked from one to the other of them. He and Bull were the only two who knew he'd come home. The only two he wanted to know. His old friend probably thought he'd been doing Rowan a favor by not warning him the detective he'd come to see was six feet of luscious curves. No way could Harry know they had a history together, or that most of his friends blamed Jo for his departure from the force. The way they told it he would have done the same for anyone. Anyone stupid enough to become a target. He wasn't so sure. He'd only known he couldn't let the bastard shoot her.

"Bull has given *us* a week to pull it together. Then I can okay Skelton's payment." The black look he'd expected from Jo didn't materialize. Instead her attention focused on a little redhead, sitting on a bench by the far wall staring at him with her mouth gaping. He gave a mental shrug. Kids.

"Harry. Why is Ginny still here?"

The sergeant's voice dropped a notch while he spoke to Jo, "Her mother had to work and her father won't be home till later. Ms. Wilks said to send her on home, she'd be all right. But I had a feeling you'd rather see she got there."

"That's for real. Thanks, Harry, I'll still have to speak to the mother, though. Where does she work?"

"The Hard Luck Inn."

One black eyebrow rose as Jo's gaze left Harry and zeroed in on him. "Looks like we've got two birds to kill tonight." The lopsided smile quirked her lips, producing a dimple. "That will be Ms. Wilks's *hard luck.*"

The conversation was interrupted by Bull and Jake bringing two men through the door from the cells under protest.

"Uh-oh, gotta go," muttered Jo, her gaze on the girl. "I'll catch you tonight, McQuaid. For now, I have to baby-sit."

Harry let Jo get out of earshot before he produced the question Rowan could see hovering on his lips. "You two got a date tonight?"

"Not so's you'd notice. We're going to visit Jo's chief suspect." As soon as he'd said it, he remembered Bull's reaction and wished he could pull the words back.

"You mean Rocky?"

"Yeah, but keep it under your hat. I don't think it's for public consumption. You know the guy, Harry. What do you think of him? Is he capable of flights of fantasy? Satanists?"

"Must admit I thought it far-fetched when I first heard the story, but everyone else was convinced."

"Everyone but Jo?"

"I guess you could say if I took it with a pinch of salt, she used a bloody ladle. But then, she never worked with Rocky, didn't know him the way we do."

"And what do you know?"

Harry's mouth twisted as he considered. "He can be pretty sharp, and if that's how things are shaping, watch you don't get cut."

"Thanks for the warning." He hitched one trouser leg and sat down on the corner of Harry's desk, getting comfortable. "Talking about warnings, why didn't you do me the same favor with Jo?"

"Made your heart jump, did she? She's one beautiful woman."

"There are lots of beautiful women."

"Yeah, but you still haven't married any of them."

"Hell, you're as bad as Scott—"

"Oh, I can tell you and him are the same. Time you were both married."

"Well, he's decided he doesn't need an heir as long as Taine and I are around, but Taine can't do the same for me, so *I* ought to marry and beget heirs."

"Been matchmaking, has he?"

"You could say that. Now that I've left the force, he feels obliged to introduce me to all the eligible women in his circle. He never once said anything against me leaving him to look after the firm to become a cop, but I can tell he's glad it's behind me now. I guess he'd always had this idea I was invincible because of being so much bigger."

"Yeah, it always was *you* who got him out of trouble."

"Well, he's turned that around now with the firm." He slipped Harry a wry grin. "If it hadn't been for Scott, we wouldn't be living in the style we've become accustomed to."

"Scott's done well by us all."

"Have you got shares as well?"

"I've got the ones your father gave mine, when he worked for him. Probably thought Dad earned them putting up with you lot."

"Come off it, you spent as much time at our house as you did at your own."

Harry had the grace to look sheepish. "I helped Dad."

"Is that what you called it? Well, I'm helping Jo and I'll probably be about as much use. You can't find what's not there."

Heaven help him, was he starting to think like her? The last thing he wanted was to suspect Rocky Skelton of fraud. If that happened he could be here for longer than a week, long enough for the woman to get under his skin again.

Hell, she was under there now.

Damn, this was a complication. No matter how much he treasured his own hide, he had a dislike of paying out the firm's money for nothing, probably part of the Scottish heritage he'd been so quick to deny after what his mother did. It was all right for the hierarchy to say, "Write it off as public relations." In this district most people put their money with the Stanhopes, thinking it would benefit them in the long run.

Rowan stood. "I'd better get going. I'm living on the *Fancy*. Scott said he'd have someone leave it ready for me, but you never know with him."

"I for one never thought he'd play matchmaker. Shows how wrong you can be. It's usually us married guys who're pushing all their mates into the same boat. Has he managed to set you up with someone then?"

Hoping it would keep Harry off his back, he told him, "There's a woman I've taken out a couple of times, but it's early days. Might never come to anything." Hell, he knew it wouldn't, not now he'd met Jo again.

The shame of it was, he liked Barbara, and had thought maybe he could make it work, since she filled all his requirements. A woman he could be friends with, but who didn't stir his blood. It was a decision he'd made a long time ago. He wasn't looking for love. That way he wouldn't be hurt when she found someone else. The pain his father went through when his mother left wasn't going to be part of his inheritance.

No, it definitely wasn't for him.

Harry pushed back his chair and stood up to face him. He was two to three inches shorter, but he'd never carried the bulk that Rowan had, even when they'd both been desk jockeys. "No problem then. I wasn't really shoving Jo your way."

"No point. Jo and I have known each other for years. We worked together in Auckland." It didn't take more than that for Harry to cotton on. Not that he liked doing it to Jo, but if it would help his old friend mind his own business...

"So, she the one...the one who... Look say the word and I'll get Bull to put Jake back on the arson job."

"Hell, no!" He leaned over the desk and stared Harry in the eye. "And if word of this gets out I'll know who to blame. Right? I've no animosity toward Jo. I threw myself in the way of that bullet. My choice. Okay?"

"Sure thing. But if you know each other so well, how come she didn't give you an earful for pinching her parking space?"

"I didn't know I had."

Harry's chin jutted slightly, his eyes narrowing as if hiding the wheels turning behind them. He'd always been easy to read.

"Look, to Jo, I'm simply Rowan McQuaid, and I'd like it to stay that way. I won't be here long enough for involved explanations. And as much as she thinks she knows me, I know her better. Her mouth is inclined to go into self-destruct mode at the most inopportune moments."

A grin split the sergeant's face. "You really do know her."

"Let's put it this way, it's not so much Jo I'm worried about, but if Molly Skelton finds out who I am my life won't be worth living."

"Got it in one, mate."

Outside, Jo was saying, "Will you stop looking like a sick puppy, get into the car and shut the door?" Ginny's pathetic show of reluctance was ruffling Jo's patience. The girl was lovesick. Jo sighed, then clamped her lips on the smile forming as she watched the teenager's crablike shuffle. Each time Ginny's feet crossed, Jo held her breath, waiting the inevitable tumble while doing a mental inventory of the first-aid stuff she carried in her bag.

Eventually the kid made it to the passenger's seat without taking her star-glazed eyes off the exit, and fastened her seat belt. Heaven help the boys when the girl grew up; Ginny wasn't backward at coming forward when someone took her fancy.

"He's not going to come out. He's too busy. Besides, his car's parked out front." And he would pay for pinching her spot. A chance to drive his Jag would just about cover it. A decision punctuated with an ellipse as her car crawled into Main Street. Hers had to be the oldest model in the fleet. Not simply a case of first come first served, more that with her work schedule, they didn't expect her to be in any high-speed chases. And in the unlikely scenario of them presenting her with a newer one, she'd have to make do with a tune-up.

Finally, Jo had Ginny's attention, albeit secondhand. "You mean that beaut car is his? Isn't he just, just too awesome?"

Awesome was hardly a description she would have used herself, but Rowan was definitely *something*. She just couldn't make up her mind what. She wouldn't go so far as to agree with the hoary old saying that absence made the heart fonder, but in her case it certainly beat faster.

"I think your earlier description was more apt, Ginny. The man is definitely a babe."

It was as if she'd been given a new and improved pair of eyes that saw past the facade he'd used before. Details she'd missed took on a shimmering quality that beckoned her like a light in the window after dark. Like going home.

God, was that it? She was homesick for Auckland?

No way. The rest of her symptoms were definitely hormonal.

"What's his name, Miss? Has he come to live in Nicks Landing?" The words came out in a breathless rush.

The title *Miss* hurt, like suddenly being reduced to the status of maiden aunt, or schoolteacher instead of teen idol. "His name is Rowan McQuaid, he's only in town for a week, and for heaven's sake, call me Detective…Jo," she compromised, on the spur of the moment.

"Is he a detective, too?"

"He's a private investigator."

"A private eye…wow, even better. Is he here…like on some big case?"

The child definitely watched too much TV. Philosophical at being reduced to second fiddle, Jo got ready to disappoint the kid. "Nothing exciting, a case of arson, is all. We'll be working on it together."

She glanced at Ginny to ask, "It's the next left, isn't it?" only to find her status had been restored.

"That's ace," she said, all big eyed. "Yes, turn here, it's just two blocks down. Top apartment on the corner."

Jo pulled up outside a run-down apartment building crying out for refurbishment. It was a shame. A lick of light-colored paint over the sea of won't-show-the-dirt-khaki could give the whole neighborhood a face-lift and send it rocketing up a price bracket.

"Okay," she said, catching her breath as the dung-colored entrance door creaked open and a woman with a frown carved into her features came out. No wonder the kid had tried to heist pink barrettes. They were an antidote for living here.

"When I visit your mother at work, I'll discuss which form

your punishment will take. Though I guess grounding would be as good as any."

"Oh no, not grounding, it's almost Halloween. My friends and I have something planned."

"Even better."

Ginny's jaw dropped. "Can't I just help someone? An old lady or something? Granny Monroe lives down the hall from us. I could do some cleaning for her."

Jo pretended to consider a moment. She couldn't blame the kid not wanting to miss out on a night of trick-or-treating. "I'd have to check with her that you'd done a good job."

"Sure. No problem. I'll go right in and ask her now. I can phone you when it's done. Will that do?"

"Sounds good to me." Jo dug into the pocket of her shirt and pulled out a business card and gave it to Ginny. "My number's on there. That doesn't mean I won't talk to your mother, but I'll tell her I've okayed you helping Granny Monroe."

The weight of the world seemed to pull Ginny's mouth down at the corners. "Molly's okay, but Rocky doesn't like it when people take Mom's mind off her work."

"Don't worry, kid. I'll flash my badge and tell them it's police business." She winked at Ginny. "So, what's wrong with the inn? Don't you like her working there?"

"I guess it's all right, but Dad and I hardly see her. Mom says it's the only way we're ever going to get out of this dump." Unfastening her seat belt, Ginny sat with fingers on the handle as if reluctant to press it down.

"Sounds like a wise woman. I'll talk to her tonight. Rowan and I were going there anyway, but if I were you, I'd tell my Dad what I'd been up to, *before* your mother gets home."

The teenager brightened a fraction, her eyes dreamy at the mention of Rowan. "Have you got a date?"

"No, it's business. We're working together this week."

Ginny's shoulders drooped as if she'd been hoping to live out her fantasies vicariously. "Have a good time anyway."

"I'll try." And she would; hanging around with Rowan for seven days wasn't her idea of punishment.

Ginny was halfway out the door, her face glum when Jo attempted changing the direction of her thoughts. "So, what are you and your friends doing at Halloween?"

"It's going to be real exciting. We heard where the black-magic cult have their meetings. It's at Te Kohanga National Park, and we thought it would be a hoot to spy on them. They're bound to be up to something on Halloween."

Chapter 3

Eight o'clock. If Rowan was still on board surely he would be ready, waiting for her call? A call that frankly refused to go through. If Jo heard that computerized voice saying the number she'd dialed was either switched off or out of range one more time, she would spit. But then that's why she was walking down one of the floating wooden fingers of the marina. To see for herself.

The sea was remarkably calm, due to the huge anticyclone covering the country. A circumstance she gave thanks for. She hated that feeling, as if the bottom had dropped out of her world when she put her foot down, and the floor disappeared. Besides, these were her best high-heeled shoes.

At last she spied it, *Stanhope's Fancy II*. Larger than life and twice the size of the boats moored alongside, it was hard to miss its gleaming white hull. On the couple of occasions she'd ventured out on one of these, she'd learned this type of craft was called a midpilothouse motor yacht.

With one arm wrapped round a mooring post, she leaned out over the wooden lip to peer inside. No one around.

Hmmm. She looked down at the toes of her red-and-black, faux-lizard shoes, and past them to the flotsam floating in the gap with a sinking feeling. They would have to come off.

Her bag landed with a thump on the boarding platform, but no one came to investigate. With a grin, she did a quick scan of the area, imagining the headlines if she got caught: Detective charged with indecent exposure.

Her red skirt hit just above the knee. Hands on both sides, she hitched it eighteen inches higher, just below her panties, and stepped into space, shoes clutched in one hand.

"Easy," she told herself, balancing by a fingertip on the stern rail, ignoring the slap of water against the hull as it slopped over her feet. Happiness was planting them on the other side of that rail.

She gave the glass door two loud bangs, then tried the handle. Like a hot knife through butter, the door slid open.

"Hey, Rowan! It's me, Jo. Can I come aboard?"

Silence spiked tiny tremors of fear at the base of her skull. From the depths of her overactive imagination, she culled the ghost ship, *Marie Celeste*. And the thought gelled as she took in a galley to one side of the entrance; it sparkled as if neither dish nor spoon had ever cluttered its counters.

Mmm. Her feet sunk into thick blue-gray carpet. She curled her toes into it, drying her damp panty hose. Sheer luxury. So this was what it meant to be a Stanhope. Rowan had landed on his feet working for Allied Insurance. On her side of the line this would smack of corruption, but from Rowan's the label read, *perks of the job*.

On the lush, woolen pile, she crossed the main saloon as if walking on water, then drifted up two short flights of steps, passing the upper saloon by, and into the pilothouse. Silence thundered in her ears as if the soft suede walls swallowed every sound she made. Her skin prickled. The horizon slid up and down the outside of huge wraparound windows as the boat tugged at its moorings as if eager to be gone.

"Good idea, I'm outta here, too," she muttered, spinning on her heel to retrace her steps, coming to an abrupt halt on the top one. Shaking her head, she laughed. "Good Lord, you need a change of reading material. You didn't used to be so easily spooked."

The briefcase on the dining table didn't catch her attention until her return journey. Immediately, she reversed her decision to leave. Rowan had to be around. He wouldn't go off, leaving the place open for just anyone to enter the way she had. Once more, she called his name, "Rowan!"

At the next set of steps, she hesitated. The sleeping quarters lay below. No problem, all she had to do was knock first.

She went on down.

The door on her right stood ajar. L-shaped bunks took up two walls, all of them made up as neat as a new pin. Across the companionway the door was closed. She rapped on it with her knuckles, then gradually eased it open, but saw no signs of occupation. Her choices narrowed to one last door.

Her shoulders drooped as she spied another neatly made-up bed without even a hollow in its surface to say someone had sat there. Expelling a gusty breath did nothing to relieve the disappointment threatening to swamp her. "Wrong darn boat!"

"Depends which boat you were looking for."

"Rowan!" she gasped, caught off guard, her mouth gaping at his half-naked figure framed in wisps of steam in a doorway that was hidden among the paneling.

"I...I did knock," she stammered, trying to make sense of a breathless response that tied her larynx in knots, cutting off the air to her lungs.

Water darkened his hair to burned sugar, molding it tightly to his scalp, until it fell into damp curls at his nape. His broad, broad shoulders glistened where diamond-bright drops of water beaded, pausing momentarily before the slide down the long muscles of his arms.

She had never seen Rowan without clothes. Had never expected to. Never even imagined it before today, and still she couldn't believe her eyes.

Was it any wonder he'd taken her breath away? Sculpted

satin-smooth curves and hollows fitted his upper body as God had intended. Perfectly.

His chest shuddered lightly on the aftermath of a sigh. Even as she watched, his flat, male nipples set wide on the curve of his pectoral muscles, crested, tensing in the wake of her gaze.

Jo's blood leaped from her heart to her face.

Embarrassment was no hindrance to eating up his manly beauty with her eyes. No power on this earth could make her drag them away.

A narrow white strip, edging his charcoal-gray shorts, deepened his tan in contrast. Languor weighed her eyelids, a sensual heaviness. She knew she should look somewhere else, up…down…anywhere and pretend his body hadn't responded to her blatant voyeurism. But Lord, the sight of cotton knit molding his form stole her breath away.

Jo swallowed. *Oh, my.*

The seconds it took to remove her gaze dawdled like hours. Yet one glance at his thighs sent her reeling back to the safety of the companionway. Her stomach shot up to meet her throat and devoured every particle of heat from her body.

Cold. She felt so cold.

And sick.

She had done that. Blighted all that perfection in one unthinking second, with no other justification than she had been focused on Max. But after Rowan's sacrifice, how could she make excuses? And whom could she make them to?

The scars alone mightn't have been so bad, time would take care of them, turn scarlet into silver. The missing muscle, though, could never be replaced. Not after the bullet that should have been hers, had ripped it apart, spraying it over the grass where she stood.

"I'd better go back up…" she whispered through chattering teeth "…until you get dressed." The complete understanding in his eyes was worse than anything she'd ever experienced.

God help him, he hadn't been able to control his body's reaction to her. He'd stepped out of the shower, thoughts of her running through his mind, and suddenly she'd been there, as if he had conjured her out of thin air.

The same but different.

Her dark curls, as riotous and ruffled as a black, Oriental poppy after a storm, caught in a tangle at the back of her collar, unveiling a secret. Revealing another layer of the mysterious sway she held over his libido.

If he'd had the courage to ignore the danger of her thrall, when he'd first known her, he would already have pushed back that black silk curtain to discover for himself the smooth tender hollow where her jawline met her neck.

Instead, he'd been in control. Hell, he'd congratulated himself on it. So he'd never known that the pink slashing her high, Slavic cheekbones would match the rose of her earlobes.

The loss had been his.

Rowan's chest heaved. Until today he'd never known her ears were pierced or that she'd choose anything as feminine as creamy pearls to highlight their petal-soft lobes.

Damn, why was he torturing himself?

An unwelcome hunger prowled his reason like a ravenous beast full of suppressed urges and needs. Habit pushed it back into the black cave at the back of his mind where it had hibernated for the past two years. Too late, far too late. The mere thought of claiming one of those glowing pink morsels with his mouth, and circling a pearl with the tip of his tongue, made him hard.

Harder.

Then she'd blushed.

In all the years they'd worked together, he'd never known Jo to blush. It gave him a whole new take on her. A fresh angle corroborated by the way her cocoa-brown eyes had darkened to onyx. Arousal.

The other signs might be hidden from view, yet he'd bet bullet-hard nipples strained against her bra and her female core would have been slick and damp to his touch. Yeah, she'd been ready, every bit as ready as himself, as ready as the bed waiting in the corner of the cabin.

All he'd had to do was reach out, cup the back of her neck and the wanting would have been quenched.

Jo would have been his.

The salutary lesson had come with a look that took in his mangled leg. What else had he expected?

Yet he still wanted her, ached with it.

Shielding his unrelieved erection with one hand, Rowan zipped up his jeans. He'd given himself away. Years of self-discipline blown in a heartbeat.

Time for more damage control.

One large, black loafer slipped on to his feet followed by the next. He stood up, patted his belt buckle and pulled in a breath, ready to face Jo. From outside, the crimson tails of day's end whipped color into the steamy haze as he left his cabin and followed the scent of freshly brewed coffee up the stairs and into the galley. Jo had made herself at home.

She stood at the counter, staring out the window. "Just what the doctor ordered," he said to the back of her head.

The low hills behind the town were aflame with red, orange and purple. His mouth twisted slightly. *Red sky at night, shepherd's delight.* So, they were going to have a good day tomorrow. He could certainly use one.

She turned to face him, her eyes slightly red as if they'd captured the sunset. A smile poised precariously on her lips as if afraid the arms she'd folded across her breasts weren't her best defense.

Looking down the length of her body, he noticed what he hadn't seen before, when his gaze had been fixed on her face. Jo had dolled herself up for their outing. The sleeves of her pearl-gray twinset were pushed up, businesslike, to her elbows, and the hem of her red skirt kissed the crease at the back of her knees.

Her shoeless feet nearly floored him. The way she crossed the toes of one over the other, like a little girl awaiting punishment, and through the nylon he could see she'd painted her toenails red. Any ire or anger left inside him washed away as she changed from one foot to the other.

He'd never thought he'd want to smile at a time like this, when life as he knew it hung in the balance, but he did. "Lost your shoes somewhere?"

"They're outside...on the deck..." She trailed off, and her explanation turned into a jumble of words and a spill of tears.

Though he understood the risk, he had to go to her, comfort her. Place his hands on her shoulders, and feel her flesh mold beneath them. "Hey, hey, what's all this?"

"Don't hate me, Rowan. Please. I didn't know...it's dreadful what I did to you, and I don't know how to make it better."

"Aw, hell, Jo. Not pity." Not from you. "I'm a tough guy and I've learned to live with it. I even made a New Year's resolution. No pity allowed."

Though his mouth felt dry, he chanced a rendition of the phrase, "Big boys don't cry." His voice was husky and off-key from the lump strangling his throat, but it achieved the desired result.

Jo smiled. "Don't take up singing. You just murdered that."

He threw a quick retort into the ring. "Maybe you ought to call a cop."

His mind went back ten months, to New Year. He'd been two weeks out of hospital, in time for Christmas, taken a good look at himself and disliked what he'd seen.

Life didn't come with guarantees. Bone reconstruction, either, as he'd discovered the morning he'd put his foot on the floor and found the pin in his thigh had slid up inside the bone. Having one leg that was four inches shorter played hell on the ego.

As the year began, he'd decided to get on with his life and make the best of what came. Meeting Jo again had thrown a spanner in the workings of his brave new life with the discovery he still hurt.

"Want a cop, you've got one," said Jo. "What can I do?"

"You can pour me a cup of that delicious-smelling coffee and we'll call it quits," he said, not blinking at the lie.

"That's not near enough. If you'd like me to give up beating this dead horse of a case, it's yours. Just say the word."

Hell, she was serious. She'd been so hung up on proving Rocky was guilty a few hours ago. Now, she was offering to stand aside, and make his problems with Skelton fade away. His leg must look a helluva lot worse than he'd feared. For as long as he'd known Jo she'd pokered up at the faintest whiff of payback.

"Look, it's no big deal. As long as I don't try to run the mile in under four, I'll be okay. I'm used to it."

She swallowed. Hell, he hoped she wouldn't cry again. His resolve couldn't cope with drying her tears.

"That's the problem, I'm *not* used to it. If only…"

Rowan held up a hand as if to ward off the flow of regrets he could see coming. "Okay, I won't keep on about it. Let me pour you that coffee."

Jo was rinsing their cups and saying, "Tomorrow, I'll take you to Rocky's house, what's left of it, at Lonely Track Road. I'll walk you through his explanation of what happened."

"I'll want the afternoon free to check into his finances."

"That's okay. I know Bull's only given me a week, but that doesn't mean I can put the rest of my cases on hold. He'd be chagrined if I didn't keep up with them. That said, I received some new information this afternoon. No guarantees, in fact it sounds a bit iffy, but I should follow it up." Her lip quivered. "If it comes up trumps, you can wipe out two with one blow, pay Rocky off, and still keep your bosses happy."

She sounded defensive and he couldn't understand why, but she didn't keep him in suspense for long. "Don't think I made you that offer because I realized Rocky might be telling the truth. I don't trust the man. If I'm wrong about this, I'll admit it. I'll even buy you dinner. But, if Rocky isn't concealing the truth about the fire, then it's something else. It might take me a while to suss exactly what, but I'll do it. My biggest hurdle is Bull. The dope thinks the sun shines out of Rocky's sorry behind and refuses to hear a word against him."

Wondering when she'd get around to hitting him with the punch line, Rowan asked, "Is this new information secret, or are you gonna share?"

By the time they'd walked the length of the harbor wall and reached the Hard Luck Inn on the corner of Main and Broad Streets, she'd talked out Ginny's information about Halloween with Rowan.

"You're right," she told him. "Even though it disses any hope I had of pulling Rocky in, I can't *not* check it out."

"From where I stand it looks like we've got Tuesday and Wednesday scheduled. Friday night we could be crawling through the bush in the dark, Saturday looks like a day off. Any thoughts on Thursday or are we just gonna go with the flow?"

Though Rowan's tone was conversational, Jo got the message. "I'm doing it, aren't I? I'm organizing you. You did say I could be in charge."

"Remind me next time to think before I speak. It's the only way to stay out of trouble." A white grin split his face between the dusting of gold designer stubble and slightly darker moustache, softening his words. "One thing I insist on. We take my car to Te Kohanga. It'll be quicker."

"Can I drive?"

"I don't know, can you? You looked a bit shaky getting out of the station house car park this afternoon."

"Oh, you...were you watching?"

"Came out to apologize for stealing your space."

"My car gets that way when the engine's cold. Once it warms it's hell-on-wheels," she said sticking up for the car she cursed six days out of seven.

"I've known people like that."

In the lights from the bar, Rowan looked serious. Too serious. Tension that hadn't crackled since she burst in on Rowan, half-naked in his cabin, and devoured him with her eyes, was suddenly alive and well and sparking between them.

Confused, Jo sought to diffuse the situation by putting on a tough act. "Yeah, yeah, McQuaid, don't think you can get away with distracting me. It's payback time, buddy. At the very least, you owe me a drive for not giving you a parking ticket."

The tangle of emotions in her chest almost unraveled her. It didn't matter which string she pulled, the knots just fell apart. Man, could she pick her moments. Her timing was always off. It was as if the minute puberty hit, they had handed her a certificate with an F in Relationships 101.

Rowan raised his thick brown eyebrows. The creases at the corners of his eyes looked pale in contrast to his face. "Okay, I'll think about giving you a turn at the wheel. Now let's go inside and get this over with."

Jo turned the handle and Rowan stretched a long arm overhead, pushing the heavy door open. As she stepped into the noise and smoke, she turned, glancing at him. The strafe of lights flashing round the bar caught him square in the face. He looked like a stranger. What if they'd met for the first time today, this afternoon, as strangers? Would she still be having these feelings? Or was the fact that they weren't strangers the reason she felt all screwed up inside?

Rowan stopped just inside the bar, lifting his voice to be heard over the heavy-metal music blasting from the sound system. Rowan yelled, "What?"

"I was just wondering why the moustache?"

"Maybe I'm hiding behind it."

"Come off it. The Rowan McQuaid I know never hid from anything in his life."

He tagged her with a look that had "that's what you think" written all over it. "All right, you got me. I was scuba diving up in Fiji and my brother thought he was being funny and grabbed me from behind. I turned too quick and my momentum thrust me into some jagged coral that cut my lip." A wry twist pulled at his moustache. "I don't know what frightened him more, all the blood from the wound, or the chance of it attracting sharks. He had me out of there and onto the boat in no time flat."

As if he couldn't resist touching it, Rowan ran one finger

cross the toffee and gold bristles covering his top lip. Jo
wished she had the courage to repeat the move.

"Anyhow, I couldn't shave until the stitches came out and
by then I'd gotten used to it."

"It certainly changes your appearance. I guess that's why I
didn't recognize you at first. So tell me, who is this brother?
I never heard you mention him before."

This time the look said, "See? You *don't* know me as well
as you thought."

Rowan took his time about answering. The biker paraphernalia hanging round the walls finally caught his eye. He
blinked, twice, then looked back at her and finally answered
her question. "He's just a regulation-size big brother who
thinks he can boss me around."

But Jo had already lost the scent, and set off down another
trail. "So what do you think?" she asked. The black painted
ceiling and walls were hung with a mass of number plates;
helmets, handlebars, front spokes even. A selection of chrome
wheels looped in chains glittered like tinsel alongside bril-
liantly polished Harley signs being given pride of place. And
among the clutter, a tangle of red-white-and-blue tattered flags,
a mix of Confederate, Stars and Stripes, and New Zealand's
Southern Cross, added color where the spotlights caught them.

"Bloody amazing. I never thought I'd see anything like this
here in Nicks Landing."

Her eyes narrowed curiously, then she shrugged as if the
thought evaporated in the booming noise. "Well don't let it
turn your head. Remember we're here on business."

For the first time since he'd helped her off the boat, Rowan
touched her. As his arm went round her shoulder, she felt the
weight of his gaze slide over her body like a living, breathing
thing. "Too bad you haven't dressed for it."

"Maybe I'm hiding, too."

His arm stayed put as he walked her up to the U-shaped
bar, and she couldn't prevent slanting an obvious glance at his
fingers cupping her shoulder. "Camouflage," he said, giving

her a squeeze. After the excuse she'd made for her own attire she could hardly complain.

"I take it that's Skelton?" he asked, lifting a brow in the direction of a man drawing a beer from the tap, dressed in a black T-shirt emblazoned with a long-dead singer's face.

Jo's gaze slid between the customers leaning on the dark-oak edifice Rocky had bought at a demolition sale and transported to Nicks Landing in sections. But before she could answer, Rowan's eyes latched on to a woman serving at one of the tables. "And that would be Molly. The woman who's been blighting the life of everyone at head office."

Jo followed his gaze. As soon as she saw the red hair, she knew she'd found Ginny's mom. "Sorry, that would be Ms. Wilks. I need to discuss her daughter with her. Molly does all the cooking. No doubt you'll find her in the kitchen."

Jo accepted one of the stools Rowan pulled out from the bar, hooking her toes under the brass rail that ran a foot off the floor to pull herself in closer. She kept her bag over her shoulder instead of dangling it from the back of her stool. With the 9mm Glock she carried, she couldn't afford to be careless.

"What can I get you folks?" Rocky rubbed his hands together as if expecting a big sale. She wasn't sorry to disappoint him. He was just short of being tall, but built wiry. He'd never have escaped the flames otherwise. One of the firemen had given her a lurid male description of how he'd found Rocky, trussed up like a chicken with duct tape wrapped round his sorry carcass. All plucked and dressed, ready for the oven.

"I'll just have coffee."

"Oh, c'mon, Johanna. Surely we can tempt you to have something stronger. A glass of wine." Rocky smiled at her and the steel-gray sideboards he affected, bunched on his cheeks. There was more hair on his face than on top of his head, where he wore it long in a comb over.

She hated when he used her full name, taking advantage of his supposed friendship with her father to hint at a familiarity that didn't exist. And she hated the noise which made it necessary to lean forward to hear him. Her hands fisted on the bar and she ground out, "Bring me a cup of coffee" *or else*.

"I'll have coffee, too," Rowan bit out in a way that brooked no opposition.

"Aren't you going to introduce me to your friend, Johanna?" wheedled Rocky.

Thankfully, Rowan let her off the hook by thrusting his hand out. "Rowan McQuaid."

"Rocky Skelton, owner. Glad to meet anyone who can drag Johanna in here. We don't see enough of her."

Jo found it hard to keep the glee out of her voice as she butted in. "Rowan's from Allied Insurance. He's come to investigate your fire."

She watched Rocky closely. Tension bunched in his shoulders as he wiped his hands on the towel he kept hanging at his waist for polishing glasses. Though his body language said flight, he hadn't been a cop all those years without learning how to bluff.

"About time. Maybe we'll get some action round here." His friendliness wasn't apparent in the look he darted at Jo. "I thought you two were an item when you came in. Sorry, my mistake," Rocky said.

"You weren't too far out. Jo and I have been friends for a good many years."

"Give me a second and I'll get those coffees. On the house, of course."

Rowan didn't bat an eye as he refused. "No need, I'm on an expense account."

Rocky grabbed a couple of cups from the top of the espresso machine and began making noises with milk and steam.

With his elbows on the bar, Rowan angled his body to face her. It put them close, close enough for his breath to brush her cheek. Close enough to taste it on her lips. But soon it became clear he only wanted to speak without being overheard. "Bad news, we've given him time to get his act together."

"Sorry about that."

"You didn't tell me you were friends with Skelton, *Johanna*. Anything I should know about?"

"It's a long story, nothing that affects this case." Whoa, back up girl. Lord, she'd nearly caught herself out on a lie. "Well, only indirectly, but this isn't the place."

She drummed her fingers on the bar impatiently. The coffee was taking forever. Rocky kept breaking off to serve someone else. At this rate the coffee would be cold before they were served. She watched Rocky scowl at a grungy-looking kid who hardly looked old enough to be in the bar. Should she check him out? The kid kept on calling and Rocky just kept on ignoring him.

She noticed Rowan watching the byplay. "Interesting, don't you think?" Sliding down off her stool, she said, "I can't wait any longer for that coffee. Tell Rocky I've gone to speak with Ginny's mom."

With one eye on Ms. Wilks and her one-handed balancing act with a tray filled with bottles and glasses as she wiped up spills from the table, Jo walked idly past the kid sitting alone on the far side of the bar. The closer she got, the more she thought she knew him from somewhere, but she decided not to approach him. Instead she salted his features away in her memory for future reference.

She'd always had a nose for sussing if something was out of kilter, but the whiff of cannabis was unexpected. The air in the bar was quite blue with smoke, even in the nonsmoking area, it hung close to the ceiling. But this was different.

Without making it too obvious she checked out his hands for a cigarette. He wasn't holding one.

No matter, fire was needed for smoke and a pinpoint of flame glowed at the back of her mind. Let it burn long enough… Oh yeah, sometimes her patience surprised her, only look at this business with Rocky and her dad.

The waiting would simply make a positive result all the sweeter.

Chapter 4

Rowan watched Jo, his hackles rising as he saw several other men in the bar do the same. He couldn't control the spurt of possessiveness awakening the sleeping beast in the back of his mind. And he had to admit, letting it stretch a time or two before reining it in lessened the strain acting so damn *nice* all the time put on his back teeth. They ached.

Hell, he wanted her.

What man wouldn't? She was so easy on the eye.

For an extratall woman she gave the appearance of being comfortable in her own skin. No hunching her shoulders. No wearing flat-heeled shoes. No pretence. She was simply herself. Beautiful without seemingly aware of it.

Casually, she walked by the stools on far side of the U-shape, hardly appearing to notice the guy whose clenched fist vibrated with impatience on the bar top. Yet, Rowan knew she wouldn't forget him in a hurry.

The intrusion of china clattering on the counter by his elbow broke his concentration.

"Worth looking at, isn't she, McQuaid?"

Eyes off, you sonofabitch! It was all he could do to hold the growl at the back of his throat and swallow it down.

Skelton wasn't finished, more's the pity. "Reminds me of her old man. He was a looker too, a real babe magnet. Pity."

He leaned toward McQuaid, confidential-like. Intuition told Rowan he wasn't going to like what was coming. Looking away, he took his time, ripping open the paper tube, pouring the sugar into his coffee, stirring until it dissolved.

"You probably know the story. Milo, her father, was my partner, but I don't think I ever really knew him. He was the kind of guy who played his cards close to his chest. That's another trait Johanna gets from him. I'll tell you it shook me up when he committed suicide."

Rowan had heard enough. He jerked his head toward the other side of the bar. "There's a guy over there so dry looks like he could spit tacks."

Skelton didn't need telling who Rowan was referring to. He looked over his shoulder, saying, "He'll keep."

"I don't think so, you deal with him, then come back and we can *deal*. No more interruptions."

"Sure, no worries," said Skelton. Moving with the smoothness of long familiarity, he slid open the glass fridge door, grabbed a long-necked bottle, an import, and cracked the top.

The round base hit the counter loud enough for Rowan to hear, but their conversation was another matter. The guy scowled down at the beer. It lasted maybe two seconds then his gaze widened fractionally before his pale lids shuttered his eyes, masking his expression. Skelton turned his back on him and like cock-of-the-walk, chest and biceps pumped, stretching the face of the dead rock star on the front, he stalked away. Behind him the guy twisted the top off the bottle. A fountain of froth spewed up the neck and over the counter.

Rowan saw the shape of the curse on his lips, but couldn't hear. Skelton could. Turning, he glanced over his shoulder as the guy slouched away, leaving the bottle slicked in foam, and untouched by human lips. Skelton simply shook his head, saying, "Kids. You can't win. Now what do you want to know?"

"Not a lot." Rowan took a long swig of coffee, checked out Jo over the rim of his cup, and said, "I've read your police statement, and I've brought a copy of your claim. Tomorrow morning I'll check out your house. And in the afternoon, with your cooperation, I'll do the same to your financial situation."

"You what?" Skelton shrank inside his black T-shirt and the white plastic face of Jim Morrison on the front sagged.

"Cast your mind back to when you took out the policy on your house. Remember the privacy waiver?" Rowan reached into the pocket inside his leather jacket. The papers were folded in four. He spread them out on the counter, rubbing out the creases with his thumb. "Unless you sign this form giving me access to all your accounts, your policy becomes null and void."

Five minutes later, Rowan had an inventory of all Skelton's banking, and the name of his accountant. He knew he'd been coming on strong, but the man had brought it on himself with his oh, so innocent, throw-away remarks about Jo's father. The jerk knew what he was doing; he was just too dumb to realize Rowan knew it, too. At last he had an inkling, if not all, of why Jo didn't trust the guy. He knew if he'd given the jerk another inch he'd have stabbed her in the back.

Hell, he was banking on being out of Nicks Landing in under a week, could hardly wait. But if Jo's secrets were going to be blabbed, he'd prefer to hear them from *her* lips.

And as for his secrets…same goes.

Jo recognized that the resemblance between Ginny and her mother was more than a mass of red curls. As she walked up behind Ms. Wilks, she heard her talking to the patrons in the same gotta-get-it-all-out-in-one-breath style as her daughter.

"Ms. Wilks?"

The woman gave the table a last flick with her cloth and turned, balancing the full tray on her hip. "Get yourself a table, hon. I'll take your order in a sec."

"No. I don't want to order. I wondered if I could have a

word?'' She wasn't a short woman but she looked up at Jo, giving her a familiar wide, blue-eyed stare.

"I'm sure the check's in the mail...." She laughed then, but there wasn't much humor in it, only the ring of resignation. "I bet you hear that all the time."

"Actually, no. It's usually some other excuse. I'm a cop."

"Omigod! Something bad's happened. Who is it? Carter or Ginny?'' All the color leached out of her face, and in contrast, her hair swung in bright flames as her eyes flicked from side to side as if wondering where next to turn. "Has Carter taken another of his spells?"

Jo felt dreadful. She spoke up quickly, wanting to reassure the distressed woman. "Relax. It's okay, nothing major. I only wanted a word about Ginny."

Ms. Wilks released her white-knuckle grip on the tray and Jo made a dive for it, before its weight could send it crashing to the floor. Color returned to the woman's face as they faced one another, each with a hand on the tray.

"Thanks," she said shakily. "I couldn't afford to pay for that lot." She nodded toward Rocky. "Not out of the wages he pays."

"My fault. I could have picked my moment better."

"So what's Ginny been up to this time?"

"Nothing too awful. Look, why don't you put down that tray and we can talk about it?"

"Sorry." Ginny's mother looked in the direction of the bar again. Rocky was serving the guy Jo had been watching. "I have to keep moving. He'll dock my wages if I fall behind with my work."

"How about I walk round with you and we can talk as you work." Jo asked as she carefully framed her next question. "See that young guy Rocky's serving, do you know his name? Is he a regular in here?"

"Who, Jeff Smale? Yes, he's pretty regular. Not that I have much to do with him." Her nose curled as she sniffed. "Always looks as if he needs a good wash. So, what's he done?"

"Nothing." Nothing that she knew of, at the moment. "I

thought I'd met him someplace but I don't recognize the name."

"Maybe it was one of his brothers? There are three of them, and they all look alike."

"Maybe that's it, thanks for your help, Ms. Wilks." Jo said, but Ginny's mother was already heading for another table.

She looked over her shoulder. "Call me Betty. I'm more used to it than Ms. Wilks. Now, you were going to tell me about Ginny. I take it she's in trouble again. She's not a bad kid, but she's impulsive. Doesn't stop to think things through."

It was like déjà vu, hearing an echo of Grandma Glamuzina's old warning. *Think before you speak, girl.*

Some role model she would make, when she still hadn't learned that herself.

Rowan tucked the signed form back where it had come from and smiled at Skelton. "Wise move. Less painful than drawing teeth."

He threw Rowan a look with a lot of stick behind it. "Some things are sacred."

"I'm afraid that cow died the moment you signed the insurance agreement." And it wasn't even fine print. "Where can I find your wife?"

"Molly? She's in the kitchen." Pale blue eyes swiveled in the direction of a door practically invisible against the dark wall, except for a small round of safety glass. Skelton cracked a smile. "Reckon she'll be pleased to see you. Been getting on her nerves all this waiting."

Putting his empty cup down alongside Jo's untouched one, Rowan slid a ten out of his wallet and placed it on the counter.

Indecision hovered over Skelton's features, and flicked between his expectation of Rowan's reception when he entered the kitchen and the studied insult in the ten which diminished him. His ego won. "It's on the house."

"No, thanks. Company policy, but keep the change."

A quick glance through the glass to confirm there were no

bodies on the other side, and Rowan shouldered his way through the swing door.

Molly lived up to her name, contrary to his expectations after reading the crazed letters she'd bombarded Allied Insurance with. Silver-blond curls bobbed on her forehead and her cheeks were pink with exertion as the knife in her hand made short work of the carrots sitting on a work table too tall for someone of her diminutive size. "Mrs. Skelton?" he inquired.

She looked up, swiping at a lock of hair dancing in front of the bluest eyes he'd ever seen. Molly smiled and the dimple in her chin deepened. Only the series of lines tracking either side of her mouth and eyes showed her true age. "Sorry, we don't allow the public through here. Health regulations."

"Your husband sent me through. I'm from your insurer."

The knife in her hands froze midstroke and her smile faltered an instant then widened. Fluttering her eyelashes, Molly laid the knife down carefully on the scrubbed, pine butcher block at one end of the work counter. Right there and then Rowan decided Rocky had sent the abusive letters in his wife's name.

She wiped her hands on the navy apron she wore over a pink frilled blouse. "If I'd known they were going to send you, I'd have insisted on getting face-to-face sooner."

Hell, she was flirting with him. "I'm sure we'll be able to resolve all your problems within the week."

Her pert mouth pouted. No trace of the childish protest touched her eyes. Instead of sparkling, a dearth of emotion flattened their blue depths.

"I take it you haven't brought the check?"

A wiser man would have backed off when he caught the look in Molly's eyes, but sometimes it was easier to be wiser after the event. "I'm afraid not, but I do want to thank you for writing to Allied Insurance about your concerns."

The slash of overbright pink lipstick disappeared as she bit her lips. Aw, hell. She was going to cry. "I don't want thanks. A thank-you will never replace what I lost. All my pretties."

That flummoxed him. He hadn't heard about the lost pets

in the fire. "I'm sorry Mrs. Skelton. I know it's hard to lose a pet—"

"Pets?" she sobbed. "I didn't have no pets. It's my collections, my crystal, my *Lladro*. What didn't smash when the beam fell onto my glass cabinet, the firemen finished off with their big feet." Molly grabbed her apron and buried her face in it, which muffled the sounds.

"You'll be pleased to know I've come here to give the local cops a hurry up." He could imagine Jo's face if she heard him now, but he picked the tool most likely to get the job done.

Molly's eyes peered at him over the apron.

"You have to admit it's not your everyday kind of case. Do you have any thoughts on what could have provoked…"

She sniffed and dropped the apron. "I'm done thinking about it. All I want is to make a start at replacing my stuff. Not that I'll be able to. Not all. Some of my pieces were irreplaceable. For starters there was…"

It looked like being a long list. Rowan started to brace himself against the boredom of a minute description of everything Molly had lost in the fire. But as he listened, it became easier. He felt sorry for her. The woman had no children, was stuck with a husband whose idea of beauty appeared to be the badge of a Harley-Davidson, or a crash helmet with a dent in one side. Everything beautiful in her life had been destroyed in a few short minutes.

He could empathize with that.

Molly's attitude toward him slipped from tearful to reasonable. Any tears she swiped now were on account of an onion.

"As soon as the police are satisfied, and we're looking at days here, you'll be paid out."

Molly sniffed. "When you say police I take it you mean Jo Jellic? Everyone knows she doesn't like Rocky. Believe me, she'll do her damnedest to see he comes off worst." She shook her head, blinking at the strong fumes. "As if a man would do that to himself. My Rocky was in agony. Slept on his stomach for weeks."

"Understandable, I saw the photo." He'd had another look at the photos after he'd dumped his duffel on board. That was the weakest link in Jo's case. It took guts to deliberately set fire to yourself. Rocky didn't seem top-heavy in that department.

Nodding her agreement, she said, "Could have been worse. His burns stung, but he could be dead now." She scooped the onions into a bowl with the rest of the vegetables, then turning her back on Rowan she tipped them into the stew and gave it a stir. "Can you imagine the sort of low-life it takes to even think of doing that? They had to be mad. You should look to the loony bin for suspects. That's the place for devil worshipers."

"Somehow I don't think we need worry about anyone locked up, the ones walking the street are harder to get a handle on. We got a lead today. Could be we'll bring this to an end quite soon."

"And you think Jo Jellic will follow it up?"

"Yes, I do. And I'll be right there alongside her." Right or wrong, it seemed Jo had something to prove, and not only to herself.

Skelton's wife never stopped working. She was gathering together the makings for pastry, piling it into a huge mixer. "Do you do all the cooking for the bar by yourself?"

"Every last bit. I don't trust nobody else to get it right." She switched on the machine and little puffs of flour rose from its bowl. "This is for my steak pies. I have to make plenty, they're my best sellers."

"Well, if they taste as good as they smell, I'll be in to taste some for myself tomorrow." He earned a smile for his compliment, and promised himself he would come in tomorrow and sample her baking. A few brownie points wouldn't go wrong.

The back of his neck prickled as if he were being watched, then the door behind him swung open and he heard Jo's voice.

Molly stopped smiling.

"I'll hold the door," Jo was saying as he turned around,

laughing with the woman carrying the tray. His chest tightened. She'd never laughed with him that way. So naturally.

When had he ever encouraged her to? It had been safer to poker up when the jokes were flying, and keep his distance.

Safer for his peace of mind.

"What do you think this is? Central Station?" Molly slapped the cloth in her hand down on the bench and began rubbing hard enough to wipe six inches of splinters from the butcher's block.

One word from Molly and he had his reprieve. Jo raised an eyebrow. Flame flickered in the dark brown of her eyes. A cold flame, one that stripped the flesh off your bones. He was glad not to be on the receiving end. If Rowan had needed confirmation that there was no love lost between these two, he had it now.

"Jo was just holding the door for me, I'm pretty loaded up."

Jo? If they were on a first-name basis the talk between her and Ginny's mom must have gone well.

"No problem, Betty. I don't like to see anyone overworked."

Betty, the peacemaker, spoke up again, "Oh, Molly would never overwork me. She's very good to me and Ginny. I like to earn my wages, though. That way no one can complain."

From the look Betty cast Jo, Rowan gathered she was implying Skelton was a different proposition. "I was telling Molly we'd gotten a lead and she'd probably be paid out soon," he mentioned, hoping to put his weight behind Betty's conciliatory remark.

"Actually, Jo came to see me about Ginny. Wouldn't you know it? She's in bother again."

Molly just laughed. "She's a hard case that girl. What's she been up to this time? Not much, I bet. Some girlie nonsense. The child doesn't mean anything by it."

"Ginny's a favorite with Molly," said Betty, stating the obvious. "Jo picked Ginny up for shoplifting this afternoon."

"And charged her, no doubt. As if the cops haven't got better things to do than go around chasing kids."

"She's been given a warning. That's all. Her mother can see to her punishment. I'm sure Ginny is really a good kid. At least she didn't lie about it when she was caught. I appreciate *honesty*. I've been thinking about what Ginny told me. Betty was saying the kid has a great imagination, Rowan. Maybe it's not worth the trouble of going all that way, because of what Ginny thinks could be a satanic cult. The boys at school could have been teasing."

Betty rattled glasses as she filled the dishwasher, and the pastry dough slapped against the sides of the bowl, making it rock on its stand. Jo's indecision hit a lull and sounded the louder for it. Molly stopped scraping up flour with the edge of the knife. "What did I tell you? She's got no intention of finding out the truth. She's no more use than Bull and Jake. They couldn't find a suspect if he was under their noses."

The knife shuddered as it clipped the edge of the mixer, sending it spinning. The reflection from the fluorescent bounced off the blade, making fairy lights dance on the ceiling.

Molly watched the knife as if mesmerized until Betty walked over and picked it up, saying, "I'll put this in with the glasses." The moment passed.

He could see the quick rise and fall of Jo's breasts and knew he wasn't the only one breathing fast. Skelton's wife balanced on the edge of her stress like a tinker-tot doll, not quite falling over. He just hoped they weren't around when she did.

"Don't worry." Jo's tone was even as if she'd never had any doubt about the way Molly had eyed that knife. "If the truth's out there, Molly, I'll find it, no matter who's doing the telling. And don't be so hard on Bull and Jake. Only this afternoon they brought in a couple of bad guys who'd been growing dope. Not content with growing it out in the bush, these guys had set up lights and tinfoil, and were growing it indoors."

Through pinched lips, Molly said grudgingly, "'Bout time

they did something to earn the money us taxpayers pay them. They lost a good man when Rocky retired.''

Before anyone could comment that it was actually redundancy, the timer on the oven began to ping. Molly grabbed a tray from under the counter. "If you'll excuse me, I have to go fill up the pie warmer in the bar."

"I can do that for you," said Betty.

"No need. I'm sure these people haven't any more questions. I expect they'll be gone when I get back."

"Well, I'm one who can take a hint," said Jo, as the door swung shut with Molly on the other side.

Betty closed the dishwasher and spun the dial. "Molly's not always like this. She just hasn't been herself since her house was torched. She had it beautiful. Lived for that house, always planning what she would buy next. Got a pile of catalogues in the storeroom that she shopped through. No place in Nicks Landing for that sort of quality. Nothing but the best for Molly." Sighing wistfully, she looked at Jo. "She never had any children. I guess the house and those collections were her compensation."

"Molly never struck me as the motherly type."

"Oh, she wanted kids all right. Molly told me how Rocky and her tried for years. She even went to specialists. None of them could find a thing wrong with her. It was just one of those mysteries that no one can explain."

The conversation between Jo and Betty was heading in a direction guaranteed to make Rowan uncomfortable. He'd never been married, never had a sister either, nothing to help stop him breaking out in a sweat as the talk turned to women's troubles. He began edging toward the door, hoping Jo would follow him.

Jo took a couple of steps back in his direction, waving goodbye to Betty. A wry smile creased her lips as she lifted her face to his and spoke softly, cutting Betty out of the circle. "The biggest mystery is how Rocky hoped to father a child when he'd had himself snipped."

They hadn't heard the door open, or counted on Molly standing behind them. "Are you two still here?"

Rowan didn't breathe till they got outside. "Do you think she heard?"

"Heck, no. I'm still standing, aren't I?"

Chapter 5

Jo scrubbed her hands till they glowed pink. If anyone had told her three years ago that she'd spend the best part of a morning looking at a dead bull calf's innards, she'd have laughed in their face. If Rowan had suggested it last night, she'd have given him one of her I-don't-think-so looks and dismissed the possibility.

Compared to this morning's outing, last night's visit to Rocky's Hard Luck Inn had been an adventure in Sin City. Wanna get down to basics? Visit a farm.

Thank heavens she'd taken Harry's advice when she first arrived in Nicks Landing and invested in a pair of rubber boots. She kept them in the trunk of her car for visiting farms and the like, but usually by the time she got home it was mud and manure needing to be hosed off, not blood.

Taking a deep breath, Jo centered her equilibrium. A few swift strokes of the brush through her hair, a spray of her favorite perfume, the one her friend Maggie had sent her last Christmas, one squirt behind each ear and another inside the front of her bra and she felt almost normal. Ready to face anything—except maybe Rowan.

A quick look at her watch told her she was already five minutes late for their appointment. The one she'd already set back by four hours.

The sight of Harry sitting behind his desk was comforting somehow. Steady. Reliable. Unweird.

She'd come across a lot of peculiar things during her stint in Auckland, but luckily, nothing as bad as this morning's little entertainment.

Harry brought up his head and gave her a grin. "Feeling better?"

She looked at her hands. "Some carbolic would have come in handy. Lady MacBeth has got nothing on me. I don't think my hands will ever be clean again."

"Didn't you wear gloves?"

"What difference does that make? It's the thought that counts. And if Bull and Jake hadn't stayed overnight in Gisborne with those cannabis growers, this job would have been right up their street. I don't think I ever saw so much blood in all my life."

A puzzled expression drew some extra lines round Harry's eyes. "Didn't you work on that serial killer case up in Auckland?"

"I did. But *he* was a very tidy fellow. Hated the sight of blood, unlike our friend at Rimu Downs farm."

"So, are you going to fill me in on it then, or do I have to wait until you put in a report?"

Jo checked the clock on the wall behind Harry. She could spare maybe two minutes, that was all. It would take five to reach Lonely Track Road. Any more and Rowan would give up on her.

She hitched one hip onto the corner of his desk and began. "Okay, I'll give you the gist of it, then I have to run. The bull calf was worth ten thousand, minimum. It was part of a special breeding program they've got going up there. Its sire—" She paused a minute, thinking. "Do they call bulls sires?'' Harry looked blank so she carried on. ''Anyway, its father was worth about ten times that, and they'd had high hopes for the calf.''

''You'd better tell McQuaid that.''

''Why?'' Had Harry come to the conclusion bugging her all morning? That maybe, just maybe, Rocky hadn't been lying. How many calves get killed by ritual sacrifice?

''Rimu Downs belongs to the Stanhopes. The guy running the farm is only a manager.''

''And?'' she prodded him.

For a second he looked like a goldfish drowning on air, then he spat out the words. ''It's obvious. McQuaid works for them. Allied probably handled the insurance.''

Logical, but something told her that hadn't been Harry's first choice of words. ''I'll tell him about it when I get to Rocky's house. He's meeting me there fifteen minutes ago, so the rest of the gory details will have to wait.''

''Speak of the devil.''

''Who, Rowan?'' She swung around. The sergeant's chair was positioned to give him a view of the comings and goings at the front counter through the open door. Rocky was there talking to Seth. ''What does he want now?''

Harry sighed loud enough for it to have come from way down in his boots. ''Knowing him, it won't be anything good.''

That was what Jo liked about the Sergeant. He was the only other one in the station house who didn't think daisies sprouted in Rocky's footprints. Yeah, she really liked that about Harry. He was a man of extraordinary common sense.

Seth stuck his head round the door. He looked from Harry to Jo. ''Rocky wants to talk to Jo, I mean Detective Jellic.''

''Let him through...''

''Don't tell him I'm here,'' said Jo at the same time. It was no use. Seth knew which side his bread was buttered on, and obeyed Harry. ''I don't have time for this. I should have left earlier.''

''If it's of no importance, tell him you'll get back to him.''

"Have you ever known him to listen to anyone but himself?"

Rocky appeared from the foyer. Harry spoke. "What's important enough to drag you from the bar during the lunch trade?"

"They're back." One bald statement as if she and Harry were mind readers. Maybe so. Icy drips trickled down her spine.

"Why don't you start by telling us who *they* are?" suggested the sergeant. He was nonchalance personified in contrast to a harried Rocky whose thinning hair stood on end as if he'd run his fingers through it. His gaze dodged a long strand of hair hanging over one eye and focused on checking her reactions. Only natural. He *knew* she thought him a liar. She'd told him to his face less than two months of arriving in Nicks Landing. Honesty had become her creed. She practiced it well and in no uncertain terms Jo had let him know, she thought he'd lied about her father. She'd followed Max, her old sergeant's example. Jo used to chide him about it, say it was his there's-a-new-Sheriff-in-town warning. It hadn't worked with Rocky. He'd laughed it off. Of course that was before she knew he considered himself bulletproof. Who wouldn't with half the local cops backing them?

"The satanists, they're back."

"What happened? They set fire to your bar this time, or just your shirttail to send you rushing over here in a tizz?" Harry's drawl grew more pronounced, emphasizing his country roots. It always did when he spoke to Rocky. At a guess, it was part of a running battle. One that had gone on in the days when Rocky had been Detective Sergeant, city trained and a big wheel in Nicks County police. Harry hadn't aimed any further than the town he'd been born in, hadn't wanted to.

"They've been back to my house. My neighbor, Jenny Gilbransen, came in this morning. Not for a drink, she doesn't drink, and anyway the bar wasn't open." He paused for breath, giving the impression he'd run all the way, which would be a first.

"She said she heard a car outside my place in the middle of the night. Said it was there awhile before it took off."

It was time Jo got involved, so she asked, "Did she get up and take a look? Did she see anything?" See you, maybe? First the calf, now this. Coincidence or what?

"No. She's on her own in that big old house next to mine. I bought my land off her. Jenny said she just pulled the covers over her head and waited till she heard them pull away."

"She didn't think to call you?"

"No. She got up when they left, had a look to see if my house was on fire, and when it wasn't she made herself a cup of tea and went back to bed."

"So why the panic if your house is okay?" Or as okay as it's ever going to be till they pull it down? Something was going down. Something distinctly fishy. If Rocky Skelton was cool enough to get himself out of a burning building with his skin still intact, or practically intact, why fall to pieces over a house that was hardly more than a burned-out shell?

"I went up there. I thought I'd find you and McQuaid, but there was no one around. Someone had been there all right. They'd scattered newspaper all over the floor."

Jo let a raised eyebrow speak for her. A yawn would have done it better, but she could control herself. She hoped the punch line was better than the rest of his story.

"The papers were covered in blood."

Harry looked in her direction. She could tell they were on the same wavelength but he was leaving the questions to her. Both of them throwing a two into the pot, hoping to come up with five.

She stared pointedly at Rocky. "But there was no body?"

"I didn't see one. Just an old newspaper with my picture on the front. It was smeared with blood and someone had drawn an inverted pentagram around the picture." His Adam's apple quivered among the lines on his neck. "Like it was a target."

None of his drama touched her. If it had been someone else she might have felt for them, but her sympathy button had been preconditioned, and Rocky just couldn't push it. "Two questions. How long ago was this? And what did you do with the paper?"

"Twenty minutes ago. I started to pick it up then dropped it back on the floor and got the hell out of there."

Rocky, Molly's *parfait* gentle knight, what a joke. She'd once gone into the kitchen of the Hard Luck Inn and caught Molly watching *The Bold And The Beautiful* on TV. Though Jo had scoffed to herself, she understood Molly's need for distraction, being married to a man who was anything but bold or beautiful.

It suddenly dawned on Jo that twenty minutes ago, she should have met up with Rowan. "You didn't see McQuaid at the house?"

"No, no one. I thought I might run into him because he said you two were going there this morning."

"Our plans got changed."

Ratchett! She gave herself a mental slap. Her nose twitched as it always did when she was annoyed with herself. Should she believe Rocky or not? If this was another of his cons...

"I've got to go," she said more to Harry than Rocky. "You see Rocky out and I'll see him later."

She hurried through the lockup, silent today, and out to her car. Dust from her trek to the farm covered it so she'd hidden it out back. Her heels left short, sharp, snapping echoes on the concrete as her mind assessed the pros and cons. The bloody newspapers and eviscerated calf cried out to be connected.

If she was wrong about Rocky, bang went her chance to show the man up for what he was. What she knew he was, firsthand. Who else but a scumbag would tell lies about his dead partner? A partner and friend who could no longer defend himself. That's why the job had fallen to her, his partner's daughter. If she was wrong, Rowan could be stepping into a trap set for Rocky.

And if she was correct about said scumbag? Rowan could

be stepping into a trap set for both of them…or maybe just for her. Rocky hadn't been whistling "Thank Heaven For Little Girls," when she'd taken over the case.

Jo put her foot down, accelerating out of the car park with more haste than style. Whichever side of the line the truth fell on, she needed to get the hell out there and warn Rowan.

If only she could remember where she'd stashed his business card. At least then she could have called him.

Rowan checked the clock on the dashboard as he pulled up in Lonely Track Road. He was late, but Jo was later. He'd give her five minutes, then go take a look for himself. He was a big boy, and whatever bug she had in her brain about accompanying him, he didn't need her holding his hand.

She'd been very insistent. "I want to show you the exact route Rocky took to get out of the house," she'd said when she called at some godawful early hour of the morning. Not that it mattered, he hadn't been asleep. Too busy planning his retreat to catch more than a few z's at a time.

No mention had been made of the unspoken disagreement that had driven them apart the moment they'd hit the sidewalk in front of the Hard Luck Inn.

Molly Skelton, God bless her, had a good excuse for her sour outlook on life and the rings she'd been running round the staff at head office. Rowan shook his head as he remembered his meeting with the CEO of Allied Insurance. He didn't know where the management got off employing such a bunch of wimps in a job where abusive letters were run of the mill. Yet Molly Skelton had inundated them with faxes and phone calls till they were almost ready to pay her the money just to get her off their back.

For the first time in seventeen years, Rowan had come home to Nicks Landing as a peace broker. All that changed the moment he met Jo. He just wanted to pay up and get the hell out of Dodge.

Sure, he could turn tail and run before concluding his business. But it would look too suspicious. Jo was *too* smart, and didn't need ideas put in her head.

She already had enough of them for two people.

Rowan looked up at the burned-out shell as he stepped from the car. Red chip crunched under the soles of his boots as he trudged up the fairly steep drive, intending to walk around to work out the easiest way to get inside, if Jo didn't arrive.

A car changed gears behind him. A quick glance was followed by a sharp twist of disappointment in his gut when he saw it wasn't her. For years he'd been telling himself he didn't need her.

What was so different now?

She'd taken him by surprise, and he'd still to decide if it was pleasant, or what?

The house stared down at him with dark vacant eyes. A sad Cape Cod with a hole in the roof that had seen better days.

Hadn't they all.

The sign nailed to the porch read, Danger. Keep out.

He knew all about danger. He'd lived with it for years, working in the same building, never knowing when he would bump into Jo in the corridor. Except he never had. Bumped into her, that is. He'd always made sure never to encroach on her personal space. Ironically the only time he'd ever gotten up close and personal with Jo was the night he'd been shot, and that memory he associated with pain.

A car door slammed as his foot hit the bottom step. He turned and it was Jo, running toward him shouting, "Wait up!"

She moved gracefully for a tall woman. A tall woman in a hurry as she didn't slow down, knowing he'd seen her. Her breasts swayed, captured by the bonds of a lime-green shirt Jo had tucked inside dark khaki pants. She'd topped the outfit off with a cream marled waistcoat barely reaching her waist. Hanging open, it didn't impede his view of her full breasts and lush hips.

Would he ever get the chance to touch them?

Would he ever *take* a chance and touch them?

Jo was so beautiful. Hell, he got turned on simply watching her.

The closer she got, the more his annoyance dissolved. He'd almost had Molly eating out of his hand last night—well, if not that, at least being agreeable—until Jo's blunder.

"Thank heavens I caught you." Her voice had a husky, breathless rasp. He wished it was on account of his presence instead of the grassy slope.

"What's the rush, I got here late myself."

"I know, Rocky told me, at least he told me you hadn't arrived earlier."

Her scent caught him with a right cross to the esophagus. She smelled of limes and passion flowers warming on a vine in the summer sun. He breathed deeply. An indulgence. One he could ill afford if he meant to stick to his original plan of staying out of danger and where danger dwelled. "So, he's been up here? What did he want?" Frankly, he didn't give a damn what Skelton wanted.

The sun was shining on Jo's hair and it reminded him of a lake he'd once camped by, the way the moonlight had crested the top of the ripples when the wind disturbed its surface. How easy it was to let his mind slide from there, to him and Jo, getting cozy together in a small tent. A very small tent. Oh yeah, it was tempting danger, but he was getting to like it.

"You can't get in that way. It's boarded up because the floor is dangerous," Jo was saying. "I have a key to the back door of the garage. It's easier to get in, less damage."

She grabbed his hand, oblivious to the effect of her touch on him. Seemed she wasn't holding any grudges over his dismissal of her the night before.

"C'mon, I'll tell you what Rocky *said* he wanted as we go. Then I'll give you a blow-by-blow description of my visit to Rimu Downs farm this morning and see what you make of it."

Jo pulled him away from the steps and down the path and he let her. Her grip was firm for a hand much smaller than his, but he lapped it up, wondering if the proverbial lamb felt this good as it was led to the slaughter. Maybe there was more of the masochist in his makeup than he realized.

"So there we are, me and the farm manager, we're standing inside this circle of white lime." Jo stopped and opened a door. "Through here," she said to Rowan.

Her panic had subsided on the drive to Lonely Track Road. In fact she'd begun to feel a little foolish about the situation and didn't want Rowan to know. That's what came of taking anything Rocky said at face value. Now if she could only stop talking. Heck, she could sympathize with Ginny. Seemed they both ran off at the mouth when they were nervous.

Nervous?

Was that the true cause of her girlish reaction? So? She wasn't as blasé as she liked to pretend.

"This calf is in the middle." They were walking down the hall now and the walls on either side of them were covered in soot. "Watch you don't brush up against anything. You'll never get it off. I think it's residue from the polyurethane foam inside the lounge suites. The only way to remove it is with soap and a wire brush. You scrub the stain till all that's left is a hole."

Rowan's features looked carved out of rock. She guessed he still hadn't forgiven her little faux pas—well all right, big faux pas—in front of Molly last night. There had been a moment when she'd run up to him outside, that she'd thought he looked pleased to see her, but it was probably only a trick of the light. She just wished he would add his two cents worth to the conversation. So, shut your mouth and give him a chance.

"Anyway, the calf's throat's cut and it's been slit open from top to bottom, lying there with its poor little legs sticking up and everything hanging...well, I don't have to describe it. Use your imagination."

They'd reached the family room. She took a good look round, couldn't see any newspapers, and carried on to where bifold doors hung lopsidedly on their hinges separating the room from the entrance hall. "I didn't know whether to be sick or swear." Or give way to hysterical laughter. "The farm manager, he was practically crying, and his voice squeaked every time he took a gander at the region where the calf's male parts once resided."

She stopped in the entrance hall.

Rowan came to a halt beside her, folded his arms and looked around. "Something special I should know about?"

He looked calm enough. Patient. Waiting. Tension strung the muscles of his lower arms where sun-bleached hairs caught the sunlight coming through the hole in the roof above the two-story-high foyer. They were the same color as the gold streaking the moustache that made his expression hard to read. For all he'd shaved last night, *it* still resided on his upper lip.

"This is the way Rocky got out. The floors in the entrance and living room used to be polished rimu." She pointed into the living area. "See that plank there? That's where he said they left him tied up."

"With duct tape?"

"Yeah, the firemen removed it before the cops got here. We've got the tape, but no photos of how he was tied up."

"Don't sweat it. This is another time when I'd rather use my imagination." His teeth flashed white, acknowledging her earlier throw-away line.

He'd actually smiled. Was this the same gruff Rowan she'd known in Auckland? If he'd hit her with a smile like that then, maybe she would have given him a second look. Or even a third. She mightn't have gone as far as shouting *babe alert*, or whistling, but she'd definitely have looked. A sigh crept up from the soles of her feet. Time to get back on course.

"Well, imagine this. He's doused in gasoline."

"Initials carved in his back."

"Yeah, so he said. The jury's still out on that one, remember? But I guess it would have stung."

"Not to mention the small matter of a fire chasing his tail."

"Let's not. There's gasoline all over the floor, but conveniently not beneath the curtains that they set fire to."

She turned and looked up, her shoulders at ninety degrees to the center of Rowan's chest. But before she could set him straight on the rest of the story, he said, "Could be that was to give them a chance to escape, or to make Skelton sweat watching the fire coming nearer."

Logically, Rowan was one hundred percent right. The trouble with this case was that all the evidence was circumstantial. What she needed was something positive, then she'd have Rocky. Or not.

"Good point," she conceded.

Rowan nodded. "Okay. He's out in the foyer. Where does he go from here?"

"C'mon. I'll show you. Someone's closed this door, but Rocky says it was open." Jo flung the door wide. "I can't imagine Molly leaving this open as it can be seen from the entrance. But then, she wasn't at home. This is the utility room. The washer and dryer don't look too bad, but I suppose she's claiming for them, as well. The door that's boarded up is the one he dived through. The flames caught up with him and gave him a bad case of sunburn. He put them out by rolling around on the back lawn."

"Don't you think if Skelton had set this up himself he'd have *conveniently* left that door unlocked?" Rowan stepped round Jo and measured himself against the door. Would *he* have made it through?

"No, because he didn't have any way to open the door. Look at it this way. He's wriggled in here on his belly, pushing with his toes. His ankles are bound and his hands are tied behind his back. The space between the tub and this wall is about three feet, so he pushes himself up the wall, digging his toes into the baseboard at the bottom of the tub, and gets upright. How does he turn the handle—with his teeth?"

Rowan took a good look at the hexagonal-shaped handle. His jaw worked slightly as if testing the theory. "You're right. No way could he open that without hands, but if he'd set it up himself, why didn't he leave the door open?"

"Puleeeze. That would have been too obvious. Either way

he had to take a dive through the glass. I'd say the only thing stopping him from being cut in half was the three smaller panes. They don't have to be as thick as the large expanses.''

The three feet of space which had made it simple for Rocky to push himself up, was about three feet too small with two of them trying to get out. They did a slow dance, elbows bumping, turning, fronts brushing. His breath tickling her face. Oh, Lord! Perspiration ran down her spine. Could Rocky have felt any hotter with flames at his heels?

With a jerky movement she brought her chin up, wanting, needing to see his reaction. Her gaze met his enigmatic, green stare head-on. His nostrils flared, his chest lifting on a sharp breath. Embarrassed, she felt her nipples crest as if chasing the elusive hardness that had made them tingle. She felt herself shake. Was that a hint of mockery round his lips? She looked away, dreading to have her suspicions confirmed.

"We'd better get on," she said, her voice huskier than she would have wished. She put a hand out to push past, discovering his heartbeat under her palm, slow, heavy thuds that reverberated in the nerve endings of her arm. The sensation giving her ideas.

"I'll go first." *Second. Anytime. Just give me a sign.*

"You're the boss."

Jo swallowed as she thought of all the ways she could take that. Take him. Lord, she was going loco.

Dragging her mind out of the bedroom and back to work, she said, "In that case, let's go find those bloody newspapers that had Rocky so worried."

Inwardly, Jo knew she'd been postponing the moment that might confirm or deny her suspicions about who was behind the fire, Rocky or someone else. Looking over her shoulder, she surprised Rowan's gaze somewhere around the level of her butt. A rueful glint tinged the admiration as his eyes lifted and met hers. All one-sided? She didn't think so.

"If you see a plank, walk on it. Chances are the floor won't take your weight." How heavy was Rowan? She turned away swiftly and quickened her pace into the living room as she felt heat color her cheeks. That's what she got for wondering how it would feel to wake up with Rowan's weight covering her.

Her womb clenched and she almost doubled over from the intensity. It took almost six deep breaths to return to normal. By then she was surrounded by bloodstained newspapers.

"What is that bad smell?" Rowan asked, his tawny head lifting, scenting the air like a huge lion as his hair tossed like a mane, completing the analogy.

Jo recognized the odor. Dead meat.

Shades of her time on the farm that morning. Lord, she hated the country. It was too basic, too down-to-earth for her. Everything stunk to high heaven. The buzzing was familiar as well. Darn flies, they had better radar than a bloodhound. At last she sighted her quarry. "It's the brown paper, grocery sack in front of the window."

Digging into her pocket she sighed with relief to find a spare pair of latex gloves. "At least I won't have to touch it. How kind of them to leave it where I can reach from the plank."

Rowan's big hand settled on her shoulder. "Give me the gloves. I'll do it."

"No, this is my job. I won't have anyone say I shrank away from whatever needed doing. Just don't ask me to like it." The latex snapped as she pulled the gloves tight over her wrists. Then for good measure she took the precaution of rolling her cuffs up to the elbow.

Keeping it light she said, "I wouldn't say no to a can of fly spray if you have one." Then began walking the narrow length of the wood. A deep breath solidified the lack of substance in her knees. It wasn't as if the solid strip of twelve-by-two pine was higher than the floor. Now if she'd been on a pirate ship, with sharks circling below, she'd have an excuse for the wobbles. A chance of crashing into the basement didn't have the same impact.

Just past the halfway mark, Rocky's photo stared up at her from the center of a pentagram. She could read the date above the headline, "Ex-cop attacked by satanists." The day after the fire. Two and a half months and already its folds were yellowed as if it had been part of a pile sitting somewhere sunny. Or had someone simply treasured it for their notoriety? Bringing it out at the appropriate moment.

"I see what Rocky meant about a target." Balancing on one foot, the other hovering six inches above Rocky's face, she eyed the newspaper the way a darts player sizes up the bull's-eye.

Rowan's weight made the plank sigh as he stepped on it, calling out, "No, don't," as if reading her mind. "I know it's tempting, but maybe that's the idea. Better to turn around and come back."

"Easier said than done, wise guy. Let me get to the end and pick up the goods, then I'll come back. It's only another yard or so." She took one long stride, clearing the paper, and a smaller one to land in front of the sack.

Consciously, she'd put the flies out of her mind, but this close they were noisier than a lawn mower on a Sunday. She stooped over, gripped the rolled brown paper edges between finger and thumb. A wave of black dots flew off to explore the disturbee.

"Oh, gross." She waved the dive-bombers away from her face, flapping her hand. "Urk, let me out of here," she moaned, straightening as the bottom fell out of the bag. A heart fell at her feet. She screeched as it rolled, jumping back a step.

The wood underfoot vibrated from Rowan's heavier tread. "What on earth have you got there?"

Jo knew he couldn't see what had happened. She was blocking his view, after all. But he could no more hide the alarm in his voice than she could stop her anxiety spilling over. Taking a calming breath, and feigning an insouciance she didn't feel, she asked Rowan, "Did I ever get round to mentioning which part was missing from that calf?"

Her two-fingered grip on the sack hadn't loosened, and panic soon replaced nonchalance as she flapped it at the ferocious little followers. Anyone in their right mind would have dropped the sack, but sadly, her common sense had gone the way of the heart and hit rock bottom.

Dry newsprint rustled as she was forced back another step. Her heel landed as Rowan caught her round the waist.

"I've got you," he said. She felt his head come around as he looked down. "And you got him."

She twisted, following his gaze. Bull's-eye. The solid heel of her work shoe had landed dead center on Rocky's face.

Not only that, she'd pitched backward with all the grace of an inline skating newbie, lower half at 110 degrees and one foot in the air. Her head leaned into the curve of Rowan's shoulder, his hands and arms circling her ribs. Two inches higher and her breasts would have been the recipient of all that raw power.

This wasn't the moment for wishing his aim had been better, or worse. She hadn't time to ponder the possibilities right now. The question of whether he'd expect her to say "Thank you," or "Will you please remove your hands," uppermost in her mind.

Then came the explosion.

It didn't come with a bang. It was more the sort of noise a barbecue starter makes when you throw in the match.

Though the blast was big enough to send them both reeling as the floor lifted on a cushion of hot air and flames shot up the wall underneath the window.

Rowan's body was too hard to actually soften her fall as she landed on top of him, but it did break it, sending air from his lungs whooshing through her hair.

It appeared every time she and Rowan got up close and personal, they were fated to roll around in a heap.

This wasn't good. It was either the beginning of the end of any hopes she'd nurtured, or it was the end of the beginning.

Chapter 6

"Will you *please* drop the damn sack?"

He'd imagined holding Jo, but it hadn't been like this, with flames licking at their heels and every fly within a square mile dive-bombing the bloody paper sack in her hands.

Lifting Jo, he let their recent discussion of Skelton's escape route guide him through the smoke into the utility room.

Her arms clung round his neck, but he refused to read anything into it. She was probably simply wary of being dropped. A smoky haze shadowed her eyes as if the fire were inside her instead of behind them, gobbling up portions of house it had missed before, like a starving priest after Lent.

In these circumstances, lust ought to be the last item on his agenda. He just wished someone had informed his body. The female softness warming his chest warred with his emotions until he couldn't tell if his heart raced from exertion or excitement at having achieved the ultimate. Being pressed against her lush curves combined his deepest desires with his worst-case scenario.

Slipping his hand out from under her knees, he let her slide to the floor. He was the one who peeled her hands from his neck, yet as she turned her back on him and stepped away, it felt as if his secret fear had come to life by the heightened tension of the moment. Her walking away, and him letting her.

As his father had done with his mother.

Everything he knew would happen, coming true. It seemed a lifetime before he came to his senses to hear Jo saying "Darn, I left the evidence behind."

Her hand gripped the door frame as if she might dash back into the foyer. He reached for her, his fingers tangling in her hair. "Don't be a fool. You'll fry out there."

They could barely see. Acrid smoke blocked the light that had once poured through the hole in the roof and at his back the boarded-up door and window let nothing through. Grasping the door handle, he jerked it round with a sharp turn of his wrist. Pain ricocheted up his arm. The bitch was locked.

The color drained from Jo's face as he gave it another futile twist. Stinging tears filled her eyes as she started to cough. "Close the door, or the fumes will kill us before the flames."

He heard it shut with a snap as he sized up the exit. Luck hadn't abandoned them completely. Whoever had boarded up the door had nailed the plywood to the outside of the frame. The theory being people were more likely to want to break in than break out.

Jo pushed at his shoulder, swinging him back against the soot-blackened wall and if his shirt hadn't been ruined before…

"Stand back and let me kick it out," she wheezed, running her hand down the plywood as if testing its strength.

Her insult thundered in his ears. It always came back to his damn injury. Vexation almost choked him. "No need, I can manage."

In the thin whispers of daylight squeezing through the slits in the board, he felt rather than saw her gaze rest on his thigh, confirming Jo still hadn't gotten over the horror of it.

Damnation, he knew Jo hadn't aimed to unman him. Call

him supersensitive, but he had an overpowering urge to flex his muscles and did, feeling his shirt tighten around them as if he were the Incredible Hulk's alter ego.

No sense in taking deep breaths, even shallow ones hurt too much. His only option was to lead with his shoulder. The plywood shuddered but didn't budge. A curse ripped from his lips in a mixture of pain and frustration. Skelton broke out with his hands tied behind his back. He'd be damned if the place would hold *him*.

"I can hear flames on the other side of the door." Her palm slid down the wood. "Oh, yeah, that's hot. Real hot."

A glance over his shoulder was enough to harden his resolve. Her waistcoat was off, and she tucked it along the bottom of the door to block the smoke. On second glance, she shrank back into the corner, giving him room. One hand waved in front of her face, battling smoke and heat, and she loosened her shirt as the high temperature turned the confined space into a blast furnace.

They had to get out or a lack of oxygen would suffocate them.

Two kicks were enough. The barrier fell outward with a soughing and screeching of nails ripping from their sockets. Rowan turned to Jo, laughing on a surge of pure adrenaline, and swung her into his arms. Jo weighed almost nothing, a featherweight. With her clasped to his chest, he ducked his head and stepped sideways through the gap into the sunlight.

God, life was great!

And with that thought ringing in his head, he took the back steps in one bound, feeling no pain in his thigh or anywhere else for that matter. On the lawn, with his lungs heaving, he halted and watched the fire swallow up the room they'd fled from with less than a second to spare.

Hallelujah! They'd escaped. Rowan threw back his head as relief ripped a huge bellow of glad-to-be alive laughter out of his throat. Jo's fists beat against his shoulders but she didn't join in. He held her away till he could see her face, amazed to find no sign of his own knee-jerk reaction of joy.

Perspiration beaded her forehead and smoky trails of tears painted her cheeks. She'd never looked more beautiful. She was alive. They were alive. For once in his life he let his feelings take over and spun her around in circles.

"Rowan," Jo called his name, her hand tugging at the collar of his shirt. He slowed down, stopped, but the garden kept spinning.

"Rowan..." Her lips seemed to tremble on his name. Her mouth, her beautiful mouth filled his vision. His head dipped to take her lips with his own. A kiss. One kiss. A hero's kiss. He was entitled, and this time he could claim it.

Could a person feel happy and mad at the same time? Happy to find she was able to feel mad, and mad because he was so happy about having rescued her again, when she could have just as easily have gotten out under her own steam.

She felt his breath, tasted it as his face came nearer and put her in danger of discovering exactly how his moustache felt against her mouth, but even the anticipation of such a treat couldn't put the flash of temper she experienced on hold. "Rowan. How do you think this will look on my record, you having to rescue me again?"

His head shot back, all jutting chin and machismo, with no defense against the verbal right cross she landed.

"The powers-that-be will think I can't do my job." Hands on his shoulders, she pushed and this time he let go. Her limbs didn't feel as if they belonged to her, but at least she was on her feet looking up at him. The five inch difference in height had never seemed so great.

"Well, pardon me for not wanting to watch you die."

God, she knew the feeling. She'd prayed harder the night Rowan was shot than she ever had in her life. With his blood on her hands, she'd made promises she couldn't remember and could only hope she'd kept. But she couldn't lie about her feelings. Already in Rowan's debt, the interest rate was growing too steep.

Drawing her dignity and herself up to full height, oblivious to her sooty appearance, she protested. "Look at me, Rowan."

He obeyed her peremptory command, yet the flat, glassy green gaze he inflicted on her made her flinch.

"I'm a big girl. Hell's teeth, I'm a cop. You have to let me fend for myself. So, maybe I couldn't have kicked the door down, but sure as I'm six feet tall in my socks, I could have walked out of that house on my own two feet."

"You're absolutely right," he apologized stiffly, arms akimbo, his face as expressionless as an Easter Island statue. "I guess I got carried away with the buzz of escaping the flames."

Oh, oh. She'd done it again. "No, I was the one who got carried away." Her smile was feeble, without life. It didn't soften the blow of words regretted as soon as spoken. He hadn't meant to put her down, or make her feel diminished. She'd achieved it herself.

Her fingers rested on his forearm, curling around steel-banded muscles folded across their match. Had his tension lessened?

Desperate to make amends, she sighed, a feminine ploy.

His lips quirked, putting a kink in his moustache.

She followed through. "I apologize, it's not your fault. You just got caught in the backlash of my beef with the guys at work. Back in Auckland I was one of the team...."

She swallowed quickly to release the tightness in her chest as she realized this could be the end of her plan, her dream. If the combination of this morning's call out, and the trap they'd walked into were for real, it might force her to abandon an ambition she'd nursed since she was a teenager.

"Down here on the East Coast I'm just the little lady."

He shook his head slowly and reached for her face. "I didn't notice a plethora of men carrying white sticks." Swiping his thumb across her cheekbone, he said, "The male population of Nicks Landing must be blind." Then he held up his thumb and showed her a black smudge.

"Guess I'm just lucky they're not here today," she whispered, past a larynx rough as sand. She covered his knuckles with her hand, rubbing her thumb sinuously against his larger one where his print was just right for the taking.

And what about her? Was she ripe for the taking? Staring into his eyes, she looked past the shadows of old hurts, falling fathoms deep into his soul.

A crash behind her broke the spell, and she turned to see the roof falling through what was left of the second floor, down onto the first.

She shuddered. "We walked into a booby trap, didn't we?" Rowan nodded and left it at that. It was impossible to figure out whether it had been meant for Rocky or them.

Being an ex-cop, Rocky had known all the right buttons to push when he'd rushed into the station this morning. Maybe even been *too* convincing?

Ever the optimist, she acknowledged she hadn't given up. Never would. Her eyes narrowed, studying the thick black pall of smoke with Rowan's arm bumping against hers. A reminder that they'd survived together. Again.

As if the thin wail of a siren in the distance was a signal, they turned to each other. "Did you call them?" he asked.

She raised her eyebrows. "No, you?"

Rowan shook his head. "I was too busy being thankful we got out alive."

"And I was feeling ticked off. But you're right, we *were* lucky to get out alive. I'd no business feeling that way. But you need to understand, I'm not in the market for a hero, but I'm wide open for a partner."

Rowan's gaze clouded, hiding his thoughts. He never moved, yet she felt the distance between them widen.

"Hey, don't sweat it. I'm talking a week, seven days max. Not a commitment. Everyone knows you don't play on the romance circuit." She sweetened it with a smile, but it didn't take, sliding off her lips when she could swear Rowan growled.

He certainly had the haughty, king-of-the-beasts demeanor down pat. "Everyone?" he drawled.

"Well, I don't know about *now*..."

"Or maybe you simply don't *want* to know."

When had she given that impression? she wondered with more than an ounce of regret. Was it in the heat of the moment when his mouth had hovered close to hers? Had he *actually* wanted to kiss her? She'd never know now.

The arrival of the fire engines ended any further soul-searching. They roared up Lonely Track Road as if the end of the world was nigh. Jo squared her shoulders, telling herself the job called.

Then how come when she turned to Rowan, all she remembered was his lips descending toward hers?

She fished in a pocket for her cell phone. "I'd better give Harry the news," she explained, starting to dial. Silence. It was dead. "Blast, I think it broke when I fell."

"No, I'm sure it was me that broke." He ran the palm of his hand over his ribs. "Yeah, it was me."

"Okay, so I'm no lightweight, but trying to keep my balance on that plank wasn't easy. Lord, when that heart fell at my feet," she chuckled. "It was so gross. Who'd think like that?"

Icy fingers traced her spine as she replayed the moment.

"I'm sure that heart came from the Rimu Downs calf. It will be roasted to a cinder now. If only I'd hung on to the sack, forensics might have made a match." She shrugged away her regrets. "No point in crying over spilled blood."

"Once the fire cools get them to take a look for a pressure switch. If it wasn't hidden under Skelton's picture then my name's not McQuaid." Rowan made a choking noise.

She thumped his back as he sucked in breath. "You're right, it had to be a setup. But who was it meant for?" Who knew she'd like nothing more than to stomp on Rocky's face? If she and Rowan had become targets it could mean spending more time together watching each other's backs like the old days.

A smile crept out of its own accord as she complimented him, "Good thinking, Batman. I guess I should bone up on the technical stuff. It just hasn't seemed to matter since I moved away from the city. Guess I underestimated the local bad guys." She began to move away. "C'mon, let's go get my notebook. It's in the car and I don't want to forget anything."

"Talking about cars, we ought to move them out the way."

"Now there's a thought. I would hate to see that Jag of yours with its nose put out of joint. At least, not before I've had a chance to drive it."

He punched her lightly as they marched toward the fence line, keeping their distance from the fire. "That's one of the things I like about you, Jo. You don't call a spade a shovel."

"It may sound like I'm caught in a time warp, but I still contend honesty is the best policy." She stopped walking and squinted up at him. "While we're on the subject, you have this smudge, right about here." She stroked her fingers lightly across his cheekbone a few times more than necessary, simply for the pleasure of touching him. "There, all gone. How do I look?"

He took her question seriously. "Just a few sooty tear stains." A handkerchief appeared as if by sleight of hand and he held it up to her mouth. "Damp it, it's clean."

When she'd obeyed, Rowan wiped her face. "That's better, but if I were you, I'd button up your shirt. You wouldn't want to take the fire team's mind off their job."

Jo looked down and flushed. The view of her breasts curving up from the pink lace edging of her bra must be pretty good from Rowan's angle. Quickly, she fastened her buttons, not so much worried about putting the firemen off their stride, as wondering why she hadn't had the same effect on Rowan.

"Thanks, I'm in your debt. Again."

A frown creased his brow and the angle of his jaw tensed. "I'm not keeping score, Jo. But if I was, at a guess we'd be even. I would have died if it wasn't for the first aid you gave me at the vineyard. That's what counted. We were miles away from a hospital and you know they say it's the first hour that counts. The golden hour."

"There's still today."

"Consider that one a freebie. Besides, it doesn't count. As you said, you could have walked out yourself."

"Oh, no. I wouldn't have been walking. I'd have been flat out running. I'm not stupid."

Rowan reached the front of what used to be Rocky's house, when Jo's shaky sighs finally caught up with her.

She stopped abruptly, frozen to the spot.

"What's wrong?" he asked.

Firemen were running out hoses and water cascaded onto the steaming remains that had tumbled into the basement, but Rowan's attention was fixed on her.

"Did you ever feel you were running up and down on the spot?" She gestured in the house's direction. "All this work and we're no farther forward. It still could have been Rocky...or not."

She rubbed her hand over the bridge of her nose, frowning. "When it comes to the bull calf, do you think he has enough guts to eviscerate an animal that big?"

"I think he has guts enough for anything, except maybe standing up to his wife. But then again, if it *was* Skelton, who's to say he didn't have help?"

God, it was right under her nose and it had taken Rowan to clue her in. She'd been too focused on Rocky as chief suspect, she hadn't even contemplated the idea of him having assistance. Suddenly the world seemed brighter. She didn't mind looking for more than one culprit.

Filled with renewed fervor, she thought, *bring them all on. I don't care how many as long as one of them is Rocky.*

That's when she recognized the local fire chief heading their way. "Show time," she said to Rowan.

"Well, before we get too busy, what time do you want to meet me tomorrow?"

The fire must have turned her brain to jelly. "Tomorrow?" She couldn't remember making any arrangements.

"Te Kohanga."

Blast, another day in the country. "Let me get back to you

on that," she said. "I have to check the directions with Ginny and see if she's still telling the same story."

A quick tingle of annoyance brought her up short again. Was Rowan too fixated on proving these satanists existed? On the other hand if they found nothing, the scales would dip down on her side.

A few hours tramping through the bush was inevitable, she decided. What the heck? That kind of sacrifice, she could deal with. The ones that required rubber boots, she'd rather *steer* clear of.

Good grief, she must be tired. Another dreadful pun.

Jo reached Ginny's school just in time to watch the rainbow-colored stream of teenagers in their summer clothes, spill out of the high school barely moments after the bell sounded.

Picking out Ginny wasn't going to be as easy as she'd thought.

Finally, after thinking she'd spotted the redheaded girl five times, she caught sight of her in a group, walking slowly, heads together, giggling.

"Hey, Ginny, got a moment?"

Color swooped across her cheeks as she saw Jo. Quickly, she broke away from the group with no more than a perfunctory wave and an embarrassed glance over her shoulder at her friends. Her actions weren't those of a kid who'd laughed over being caught shoplifting with her peers.

Hoisting her bulging backpack more securely onto her shoulders, she lifted her gaze to Jo's almost defiantly. Her mouth cut a pale thin line across her face, and the rush of color had disappeared, making her freckles stand out. "I did what you asked, Detective Jo. Granny Monroe said she'd call you."

"And she did. Very pleased she was, too. You might want to look in on her now and then. She sounded as if having company was a rare occurrence."

"I know and I will, she kept wanting me to stop working to sit and have tea. I didn't mind," she hurried to assure her.

"And I will go back. She was nice and I don't have a grandma."

"Good idea, but that wasn't why I wanted to speak with you. I don't want you and any of your friends going up to Te Kohanga Park at Halloween. If what you heard was true, it could prove dangerous and I don't want to have to go chasing through the bush looking for you."

She grinned at Ginny, pretending to shudder. "Too many creepy crawlies. I just hate bugs."

That made Ginny laugh. How was she to know Jo was telling the truth? A truth that fell way short of kidding.

"I wanted to tell you about a Halloween party that St. Michael's church is throwing. All are welcome, so take your friends. It'll be fun."

Yeah, right.

Ginny didn't need to say the words, they were written all over her face. "Listen, I kid you not, no fuddy-duddies, just cool fun like bobbing for eyeballs, pretty gross stuff like that. It's run by the youth group and from what I hear there are a lot of potential babes among them. You should try it out."

Ginny's demeanor brightened at the mention of babes. Jo sighed. Did she know how to read her or what?

"Maybe I'll give it a look in. I can't be too late anyway. I'm doing a paper route, filling in for someone who's sick so I have to get up early," she informed Jo, making sure she realized visiting the park had been out anyway. "If I do a good job, they said I can have a route of my own."

"Well, that's excellent news. I knew you had a good head on your shoulders." Slipping her hand into her pants pocket, Jo pulled out a small paper bag. "Here," she said handing it to Ginny. "You might want to wear these."

She could tell Ginny realized what was inside long before she ripped open the bag. "Oh, the pink ones. Thanks, they're so cool!"

"No problem. Now, would you like a ride home? On the way, you can tell me exactly where you heard that cult was meeting."

Chapter 7

The morning after the fire, Rowan stood outside Jo's address, ready for a day of trekking through the bush. To the rhythm of his boots on the brick path winding between intensive plantings, he weighed up Jo's seeming unwillingness to discuss today's project.

Fact number one, they were going at his insistence. Fact number two, if he'd given her the slightest excuse to bail out, she would have jumped at it. He'd never found Jo to be quite so fixed in her ideas when they'd worked together in Auckland.

Yet, she had tunnel vision when it came to Skelton. One had to assume the man's past association with her father in Auckland to be at the root of it. So far, she hadn't brought him up to speed.

Some would say he'd been paid in his own coin.

Secrets, everyone had them.

No matter. If the cult, satanists, black magic, whatever name they went by, were liable to meet in Te Kohanga Park, he'd rather check out the lay of the land in daylight. He was a planner. Always had been. Give him a pencil, paper and a situation and he'd do the groundwork and come up with a scheme. Stumbling around blindfolded wasn't his thing.

And truth be told he'd enjoyed pulling the rug out from her reluctance. Seeing Jo at a loss for words had been a new experience. Before they'd parted company last night, he'd arranged for an expert to check out the fire, and the farm manager, whom he'd known for years, to deliver the bull calf to the pathologist's door.

Rowan leaped up the four steps to the porch. He'd barely caught hold of the wizened face decorating the knocker, when the door swung open. Until that moment, he'd thought himself familiar with every shade of red hair in existence. But one look at the mass of vermilion curls, flaring like sunbursts against the shadowy background of the hallway, and he did a double take.

A quick indrawn gasp, tangled with the words in his throat and his, "Does Jo Jellic live here?" barely scraped out in some sort of order.

Birdlike, the woman's bright blue eyes scrutinized him with open curiosity tempered by the warmth of her smile. Looking him up and down, she nodded in a way that told him he passed muster.

"You'll be Rowan, then. Jo will be out in a second." Her soft burr caught him a sneaky sucker punch, echoing his mother's accent and the way she'd pronounced his name. She'd always turned the first syllable into an *ow* instead of an *oh*.

"I'm Moira MacGregor," she introduced herself, slipping a fine-boned hand into the one he'd offered automatically. Her warm dry skin felt as if it would crush like tissue paper, but it was her long purple nails that drew his gaze. As he glanced down, Moira's skirts, which were reminiscent of a seventies op-shop relic, swayed outward revealing a ginger cat. The final touch of eccentricity.

Tail held high, the cat shimmied against his legs, winding in and out between his boots. The thrum of its purring vibrated in its chest like a boom box. "Nice cat." *Long claws.* Its tail twitched, flicking his shin as if it read his mind.

Moira cocked her head and nodded decisively. "You'll do. Spoiler likes you."

"Spoiler?" he repeated. Strange name for a cat. Then he remembered those claws and had a vision of a sofa with its stuffing spilling in all directions.

"Once I had him he spoiled me for any other cat."

There was no answer to that, but he needn't have worried. Moira hadn't finished. "It was time you got here."

He flicked his wrist. Eight fifty-five. "Actually, I'm early."

"No, no, I meant time you got here *for* Jo. Her sex life has been sadly lacking since she got to Nicks Landing."

Stumped again. But he wasn't about to discuss Jo's sex life with a woman he'd known less than two minutes.

Thankfully, Jo appeared behind Moira. Saved! He could have kissed her, but that would only have encouraged Moira.

One heart-stopping glance at Jo's glowing features and he wondered why her sex life was nonexistent. What man in his right mind could look at her and not want her the way he did?

"I guess we'd better make a move," said Jo.

"I'm ready if you are." Damn right he was ready.

He'd been thinking of her more and more since he came to Nicks Landing. In fact, she was never far from his mind. If he wasn't thinking about working on the case with her, he was wondering how she'd fit in his arms. His bed.

Dipping her head, Jo bussed Moira on the cheek, then sniffed at the back of her hand as she straightened. "Ooh, this bug repellant you mixed is disgusting. I just hope that it works."

"It'll work...but only on the bugs," she said with a laugh, then pulled Jo closer and whispered in her ear.

"Okay, I'll remember," she said, but as she didn't color, he gathered Moira hadn't reopened the subject of Jo's sex life.

Letting Jo lead the way meant having to grin-and-bear the enticing view from behind. Someone ought to fine jean makers for using too little cloth. They played havoc with his equilibrium.

His resolve was all but shot.

The sooner he was out of Nicks Landing the better. The longer he stayed, the more his resistance weakened. And no way did he intend turning his life into the living hell his father had endured the last two years of his life.

Jo settled back into the softness of the fine leather seat, watching Rowan's hands on the steering wheel. Capable and controlled, that was him in a nutshell. Just once, she'd like to see him let go. "Now that we're outside the town limits, are you going to let me see what this baby can do?"

"Ah-ha, police entrapment? I go over the limit and you hand out a ticket." He threw her a white grin, but kept the Jag slightly below the allowed speed.

"That's the difference between us, McQuaid. I can be tempted. How can you *not* let this dream machine rip?"

"What? You think I'm not human? I can be tempted all right."

Talk about the pot sniping at the kettle. Who was she to imply Rowan needed to get a life? Until he hit town she hadn't realized how lonely she was for someone who understood her, who spoke the same language. Until he hit town, she hadn't realized how ready she was for a loving relationship, or remembered the last time her blood fizzed in her veins at the thought of seeing a man.

"You didn't tell me that your landlady was a hippie."

She spun in her seat. "Moira? Lord, she's not a hippie, she's a naturopath, a woman with her own individual style. So what if it's colorful? She's comfortable with it."

Rowan's glance left the road for a second, and a smile tugged the corners of his mouth. "I've no doubt that she's a law unto herself, but how do you get used to that hair?"

"Same way I got used to your moustache."

Curious, she licked her lips. How would it feel? What were the chances of tasting his mouth before he shaved it off? There was that moment yesterday when he'd bent toward her and the flame in his eyes definitely hadn't been the reflection of Rocky's house burning. Then she'd blown it. One of these days she'd learn when not to speak out of turn. Now she'd probably never know how it felt to kiss Rowan. Unless she took the initiative.

Time to get real. "I don't notice Moira's little foibles anymore, they're just part of who she is."

"Hopefully growing cannabis isn't one of her foibles. That's some garden she has."

"I think I'd notice if she'd gone to competition with the Smale brothers...." Oh, darn. The guy in the pub had the same name as the guy Bull arrested. It just went to show her instincts still functioned even if they hadn't clicked straight off. Oh well, better late than never. Bull had stuck her with the grunge jobs for so long, it was a wonder those instincts hadn't atrophied.

"You were saying?" Rowan asked as the yellow finger of a road sign appeared ahead.

"Nothing important."

The subject dropped out of the conversation as quietly as Rowan slipped the stick shift down a cog, saying, "This is the turnoff for the park."

The scenery merged from fields to tall trees, and the view of the local volcano, Tane's Throat, hugging the shoreline as the south side of the park became hidden behind them.

"What was all the whispering as we left?" he turned his head slightly, one eyebrow lifting mockingly.

Right about then, the Jag hit a patch of rough gravel. The wheels spun as clouds of dust concealed the road behind them.

"From here on in, McQuaid, you'd be smart to keep your eyes on the road. It would be humiliating all round if we had to call in to have someone tow us out of a ditch. You wouldn't want Moira's prediction to come true."

"Prediction?"

"She's very superstitious. Seems there were rings around

he moon last night and she says that means trouble. She told me to take care. By the way, she thinks this is a social outing."

After half an hour of riding the bare ruts in the gravel, the road ended at a fenced-off parking lot with a sign on the five-bar gate which read, No Cars Past This Point.

"Make sure your boots are laced up tight," he said, swinging the Jag into the shade of a tree. "It's rough going from here on. I wouldn't want you to sprain an ankle."

She rested each boot in turn on the wooden bench of a picnic table to redo the laces. "How come you're such an authority?"

"Didn't anybody tell you? I grew up round here."

For once, she didn't blurt out the first thing that came to mind and settled for the second. "So, that explains Bull and Harry being so cooperative."

"From Ginny's description, this looks like the path we want."

"I guess you'd know since *you* grew up in Nicks Landing."

"You're not going to let it go, are you? Personally, I can't make out what the big deal is. I didn't lie to you. The subject simply never came up."

Too bad he hadn't thought to claim Nicks Landing as his hometown the day he arrived. Rowan would be the first to admit his life wasn't an open book; some of the pages had stuck together, their contents hidden. Things he'd avoided dealing with. Others he'd turned the corners over, places to remember, like the day he met Jo. And where the words blurred? Well, that was the difference between secrets and lies.

He planted his boot firmly on the ground and pushed on, up a path crowded with ferns and seedlings. As if his conscience wasn't troubling him enough, walking side by side, continuously, trying not to brush against her had become torture. Easier to suggest, "You go ahead. I'll follow."

Her gaze flicked uncertainly from him to the path ahead. "Maybe you'd better lead. I'll only slow us down."

Her obvious reluctance might have been amusing, if it

hadn't been threaded with fear. What was up with her? It was so beautiful here, especially at this spot with the sun slanting through the gap in the treetops where a giant puriri had been toppled, in a storm no doubt. Even in the green shade, the air was steamy enough to bring him out in a sweat, yet Jo had been walking for thirty-five minutes, and the sleeves of her shirt were still buttoned up tight, as tight as her mood.

"Maybe you could travel faster if you loosened up a little." He flicked a finger at the top button of her denim shirt. "Aren't you the least bit hot?"

She patted the button as if to make sure it was shut tight. "Just a little," she replied, eyeing the path ahead.

Brushing his fingers through his sweat-dampened hair, he asked, "What's worrying you? You know there aren't any snakes in the New Zealand bush."

"Bugs." A visible shudder rippled through her. "I hate them. Have you seen the size of some of those wettas?"

The expression on her face startled a laugh out of him. He kicked at a rotten log, testing. "Like those you mean, with the long wriggly feelers?"

He regretted it the moment she squealed and danced back. "Joking, just joking."

Remembering Jo, heart rolling at her feet while she batted the flies with the bag attracting them, he shook his head, saying, "I never thought you'd be scared of anything."

"You didn't have four brothers who thought dropping spiders and beetles down your back was a great joke."

"No, I didn't. Didn't know about your brothers, either," he replied, insinuating that her past was as much a mystery as his. "I had two brothers. One older, one younger, but they never played those tricks on me. Something we used to do, though, you know the house where you're rooming? Haggetty House?"

"What about it?"

"The house stood empty for years when I was a kid. The grass even grew through the floor of the porch. In fact it was so long, it practically pushed down the fence.

"We used to dare each other to see who could run through all the rooms without getting caught or peeing their pants. You see, we always thought the house was haunted."

Now Jo lived there.

He guessed in his case, time had proved him right.

A residual shiver from his youth ran through him and he laughed. "I remember the last time I dived through that door as if my shirttail was on fire. Those were the days."

Before everything turned to crap.

"I'll tell you what, if you lead, I'll watch your back for bugs. Okay?"

Big mistake. The way she filled out those jeans was making him damned uncomfortable. For him, watching her back pockets sway in front of him was a mating call. Jo might be tall, but no one could deny she was womanly. Her waist narrow; her bottom heart-shaped where her jeans hugged it tight. Using his eye to gauge her size, he bet she'd fit his hands like a pair of gloves.

Luckily, for sanity's sake, he'd eased back a few paces so when she stopped abruptly he didn't bump into her. "What's up?"

Her voice was whisper thin. "There's something in my hair."

When they'd started off, her hair had been knotted at the back of her head, and though the terrain wasn't particularly rugged, a run-in earlier with a tree fern had pulled a few strands loose. Rowan moved closer. "Are you asking me to rescue you?"

Her voice quivered between laughter and fear, "Please."

Two little feather-shaped fronds clung to her hair. " It's only bits of tree fern. I'll get it for you," he said, capturing one of the delicate green culprits to hand to her.

Taking the other miniature frond, Rowan drew it gently down her cheek, tickling her under the chin, before he realized what he was doing. These last few days had to be the longest he'd spent continuously in her company. Continually avoiding temptation.

For a moment neither spoke. The air crackled like a storm was about to hit. Way back, in his subliminal mind, Rowan acknowledged it would be so easy to grasp the moment, take Jo in his arms and kiss her till she clung to him and begged for mercy.

A great rush of heat blistered his skin from the inside out. Then the breeze picked up, shivering through the tops of the nikau palms and making the tall slender branches of the kanuka clack against each other, like warning drums.

An answering beat thrummed in his temple. Do it…do it…do it. He'd had years of practice at not responding to that inner voice. Years of wanting Jo. What would another few hours or days matter? The voice in his head laughed.

Both of them knew there was more going on than a surfeit of self-control, but neither of them was game enough to admit the truth. He handed her the other frond. "The rescue's on the house. After all the excitement I could murder a drink. Want one?"

He watched her swallow hard as his fingers ripped the Velcro fasteners apart the way he'd torn the tension building between them. Digging deep inside the pack, he grabbed the water bottle, his knuckles brushing the fruit he'd pushed in the pack as he left the boat. "Or would you rather have an apple?"

Her face relaxed, her eyelashes fluttering on her cheek and the tension fled on a mutual release of breath. "Haven't you got your genders mixed, McQuaid? It was Eve who offered the apple." Her eyes widened and sunlight flickered in them. "Or maybe there really *are* snakes in the New Zealand bush."

He watched her teeth dig into the red skin. Heard the crisp snap as the white flesh broke away and the sweet juice dribble down the side of her palm. Stared like a man dying of thirst as she licked her hand.

Playing the if-you-can't-beat-'em-join-'em game, Rowan bit down hard on a second apple and sucked up the juice. It was probably the closest he would get to sharing the same sweet taste as Jo.

* * *

Rowan let her get a few steps ahead before she heard him follow. She wasn't sure what had happened back there. Suddenly, she no longer felt the urge to jump each time a twig or frond snapped back into place.

Taking one last bite of the apple, she wrapped the remains in a tissue she had in her pocket and stuffed it into the small waterproof pouch on the side of her backpack.

Paying more attention to her surroundings, she became aware of a profound truth. In the rain forest, life and death existed hand in hand. Fallen leaves and branches rotted on the ground feeding the trees, while high up in the canopy birds dined on their berries, letting their droppings fall to the moist humus below. And so the cycle continued. Everything had its own part to play in the rhythm of the bush.

Lord, her thoughts were melancholy, yet she felt exactly the opposite. The day had taken an unexpected twist for the better and she'd begun enjoying herself.

Maybe it was the company? For *sure* it was the company.

For an exquisite moment in time earlier, she'd been completely aware of Rowan and nothing else. Not the bush, or the bugs, only the way his mouth opened around the apple and the relish he'd eaten it with. She'd wanted him to kiss her. Known she'd wanted him to. Prayed he'd take her in his arms.

The setting of the park was magical. Its full name, *Te Kohanga o Nga Atua* translated into "the nest," or "birthplace of the gods."

One night, Moira had told her of the legend, of a beautiful young Maori *wahine* seduced by one of the gods, perhaps Tane. The sad part of the story was the maiden died giving birth. As for her son, he leaped off the cliffs onto the wave caps to join his people. Even today, the birds skimming the waves called his name.

She could hear those waves now, washing over the rocks. It had to be high tide. Looking back over her shoulder, she hesitated and Rowan almost fell over her. Reaching out to steady himself he gripped her shoulder.

She'd been too deep in thought to realize he was virtually

walking on her heels. The heavy green smell of the bush couldn't compete with the mix of Rowan's spicy scent and good honest sweat. She gulped. Instead of calming the tingling sensation in the pit of her stomach she tasted him. Rowan.

It took all her willpower to ask, "Do you think we ought to call this track a nonevent and turn back?"

"No. The path hasn't narrowed any and that, to my mind, means there has to be something at the end of it."

She should step away, but couldn't bring herself to move. Her position was awkward, looking up at him from over her shoulder, the cords in her neck taut from the tension whirling inside her.

This close she could see the pores in his skin and the stark maleness of the new growth of beard shadowing his chin below the tantalizing challenge of that moustache. Would she enjoy the feel if he kissed her? Would it mark her skin, leaving a reminder of how good it had been? Somehow, she just knew it would be good....

"Do you want me to take the lead now?"

Duh! How was that for getting her wires crossed? While she'd been salivating at the thought of his kiss, Rowan had more fitting matters in mind. "Yeah, sure. You go on ahead."

If the measure of his stride was anything to go by she'd definitely been slowing him down. Not that she was complaining. From this vantage point, she had a good eyeful of the length of the legs taking those strides. Like her, he'd pulled on jeans that weren't quite past their use-by date, but close enough to it that a snag or tear wouldn't matter. The jeans fit him like a glove, the soft denim cupping his butt, clinging lovingly to his thighs.

One second she'd been considering Rowan's butt and the next he'd disappeared. An intense feeling of déjà vu brought her up short as she remembered the time she'd lost track of Max.

She plunged after him and was on her second "Rowan!" when she hit something solid. Warm and solid. "Lord," she breathed out shakily, less from anxiety than from feel of muscle rippling under her palms. "I thought I'd lost you."

Just when the temptation to wrap her arms round him and cling became overpowering, Rowan looked down at her and grinned. Taking a few steps forward, he let her through until they stood shoulder to shoulder and she saw what had stopped him in his tracks.

About five of Rowan's strides from where they stood was a tall, straight tree covered in flowers. Fascinated, Jo drew closer.

On any normal tree the bracts would have grown high overhead, surrounded by leaves. These pale green beauties on long delicate stems sprang from the bark itself, flowing down the trunk and cascading from the branches overhead. "I've never seen anything like it," she murmured. Tilting her head back, she looked up into a shower of soft, green-tinged blossoms.

Rowan joined her under the tree. "It's a kohekohe. We used to have one in the garden at home when I was a boy." He lifted one hand and caressed a stream of velvety blooms, letting them flow through his fingers. "We're lucky to see this. Most of them have died out in the wild."

"They remind me of the decorations on a Japanese bride's headdress," she said, with a breathless sigh.

"I never knew you were a romantic."

She slipped around the tree, refusing to answer till she'd sorted out her feelings. Romance led to things she no longer craved, or so she'd told herself. Things like wedding bells and commitment. Oh no, she was too wise to let her hopes turn in that direction. She'd been burned too many times by men with smart talk and even smarter lies.

Yet, her heart began to pound as her gaze caught sight of another kohekohe and another. A whole ring of them, each separated by a tree where no flowers grew.

They had come to the end of their search.

The magic circle.

Suddenly the trees lost some of their charm.

"Looks as if Ginny was spot on," said Rowan.

While her glance had encircled the margins, his had been snagged by a ring of stones in the center filled with cold ashes. Not a blade of grass grew between the trees and the stones, not even a bird-sown sapling, yet life-giving sun shone through the hole in the canopy. Jo smartly covered the ground between the tree she'd been standing under and the one next to it. Ugly red fruit grew out of its trunk like weeping boils. A more fitting tree than the other for guarding the borders of a demonic haunt. "What type of tree is this? Do you know?"

Rowan glanced over his shoulder as he paced the distance between the stones outside the ring round the fire. "That's still the same tree. One in flower, the other in fruit. Harry's father used to say the kohekohe had a longer gestation period than an elephant."

As Rowan turned his attention to measuring distances, she fumed inwardly over nefarious louts using loveliness for evil ends. "I don't think I like this place."

"Yeah, it's kind of lost its glamour for me, too."

As Rowan paced, Jo picked up a fallen twig by her feet and walked into the center, saying, "You're doing it all wrong. Here, let me show you."

Poking the stick into the dirt she began to draw a line. "See, like this. There are five rocks, which means they're probably the points of a pentagram with the fire in the middle. The line stretches from here to there and on round the boulders in a continuous line."

A longer twig might help, she thought, swiping at a strand of hair blocking her vision. She was at the fourth point when the blood started pounding in her head. It's only from bending over, she told herself, yet her breathing grew more shallow until it barely reached her lungs. Perspiration bathed the back of her neck, her breasts grew heavy and the tops of her thighs ached. Still she kept on; she wanted to finish. Had to finish.

Her eyes lifted to Rowan. He stood statue still, staring at her. Energy jangled the air around him. His stillness was that of a jungle cat studying its prey. A glow lurked deep in his eyes, penetrating, intense, escaping shadows of his brow.

Stumbling slightly, she dropped the marker, overcome by a feeling of giddiness. A rushing filled her ears as she bent to retrieve it. She had to finish. Only a few feet to go.

Rowan was there before her, grasping the stick, throwing it aside. "No more, Jo. No more," he growled. His hands circled the tops of her arms, drawing her hard against his chest.

Her gaze swam and Rowan's features with it, but it couldn't disguise the intense hunger shaping them. His heart pounded against her palms as they slid up his chest to twine around his neck. The heat inside her spiraled near flash point, and surges of desire repeatedly jolted her until her body shook.

"What's happening, Rowan?" she asked breathlessly. "I don't understand. What is this place doing to me?"

His answer roared through her head as if carried on a tempest. "Damned if I know, but it's brought out the devil in me!" And with that, he covered her mouth with his in a knee-buckling kiss draining her life force, leaving her weak, wanting more.

It felt as if all his life, all he had ever wanted was this.

Jo.

Her hands on him. His hands on her. And her taste? There had never been anything like it for him, never would be again.

Her mouth tasted of flavors he'd only dreamed about, never expecting to indulge in. Sweet flavors. Honey, bloodred wine and spices that heightened the senses. One sip alone would live on in his memory, but would never fill him.

The velvet touch of Jo's tongue brushing his wasn't enough.

He wanted more.

He wanted deeper.

Rowan angled his mouth over hers.

A flash of pain smote his head with the knowledge he would never get enough. Never be satisfied. Never fulfilled.

The thought drove him crazy.

Her hands gripped tight on the back of his shirt and ripped it out of his jeans. He felt her nails anchor in his skin, holding on to him like a lifeline. They both shook and he couldn't tell where her shudders ended and his began.

He cupped the nape of her neck with both hands and pressed his thumbs under her jaw until her head tilted back farther. He drove his tongue inside her mouth, mimicking the end they both sought, both fought for.

The inside of her mouth was a potpourri of textures laid out for him to enjoy—velvet, satin, pearls. The rasp of her tongue. The softness inside her cheek. The hardness of her teeth. He savored them all. Her swollen lips throbbed from his caresses. He sucked the lower one into his mouth and caught it between his teeth.

Jo moaned and the sound filled his insides with a fire that threatened to consume him. Consume them both.

His hands raced down her back and dived under her T-shirt. There was more to come. More to experience.

Jo's hips thrust against his and the terrible ache in his groin flexed, seeking the curve of her belly even as the fullness of her breasts filled his hands, pebbling against the center of his palms.

He squeezed tight. Tighter.

Jo let out a desperate mewl from deep inside her throat. He swallowed it down. Swallowed her passion and thrust his thigh between hers when it looked like they might fall as her hands scrabbled to undo the buckle at his waist.

An intrusive vision blasted Rowan's mind. Jo naked, spread-eagled on the dirt and himself over her, the marks of her nails like bloodred scars on his back as they lay in the center of the pentagram she had drawn.

A pounding grew in his head and paced him thrust for thrust. Pounding…pounding…flesh slapping against flesh in a feverish animalistic search for release.

Lashed by lust and almost blind from the fires the picture lit in his mind, he gripped Jo by the shoulders and pushed her away. The anguish and frustration roaring inside his head poured out of his mouth in a curse. He could hardly tell real from imaginary.

He only knew that if he didn't get them away from this place, the vision would become fact and the ritualistic undertones made him sick to his gut.

Only the superior length of his arms protected him from Jo's protests, her eager hands reaching out to touch him. He dare not let her near, or all his good intentions would come undone.

"What are you doing?" she yelled as he frustrated her attempts to draw him back into a carnal whirlpool of selfish needs that would suck them under; steal their humanity and spit them out, having taken the best of them.

He gave her shoulders a short, sharp shake. "Stop it, Jo. Stop it now. Look at me. This place is evil. It's put us under a spell. Bewitched us. We have to leave while we still can."

If he'd taken an old black-and-white photo and painted the lips scarlet that would have been Jo. Her eyes were huge, dark and dazed. Her face drawn and white. Yet, the red fullness of her lips had come from his teeth mauling them. At some stage he'd removed the pins from her hair and it hung in wild, tousled abandonment round her shoulders where his hands had done their damage.

She was breathing hard. They both were.

Their ragged breaths filled the silence between them as he kept her at arm's length and watched her breasts tremble on a long drawn-out sigh, remembering the weight of them in his hands.

They had to get out of here. Now!

Loosing his grip on her, Rowan bent down and snagged both their packs from the ground where he'd tossed them aside without even noticing. Standing up, wrapping his other arm round Jo, his hand tight on her shoulder, he walked her out of the circle.

Beyond the ring of trees at last, he turned and let his gaze rest on her face, gratified to find an uncertain, half-embarrassed smile. After such an experience, fear might have been the result. Fear of him. He couldn't bear the thought of her cringing away from his touch.

His hands trembled, grazing the tops of her arms where he held her steady. "You were right about that place. We're better off standing on the outside, looking in. What do you think, are you starting to feel somewhat normal?"

Nodding, she called his name as he headed toward the ring of trees. "Wait here. I'll only be a moment." His hands fisted inside his jeans pockets, as if that was the only way he could keep them off her. He needed this time away from her to calm down. The whole situation was just plain weird.

What the hell had gotten into him?

"I'm going to use an old Native American trick I learned at the movies. Once I've brushed away that pentagram no one will know we've been here," he called out.

The most handy twig was a length of manuka covered in black, honeydew mold that stained his hand. However, he willingly conceded it was better than the darkness that had stained his soul when he held Jo in his arms inside the accursed circle. Even now, he could feel it prowling the air, waiting to pounce the moment he let down his guard.

Never again.

He wanted Jo. And doubted that would ever change. But if they ever got to know each other in the biblical sense, he didn't want their first joining driven by some outside force. Driven by feral lust. How could he make a memory he didn't dare remember or retain his integrity and Jo's trust?

Tossing away the twig, Rowan dusted his hands on his jeans, then tucked in his shirt and fastened his belt. His back stung where her nails had gripped him, but didn't feel sticky with the blood he'd seen in his imagination.

His conscience eased slightly when he noticed color had seeped back into Jo's face. She'd tidied her hair, though it would never look the same to him. Who could forget their first encounter with perfumed silk?

Not him.

"I don't know about you, but I could go for a cup of coffee." Then he remembered tossing their packs. His mouth pulled to one side on a rueful, "Aw, hell. I hope I didn't break the vacuum flask!"

"You're in luck. It's a stainless-steel one. Unbreakable," she said, her smile playing hide-and-seek with him as she took her pack from his hands.

Thankfully, the coffee was safe. He wished he could say the same about Jo; he'd never seen her look so fragile. "Let's head for the sea. I've a sudden yen for fresh air, sunshine and the feel of wind on my face."

"Me, too," she said, looking up at him. Her eyes were huge and darkly luminous in the dim light, as if washed with tears.

He felt he'd been ripped open and a giant fist was squeezing his heart. Aw damn. What had happened to his defenses? Sucking damp green air into his lungs as deep as it would go, Rowan slung his day pack over his shoulder. "Let's get out of here." As far as he was concerned it couldn't be a minute too soon.

Chapter 8

Wow! The situation back there had gotten pretty scary. When was the last time she'd tried to rip a man's shirt off his back?

Never.

Jo colored up at the thought, glad she followed in Rowan's footsteps. She'd much prefer to be alone when she downloaded the memory of her incredulous response to Rowan's kisses. The most erotic five minutes of her life. Five minutes she wouldn't forget in a hurry. Five minutes better viewed from a distance.

Lord, just thinking about it made her heart race.

"Watch where you put your feet. There are a lot of roots breaking through the surface. Mind how you go."

Too late. She'd already turned off at a side road filled with twists and turns. Heaven only knew where it would end.

The situation had been explosive. One touch from him and she'd gone off like a stick of dynamite with a short fuse. Who'd have thought after all that time, working side by side? She'd never imagined his kiss could pack such a wallop. Never thought of him in that light. Never once, until he'd arrived in her office.

Since then, the attraction had been skirting round the edges of her mind, but she'd refused to give it its head.

He was only here for a week, after all. Not even that, now that they'd discovered the ring of trees wasn't a figment of Ginny's imagination. But what if there was a way…a way he could stay a bit longer….

The sooner she forgot how it felt to be plastered against the front of his body, the sooner she could set her mind to work out ways and means to keep him here.

However convenient an excuse—and why should they need one?—she couldn't go along with Rowan's bewitched theory. No sense in making excuses. The desire they felt for each other had existed pre-Te Kohanga Park. The heat and the lush tropical setting had simply magnified it.

Rowan would soon come around to her way of thinking. He'd been a skeptic from way back. Good grief, she'd even known him to raise an eyebrow at some of Max's comments about Maggie's psychic powers. "Hell, Max," he'd said, "sure she's beautiful, but we all know her history."

Now Maggie she could believe in. She'd known her forever. The two of them had roomed together at St. Margaret's boarding school. And Rowan couldn't argue about Maggie's dreams being instrumental in catching a serial killer. The last case they'd worked together on in Auckland.

It was laughable that now he'd have her believe some nasty spirit had had them in its power. She'd give him maybe half an hour, an hour max, to change his mind.

She trailed after Rowan, both of them lost in their own thoughts, until his "Will you look at that" made her stop.

Rowan stepped aside. Light, so bright after the dim green bush, made her eyes squint as the reflection of sun on the water dazzled them.

"What a view." She walked forward carefully to the top of the cliff, letting the breeze turn her hair into a mass of tangles as she stood watching the waves. Amazed at her own intrepidity.

Next stop Antarctica.

With her history, the simple act of looking out to sea, on this East Coast cliff top, knowing there was nothing else out there was like taking away a child's security blanket. She had this standing-on-the-edge-of-the-earth-ready-to-fall-off feeling.

Away from the city lights she got the same sensation, looking up at the dark velvet of a clear night sky, studded with stars close enough to reach out and pluck down. But, the moment she remembered some of those twinkling lights were bigger than the sun, she started to shrink.

She'd hate anyone to know she could be so vulnerable. At six feet tall, she'd always had to be one of the big-enough-to-do-it-for-herself types. At least, that's how the three youngest of her brothers *and* her male colleagues in the force had treated her. Like a no-nonsense woman, both feet planted firmly on the ground with nary a thought of shooting stars in her head.

Boy, she was getting maudlin.

"Let's move on and find a spot sheltered from the wind."

Glad of the distraction, she merely nodded her agreement. They walked south along the cliff top in the direction of Nicks Landing until she moaned. "Aren't you hungry? I am. So hungry I could eat my boots if forced to…maybe even yours."

Rowan had always been famous for his big feet, so he just grinned, asking, "Will this spot do?" He swung the packs toward a clump of shrubby pittosporums, heaving them onto the grass.

"Looks good to me. Plenty of sunshine and sheltered from the wind." Jo opened her backpack, the one with the coffee and sandwiches, and tossed the largest packet to Rowan who had thrown himself down on the grass. Taking an orange nylon parka out of a zipped compartment, she spread it out to sit on, thus avoiding any creepy crawlies, facing Rowan, elbows balanced on her knees.

She was fascinated by the movement of his throat as he

wallowed, but tickled by the way his fingers wiped his mous-
ache, taking care of any crumbs. She touched her top lip remembering how it had brushed against it.

"Mmm, these are good," he said, as she handed him a cup
f coffee and he settled back, leaning against a clump of spiky,
ellow grass, content to eat in silence and soak up the sun.

Rowan had demolished eight sandwiches to her three and
owned two cups of coffee while she was still on her first.

"Are you ever going to shave off that moustache?"

"Why, don't you like it?"

"I don't know. I haven't tasted you without it," she said,
eeling safe to be slightly bolder, sitting out here in the open.
he lowered her lids as she realized it was happening again.
Vith Rowan she felt like a butterfly newly escaped from its
ocoon, testing its wings. In other words, she had that fluttery
ensation round her heart again.

She saw none of her own insecurities reflected in Rowan's
yes. Instead he said, "Maybe once the scar fades, you can
ome up to Auckland and find out for yourself."

The rough, dry, crenellated edge to his tone proved beyond
doubt he didn't believe it would ever happen.

She balanced her chin on her arms and looked at her toes.
Ie meant to leave soon. Now that, too, was out in the open.

Had it only been three days since he arrived? How would
he stand it when he was gone? The thought of going back to
onely days and even lonelier nights overwhelmed her. Soon
he'd need to decide between staying in a much-loved career
hat was killing her, and giving it up to return to Auckland
nd a new life.

Maybe she'd surprise Rowan yet. She flicked a glance at
im through her lashes and found him staring at her.

"Know what's been bugging me?" His question was as
azy as his body language. Rowan's feet crossed at the ankles,
nd with his legs at full stretch the distance between them
hrank. Soft, worn, bleached-at-the-seams denim clung to his
highs and cupped the maleness he had pressed against her.

She knew she was staring but couldn't drag her eyes away

as she responded to his question. An answer as brief as it wa
hard to drag out. "Not a clue."

"How'd you know about Skelton's vasectomy?"

The question popped into the conversation with all th
aplomb of a ballerina picking her way on points across a barn
yard. Jo felt about as steady, lifting her gaze to his face.

The other night, she'd known as soon as she'd made th
remark it was a mistake. And now she was going to have t
pay for it. "It wasn't through any personal association, i
that's what you're thinking."

"Nothing was further from my mind. It's obvious you can'
stand the man. Hell, you've been doing your damnedest t
nail him for fraud and arson since I got here, and probabl
before. Guess I'm pretty safe in thinking there's no love los
between you two."

"That's not even the half of it. Did you know my fathe
was a cop and Rocky was his partner?"

"Skelton mentioned it."

Huh, it was worse than she thought. Rocky had got in firs
with his poison. "I'll just bet he did. And I'll stake my lif
on him giving you the old wink-wink-nudge-nudge-know
what-I-mean routine."

Rowan sat up, alert, the laziness dropped from his manne
and his voice. "He tried, but I wouldn't listen. If you can'
bring yourself to tell me, then I don't want hear it from anyone
else."

"Well, it's a matter of record. Not mine, but it might wel
have been. I had a lot to live down when I first joined the
force, but I made it. Sometimes it's harder battling what people think they know about you than the actual truth."

"Tell me about it," he said, slapping his thigh.

Jo caught his drift immediately. She'd heard the rumors they
were going to amputate his leg and they'd scared her spitless.
She'd felt like a rookie pitcher with all the bases loaded and
the other team's best man up at bat.

All the air in her lungs came out in one big huff. Revealing her past wasn't something she did every day. Not even every year.

"Getting back to Rocky. I discovered his secret by eaves-dropping. Don't get me wrong, I'd have been around eleven at the time, griping to my grandmother about too many chores. She brought me up, and had this saying about idle hands—"

"What happened to your mom?"

"I never knew her. As I came into the world she went out. We were a close-knit family then, even though my father had to work all hours. The budget was pretty tight back then and with five kids, the overtime didn't go amiss." She didn't want him thinking she was looking for sympathy, so she looked away, avoiding his eyes.

Blades of yellowed grass drifted across the toes of her boots. As she watched, a seed head tangled in her bootlaces. It was then she realized her hands were plucking nervously at the dry stalks.

Jo dropped the grass and wrapped her arms round her knees. "Anyway, I was sitting on the window seat that day, hiding behind the curtain and reading a book. It was dinnertime and Dad had just come in." She didn't mention she'd been ready to leap down with a demand to hear the latest on the big case he was working on. Or that she'd held back when her father had begun telling Grandma about Rocky. Her long-held romance with becoming a cop sounded kind of childish from this distance. Like a fairy tale without the happy ending.

"I remember him saying he'd been working on his own that day as Rocky had gone for a vasectomy. Not that I knew what it meant at that age, but when Grandma went off the deep end, saying it was a sin against God and Rocky should be ashamed... Well, as you can imagine, I had to look it up. That's why it stuck with me."

She laughed at the memory. "When Grandma started ranting about sins against God, you just knew it had to be something *really* bad. How the world has changed."

"Stop talking as though you were ancient. I know you're four years younger than me. So that would make you thirty."

"Next January, Aquarius. What are you?"

"An idealist, eh? Mine's Taurus."

Was that how he saw her? To her mind idealists were the dreamers of the world, whereas she believed in action.

Her lips quirked slightly. "That would explain it." She tossed the statement back in his court.

"What?"

"Rowan, you must admit you can be pretty stubborn."

"Only when the cause demands it." He stood up and closed the gap separating them. "Time to go. Here, give me your hand." Jo slipped her hand in his and let him pull her to her feet. Mistakenly, she'd thought herself strong enough to touch Rowan again without reacting, but the sensitive, tactile memories in her fingers had other ideas. She dropped his hand as if it burned. The emotion he'd wrung out of her didn't look to be fading anytime soon.

Turning her back on him, she speculated, why now? Why did Rowan's touch make her backbone turn to jelly and her brain to mush? Right now, every mental facility should be concentrated on clearing her father's good name. Not wondering how good Rowan would be in bed. Besides, without handcuffing him like a felon and locking him up, he'd be out of Nicks Landing before the dust from the bush had been stomped off his boots.

She took a last look over the cliff. Just beyond where they'd been sitting an old landslip covered by scrub and spindly manuka flowed down to the water, making a tough but manageable climb to the beach.

The bay below was beautiful, more traditional than the black iron sands to the west of the North Island. It was hard to imagine a car lying at the foot of these cliffs as it had at Torbay. The words tumbled out of her mouth without thought. "My father's car went over a cliff. They said it was suicide but I never believed them."

That was the difference between him and Jo. Different yet the same. They'd both had to get over the tragic death of their parents, but he'd always *believed* his father had committed suicide and taken his mother with him.

He looked at Jo, not saying anything, knowing he didn't need to, waiting for her to fill in the gaps about her father.

"They said…*Rocky said,* he'd been dealing drugs and when he got caught he couldn't stand the shame so he drove off the cliffs. Rocky lied." Jo's eyes blazed with conviction. "My father never killed himself. He loved us, loved his family. He would never leave us that way."

Substitute me for us and those were the same damn thoughts he'd had when his mother had taken off, gone back to Scotland and left his father. *Left him.*

He wanted to take her in his arms, give comfort, take comfort, but he couldn't. The shadow of what happened between them earlier hung over him like a dark cloud. He'd lost control once and it could happen again. And without control, what else did he have?

"And if you'd nailed Skelton, what would it have proved?"

"The kind of man he was…is. A man who will lie for his own advantage. Did you know Rocky came down here shortly after Dad died? Hell, they had to drag me away from Auckland. Why would a cop come voluntarily to Nicks Landing unless things had gotten too hot for him?"

"Is that what happened to you?"

She let out a sharp puff of air from her mouth that lifted the hair hanging over her eyes, only to glide back into place again until she caught the errant strand and secured it behind her ear. "No, Rowan. I didn't jump. I was pushed."

"Believe me, I'm sorry. I didn't want that to happen."

"Don't be sorry. It wasn't your fault. You saved my life."

And he'd do it again in an instant, less than that, a microsecond. "Then you saved mine. That's what teams do. You rescue me, I rescue you. Partners now. Wasn't that the decision?"

She shook her head. "You're too generous, Rowan."

"No, I'm not, but you could set my mind straight on one thing. What in hell got into you that day? That wasn't like you…to deliberately step into danger had to have been an aberration. You were too good a cop. Still are, to my mind."

"Didn't you hear the rumors?"

He shrugged. Jo was holding out, but if anyone deserved to know the truth it was him. "We already covered rumors. I don't listen to them."

"It was Max."

Did he really want to hear this?

Damn, he'd known she'd loved Max, had embraced the fact with open arms, while it helped him see that wanting her would have been a lost cause even if she'd known. That didn't mean he had to like it.

"I caught sight of him heading toward the back of the house. And then I saw the gun. It was pointing straight at him. All I could think to do was distract the gunman."

She looked him straight in the eye. Hers were clear, unafraid. "Everyone thought I was in love with Max and that's why I acted so dumb. But I'd realized, just that afternoon when I talked to Maggie, that all I'd had was wishful thinking, and it didn't compare to what she and Max felt for each other. I was looking for an honest man. Max was handy, so he got nominated."

What if she'd nominated him? Where would his famous control have been then? Rowan pushed his fingers through his hair. "Why in heaven's name didn't you explain, about Max, that he could have been shot?"

"Partners. Max was mine, then. He shouldn't have done what he did, but I couldn't drop him in it. Besides, by the time I got home from the hospital, it was too late. The word had already done the rounds. It would have sounded like an excuse. When your father's been labeled a dirty cop, excuses won't cut it."

He heard the last couple of sentences, but didn't take them in. All that counted was the reason she'd given for getting back late to Central. "You were at the hospital? No one told me you got hurt."

Jo stepped right up to him. She shook her head as if exas-

perated and gave him a lighthearted punch on his arm. "*Stupid.* Of course I was at the hospital. That's where you were.
visited a lot, but you were always out of it."

Why had no one told him? His brothers should have told
him. It mightn't have made any difference, but at least he
would have had that. He would have known.

She'd been at a bad place in her life while he was in the
hospital. She'd gone in regularly after her shift and visited the
intensive Care Unit. Dim and silent except for the rhythmic
swoosh of air from ventilators and the rubbery squeak of the
night nurses' shoes, it had seemed a place apart from daily
life. Standing there, in the half-dark with guilt churning in her
gut, she'd felt the weight of the world on her shoulders. But
gradually guilt had been overtaken by the peace of just being
with him, and the certainty he would be all right. Would heal.

The only occasion she'd seen him after that had been Maggie's wedding and the atmosphere had hardly been conducive
for telling Rowan how his being shot had affected her. All she
could do was say, "Sorry," and let it go.

This wasn't the place, either. Maybe one day she would tell
Rowan how sitting beside him, holding his hand, had helped
heal her, too.

"I suppose we should make a move," she said without
looking at Rowan. She wasn't used to letting it all hang out.
Never had anyone she felt she could trust with her innermost
feelings, until now. She'd told him she'd been looking for an
honest man. And as her eyes scanned the bay, and beyond it
the volcano that hid it from Nicks Landing, she realized she'd
found one.

"I guess you're right, Bull will be sending out a search
party if we don't get back soon."

"That's it for you now, isn't it? You've got enough to make
Rocky's story sound believable, and you can hop off back to
Auckland. Whereas I—"

"Whereas you?"

"I still have to find out who these people are, and to be

honest, I could do with your help.'' The solution had come to her in a flash. A lightbulb moment.

Rowan's brows lifted. ''In what way can I help? If you're talking about catching the members of the cult, why do you need me when you have Bull and Shane and a few other assorted cops back in town?''

''You have the one thing they don't. A boat. Besides, can you really see Bull and the others creeping stealthily through the bush? They'd hear them coming a mile away.'' She stared up at him, considered batting her eyelashes, then decided against it. Sex wasn't the way to get what she wanted. She'd only end up feeling stupid. Especially if he turned her down. ''I just thought how much simpler it would be to come up here by sea on Halloween. Tell me you know how to drive it.''

For a moment he froze with his hand halfway to his face, but only a moment. Then his fist supported his chin while his thumb brushed the corner of his moustache. She could tell he was considering the idea, but he still didn't speak.

''I'm sure I could get you a voucher for gas, so it wouldn't cost you, but I don't think I could up the ante to hire the boat. Would your boss object to you taking it out?''

Rowan's brows drew together and his eyes narrowed to green shadows. ''That's not the problem. I have the use of the boat and I can drive it. What I want know is how important is this case to you? Do you really need to nail these bastards? It could be dangerous.''

A buzz of anticipation flowed through her, making her skin tingle with excitement. Rowan was going to help her. She just knew it. ''It wouldn't be too dangerous if we limited our contact to taking photos. Once we're sure, I could warn Harry, and get some cars to meet them as they leave. There's only one way out.''

''How would we get up here?''

She pulled at his sleeve, impatient now. ''Come and look. This is what gave me the idea. If we anchored in the bay, we could climb up the landslip. There's plenty of trees to hang on to but we'd need to wear gloves."

Rowan studied the slip for a few moments. His eyes measured its position and looked farther afield as if comparing a few others. "It's a fair climb, we'd need a rope."

"If you think it's too steep I could try it on my own as long as you got me here." Straight off, she knew she'd put it the wrong way. Rowan's mouth pulled into a narrow line and his hand squeezed hard on his day pack's strap.

"I've told you there's nothing wrong with my leg, but we don't want to go off half-cocked. No sense in getting killed before we can take any photos. And no more acting on impulse, okay? Sure and steady, that's the way to tackle that slope. We'd better mark this in some way, so I can pick it out from the water."

"My parka." Jo pulled the small bundle of orange nylon from her pack. "Will it be bright enough?"

"Bright enough?" He rolled his eyes and grinned at her. "I should think they could use it as a beacon to guide planes flying back from the south pole."

She looked at her pack. "What can I say? They came as a set. Find me something to tie it on to."

They fastened it to a half-grown manuka, waving its arms like some half-pint scarecrow that would glow in the dark.

"Howzatt?" he asked stepping back to admire their handiwork.

"Perfect." Jo slid her arms round his middle as if it were the most natural thing in the world now that they were truly in this together. A team. As for the buzz she got whenever he came near, like the one tingling through every nerve in her body, she had a feeling time would take care of that, now that they had some.

"I never told you why this was so important to me. I know falsely, I'd been pinning my hopes on proving Rocky did this himself. But since it appears I was wrong, maybe I can salvage something from it. Like catching the real bad guys. A story this weird is bound to make the papers again. And who knows? If Bull takes me off the shoplifting circuit, I might be able to earn a few more brownie points and get back home to Auckland.''

"I hope you make it," he said, surprised to find he really meant it. He placed his hands on her shoulders, needing to push her away before she discovered just how much being close to her aroused him. He was rock hard and aching with it, yet his heart squeezed as she leaned forward, her hair brushing his wrist like a silk rope she used to bind him to her. He could feel her breath, damp and warm on the skin at his throat. Then her mouth as she kissed him. Once, twice, three times he felt the slow heat of her lips on him.

And between each of them she murmured words so soft he had to strain to hear them. Words that almost tore asunder the bonds he had placed on his feelings for Jo.

"I'm going to miss you when you leave, Rowan. It'll be like leaving home all over again. Maybe I can visit with you when I come up to Auckland. I have some leave due."

How could he say no?

How To Play

1. With a coin, carefully scratch off the 3 gold areas on your Lucky Carnival Wheel. By doing so you have qualified to receive everything revealed—2 FREE books and a surprise gift—ABSOLUTELY FREE!

2. Send back this card and you'll receive 2 brand-new Silhouette Intimate Moments® novels. These books have a cover price of $4. each in the U.S. and $5.75 each in Canada, but they are yours ABSOLUTELY FREE.

3. There's no catch! You're under no obligation to buy anything. We charge nothing—ZERO—for your first shipment. And you don't have to make any minimum number of purchases—not even one!

4. The fact is thousands of readers enjoy receiving books by mail from the Silhouette Reader Service™. They enjoy the convenience of home delivery...they like getting the best new novels at discount prices, BEFORE they're available in stores. and they love their *Heart to Heart* subscriber newsletter featuring author news, horoscopes, recipes, book reviews and much more!

5. We hope that after receiving your free books you'll want to remain a subscriber. But the choice is yours—to continue or cancel, any time at all! So why not take us up on our invitation, with no risk of any kind. You'll be glad you did!

A surprise gift

FREE

We can't tell you what it is...but we're sure you'll like it! A

FREE GIFT!

just for playing LUCKY CARNIVAL WHEEL!

Visit us online at

www.eHarlequin.com

The Silhouette Reader Service™—Here's how it works:

Chapter 9

Were blisters on top of blisters possible?

Jo did a mental calculation of how many Band-Aids she had in her pack and decided the way her feet felt, there wouldn't be nearly enough. Gravel rolled under her boots as she quickened her pace across the parking lot, nearly embracing Rowan's Jag with open arms as the remote key bleeped a welcome. Would Rowan think she was nuts if she kissed his car?

She was halfway round the bonnet to the passenger side when he said, "You drive."

Jo stopped short in surprise, almost missing the keys he'd tossed casually in her direction. A shiver of anticipation snaked up her spine. Rowan trusted her enough to let her drive his car. Oh, boy! This car tempted her like the apple did Eve. All that power under the hood, just waiting to be released by the touch of a hand. Her hand.

Shortening the distance to the pedals, Jo adjusted the seat, and straightened the back till it fit snugly against her shoulders. She shifted, easing almost sensually into the soft leather and took a deep breath. "Lord, I love that smell." She took another sniff for good measure, and held it, allowing the earthy smell of new leather to seep into her—bone deep.

A random memory, a scent, powerfully, muskily male, overlaid the other as the engine began to purr and found an answering echo inside her. Rowan and his car were a good match. They both stirred her senses. She turned and ran her gaze over him, letting the sensations she felt spill over into her smile.

Rowan shook his head, the wry twist to his mouth reinforcing his words. "If you've finished drooling, maybe we could leave."

"Yes, sir. Whatever you say, sir." What would he say if he knew he made her mouth water every bit as much as his car? More...

She put her foot on the gas pedal. The engine growled. She couldn't resist. "Do you hear that?" She licked her lips wickedly, teasing him. "Hot sex on wheels."

His eyebrows rose, feigning an impatience that didn't reach his eyes. "Are you gonna drive, or do I have to take over?"

Jo took it easy at first, careful not to spin the wheels and send any gravel flying that might chip the paintwork.

Her skin prickled lightly as if it glowed from an excess of static in the atmosphere. Not solely her doing. Something new proliferated the air between them. The attraction was a given, but an extra element had been added. The word *trust* popped into her mind. Yes, that was it. A new trust had grown between them.

"I really appreciate you letting me get behind the wheel of your new toy." She turned her eyes, hardly daring to take them off the road. Rowan looked large and safe. Safe to confide in.

"No problem."

She'd opened up back there on the cliff top, told him stuff about herself, about her father. Stuff she'd never discussed with another soul. Not her grandmother. Not her brothers. And

Rowan? Well, he'd listened, and he hadn't laughed. Hadn't said, "You're just imagining things."

She thought back. The sharing hadn't all been one-sided. He *had* told her he'd been brought up in Nicks Landing, and he *was* staying on a bit longer to help her. What more could she ask?

Men couldn't bare their souls as easily as women, but if ever there had been an opportunity to get anything off his chest, like a grudge he'd been holding against her, anything important, that had been the time. "What I really wanted to say, was thanks for trusting me with your car. I know how much these babies cost. And I wanted to say the feeling's mutual."

"It's what?" Rowan's shoulders cut out the light from the window, increasing the space separating them. "What's mutual?"

"I trust you, too. You've always been one of the good guys, Rowan. Honest. Straight. That's pretty unusual, these days. Believe me I know what I'm talking about."

He shrugged, but didn't respond until she'd taken her gaze off him as they approached a T intersection. "You need to get out more, out of the station and away from the criminal environment. I'm just an average guy, don't try putting me on a pedestal."

Yeah, sure. The average guy goes around saving lives every day of the week and twice on Sundays.

Jo checked for traffic then took a left. As far as she was concerned his modesty was all part of the same package. And the slight dent in his comfort zone only needed a few gentle taps with a hammer to smooth it out.

"Hey, don't get me wrong. I'm not resorting to flattery on the off chance you might change your mind about helping me."

Her foot increased its pressure on the gas pedal and the speedometer needle inched closer to the speed limit. "Allied Insurance sure must think a lot of you. I'll bet they don't supply many of their employees with cars like this."

"Not many."

She should have stopped there, but curiosity got the better of her. "I suppose cops aren't usually in the same league as the Stanhopes, but I guess you've known them most of your life."

"How did you know?"

"An intuitive guess. From what I heard, the Stanhope brothers ran pretty freely around Nicks Landing when they were kids. You're bound to be the same age with at least one of them."

Rowan shifted his hips in his seat. The soft leather made the kind of groan she had wanted to, following that denim-covered butt through the bush.

"Got it in one. I'm the same age as the middle brother."

She couldn't prevent a small, smug grin as a line from a song hummed through her brain. Her thumbs tapped out the beat on the steering wheel and her head moved in time to the rhythm. "I guess my detective genes haven't completely seized up through lack of use, after all."

Under her breath she sang, "I feel good."

Only a jerk would choose this moment to disillusion her.

Rowan felt the weight of Jo's trust settle like a three-pound brick inside his chest. A weight that would take more than antacids to shift.

"Where to now?" she asked as they came over the last rise and entered the outskirts of Nicks Landing.

The small town looked almost beautiful from this distance, spread out before them like a block-patterned quilt. Hard on the heels of the thought, he experienced a moment of nostalgia. He'd stayed away from it for years, but it wasn't the town he hated...only the memories of his last few years there.

"We can go pick up your car, or carry on into town and your office. Makes no difference to me."

Jo had left her hair loose on the walk back, and as she turned to smile it skimmed her shoulders, sending a drift of evocative fragrance in his direction. He quieted an urge to reach out and twist the black rope of hair round his hand, just for the feel of it. Yeah, he'd like that, though he couldn't deny it would bring that mischievous smile close enough to taste.

"You know what?" she said with a naughty smirk. "I'm going straight to the station house. Bull and Jake might just catch a glimpse of me driving your car. Now wouldn't that be something."

"You think they'll care?"

"Jake will. He's always going on about fast cars and what he'll do when he owns one. You wouldn't begrudge me a little female chauvinistic one-upmanship, would you?"

He couldn't begrudge her anything. That was his problem. For the past two years he'd convinced himself he was doing great without her in his life. Well, maybe not great, but okay.

He'd been back home just three days and already he'd given up an opportunity to escape to the city, back to where it was safe.

One taste, one kiss and he'd given up the fight like a wimp. Hell, he'd been fooling himself back there in the bush. Fooling them both with tales of being bedeviled.

The devil made me do it. What a crock!

But he still wasn't ready to admit what had driven him.

Temptation…oh yeah.

The word echoed. *Temptation.* Not from inside his head, but seated somewhere deep inside his chest. He tried blowing a sharp puff of air through his nostrils to clear his system.

"All right, Jo. Let's go make Jake jealous."

Entering the station house with Rowan following behind her, Jo felt happier than she had in a long time. A very long time.

Even the knowledge that saving her father's reputation had once more been put on hold, couldn't dull her exuberance.

On hold didn't mean the same as giving up.

From the look Seth slanted at her from behind the reception counter, he'd seen her drive up. And she knew that if Rowan hadn't been there, he'd have pestered her with questions.

Rowan was at her shoulder. She turned to look up at him, inches shorter in the comfortable sneakers she'd changed into. "Do you want to go straight upstairs and work out our plans, or would you rather check in with your old mate, Harry, first?" She punched the code into the lock.

What Rowan might have answered was lost in the shuffle as Seth called her back to reception before they'd gone through the door.

"Jo, Rocky Skelton left a message for you."

Rowan held the door open by pressing his palm against it at shoulder level, but kept watching her. As she felt his eyes on her, she realized this had long since stopped being her case alone; she no longer resented him being seconded to help her. They really had become partners, a team. And it felt *good*. Better than good, terrific.

"What's the message, then? Did forensics find some brimstone in the ashes of Rocky's house?" She heard the sarcasm, heard the sharpness, residue from her grudge against the old scumbag. Two years of hoping to nail Rocky couldn't be canceled just like that. Old grievances didn't disappear overnight.

What a surprise.

The acid in her voice slid right off Seth. Working in reception on a regular basis, it took a lot to faze him. "Rocky didn't say. Just told me he wanted to see you the moment you got back."

She turned on her heels. If she hadn't been wearing sneakers they would have signaled her displeasure. Rocky had taken the edge off her good humor. Who was he to make demands on her time?

Rowan took one look at her face and said, "Your prejudice is showing."

"You're right." Her nose twitched at the precise moment she realized her arms were folded across her chest. Swell, her ambivalence was crying out; her mouth said yes but her body language was on the defensive. "Are you gonna come with me? Or leave me to get uptight on my own?"

Rowan read her like a book, a book in need of diversion.

"I'm with you, partner," he said with a wink, and took a shot at her with an index finger.

It worked. She responded with a feigned cuff on the chin. "Well, at least I've got one on my side."

She studied the back of her knuckles where the scrape of his beard lingered. He already needed a shave. Her nostrils flared slightly. There was something utterly masculine about a man who needed to shave twice a day. She looked up at him through her lashes and studied his face covertly.

That moustache. On a reflex, her tongue slipped out and tentatively feathered her top lip. Yeah, the jury was still out on that one. If it hadn't been for the facial hair—and the kiss— she could have pretended nothing had changed. That they were both home in Auckland.

Wrong.

Remembering her old life, the way things had been. That was partly what had spoiled her stay in Nicks Landing. But right this moment, right now, she wasn't sure if she'd swap.

The time of day was late afternoon, but in the Hard Luck Inn, darkness drew itself around the interior as if night had fallen. They entered to the usual clash of heavy-metal music. It reverberated through the souvenir bike parts like wind rustling autumn leaves.

Jo's senses were at high pitch and as soon as they crossed the threshold, the buzz in the air prickled the hairs on her arms.

At six foot five, Rowan's size usually attracted attention, and she was no small fry. Together their impact doubled, but although she couldn't put her finger on it, she knew immediately the stir had nothing to do with their height, or their entry.

Cheek by jowl on the outer rim of the U-shaped bar, a crush of men in jeans, work shirts and boots, not unlike the ones she'd been glad to take off, stood downing ice-cold beer. With a sense of timing that reminded her of a Mexican wave, they tilted an assortment of long- and short-neck bottles, poured the contents down their throats, then swiped the condensation running down the inside of their wrists onto the denim cloth of their jeans.

On closer observation she noted the icy sweat had settled in rings on the counter that could have given the Olympic symbol a run for its money. Seemed as though Rocky's mouth was working faster than his cleaning-up cloth.

"Let's get this over with," she said to Rowan, stepping up to the bar with a loud "Excuse me."

The bodies lining the counter parted after a preliminary glance over their respective shoulders, then ignored the two of them once more. Or pretended to. She wouldn't risk a five-cent bet on everyone minding their own business, even though they appeared to have developed a sudden fascination for the football game on TV.

Everyone fixed their gazes on the bright screen sitting among the clutter on the wall. Did they think she didn't realize that they could do two things at once even though they were men? Of course, the absence of any commentary helped.

Rowan slotted into the remaining space, his shoulder overlapping hers as if protecting her back and, just for once, Rocky looked happy to see them.

"You *sent* for me?"

"Not exactly sent," he answered, his initial pleasure collapsing as if someone had popped a balloon and let his features sag down his face in lines. "I've got something to show you. It came today." With a flick of his wrist, a folded envelope, slightly discolored from handling, emerged from his hip pocket.

Rowan leaned forward, his face close to hers. She felt the pressure of his shoulder as the latest development in Rocky's saga unfolded like the envelope. "Maybe we'd be better off at a table?" he said in her ear.

She eyed the inn's patrons, checking their reactions, but no one met her gaze. Too many secrets. Too much to hide. Secrets and lies were the lifeblood of a small town.

Hundreds of secrets that everyone but her was cognizant of.

She was an incomer, a city girl, and as such, not to be trusted.

As though someone had given him a shot of bravery, Rocky croaked, "I've got nothing to hide. Everyone's seen the anonymous letter."

She reached out across the counter, and set her sights on the sloppy neckline of Rocky's wash-faded, black T-shirt. Behind her Rowan tensed. A charge of electricity zapped where their shoulders met, as if he expected her to grab Rocky by the T-shirt, if not the throat.

In next to no time, she put the big guy, and probably Rocky, too, out of his misery and crooked her finger in Rocky's face. Besides, a girl would be unwise to get any closer to the swimming wet counter than necessary. "Come here, Rocky."

The innkeeper leaned forward and the breath Rowan released stirred her hair. Who had he really thought needed rescuing this time? Her or Rocky?

She spoke low, pitching her voice to travel across the bar and no farther. "Did it ever enter your small mind that one of these guys you've been blabbing to, might be responsible for the letter? They could be laughing up their sleeve even now."

Rocky's eyes widened and exposed a glimmer of fear. "Let's get a table over there," he said, sobered by the truth. The innkeeper opened the gate on the far leg of the U and ducked under, leading them to a table at the farthest side of the room. Was she the only one who noticed his gaze flitted around the room, never settling, shifting from one face to the next?

She'd always known his shiftiness was endemic, but in an I'm-the-man sort of way. What amazed her was the difference today from the Cool Hand Luke bravado he'd demonstrated the night she'd visited the inn with Rowan.

Betty was dispatched to tend the bar by a raised eyebrow and a jerk of Rocky's thumb as they passed. The whole operation took less than a minute and as Jo caught Betty's eyes,

she shrugged her shoulders as if to say, "don't blame me,"
and added a half smile to soften Rocky's gruff gesture.

Rocky Skelton sat down with his back to the wall. His bon
chest seemed to cave in as his shoulders hunched over th
table. If ever a man looked ready to duck incoming fire, it wa
Rocky.

She threw herself into the opposite chair and felt the meta
legs creak as they spread under her, then watched Rowan tes
his weight on the only other one at the table. Rowan ha
positioned himself so he had a view of the room as well a
the new and unimproved version of Rocky.

Keeping her face expressionless, she demonstrated it woul
take more than a few glances over his shoulder to convinc
her he was running scared. Hard luck, pal. Rocky's peculia
choice of names for his bar was about to ricochet and take
bite out of him.

In her peripheral vision, she watched Rowan rub his ches
as if it ached. His expression was set, unreadable, except fo
a gleam in his eyes that she couldn't help but answer. Then i
was back to business and she let her impatience bare its fang:
"C'mon, Skelton, spit it out, we haven't got all day."

"It's the satanists. They're after me." *Again!*

The strident riffles of a heavy-metal guitar that had buffete
them around the head, chose that moment to stop, leaving
gap for Rocky's cry to fill. Everyone in the bar stopped talkin
at once and Rocky's glare only succeeded in driving the sus
penseful whispers to greater heights.

A new, slightly quieter track began and restored privacy t
the table. "So, what's new?" she asked, "You've been sing
ing that song for months."

Gingerly, Rocky laid the envelope on the tabletop as thoug
it was on fire, then he flicked it with one finger, spinning i
in Jo's direction.

She picked it up by one corner, looked at the address, then
squeezed gently on the sharply creased edges until the jagge
rips in the top of the envelope yawned open like a mouth ful
of crooked teeth.

"What's this, then?" She shook it upside down until the contents fell out on the table. "I don't suppose the idea of not smearing your dabs all over entered your mind?"

Rocky's scowl deepened as he went on the defensive. "It did, but not until I realized what it contained. I didn't expect to find this crap in the mail. The envelope was in the middle of the pile and I didn't notice until I'd opened the damn thing."

She carefully unfolded the paper.

Rowan pushed his chair back and stood behind her, one hand resting on her shoulder. Like many threatening letters she'd seen in her time, each character in the message had been cut from a newspaper or magazine and stuck on the paper. It was as if they'd all taken anonymous letters 101 by watching reruns of old films.

Call off your dogs Skelton.

Next time we won't miss you or your wife.

Rowan's fingers tightened their grip. They'd signed it with a pentagram. "Have you shown this to Molly?" he asked.

Rocky shook his head. His gaze slithered over to the kitchen door and he swiped at his top lip where beads of sweat had gathered. "I didn't want to worry her. She has enough on her plate with the fire and everything. It's no fun trying to make a home in what used to be our storeroom."

Mark one up for Molly. Rocky gave no indication that his wife had reported Jo's faux pas. Maybe she *hadn't* heard.

"You'd better warn her. Both of you stick together. Don't, and I mean *don't*, go anywhere unaccompanied or leave your wife alone. Have you got that?" She captured Rowan's gaze and was pleasantly surprised to read agreement written there.

"This is the thing, Rocky. Hopefully by tomorrow night we'll bring an end to all this satanist mumbo jumbo, but keep it under your hat. If word of what we're doing gets out, the whole town will know before morning." Deliberately, she kept their intentions vague. On the one hand, she wanted to reassure him, *if* his fear was genuine. On the other, something didn't smell right.

Jo couldn't put her finger on it. Near as she could figure
after the first fire she would have sworn Rocky was acting
but he sure as hell wasn't now.

And why had Molly kept quiet? She'd never liked Jo. Wh
protect her now?

Had Rocky actually been mixed up with some demoni
weirdos and this was a payoff for some misdeed or attempt t
leave the cult? Whatever they were hiding, it would take mor
than browbeating from her or Rowan to make the jerk talk
No threat they made could top the ones he'd already receivec

"We mean it, Skelton. Keep your mouth shut." Rowa
added his weight to her order.

"Rowan and I want to talk among ourselves. It's all right
you go tend bar. I can tell from the way you're looking a
Betty, you don't think she's meeting your standards."

"Can I send her over with a drink, a beer maybe?"

Rowan sat down again and the metal scrape of his chai
added a bizarre off-key element to the music. She saw his lip
move, grumbling indistinctly, before he said, "No thanks."

"Me, neither. In fact, I think we should finish this conver
sation at the station house. We ought to see if they can lif
any prints off this." She maneuvered the letter and envelop
with the tip of a ballpoint, sliding them into a small clip-tigh
bag that she'd stuffed in her pocket this morning for just suc
an occasion.

Simply stepping outside that place did wonders for his equi
librium. The air smelled sweeter somehow. Rowan took a dee
breath and let it permeate through him.

On the short walk to the station house, he told Jo, "Sorry
if I trod on your toes back there, with Skelton, I mean. It'
really your call."

"No problem. You've got a heavier hand than mine
Whether or not he'll take your advice is another question."

"So, what was your take on Skelton? Was he sweating ove
this, or was it my imagination?"

"No, he was feeling the heat. There's something rotten in the house of Hard Luck and I don't think it's in the kitchen."

She stopped at the curb and their hips brushed as he lost his balance and swayed into her. Without rationalizing his need, he reached out and pulled her into the curve of his arm until they both steadied. Beyond all reason, he realized he only felt truly alive when she was in his arms. Beyond all the craziness and suspicion, he relished the days ahead with her.

It was broad daylight and he wanted nothing more than to kiss her right there in front of everyone on the sidewalk. Instead, he pressed one finger to the tip of her nose. "You always had a great sense here for anything slightly off-kilter. I'm positive you're right. But never mind, he's got more than satanists or devil worshipers on his tail now. You and I are going to find him out."

"Hi, Detective Jo. Hi...sir."

His first reaction to the young voice was annoyance. He'd have felt the same about anyone who made Jo flush and push away from him, taking her warmth.

One glance gave him a clue to the owner of the voice. There couldn't be many red-haired kids wearing pink barrettes in Nicks Landing. She looked up at him with a frank show of adoration in her eyes. Now *he* wanted to color up. He wasn't used to kids this age, or the way they didn't hide their feelings.

"Well, hi to you, too, Ginny. This is Rowan McQuaid."

The kid nodded but didn't say anything. "Where are you off to?" asked Jo who put a hand up to her own hair and commented, "Love the barrettes."

Seemed Ginny had plenty of adoration to go round. It shone from her face as she responded to Jo, copying her action and fingering the touch of pink in her hair. "Me, too. Don't worry, I'm not getting into trouble. I'm cooking supper for Dad and getting an early night."

"For heaven's sake, Ginny. I hope you're not still planning on hiking into the bush tomorrow night after what I said?" Jo crouched, bringing her face level with Ginny's, and held her lightly by the shoulders. "Promise me you won't go near Te

Kohanga Park tomorrow. It's dangerous...and I don't mean all those rumors that have been flying around. I'm talking about the bush. It's too easy to get lost in there and I don't want to have to send a search party out after you.''

"Oh, we changed our minds about that anyway. Sandra's mom won't let her have the car.''

Straightening up, Jo rolled her eyes at him, but he could see she was thinking, thank goodness for Sandra's mom. "That's great. I didn't want to chase through there looking for you.'' She winked at the kid. "Remember what I told you about the B-U-G-S,'' she whispered, as if he couldn't spell.

Bloody amazing. She'd pit herself against a satanist any day, but cave in the face of a bug.

Ginny wrinkled her nose the way he'd often seen Jo do. It was either a girl thing or the kid had a case of hero worship. "Not to worry, Detective Jo. I couldn't go anyway. I've got the paper route. I have to get up early in the mornings.''

Jo gave her the thumbs-up. "I'm proud of you. We've got to go, but don't forget to say hi next time you see me.''

The station house door had barely swung closed behind them when Harry got to his feet, frowning. There was little he missed, including the fact she'd been out of range all morning, her cell phone reception shaded by the volcano at the southern end of the park.

She wasn't kept in suspense for more than a few seconds.

"You get hold of Rocky?''

"Yeah, no problem, Harry. He received a threatening letter. I don't know if it'll tell us much. The idiot got his prints all over it. Still, I'm going to need it sent down the line and have it checked.'' She held the clip-tight bag out to Harry. "Did the forensics team leave already?''

One of the biggest hindrances she had found in Nicks Landing was the lack of a forensic team. They didn't have enough continuous work to warrant the expense of one there.

Sure, Nicks County was a big area, thus three detectives, but it was mainly rural. There was no knowing how many cannabis patches were hidden back in the hills. Bull and Jake were always following up leads. Especially at this time of year, when the fresh young growth of the plants stood out among the darker green bush, making it easily spotted by crop dusters or copters passing through. And often as not if they got too close, they were shot at for their trouble.

It had happened on Great Barrier Island to a friend of Rowan and hers, Jamie Thurlo. He'd been flying the helicopter the day Rowan had got shot. As far as she could make out, Jamie had taken an investigative reporter with him on one of his regular flyovers of the island. They'd been lucky to come out of it alive, though she'd heard Jamie was pretty scarred.

"You just missed them. The team's on its way back to Gisborne. I read your report. You were right to be wary of that newspaper with the pentagram, Rowan. They found the remains of a pressure switch. Looks like it was connected to the tractor mower in the basement. It only took one spark."

"That's great. Now they're getting technical, working their way up from candles to pressure switches."

"More than technical," said Rowan, "the bastards are getting serious. Did you tell Rocky?"

Harry nodded. "When he came looking for you."

"No wonder Rocky was sweating on it. From now on, ex-cop or not, I say we keep him in the dark. What do you think, Jo?"

"Definitely. I still don't trust the guy. His going up to the house yesterday might have been more of a fluke than anything else. We were the only ones who had made definite plans to visit Lonely Track Road. Rocky knew that. But, who else did he tell?

"Which makes me think we could be getting too close and the fire was a warning for us. You know Rocky once he gets behind that bar. He could have spilled our plans to any number of people. You can't keep secrets in this town."

"Somebody can," muttered Rowan, frowning, his brow as dark as a thunderhead.

"Well, I didn't tell anyone about our lead to the national

park. Not even Moira. She thought we were just having a da
out."

"On a Friday?" gibed Harry.

Jo shrugged it off. "She's got used to my insignificance i
the scheme of things around here. Why should she be surprise
if I get a day off?"

"Well, I might have something here that will cheer you up
if it doesn't piss you off first that is."

"What is it?" she asked.

Rowan chimed in. "That's the kind of attitude that got th
messenger shot, Harry," he said. "But let's see what you'v
got."

The sergeant held out an envelope, a twin to the one insid
the baggie.

"You didn't open it?"

"It's not addressed to me," he answered.

Meticulous to the last. She wouldn't have expected anythin
less. Harry was a good cop. "Got a knife?"

"Here," said Rowan, retrieving a slim pocketknife from hi
jeans, then opening the equally slim but lethal-looking blade

"Offensive weapon?" she teased, refusing to acknowledg
the letter had any power over her. She focused on Rowan, an
why not? Over the last three days it was as if he'd been he
hold on reality while everything around her went mad.

Rowan gave her a crooked grin. "Boy Scout knife."

One thought dominated after he passed it over. And i
wasn't, *hurry up and open the letter*. No! The one seducing
her concentration went, *she could feel the heat from his body
flowing from the knife into her palm!*

"It's sharp. Be careful," he warned.

"Don't worry, I can handle an itty-bitty knife like this one."

She lifted the blade to slit the fold, remembering the jagge
rip Rocky had torn in the other one. It was a short step from
there to the words with their implicit threat that she'd read a
the inn. Her hand trembled as the memory wiped out any
humor she'd found in the situation. "I think I'll take thi
through to my office. I should photocopy the note Rocky

handed over…and this one, too, if your suspicions are correct.''

From the moment Harry had spoken of a letter addressed to her, she'd been conscious of Rowan hovering next to her elbow. Not touching, but close enough that his presence became part of everything she did.

After a day spent in the bush, she wasn't certain how her deodorant was hanging in, but Rowan's spicy tang with its additional sharpness wasn't unpleasant as it might have been in a stranger. There was something very intimate in having his scent in her head. An awareness of him as a man.

Her man.

Her step faltered on the last thought.

When they reached her office, he took the knife and the envelope from her and said, ''Here, let me do it.''

For once, she gave them up without a murmur.

After he slit it open, he tipped the fold of paper onto her desk. The marks where the paste had dimpled the back of the note were visible at a glance. ''Want me to open it?''

She simply nodded and said, ''Gloves in the top drawer.'' Certain of the threat it would contain, her mouth grew dry. During her years on the force, she'd prided herself on dealing justly with those she arrested. But in all that time she'd never received a *personal* threat. One aimed at her alone.

Following Rowan's example she rolled latex gloves onto her hands. Finished, she heard his indrawn breath as his gaze skimmed quickly across the page. She could put it off no longer and held out her hand, steeling herself to read the worst.

SKELTON'S WHORE—YOUR NUMBER IS UP
DON'T BUTT YOUR NOSE INTO OUR BUSINESS
BE FRIGHTENED—VERY FRIGHTENED—WE KNOW
NO MERCY

The paper dropped to the floor as her gaze flew to Rowan. His features had tightened, throwing his cheekbones into sharp prominence. His eyes glittered angrily in the stillness of his face as his nostrils flared with each breath he took.

"It's not true...." Revulsion robbed her of breath. "Rocky and me...no way! I couldn't—"

"I never thought you could...did." Rowan came closer and his big hands cupped her face and tilted it until they stood eye to eye. "No one who knows you could believe the implication." Next moment, he held her in a bear hug, his arms pressing her against him till it hurt to breathe, but it was a good pain.

Rowan loosened his grip. His voice was gruff as if he'd hurt his throat. "It's shock tactics. They want you to back away from the case. If anyone's running scared it's them. Someone must have tipped them off."

He held her out from him. She felt bereft at the loss of his warmth. His body.

Rowan's lips twisted slightly but he pulled her head into his shoulder before she could work out which emotion was showing. "I don't like this, Jo." His hand slid over the back of her hair. "It's been a helluva day. Come back to the boat with me, I don't want you to be alone tonight."

"I've got Moira."

"And what is a ditzy little woman, half your size going to do if they come after you?"

She pushed her hands against his chest, feeling the steady life-confirming beat of his heart and felt safe. Stronger. With a half laugh, she meant to reassure Rowan she felt better, more herself. And she did. The shock had worn off. Soon she would just feel mad. Good and mad!

"I told you, I'm a big girl, I can take care of myself. No more hero stuff."

"You said partners and that's what you'll get. You need backup, Jo, and I'm it."

Chapter 10

So, this was how the other half lived. Heavens, this cabin was as large as the room she rented from Moira and twice as luxurious. Jo hung the clothes from her duffel inside the fitted locker, admiring the way the designer had put every inch of space to good use. The task barely took her three minutes and as she straightened the last sleeve, she wondered if such pitifully few clothes had ever graced its interior before.

"You can use this stateroom, the head's...bathroom, is over there," Rowan had said, then dumped her bag on the floor and left her to get on with unpacking.

Sitting down on the side of the bed, she smoothed one hand across the silky quilted fabric of the fitted coverlet. The subtle autumn hues tied in with the two shades of timber that had been used on the cabinetry and the dull apricot suede finish lining the walls and ceiling. The same decor she'd seen in Rowan's stateroom that first day, except he had a larger bed and its cover was a creamy peach brocade.

She had her own queen-size bed and private ensuite. It was perfect. Two huge square pillows rested against the headboard.

She punched one; it was soft as marshmallow. She picked up the other one and leaned it on top of the pillow on her side and gave it a punch as well. Her fist sunk deep into the center as they gave under the pressure. So, what had she expected? That he would put her in his own cabin? Is that why she felt dissatisfied in the middle of all this luxury? What more could a girl ask for than a queen-size just for one person? Perfect.

Perfectly lonely.

In the nether regions of her brain hovered the whiff of an idea that her time would soon run out. That, if she didn't do something about her feelings soon, she'd regret it for the rest of her life.

"Nonsense!" she chided herself. Since there was no one to disagree, she picked up her bag and grabbed a small squashed box of tissues too ratty to go with her luxurious quarters from the bottom. "In you go," she said opening the top drawer of the nightstand, thrusting them out of sight.

A gleam of silver at the back of the drawer caught her eye. Condoms. Fool, for all her imagining she hadn't even considered adding them to her list when she'd shopped. And with the way she was feeling anything could happen. At least she hoped it would.

Reaching in she picked up a handful of foil packets and tossed them in the air so they landed on the bed. Someone had been well prepared. What did the advertisement on TV say? *The life you save could be your own.*

It was time to go up to the saloon and see what she could do to nudge events in the right direction.

Rowan breathed in the aroma of steak broiling under the grill as he tore lettuce apart for a salad to eat with the baked potatoes he'd shoved in the microwave. He could look after himself, even if he didn't go in for anything fancy. Jo would soon see he wasn't in search of a wife simply to look after him.

Wife?

Whoa! One shot in the dark and his subconscious had taken a leap into the unknown. Time to rein it in.

He threw a handful of spring onions, sweet peppers and avocado into the mix. Sliced tomatoes followed as he sensed Jo come up behind him. Her fingers lightly snagged his belt as her head dodged round his shoulder, watching him cook. "Whatever it is, it smells delicious."

"That tantalizing aroma is broiled steak. Supper's almost ready. You take a seat and I'll pour some wine."

Rowan pulled a bottle out of the rack and held it up for Jo to read the label. Kereru Hill Shiraz.

"I couldn't resist. Look at the date, Max's first vintage. We can give him our opinion next time we all meet up."

Damn, what was he doing talking as if they'd be doing it together? The corkscrew, cork still attached, clattered onto the counter like an exclamation mark to his thoughts. He poured two glasses of ruby wine, sniffed the bouquet, then took a sip. Max had done a good job. He'd taken a chance and it had worked.

Maybe it was time for him to do the same.

Jo looked serious as he passed her a glass. A tiny V-shaped frown bridged her dark eyebrows as if she had an unpleasant task to perform. "Drink up. This is good for whatever ails you."

"Do I look that bad?"

"You've never looked bad to me, you're a beautiful woman. Easy on the eyes. I've always thought so." What more could a man want apart from constancy and fidelity.

She let out a gasp and almost spilled some wine. A small red trickle escaped the corner of her mouth followed by an explosion of need bursting inside him. It was all he could do not to seize the nape of her neck in his grasp and clean up her lips with his tongue.

Down boy, down, he warned his raging libido.

A velvety softness gleamed in her eyes, yet her smile seemed reluctant, uncertain. "I can count the number of times I've heard that on one finger. Thank you."

"It wasn't a compliment. Simply a statement of fact." He swirled the wine around his glass and let the bouquet drift upwards, rich, fruity, like black currants.

"It was a first for me. Personally, I can't see it. Mostly when I look in the mirror it's what's going on inside I see, and the rest of the junk takes a back seat."

"Sounds too philosophical. But you haven't told me, why the frown?" He touched her between the eyebrows, then smoothed a finger over both shiny dark wings to erase the small worry lines. "What's going on inside your head tonight?"

"That I always thought I would see hate in your eyes when we met up again. You have reason to hate me. Good reason."

He made a movement with his fingers, which flicked off such a suggestion as preposterous. "And now? Look in my eyes and tell me what you see now."

The danger he'd always known awaited him loomed large. His heart pounded like a jackhammer against his breastbone as if it might break out and show her his agony, past and present.

Jo stared at him. He tried not to blink, holding her gaze, hardly daring to breathe.

"I see warmth and friendship, an attraction that's reciprocated, but no hatred." Attraction. Love it seemed, wasn't on either of their agendas, but he could go with them *both* feeling attraction. It would be enough. It would have to be.

"And I see a man I don't have to fear. A man who cares for me, who could never stand aside and watch me die."

"Even when you've ordered him to do exactly that?"

Her brown velvet eyes softened. "Even then." The words rolled slowly from lips that looked fuller, redder, lush and inviting.

The smell of broiled T-bone teased his nose. Damn! "Time to eat. Our supper's ready." For an instant he'd been tempted to let it burn and follow where the conversation and his instincts led. To disaster, maybe, but at least he'd die a happy man, having trod the highs as well as the lows instead of the straight and narrow road he'd taken lately.

So, how would Mata Hari handle the situation?

Half an hour had passed since she'd come down to her stateroom, saying, "I think I'll go have my shower and get ready for bed. We have an early start in the morning."

Maybe she'd been giving out the wrong signals. Come-hither looks weren't part of her repertoire, and playing the vamp at her height had always struck her as ridiculous. Besides, there were so few men tall enough for her to look up at and bat her eyelashes.

Rowan had merely responded to her announcement with a nod. The recessed downlight overhead had cast shadows across his eyes and mouth. The lack of light made the first look brooding, the other grim, and in the end her own smile had withered from lack of nourishment.

Seduction was a game she'd never played before. Max hadn't given her the chance, and any rules—if she'd ever known them—were long forgotten. She licked her lips and pouted at her reflection in the small mirror. She tried, "Rowan," purring.

No, she decided with a shake of her head that sent her hair spinning. She couldn't do this. It smacked too much of pretense for a woman who had made honesty her creed.

Warm inside and out, from the wine, then the shower, her perfumed skin appeared to glow. It looked soft enough to the eye, to the touch. She lifted her breasts and held their fullness in her hands, imagining how they would look to Rowan.

What if all her years on the force had taken their toll, and the only softness left was on the outside? She'd spent so long proving she was as good as the next cop. Better than most. As good as her father had been, no matter what the records said.

What if she'd lost the ability to call up the softer, womanly emotions inside her? Love, compassion. When had she last opened her heart and shed a tear? *Except for Rowan.*

Perhaps there was hope for her yet.

With that thought ringing in her head, she slipped into her best underwear, wrapping a black satin robe over its red, lacy sensuality.

"Just tell Rowan the truth," she muttered over and over. He could only reject her, and she'd dealt with that before.

Her hand trembled as she held her robe tight. Her insides jangled with a mixture of anticipation and doubt. Satisfied the bra she wore underneath was hidden, she took a deep breath and grabbed a fistful of condoms from the top drawer of the nightstand, slipping them into the deep side pocket of her robe.

Maybe if his brain would shut up, he could get some sleep. Rowan should have guessed this would happen the moment he'd agreed to Jo's request that they use the *Fancy* to come up on the tree-girded circle from the seaward side.

Hell, what a cop-out. If she hadn't suggested it, he might have. No, it was the threat of Jo, sleeping a few feet away, with only a wall separating them that jangled his chain. What was it about him, Rowan McQuaid Stanhope, about his personality that all his troubles came in twos?

This time of year had always been difficult for him. A few more days and it would be the anniversary of his parents' death. It was the not knowing that he couldn't get past.

Had his father killed both his mother and himself on that fateful boat trip on the *Fancy I*?

His father had been such a good sailor, to have anchored in the main shipping lane just wasn't the act of a sane man. But what if the reconciliation hadn't taken, if his mother had hurt his father again? Rowan still carried the memory of the first time his mother had left....

He'd never seen his father cry before, and it had shaken him to the core. Damn! He couldn't lie in bed reliving that time over and over. He'd a good mind...

No, he couldn't do that either. Couldn't go to Jo and use her as a palliative to relieve the scars of hurts that still throbbed after all these years.

Rowan's feet hit the floor the moment he threw the bed-covers aside. The buttoned and belted feel of his jeans was an easy find in the dark and familiarity with the task soon had him covered in denim from ankle to waist.

Gathering her courage round her, Jo opened the door, remembering that afternoon and the way Rowan had held her.

Wanted her.

It hadn't been the result of a spell, simply a man and a woman wanting each other. "Hold that thought," she whispered under her breath.

He needed fresh air to clear his head of ancient memories and latent desires that could only lead to tragedy. When it came to love he was too much his father's son.

He crossed the cabin on bare feet in the dark and stepped into the companionway.

A soft click alerted him of another's presence in the darkness. Every hair on his body prickled with an icy chill of awareness. A superstitious man might have pondered if the ghost of his longings had come to life. Instead a sigh of inevitability left his chest in the wake of soft hands pressing dead center, against his sternum.

At his temples, the sound of his heart pounding was enough to drown the mix of irregular breathing, but not Jo's cry. "Oops, I didn't see you in the dark."

His hands reached out as if to steady them both, and encountered silk-covered skin. In an instant, he was hard. Painfully hard. He forced his apology past a larynx wrapped in rusty barbed wire. "My fault. I should have put the light on. Can I get you something, is there anything you want?"

"You. I want you." Her whisper swirled into the thick blackness enveloping them.

The world stopped and sent him hurtling into space. He sucked in a breath and held it as if it was the last he'd ever take. "I want you." The words he thought he'd never hear, rang in his ears. Their meaning more decipherable, more explicit as his head stopped spinning. This could be his last, best chance. And his gut feeling told him if he didn't grab it, he'd never get another.

"Are you sure?" It was laughable. Even now his innate caution didn't let him down. Not for himself, but for Jo. He stepped into the danger knowing it was there. Knowing what could happen. But she didn't have a clue where it could lead. Couldn't see the future as he had from the moment he knew she existed.

"I'm sure. Very sure." She stepped closer and immediately became more confident of her welcome. Her insides clenched, spasming, the moment his hard male flesh pressed into her belly.

She curved her arms around his neck, unerringly finding the way to his mouth and let their breath mingle as she said, "And I can tell you want me."

Rowan didn't answer. He let his lips do it for him. They slanted across her mouth as she gasped and swallowed the dark-coffee flavor of his breath. The brush of his moustache against her lips, neck and ears, then back to her mouth, all added to the exhilaration. The fast, furious warring of their tongues warned her not to expect a leisurely coupling.

One stem of her pearl-studded earrings pressed sharply into the tender skin behind her ear as his tongue ran a swathe of wet warmth round its circumference. She was too far under his thrall to feel the pain. It was the attention he gave the shell of her ear that nearly killed her. Her knees melted, removing their support. All she could do was fork her fingers into his hair and hang on for dear life.

Desperation drew static from the air and played like stars behind her eyelids, but she had no way of knowing if the emotion was his or hers until he stepped through the dark well of the cabin door and half carried her inside.

With his breath still warming her skin, Rowan said, "No guarantees, Jo. There's nothing here to bewitch or bedevil our minds but each other. If you come to me, you have to want what *I* have to give.''

He felt an echo of her shuddering sigh in his own as she murmured, ''That's *all* I want. Every little, last thing you have to give.''

With the soft weight of her propelling him, he found the bed more from luck than judgment. He had a growling ache in his groin which wouldn't cease until he'd pulled her under him and found alleviation inside her body.

''Touch me, Rowan. I want to feel your hands on my skin.'' The husky timbre of her voice sent his temperature up five notches. His hands slipped under the collar of her robe, pushing it aside until he found the smooth warmth of bare skin. Satin under silk. That's how it felt to his hands.

She exhaled a long drawn-out sigh. ''Ooh, that feels soo goood.'' Her voice fell like soft rain, bathing his senses, lulling the need for self-preservation. A word…an emotion trembled on his lips, but he kept it inside. He'd lost control of his body, but a small portion of his mind clutched at reason and wouldn't let go.

Perfume, hers, and the overpowering scent of sexual musk exuding from his pores combined and filled the cabin, filled his head. He undid the belt of her robe and it flowed to the floor in a puddle of silk round their feet.

Her breasts rose on an indrawn gasp of air and her lacy bra scratched his chest until he disposed of it as well.

Jo's fingers grasped the tab of his zip, jerking it down until she heard him catch his breath and cry. ''Easy now. Easy.'' She realized he wore nothing under them. Hair brushed her knuckles as she slowed down, holding her fingers between Rowan and the teeth of the zip. Air whistled through his teeth as he sprang free into her palm.

She stifled her own gasp as she discovered the length and breadth of him. One small squeeze and hot steel pulsed in her hand. His chest shuddered and she couldn't help asking, ''Better now?''

''The only place I'd feel any better, is inside you.''

"Go for it, Rowan. Make yourself feel real good."

The brief respite while she made sure not to damage him was over. Resting the tips of her fingers on the sleek skin, sheathing his collarbones allowed Rowan free rein of her body. Darkness added an extra dimension to his touch.

He turned them both round until the bed brushed the backs of her knees, then cupped her breasts, but she was blind to the movement she'd parodied in the mirror. Her hands were too smooth to simulate the scrape of masculine calluses.

She moaned as the hair on his top lip feathered the tips of her breasts and exclaimed out loud as his teeth scraped their furled crests. Rowan's hands skimmed her sides, hooking the top of her panties. To touch her, he only had to move his hand.

One finger.

Her skin crawled with anticipation. She held her breath. Then his shoulders slid from her hold as he knelt at her feet and kissed the silk keeping them apart.

Rowan started to pull down her panties, memorizing the curve of her hip as he did, breathing her in all the while. How would he ever lose the scent of her now? It was imprinted on his synapses. A panicky thought of any other man getting this close to her reared into his imagination. *She was his now.* Fear erupted in a feral growl as he grasped silk between his teeth, baring his path to her female center and buried his face in her softness.

"Dear heaven," Jo gasped, her hips thrusting forward. "I can take all you've got of that and more."

With her taste on his lips Rowan drew back. "One last thing, what's the color of this scrap of silk and lace?"

"Scarlet."

Rowan's libido spat out a prayer inside his head. Red panties. He'd never forget how she looked in them. He could see it now. Who said fantasies never come true?

He'd said one last thing, but he'd lied. How did Jo really feel? In his imagination when they made love it wasn't with him in heat and her in cold blood.

She had to want this as much, if not more than he did. As much as she'd ever wanted any man. More. He wanted it all.

The fervent cries. The impassioned moans.

He wanted her the way she'd been that afternoon in the circle of trees, climbing into his skin because she couldn't get close enough.

Stripping her of the last of her covering he clasped her to him by the hips. His breath was a caress that said, "Open for me, babe." Who would have guessed this morning how the day would end?

He nosed her thatch of hair aside and laid her bare to his mouth. Jo trembled as he placed an impassioned kiss at the core. Her insides turned soft as ice cream and began to melt.

"You taste so sweet, I won't ever get enough." Seemed whatever kind of ice cream she was serving, he was buying.

Then his tongue parted her folds and found *the* spot.

Way back in her mind she thought she heard someone whimpering, then realized she was the culprit.

Weakness invaded every bone in her body and the lock she had on her knees was the first to come undone.

"I don't think I can hold up much longer. I'm going to fall," she squealed. As her legs began to cave, Jo's fingers kneaded his shoulders and did damage with their nails.

Agony and ecstasy.

"Just hang in there, babe. I'm going to make you so happy."

"I don't think I could get any happier."

"Give me a few seconds to prove you wrong."

He found his target and circled it with his tongue as he had the pearl in her ear. Fastening his mouth over her he sucked gently, drew it into his mouth. Into the soft, wet darkness like the shell that had formed it in the depths of the ocean.

"Now! Rowan, now!"

Her impatience caught up with him and he set up an uneven rhythm, fast, slow, soft, hard. Then he slid one thumb partway inside her to join the dance.

She screamed, falling backward onto the pillows in a tangle with him sprawled across her belly.

"Hold me, Rowan. Just hold me."

He climbed over her and hauled her into his arms, wrapping her up in himself, hugging her close while the aftershocks ripped through her. The tears streaming down her face were a surprise. He lapped at the saltiness with his tongue, then covered her damp face in small kisses until her harsh breathing subsided.

She'd never experienced anything like it in her life. It was almost as if, after thinking herself experienced in matters of sensuality for most of her adult years, she'd finally lost her virginity.

Although he couldn't see them, Rowan brushed the last tears from her eyes with a thumb. "That bad, huh?"

She almost started bawling at the tenderness in his voice. Everything was new and shiny tonight. "No. That good. I never realized, Rowan...I just never realized."

"And we haven't even reached the good part. What are you going to do then, sweetheart?"

Sweetheart. When had he started calling her that? It was a good word. One that made her feel special. Forcing past the emotion clogging her throat, she responded with, "Well, if I die. Tell them I want to be cremated."

His hands were moving on her back, gently stirring her senses again. She didn't see how she could live through too much more of this excitement, but she was willing to try.

She traced his features. The darkness made sure she'd never forget the shape of them, would know him by touch anywhere. But the satisfaction she craved now was Rowan's. She wanted to return the pleasure he had given her.

Only one thing was needed to make it perfect. "Rowan, let's put the light on. I want to see your hands on me."

"No problem. I'd like that myself," he said, rolling off her. "Time I found some protection, anyway."

"There are some in the pocket of my robe. I found them in the drawer by my bed."

The light made her blink and what had been a small confined space occupied by her and Rowan, expanded in a way she didn't like and made her feel naked.

It didn't matter that she already knew it.

Rowan emptied her pocket, scattering foil packets over her and the bed. His eyes crinkled at the corners as he smiled, "Can I take this as a good sign?"

She took her time to reply. The light didn't seem as bright now, just a bedside lamp, bathing the sheen of his skin in a golden glow. If it hadn't been for the scars on his leg he might have been a shoo-in for a Greek statue. A rampantly male statue. He had the most perfect body she had ever laid eyes on, and his scars added to, instead of detracting from the whole, because she *knew* what they had cost.

"I think we should pace ourselves and think of the spare condoms as an opportunity not to be missed whether it's today or tomorrow. We really haven't got all that much time."

"No, not that much." He bent his head to hers and like an aphrodisiac, she smelled herself on his breath, stirring her, making her want him again. She parted her lips as his mouth closed over hers. Suddenly, she was drawn back into the deep dark vortex of sexual arousal. Her hands reached up and cradled his jaw. The kiss went on and on and she didn't want it to stop.

She heard foil rustle, then a stifled curse against her mouth as he fumbled with the opening. Placing her hands on either side of his face, she eased him away, whispering, "Let me do it. Uh-uh." She cut off his protest. "It's no big deal. Don't go all macho on me, Rowan. Partners, remember?"

She lifted her gaze as a sudden rush of tenderness flushed away the guilt associated with the uneasy memory. Jo traced the scar with her fingertips, less flexible than the soft surrounding skin, but no less sensual, this was a part of Rowan. Part of their shared history.

He tensed as her mouth traced the path the bullet had taken and a quavering sigh escaped as if ripped from his hide.

She'd never done this for a man before and her hand wasn't

any steadier than his had been as she sheathed his sex. By the time she'd completed the task they were both breathing hard.

Sitting back on her heels, she stared at him. Her onyx-dark eyes held a question in their depths he couldn't translate.

His heart had no such problem.

From way down inside him, emotion roiled until it burst into his chest in a rush like nothing he'd ever experienced before. His whole body tingled as it invaded every pore. And beyond all reason he knew the sensation had nothing to do with sex.

Opening his arms he pulled her into them and held her. Simply held her close and let the rigors of emotion take him. Take them both to a place where only they existed.

As the shaking eased, he pulled back till he could look into her face. Combing his fingers through the silk of her hair where it clung to her cheek, he examined her features minutely. What he saw there pleased him. Greatly.

Her lips parted as his mouth crushed them under his, and he rolled her into the nest of pillows. As her legs came round him, gathering him in, he entered her.

A groan burst from Jo's lips as his thickness filled her opening her up in one seamless thrust. Her heart pounded mating with Rowan's, breaching the walls of their chests clinging together beat for beat.

Hard fingertips kneaded her scalp until she floated in a daze of ecstasy, then slid into hollows at the base of her skull to melt her bones. His mouth whispered indecipherable endearments against her skin, her face, her breasts that made her moan with pleasure and bite down on the ridge of his shoulder to prevent a scream she felt building.

She had no will of her own. Rowan ushered her into the dance, she simply followed his lead. Had there ever been such a feeling before? She thought not, pitying those who would never experience this twist of rapture laced with fear.

Fear of not quite scaling the heights of the giant wall they climbed, Rowan pushing them higher thrust by thrust.

All thought disappeared as her reason dissolved. She no longer had to strive. She simply was.

His body flowed into hers as the gulf stream merges with the Atlantic. Two entities, one indecipherable from the other. No ending, no beginning.

Then Rowan lifted her over the wall and they fell clinging together.

As they floated in limbo, Rowan felt something tear inside him. Inside his soul. He cried out as it left him and poured into Jo, knowing his life would never be the same again.

She would always carry a part of him and if they were ever separated the piece he had left would wither and die.

Chapter 11

Five o'clock. Half an hour until dawn. Rowan got a rude awakening as the radio alarm went off. He hadn't turned the lights out. Had they even slept for more than thirty minutes at a stretch? He couldn't remember, but he'd never forget the loving.

He shared a pillow with Jo, their heads close together, her hair caressing his face and her shoulders pressing his arm into the mattress. His fingers flexed, pins and needles piercing his skin as his palm cupped a warm breast. He squeezed gently and his sex thickened in response to her nipple answering his touch. One knee lay between his and the sole of her foot massaged the back of his calf, yet her lids stayed closed. Dark lashes shadowed her creamy cheek and, though hidden, her eyes moved back and forth as she dreamed.

He blew a strand of her hair from his mouth, watching her lashes flutter as his breath skimmed her face. He repeated the procedure a few times and caught a glimpse of dark drowsy eyes in reward. Jo blinked, myopically, as her eyes tried to focus on his face.

A flash of shyness, quickly shuttered by her eyelids, sur-
rised him. "Hey," he whispered, rubbing her cheek with his
hin.

"Mmmmh, rough." She pouted. Her hand found his bristly
ace, fending it off. "You need a shave."

"Rise and shine, sweetheart." The words warmed the air
efore his conscious thought recognized the significance of the
ndearment.

Sweet—no one would ever call her that. *Tart*—didn't fit,
ither. Jo fell somewhere in between, like tasting the first
each of the season, fresh, lush. Oh yeah, that covered it. As
or *heart*—how many times had she turned his over in his
hest, by a look, by a touch?

"How about sharing a shower with me, peaches?"

Her breast rose in his hand and ebbed away in the wake of
sharply drawn breath, but she didn't speak.

"Have you gone back to sleep?"

"Why did you call me that?"

"Peaches?"

Her knuckles brushed his fingers as she fisted her hand,
olding it clenched between her breasts. An ever so slight nod
f her head gave him his answer as he felt her heart flutter.
Ie sighed; he knew the sensation well.

"That's how you taste. Like a peach," he said against her
ar, making her tremble.

"Ah, God, that feels so good."

His mouth grazed her cheek and settled over her lips. He
ursued them as her head pulled back. She drew her eyebrows
ogether in a V and twitched her nose, protesting. "Sore."

He looked at the whisker burns on her chin and decided the
noustache had to go. Who was he hiding from anyway, except
naybe himself?

"I think I'll pass on sharing the shower. Time to shape up and
hip out," she said, sliding out of his arms and out of his bed.

From up on the bridge he looked back toward the town.
Jicks Landing showed no signs of life and that's how he

wanted it. No one to see them leave. To the east a faint light ening, merely a glimmer, appeared in the clouds riding the horizon above Venus.

Time to leave.

Jo's head and shoulders appeared round the corner of the stairs. "Finished," she sang out. "Everything's cleared away."

"Be with you in a sec."

Checking that both throttles and gears were in neutral, he placed his hands on the levers of the large twin diesel engines. Moving them ahead slightly so they'd idle evenly, he turned the key and pushed in the ignition. When the dials for the revs, oil-pressure and water-temperature gauges settled he took a quick look over the stern to make sure the cooling water flowed from the exhaust.

Jo waited on the stern while he went forward. The wind had dropped away to almost nothing, relieving him of any worries about letting go both bowlines. Tall wooden pilings marked off each berth and he unclipped the lines from the bow of the *Fancy* and let them swing back with a dull thud against the posts.

A faint shiver of anticipation prickled the back of his neck as he trod the narrow deck between the port side rail and the cabin. Was this how his father had felt when he'd set sail with hopes of resuscitating his marriage?

Jo watched him cast off, stepping aside to let him pass. "Weather's looking good, just as they forecast," he said.

"Oh well, the Met. office can't be wrong all the time." She nodded toward the bowlines he'd undone. "Is that what you want me to do back here?"

"Yeah, but not till I give you the word."

Back on the bridge he returned the twin throttles to neutral and called down to Jo, "Let go the stern lines."

That done, he pushed the throttles ahead and the *Fancy* put her nose between the front poles and said goodbye to the floating finger she'd been tied alongside.

Jo appeared beside his elbow. He felt excitement radiating from her as they cleared their berth. Family trips of years gone by floated in his memory, jangling his nerves like a honky-tonk tune on an old piano. He hadn't sailed out of this harbor since his parents drowned.

Same place, same time…

He glanced at Jo and let the thought crash and burn. What he had cursed as weakness in his father teetered on the brink of understanding. Maybe he had more in common with his old man than he'd realized.

Satisfaction welled in his chest as he slid the starboard throttle into astern. They were underway. The maneuver sent their craft on a starboard turn past the moorings. Soon they had cleared the marina with only the slap of their wake on the other boats to show they'd ever been there.

"How fast can she go?"

"Well, she has two 500 hp diesel engines and a top speed of twenty-three knots. We'll cruise around twenty once we reach open water." The powerful revs thrumming beneath his feet reassured him as he stood with one hand on the wheel. Safety was everything at sea and this boat was equipped with the best money could buy. He wrapped an arm round Jo's shoulders. Ahead of them, the first fingers of sunlight clawed their way over the dateline and Venus rode above the horizon.

That darn star looked so pretty, yet if he were to believe the romantics, its influence had been responsible for all the angst he'd suffered over the last few years. He could name the time and the date it had started. The day Jo had come into his life.

If he could turn back the clock there was a lot he would change. About himself mainly. But for sure, last night wouldn't be one of them. No. That was one day he'd mark on the calendar each year. The thirtieth of October.

"I see it!" Jo yelled, quivering with excitement. While they'd done a good job of signposting their final destination,

neither of them had taken into account the size of her jacke
in comparison to the huge bush-covered cliffs.

Joining him beside the wheel, she looked round his bulk t
see the charts. "Are we safe to anchor there? No reefs o
shoals?" She hoped Rowan was more capable than her a
reading the data on the screen. Computerized charts, GPS an
sonar arrays which sketched a side-on view of the seabed
above a patchwork of colors mapping out the bottom, were a
beyond her ken.

"Everything looks fairly good. Although…" He caught he
chin with a finger and thumb turning her head then pointin,
her in the right direction. "Look at those breaks in the bus
where the yellow clay shows through, there could be som
recent slips that aren't marked on the chart. I think I'll ancho
out aways. It makes no difference. We'll have to launch th
RIB, Rigid Inflatable Boat, tender anyway."

She had no fear of running aground. Rowan worked a
bringing them in with the same kind of competence he handle
his car…handled her. Another bolt of heat flashed through her
It wasn't easy to put her hormones to rest when the man wh
rattled them stood by her side.

Time to put the brakes on her imagination before she go
carried away with her own importance in the scheme of things

Rowan slowed the boat to five knots, then gradually put he
astern until she stopped. The movement of the waves felt mor
noticeable now that they weren't cutting through them.

"We're at ten meters here. The wind is quite light and from
offshore. I'll let out thirty extra meters of chain and we shoul
be okay." She watched him do everything from where h
stood with just the chain counter and a push of a button. Th
anchors hit the water with a gentle splash as the noise of chai
running through the winches broke the comparative silence or
board without the big diesels vibrating through the hull.

The sun shone. Both sea and sky were unbelievable shades
of blue. Glowing on the steep slope, fifty different hues o

green bush flowed down to the water's edge. The weather should hold.

With its bow turned into the wind, the boat drifted away from the shore until the anchors ploughed into the seabed. Far from towns and pollution, crystal clear water surrounded them and she could count every link in the silver chains. Somehow it felt like a homily of the past they shared. Coming out to this beautiful place made the connections easier to see.

He touched her elbow. "How about a swim?"

"You must be joking—it may look beautiful but that water is cold." She pretended to shiver. "No, thanks. I'll hold your towel, though."

Ten minutes later he dove off the boarding platform, punching a hole in the water with barely a splash. When she looked at him stripped of almost all his clothes, she barely noticed his scars. Last night she'd explored every inch of his sexy body. A person tended not to notice what they were familiar with. Now it seemed as much a part of him as his green-gold eyes.

Watching him roll, turn and dive as lithe as a seal, Jo knew she could explain, but not condone the impulse, which had set the accident in motion. Never again, she vowed. She would rather she died than Rowan.

He lasted five minutes in the cold water. Out of sight one second, the next he emerged from the blue depths and hoisted himself on board.

The bottle-green briefs he wore clung to his hips, outlining his masculine shape. Water dripped from his body, turning the toffee streaks almost as dark as hers. His wet skin gleamed in the sunshine, the drops on his lashes sparkling like diamonds.

Towel in hand, she rushed over as he shook himself like a dog, spraying her T-shirt with water. One squeal followed another. The towel landed on the deck unused while he proceeded to wipe off the excess moisture on the front of her T-shirt and jeans.

"Cut it out! You're soaking me."

She pushed at his chest and he leaned against her palms and bit her earlobe. "More," he growled. "Touch me all over."

"Fool," she whispered halfheartedly as his mouth slid along the side of her neck and her knees turned as liquid as the puddle they were standing in. "I hope you're remembering I'm on duty."

Damp cotton knit delineated her breasts in waves of yellow-and-white stripes. Rowan ducked suddenly, leaving her with a view of the sodden curls. Her fingers forked through the wet strands and held on tight as his strong teeth latched on to her tender nipple, T-shirt and all. A moan of protest ripped out of her throat as he lifted his mouth away from her, taking her pleasure with him. Next moment, her T-shirt disappeared, landing at their feet, soaking up the puddle. Her bra swiftly followed.

"You can't...be on duty...if you're naked," he mumbled against her lips while his hands worked her zip.

His skin felt as cool as hers was aflame, yet she reveled in the difference where it touched hers. "You're right. Kiss me."

"Uh-uh. Not before I've shaved."

"When will that be?"

"Later tonight."

"What am I supposed to do until then?"

"Don't worry, I'll think of something." Before she realized what was happening, his arm slipped behind her knees then he knelt and laid her on the towel. One second later his briefs were gone and he moved over her, blotting out the sun.

"And this is?"

"Something."

"Well, I've got my stuff. What are you taking?"

Rowan scrunched his eyes slightly and went through the list of his gear in order of importance. "I've got water, flashlight, machete, rope, camera and light sticks."

"Light sticks?"

"Yeah. I found them in a locker along with some diving paraphernalia when I was searching for the rope."

"I meant, what are they for?"

"Finding our way back in the dark. They're low power but the glow should be enough to guide us in case we have to get out of there in a hurry."

He put his pack on the deck beside hers, which looked almost empty. "You haven't got much there. No more than would fill your pockets," he said, then taking a gander at her tight jeans, decided, maybe not. "What are you taking?"

"My gun and a couple of pairs of cuffs."

"I see, only essentials. What about water, or do you expect to share mine?"

Her teeth looked very white as her lips curled up at the corners, emphasizing her fabulous cheekbones and the sparkle in her eyes. "What's up? Worried about swapping spit?"

No doubt in his mind, Jo was referring to the swapping they'd done last night. He looked at her mouth, noting she'd painted her lips bright coral, a small feminine affectation that pleased him, considering her long-sleeved sweatshirt was a dull green meant to blend into the bush.

"I've got a bottle of H2Go in the fridge. I want to put it in my pack at the last minute so it'll keep cold."

"The last minute just arrived. Go get it while I launch the RIB." By the time he reached the deck outside the pilothouse, she was pushing the bottled water in her pack. "Right, Jo. I'll swing it over the side with the derrick and you catch the line before she hits the water."

The climb ahead of them wouldn't be easy, and his pinned thighbone had been aching ever since he'd made love to Jo on the deck. Whoever said sexual arousal masks pain knew a thing or two. Served him right for being so bloody organized he'd slipped protection into the little inside pocket of his swim briefs. And thank God, it only held one. They'd had to go back to the comfort of the cabin for the second round.

Even then he'd had to hold his lust in check. Lust?

So he was fooling himself, who better? The little voice at the back of his mind kept reminding him, he'd maybe only one more night with Jo. The danger wasn't over, he knew that, but he'd tempered foolish disregard of the truth by pretending it was him who'd walk away.

If all went well on their little jaunt, they'd end up with photos identifying their suspects. After that, it was her task to link those weirdos to the notes. He hadn't mentioned it to Jo, hadn't wanted to dampen her enthusiasm, but film filled with shots of goats' heads and masks wasn't going to further her case.

If that happened he could see his plans for the night hours foiled by hours of tracking satanists through the bush.

The RIB bumped against the hull. "You got the line, Jo?"

"Affirmative."

The tender hit the water and he leaned over the rail to check if she was coping with the line. He'd had one cold swim today and another one wasn't high on his to-do list, although the earlier one had served its purpose.

Jo was tying the line off on the rail. She twisted her head, glancing up at him with her eyes full of mischief. "You checking up on me? I said, affirmative. In case you didn't know that's cop speak for yes."

At the top of the slope Rowan put away the machete, then wiped the sweat from his eyes with the back of his glove. Jo was about a minute behind him, almost on all fours, her fingers grappling one root while her toes found leverage on another.

He undid the rope from his belt and tied it round the rough bark of a totara. The tree was sturdy enough to take both their weight on the way down. He heard Jo puffing behind him as he tugged on the knot to test it. Turning around he hunkered down and held a hand out to her, twisting the rope round the other.

They gripped each other, wrist to wrist, both grunting from exertion as he hauled her the last few feet.

She flung herself onto the ground face down. "Whose bright idea was this?"

"Dare I say, yours?" Rowan peeled off his gloves, clumped them together in his fist and tapped them on her behind. "But you don't hear me complaining. And whose brilliant idea was it to go back for the gloves?''

He'd remembered just before they'd taken off and he'd gone back to get them from the locker where the rope had been stashed.

Struggling up on to her knees, she moaned, "So, I forgot. And you didn't. That only counts as half a brownie point. Though, I'll give you one more if you pull me to my feet.''

When she finally stood beside him, Rowan pulled her in close to his chest and they just stood, hugging each other. Finally she sighed and lifted her chin so her mouth hovered just below his. "How's the leg holding out?''

His hands tightened on her momentarily. He couldn't help it. "Great. Couldn't be better," he lied.

Jo pinched him just above the waist.

"Ow!" he yelped. "What was that in aid of?''

"I'm just showing what you get if you don't tell the truth. There's no need to act all macho with me. The slope nearly killed me and it must have put a lot of pressure on your quads. If you want to sit down a little while and get your breath back it's okay by me.''

She couldn't kid a kidder. He knew her game. Her breasts grazed his chest every time she squeezed out a gust of air and her pulse beat hard and fast under his palm. "No problems here, peaches. I'm ready to go whenever you are. In about an hour the sun will be dipping down behind the trees and, look over there, the moon's coming up! Hopefully we'll be in position before they arrive.''

"Easy for you to say.''

"Do a few stretches, they'll make you feel better." Releasing her, he got down on one knee and wiped his machete on a clump of grass. At least their descent would be easier.

As he came up again, he watched Jo take his advice, and it worked better than he'd imagined, especially from his viewpoint.

A smile creased his face as he slid the blade into the sheath on his belt, then took a light stick out of his pack. Cracking the contents, he hooked it over the rope close to the knot. By daylight its candlepower didn't amount to much, but come nightfall it would be enough to light them home.

They found themselves a good spot to lie in wait, hidden by a tree fern still young enough for its fronds to sweep the ground. It was like looking through Mother Nature's veil, but once it was truly dark, instead of this thick green gloom, they should be able to pull it aside and get a good view of the circle.

Jo curled her toes inside her boots to keep her circulation going, hoping she wouldn't cramp up by lying so long in one position. She refused to even consider there might be bugs around. No way. Once her mind went down that track she'd start to fidget. She could just picture herself, racing around the circle, flapping at her shirt where a creepy crawly had taken up residence, right in the middle of some fiendish ceremony.

Now that would be funny. Funnier than a lot of the other scenarios she'd imagined happening tonight.

The whole place still spooked her, though. A breeze she'd thought nonexistent, danced through the trees on ghostly tip-toes. Branches whispered and clacked, and every little noise, characteristic of the bush or not, made the back of her neck prickle. It would be worse once night finally fell. Sounds seemed to magnify when you were blind to their source.

Her biggest problem, real or illusory, once she'd shoved her other fears to the back of her mind, was that she was left with the awareness of the heat emanating from Rowan's body. He lay alongside her, touching, burning, at shoulder, elbow and hip. They'd blamed the madness that came over them on their last visit to the circle on a mix of heightened senses spiced with vivid imagination. Now she wasn't so sure.

If someone could can the air pervading the place, they could make a fortune selling it as an aphrodisiac. She felt it creeping stealthily toward them, seeping out of the ring of trees on long green fingers that teased and prodded. Her breasts grew tight and heavy and she ached to be touched.

Just as she prayed she could get out of their hiding place without ripping Rowan's clothes off, giving their position away, his hand clasped her wrist. "Listen. Someone's coming."

Three figures cloaked and hooded in white entered the clearing. "I thought they'd wear black," she whispered.

"Hush." His hand let go her wrist, and his finger pointed in the air, level with their mouths.

Jo's nails dug into the leaf mulch they were lying in, realizing these could be the very people who had threatened her and Rocky. They'd made her puddle around in blood-soaked mud, and nearly trapped them in a burning house, not to mention forcing her to handle a roasted heart. After what they'd done, she would see they paid.

She stifled a gasp as Rowan's fingers bit into her arm. At ground level the rest of the man was invisible, but the skirt of his white robe grazed the fronds hiding them, and set the green veil shivering. Her heart pounded in her throat at the near miss. And it wasn't over. The figure reached for a branch, probably the one Rowan threw away to stop her completing the pentagram.

Two others dodged in and out of the circle, as well, collecting wood until they'd built a small pyre inside the ring of stones.

Each time they came near, she tensed. It wasn't that she was afraid, simply wary of being discovered. Recovering from one close shave, she noticed a supplicant skirting the rim of the stones with a box in her hand. Fire lighters, Jo recognized the brand, *Little Lucifers*. Tension fractured a bubble of near hysterical laughter she almost choked holding in, then Rowan gripped the back of her neck, planting her mouth over his. He tasted warm and human and the brush of his moustache was infinitely more real than the play being enacted in front of them.

Laughter no longer troubled her breathing by the time he let go. Instead she was glad of the darkness inside their hidden bower. Even the smell of leaf mold and rich humus, couldn't diminish her emotions as she reached out to touch his cheek. Not for the first time, asking herself, how could she have been so blind to his attractions?

More people began to join the gatherers. Some in white robes, some in gray. At one side, where the path they'd taken on their first visit ended, a few of the cult members moved in and out in an urgent, almost fussy manner, whispering to the apparent leader, then gliding away, robes skimming the ground.

After her lurid experience with the bull calf, Jo's mind pounced on the word *sacrifice*. Who, or what, were they preparing out there? Dear Lord, she prayed it would be animal, not human.

A goat maybe…she could stand a goat.

Dark as it was they couldn't fail to notice the ceremonial knife. An *athame*. Rowan nudged her arm. She started to nod, realized it was redundant since he couldn't see, and squeezed his hand instead.

In much the same way Jo had used the stick, the knife cut a pentagram into the earth in a continuous line from stone to stone to stone. Jo figured this guy for high priest.

Once it was done five hooded figures stationed themselves at the points, heads bowed, waiting. It didn't take long to discover who they were waiting for as two women were brought in from behind the trees. They weren't even fighting it. No struggling, nothing. Drugged…they had to be drugged or hypnotized. She'd gladly have swapped their composure for a bleating goat or a few blood-curdling yells.

Damn. Why couldn't it have been a goat?

Flames licked at the seat of the pyre, though not enough to light the circle. Jo caught back a scream as they knelt at the penultimate point and the leader raised the knife high.

Oh, God. They weren't wasting any time. Jo's hand swung behind to grasp the gun nestling against the small of her back. She had the bastard in her sights and the sound of Rowan's camera in her ears as the knife sliced through the air when the high priest threw his head back as if in exultation. And as a result of this fervent movement his hood and hair tumbled free.

Whoa! Jo did a quick reality check. *Her* hair.

A woman! Even in the dark she could make that out.

Gesticulating toward each corner in turn with the *athame*, she recited an incantation Jo couldn't make head nor tail of. Latin spelled backwards, she'd say at a guess. She should have done more research and not let her inborn dread of the whole black-magic business put her off.

The urge to make a gagging gesture to Rowan, tingled through the hands she'd wrapped around her Glock, as the hammy theatricals continued.

The priestess scooped up a handful of dust, letting it spill through her fingers as she called out, "Earth!"

The *athame* circled above her head. "Wind!" she cried. Every particle of air inside the trees seemed to follow the knife, swirling and forming a funnel. The long strands of hair spun around her head. Widening its circumference, it twisted between their robes and ripped through the fronds of the tree fern sheltering them.

Jo's pulse jolted as her gaze followed its snarling progress through the leaves and branches until suddenly it died away, and everything except her heart stilled.

With a sleight of hand worthy of a magician, a sprinkling of powder flew from the priestess's fingers onto the smoldering pyre. "Fire!" she shouted.

Almost blinding after the darkness, flames shot high, illuminating the circle and burnishing the leader's tangled locks where they floated round her shoulders.

Rowan's camera whirred and clicked. He'd loaded it with a fast film, and these pictures were their best chance of getting the evidence they needed.

A hush fell over the gathering as the priestess's attention turned to the women kneeling beside her. Others carrying flowers joined the group and laid their hands on the supplicants' shoulders.

Jo steadied her aim, looking along her arm, then stopped,

bewildered. Familiarity teasing her memory, she studied the raised faces of the women as they lifted to the priestess. *Athame* and flower garlands held high, the leader turned in a circle, stirring the dust at her feet into a fine mist at her hem. Flames glanced off her knife, casting a ripple of reflected light onto the trees as if a streamer of fire leaped through them.

Knife and flowers forgotten, Jo's aim faltered.

Rowan's gasp matched her own as they finally saw the leader's face.

Chapter 12

Like in a game of follow the leader the faces were revealed, and the worst thing about it, Jo found most of them familiar. None more so than the one holding the knife.

"Ratchett!" What a fool, the answer had been right there under her nose if only she'd bothered to look.

She didn't realize she'd cursed out loud until Rowan nudged her with his elbow. Leaning closer, her forehead grazing his cheekbone, she whispered, "Moira," then backed off before his musky male scent made her forget her purpose for being there.

There was magic in the air and it wasn't all happening in the circle.

Her landlady, the witch. Good grief, Rowan must think she was the dumbest cop around not to have known. And somehow, her not knowing only served to emphasize that even Moira still thought of her as an outsider.

But Moira was no killer.

Jo would stake her life on it.

Her landlady made a magnificent sight with her bright red

hair agleam in a tangle of firelight and curls, like a symbol of her high status. From the instance of recognition, the scene went through a transmogrification. And with change came the belief that these women, kneeling before Moira had nothing to fear from either her or this place.

Jo recognized one of them as Seth MacAllister's wife and wondered if the young cop knew what his wife was up to.

The camera clicked and whirred, reminding her she wasn't alone. Shadows tattooed a pattern over the plains and hollow of Rowan's features, disguising them in striped camouflage. He lay beside her, watchful as a jungle cat, and every bit a lethal.

Her last thought made her hesitate as she touched his shoulder. Maybe the ambience of the circle *had* worked its magic again. Even in shadow his sheer maleness aroused her. In this all-female gathering, Rowan's strength became more pronounced, more alluring. A sought-after prize in the game of mating.

Man, woman…child.

"Oh heavens," she said on a hushed breath as enlightenment dawned. And with the knowledge came the need to leave quietly, as if they had never been there, never witnessed the proceedings. The purpose behind the ceremony in the Nest of the Gods was obvious now. As obvious as the reason for Seth's departures on personal emergencies. They wanted a baby.

Time to depart and allow these women their privacy.

Leaning closer she inhaled the irresistible masculine essence emanating from the collar of his shirt. There was temptation there. Temptation to nibble on his lobe instead of whispering her decision. "We should go now. There's nothing for us here."

He nodded, tantalizing her weakened libido as the stubble on his chin scraped her cheek. Shaken by need, her whole body quivering, she finished, "I'll back out first."

It wasn't an easy retreat from their hiding place. Her mind wasn't on the job. The silhouette of Rowan's shoulders re-

inded her of the sheer strength of them, looming over her
is afternoon as he covered her body with his.

Don't go there. This isn't the time for those thoughts. Those
mptations.

Her body didn't give a damn. A spear of need twisted inside
r and coursed between her thighs. She felt as if she were in
at. Her heart pounded beneath her breast and a flush of
ousal flooded her skin.

She wanted Rowan. Wanted him now. Wanted to roll over
d open her body to—

Pain jarred Jo to her senses as her ankle banged against the
ft spongy trunk of a ponga tree fern. "Oh, boy." She'd
eeded that. No wonder they brought women who were having
hard time getting pregnant to this place. She ought to tell
oira they might have more success if they brought their hus-
nds along. Of course she wouldn't do that. She had a good
lationship with her landlady. Not as honest as she'd thought,
it she didn't want to ruin it.

Biting her bottom lip, Jo started to shuffle backward once
ore. The painful jabs of spiky little twigs towed along by
er bootlaces were more noticeable now that her mad arousal
d subsided.

A simple lift of her eyes showed Rowan would soon over-
ke her. She needed to get a wiggle on, take her mind off his
utt and those tight jeans, and circumspectly crawl out of
ere.

Not that she could see his butt, it was far too dark, but her
emory of it started a fire easier than rubbing two sticks to-
ether. She could tell the cat-that-stole-the-cream look still lin-
ered on her face by the time she was far enough away to turn
ound to make her way out headfirst. Before her, the nearest
ght stick glowed dimly. At last she could stand up.

A crackle of dead leaves preceded Rowan. Warily she
epped back among the foliage, not trusting the strength of
er resistance. Still uncertain if the circle had cast a spell, or
her libido, primed by its release from hibernation, was to
lame.

Then something fell off the greenery into her neckline.
Panic.

No, *don't* panic.

She shuddered as every hair on her body stood on en
Deliberately, she closed her mind against the peculiar inse
life inhabiting New Zealand's bush. It didn't work. Seeme
like it, too, hated being ignored.

Trying not to squeal, she struggled out of her jacket ar
tossed it aside. Holding out the hem of her sweatshirt sk
wriggled, hoping to dispatch the many-legged hitchhiker sk
sensed running down her back. Her skin tightened, shrinkir
away from it. She'd shivered over them at natural-histor
classes, creatures, part worm, part stick insect, which ran c
tiny little legs. Wettas, whose large back legs could inflict
sting.

Oh Lord. From giant huhu bugs to poisonous spiders, he
mind listed them all. By the time Rowan reached her, her arn
were high and feet stamping as if issuing a challenge with he
own rendition of a Maori *haka.*

"What's wrong?"

"Bugs, creepy crawlies. One fell down my neck."

He took the light stick from the tree. "Here, let me help.

"What is it? What can you see? Is there something in m
hair?" She fluffed out her curls, scouring them with her fir
gers.

"No, nothing there. Hold this." He pushed the light stic
at her and slid his hands under her sweatshirt.

"What are you doing?"

"Looking for bugs."

His palms skimmed her back, but it wasn't enough. He'
been dying to touch her from the moment she lay down besid
him. Every time her hip or elbow brushed against him, he'
been tempted to throw caution to the wind.

And now he could.

Rowan's fingertips trailed across her shoulder blades on th
way up. Jo trembled and he smiled, confident he could mak

er forget about bugs. His smile deepened as something prick-
d against his finger. "Hold still," he murmured.

Jo froze. "Have you found something?"

"Yeah. Let's see what it is." The light played over a strand
f rimu needles from the tree above them. "No wonder you
ought it was a bug. With those spiny needles, it would travel
round inside your sweatshirt every time you moved."

Jo sighed, letting her body lean into his. He'd have liked to
retend it was passion, but common sense told him it was
ecause he hadn't dismissed her fears. He pulled her closer,
uzzling her ear, tasting it with his tongue. "I take it I'm safe
is time."

"S-s-safe?"

"You aren't annoyed because I rescued you."

"No, just grateful, but don't you dare tell a soul that bugs
care the living daylights out of me."

"I won't. It'll be our secret." He wasn't likely to share the
ay watching her had made him feel. This visit had given him
whole new take on Jo. He'd always admired her as a dedi-
ated cop; getting shot hadn't changed that. Discovering the
oman who came apart in his arms made him want to rethink
decision made long before he knew she existed, before he
new anyone could tear his heart out the way she did. Now
e'd discovered the child in her, scared of bugs. Who'd have
elieved it? He gave her another hug and brushed a tender kiss
ver her silky tangle of black waves.

"I think I've worked out the reason for the ceremony. Re-
nember the effect the place had on our libidos?"

He not only remembered, he was still in its thrall, but this
ime he'd known what to expect.

Her hands slid up his arms and caressed his biceps through
he fine cloth of his shirt. "Maybe the legend has a basis in
act."

At her touch his muscles expanded, bulging as though strut-
ing their stuff for her approval. Not only that, the brush of
er fingers against him turned his already aroused sex hard as

stone. Given his druthers he'd take her here and now and t
hell with who heard her shouts of release.

Her palms swept across his chest, rubbing in concentric cir
cles. "There's certainly some sort of magic in the air."

"You could be right." He bent his head and took he
mouth. She tasted of desire, flavored with golden honey an
rich dark figs, holding a promise of heaven. His hands sli
down and cupped her buttocks, pulling her up tight against hi
need, so she would have no doubt of her effect on him. H
lifted his head and looked at her. A stray beam of moonligh
bathed her face as her head fell back and her hair swung free
There was no mistaking the desire on her lips or the hunge
in her eyes, shaded by half-closed lashes. "I prefer to mak
my own magic," he growled.

He let her feel the slide of his teeth on the cord of her neck
Her throaty response was enough to get them back to the boa
and into his bed in double quick time.

On the way, he gathered their guiding lights until graduall
they walked in a shimmering ball of phosphorescence bounde
on each side by trees. "And you had no idea about Moira?"

"Not a clue. I know she has lots of women visitors. I simpl
took it for granted they all came for herbal remedies."

He patted the pocket where he'd stowed his camera. "I go
some good shots of her. Do you think she'd like copies?"

"Good grief, no! She must never know. If you must develo
the film, do it when you go home to Auckland. Can you imag
ine the stir if you had them processed locally?"

His mouth went dry; this was the first mention of his de
parture. From the moment they'd become intimate it was a
though the subject had become taboo.

"What difference is this going to make to your investiga
tion? Will you still pay Rocky out? The only proof of satanist
we have now are those letters and he could have written then
himself."

He recognized hope in the way she tilted her head towar
him.

"Bull gave us a week. But I can take as long as I like." *A

fetime. Hell, he knew being with Jo had screwed his mind round. His last thought proved it. He was hedging about leaving her. What had happened to the notion that he'd be okay as long as he was the one to walk away? "I'll give it at least until we hear what forensics has to say about the letters."

They'd reached the top of the slope down to the beach and the rope he'd tied off earlier. He released the last of the light sticks from its branch and hooked it onto one of his belt loops. "Here, fasten this one on to you. It'll help a little. Even if only to show where you've been."

He shoved the rest into his pack, his movements jerky from the frustration running through him. His leg had stiffened up from lying on the ground. So far, he'd managed not to show it was giving him hell but he wasn't looking forward to the climb.

Everything seemed to be conspiring against him: his leg, the thoughts of leaving her that had been playing through his mind. No matter what time they got back on board, he wanted to love her so well, she'd never be able to forget him. Or he her. But with his leg in the shape it was in...

He shouldered his pack again. "Put your gloves on. I'll go first. Then if you fall you'll land on me."

It was near midnight and she was bone tired, yet she didn't want to sleep. The journey downhill had been worse than the one going up. Heaven only knows how Rowan had coped on his bad leg, but if he'd been in pain she hadn't been able to tell with her back to him. Any grunts he'd let loose had been no worse than her own as her arms took the strain on the rope.

More than that, the load on her quads had been tremendous and her hip joints had taken to calling her unrepeatable names by the time she hit the beach. They creaked like a dry hinge when she finally sat down on the edge of the RIB to go back to the boat.

From low down on the water, the night sky was glorious, a real midnight-blue velvet. The only thing bothering her was the ring around the moon as per Moira's prediction of trouble.

With thoughts of omens on her mind, she'd watched it sa
high above the cliff top, blighted by a red haze.

Shivering, she asked, "Do they call that blood on th
moon?"

Rowan laughed. "You're very superstitious all of a sudde
The wind that's blowing from offshore is the smoke fror
Moira's fire drifting in front of the light. Nothing to worr
about...unless they set fire to the bush."

Back on board, they stood in the middle of the companior
way as if in limbo, neither at her cabin door nor his. Slowly
his hand reached out and plucked a green sprig tangled in he
hair. Rowan tucked it into his shirt pocket. "Do you wann
shower first?"

"I can use the shower off my stateroom."

"My ensuite is larger. Use it." To settle matters he too
her jacket and tossed it into his cabin followed by his own.

His palm centered on her lower back and pushed her in afte
them. "You go get started. I'll bring the tender aboard read
for tomorrow."

If she hadn't known Rowan's was the master stateroom, hi
bathroom would have clinched it. There were no sharp corner
anywhere. A huge mirror lorded it over shiny white lacque
cupboards, curving below a brown-flecked granite vanit
counter with two basins. The heads fitted behind the sweep o
granite, and above, stacks of terra-cotta towels packed th
shelves. An almond-shaped glass wall enclosed the shower, it
base the same nonskid surface as the floor.

The mirror she could have done without.

She cringed to think she'd looked this way while Rowa
held her in his arms and made no bones about wanting her.

Man, he must have it bad.

And that was good.

She smiled to herself. A secret smile, born of a thought sh
hadn't dared voice. Not to herself. Not to anyone. With a
urgency she didn't question, she stripped off her sweatshir
boots and jeans. There was little glamour to be found in thicl
socks; she added them to the pile. Bra and panties joined then

in quick succession, then naked, she reached for one of the towels.

For less than a minute she studied her reflection. Her body wasn't the type which graced the pages of pinup magazines. Her honey-colored skin and plum-dark nipples weren't in the usual style. What was it Rowan had said last night? "You taste like Caruba rum and I'm going to get drunk on you."

The words alone intoxicated her.

She got high just listening to him.

High on love.

Was that her problem? Had she really fallen in love with Rowan? The warmth she felt inside by simply looking at him wasn't anything she'd experienced before. A look from him made every bone in her body melt and everything she was softened with a sweetness she'd never known existed.

She'd told him about her father, something she hadn't shared with another living soul. That and her phobia about bugs. Rowan was an honest man, trustworthy, and he brought out the best in her. Wasn't that what she'd always wanted?

Magic in the air or not, she'd be unlikely to find her answer in the mirror. Caught up in speculation, she hadn't heard Rowan enter, but suddenly his reflection overlapped her own, wide, tanned shoulders bare like hers.

Until he stretched for a towel on the pile, she hadn't realized he was naked. He grinned at her, tucking the ends of the towel in at his waist. His expression didn't quite wipe the pain from his eyes. Her heart turned over in her chest. She'd known the climb would be tough on his leg. "Would you like to go first? I can wait."

His arms pulled her close to his hard body as heat burned away the pain she'd seen and made her blood race. "You disappoint me, Jo. What makes you think I can wait?"

Her fingers splayed against his tanned chest as he ducked his head and nipped gently on the side of her neck. A violent shudder rocked his chest beneath her palms.

"I can't get enough of you, didn't you know that?" In contradiction he pushed her away and lifted a hand to rub his chin. "But first I've got to shave." From his chin to hers was a small leap. His thumb caressed her bottom lip, making it tremble. "Tonight I'm going to take real good care of you."

Her response was spontaneous. "Let me help. What kind of razor do you use?"

In answer he opened a cupboard and pulled out an old-fashioned cutthroat razor and a can of shaving foam. Her eyes widened and he said, "It has sentimental value. My father used this and it was one of the few things I wanted after he died."

She took the razor from him, releasing the blade from its mother-of-pearl sheath. It seemed like forever since she'd watched her father use one of these. His beard had been so dark and strong he'd said nothing else was any use. She stared at Rowan's jaw. Would she still recognize him when all the gold-flecked hair on his face had gone? Would the unveiling bring back the restrained guy she used to know, in place of the pirate standing before her? Only one way to find out. "Do you trust me?"

"With my life."

"Okay, you lather up and I'll check if the blade's sharp."

Within five minutes she was asking, "Are you sure you want to lose the moustache?"

"Positive. Just don't make me laugh anymore, or you might take my nose with it."

"All right, freeze, it's coming off."

Rowan studied his face in the mirror, checking if she'd missed a spot, as she rinsed off the blade. "Stop preening and let me look at you." She lightly touched the pink scar on his top lip. "Coral, huh? You should be more careful."

Her hands followed the trail his had taken. "Okay, you'll do. You may kiss me now."

Rowan's brows rose at her peremptory command. "What's wrong, don't you think I know this workman's worthy of her hire?"

He spoke his reply against her lips but the words were lost in the kiss as he lifted her up on to the vanity and lost both of their towels.

The cold took her breath away as he turned on the spray, but she was getting used to breathtaking, being around Rowan.

Their lovemaking atop the vanity had been fast and furious and over too soon. She'd wanted to drown in his arms and when she told him he'd lifted her into the shower. Actually lifted her and made her feel weak, trembly and utterly feminine in a way she'd never felt before. He'd said he couldn't get enough of her and she echoed the sentiment.

Gradually the water mellowed and soon she had fluffy clouds of shampoo sliding down her breasts and back.

"Here. Let me do that for you." His fingers massaged her scalp like an erotic instrument. They found every nerve ending, some she'd never realized existed, and stimulated them until she could have promised to be his slave for life.

Water fell in screeds as he rinsed her hair.

"Do you use conditioner?"

Aw, help! Did that "Yes" sound like begging?

Regretfully, even conditioner had eventually to be rinsed off. And by then, her legs were like marshmallow. Rowan turned her toward his chest, tucking her hair behind her ears out of her eyes.

She twined her arms around his waist to support herself and turned her face toward his. Her eyelashes felt thick with water, which would account for the sparkling lights flashing as she blinked to clear them. "Thanks, Rowan. You give good shampoo."

"Peaches, you ain't seen nothing yet."

The husky note in his voice rippled across her skin as she linked her fingers behind him and hung on for the ride. Soon there wasn't a particle of each other's body they hadn't washed or explored and hers vibrated with anticipation as he turned off the shower.

Twisting her towel into a sarong across her breasts, he

turned another into a turban enclosing her hair. The heated mirror hadn't steamed up and as she rubbed at her hair, she noticed him wince as he stretched out to snag another towel.

Knowing how sensitive he became if she merely hinted his leg might be bothering him, she kept her mouth shut, but resolved to have a look in the cupboards for a bottle of skin lotion. It would be interesting to see if she could turn the tables and make him melt like chocolate in a hot car.

He dried himself quickly, slinging away the towel round his hips long before she was finished looking.

There was a hair dryer built into the fittings and she'd only started to brush out the tangles when Rowan took both items out of her hands and began another sensual encounter.

Her hair felt glorious. He wanted to run it through his fingers like skeins of silk, but then he also wanted to get her into bed. "Is this all natural?" he asked, gathering in fistfuls of her curls as he checked it for dryness.

"Every bit, even the color."

"Oh, I know that's natural." He looked pointedly in the direction of her thighs, as if he had X-ray vision. A quick rush of pink tinged her cheeks. She could still blush. Amazing.

Jo was a conundrum. One he intended to solve.

He undid the knot holding her towel, but she grabbed it before it could hit the deck and tucked it back together.

"No. I want to hold on to this for now. You go through and I'll be with you in a minute."

A protest formed on his lips, but he kept it behind them. He didn't want her to think she couldn't have her privacy. If she had woman stuff to attend to it was none of his damn business.

Waiting, he tidied his clothes away in the locker and folded back the bed. By the time she appeared holding a bottle of skin lotion his eyebrows automatically leaped at the possibilities.

"I like the way your mind works," he said, holding out his hand for the bottle.

She swung away, out of reach. "That's good to know, because this is for you. Lie down."

His imagination ran riot as he followed her instructions. There was no hiding how he felt as she stood beside him pouring lotion onto her palm. The blood flooding his loins turning him into one huge throbbing ache that might just explode the minute she laid hands on him.

About the only prospect he hadn't considered was the one where she massaged his leg. Not that it didn't feel good... more than good...wonderful. Her strong fingers found every single agonizing knot in his thigh.

Painful or not, it didn't diminish the overpowering torment burning in his groin. Her fingers had only to brush close to his heat to make him groan. Each time a noise erupted from his lips she glanced up at him, leaving him in no doubt she knew what her ministrations were doing to his libido.

At last the torture was over.

Jo capped the bottle and set it on the nightstand.

He reached out and enclosed her wrist with his fingers. She looked down, her eyes glistening under her lashes as she bathed him in their warmth. "Come over here, peaches."

Instead of doing as he asked, she sank to her knees by the bed and her fingers traveled his thigh once more, but without the same intense pressure. Gently they traced the scars where the bullet had emerged. Maybe they wouldn't have looked so ugly if they could have just sewn him up, but there had been bone to mend and by the time the orthopedic surgeons were finally done with him, the red lines had spread like tentacles across his inside thigh.

Still, matters could have been worse. A little higher...

It didn't bear thinking of.

Her lips tenderly followed the path her fingers had taken until a fist seemed to reach right up inside him and twist his heart. It gave him the shakes. Overcome, he ground out, "No more, sweetheart. Come up. Come to me." He held out his arms and she fell into them. Her weight crushed down onto his chest yet her feet lingered on the floor.

"I don't want to hurt you."

He ran his lips down her cheek to the curve of her neck for

a taste of the sweetness he knew he would find there. When he spoke it was muffled by her skin. "There's no way...you can hurt me anymore...than I do now. You may have... noticed, I'm pretty much in agony down there."

Jo lifted slightly away from him and her hand moved from his shoulder down to his belly. "I can help."

"No! Not that way. It's not enough. I want to be moving inside you. Pleasuring you. That's the only way I'll be satisfied." He reached between them and rid her of the towel impeding the glory of feeling her skin against his. "Come up here beside me and I'll tell you what we're going to do."

Minutes later, Jo sighed her contentment. She was surrounded by warmth. Rowan's warmth. His chest lay hard against her back and his arms held her close. She could stay like this forever, with her breasts cupped in his large hands and his mouth, tongue and teeth nipping and nuzzling at her neck and shoulders until he transformed her into a huge bundle of quivering nerves.

Her moan was long and loud and came straight from her soul as his teeth found *the* spot again. Her body bucked, her hips wriggling against his long hot length, pressing tight and hard against the crease of her derriere.

His hand found her belly, holding her still and his moist breath panted in her ear as he sought to control her. The feel of his palm splayed over her, so near and yet so far, had the reverse influence. There was a place deep inside her that needed filling, making her undulate her body trying tempt his fingers to journey farther.

"Whoa, don't do that or I won't be long for this world."

"Then touch me, Rowan. Touch me before I disintegrate in your arms from an overdose of anticipation."

A deep growl reverberated through his chest. "I can do that for you, peaches. I sure can." He suited his actions to his words and found her female core with his fingers.

Peaches. She loved it when he called her that. It made her feel soft and tender and gooey inside as if she might melt all over him.

"Rowan," she sighed on a breath that spiraled up from the soles of her feet where her toes curled and released in time with the fingertip circling her femininity. "I can't wait any longer…I need you inside me like now!"

He heard her, and thanked providence for his forethought to see to her protection while he was still capable of rational thought. He touched the inside of her knee. "Raise your leg."

She let out a long low mewl, half human, half animal and her thighs clenched on his hand.

"C'mon. That's it, lift for me, bend your knee."

Once she complied, he gripped her ankle, tucking her foot behind his hip. She felt so open. Yet she wasn't uncomfortable. His finger slipped inside her, testing. She wanted to tell him she was ready, good and ready, but the sensations filling her robbed her of speech. He removed his hand and she felt empty. But not for long. This time he inserted two fingers and brushed between her folds. She let her feelings rip and cried out loud, her belly bucking against his hand.

The noises she made were like music to his ears. They had a magical effect on his sex. He hadn't thought it could get thicker or longer but it did, almost jumping out of his skin. As soon as he felt her first ripples circle his fingers he knew if he didn't take her soon he would miss out on feeling all that hot silk shatter around him.

"Aaaahh,' she sighed as he entered, filling her at last.

The second thrust took her to the top. The third pushed her over. All thought deserted him except one. Jo. His woman.

He growled his right of possession against her neck, lightly gripping her with his teeth as he thrust one more time.

The way down was long and scary. But they made it together.

"Rowan, it's time to get underway." His leg came over her thighs and trapped her. Obviously the man was feeling no pain this morning. "Rowan. Turn off the alarm."

With a halfhearted grunt he rolled over and grabbed his watch and switched on the light.

She pushed up and the bedcovers flowed over her knees. Although she was naked from the hips up she felt anything but embarrassed by his perusal of her attributes. Especially as he only opened one sleepy eye. The raised eyebrow told her he liked what he saw, yet the whole gesture, topped by spiky morning hair was so boyish she wanted to hug him as her thoughts fled in another direction.

She'd always wanted a son—with her upbringing, daughters didn't rate—and suddenly that son took on Rowan's features.

This was dangerous ground.

Time to move.

"Come on, Rowan." The preceding thought, wishful thinking, made her tone brusque. "Only one of us here is self-employed. I have to get back to work."

Climbing over him inelegantly, she reached the side of the bed before he stopped her, catching her fingers with his.

"Shower with me."

"Oh, no. I'm not that foolish. Once you get me in there I'll never get out." She softened her words with a smile. "Get a wiggle on, skipper. We've a lot of waves to slide down before daybreak."

By dawn they were already rounding the bush-covered cone of Tane's Throat and Rowan was on his second shot of coffee. He scowled down into his mug as he remembered Jo's cheerful smile when she'd handed it to him. Things would feel a whole lot better if she didn't seem so darn happy to be returning to civilization, such as it was, in Nicks Landing. Even now, she was down below, packing her bags. No argument from him could convince her she'd be safer staying with him until they'd caught the creep who'd sent her the letter.

The sea was rougher this morning. He heard Jo curse the chop from the foot of the stairs as they left the lee of the volcano. By the time she reached the top he'd smoothed the frown from his features.

She swapped the mug to her other hand as she braced herself against the locker beside the bridge. "Slopped my cofee,'' she explained as she sucked at the red mark forming on he back of her hand. "I should have put cream in it, then it wouldn't have stung so much."

"Go down and run it under the cold tap before it marks."

"No, it'll be okay, honestly."

Sometimes Jo could be too stoic for her own good.

The radio burst to life before he'd had a chance to reinforce his advice. "Coast Guard to *Stanhope's Fancy*. Come in." The message repeated before he could reply.

"*Stanhope's Fancy*, reading you loud and clear, come in."

"Do you have Detective Jellic aboard?"

"Affirmative." A nasty feeling crawled over his skin as soon as they asked for Jo. What could be so important it couldn't wait till they tied up at the marina?

She took over the mike as Harry's voice came over the speaker. "How far are you from Nicks Landing?"

She turned to him, her eyebrows raised in a question. "Approximately two hours at this speed, a little less if you want her to get shaken up on the outgoing tide."

"It'll be two hours, Harry. What's up?"

"Rocky's missing. Went out last night and didn't come back."

As Rowan steered them into the marina, Jo reached up till her lips touched his cheek and kissed him. "Thanks for the last couple of days. I'm going to miss you."

He took his eyes off the berths for a second and shot her a white-toothed grin. "It's not over yet, peaches."

Her heels landed back on the deck and her stomach rolled over the way it did each time he called her that pet name. If only she felt as confident. Moira and her predictions of trouble were still bugging her. She couldn't get that red haze on the moon out of her mind. Superstitious? Maybe. It wasn't her fault she'd been brought up by a grandmother who'd clung to a lot of the traditions from the old country.

"Yeah, I still have to find Skelton."

Rowan put the powerful engines into slow astern then cut

them as they glided into their berth. She'd noticed the white
and-blue police car parked at the top of the finger as the
approached and it was no surprise to see Harry jump aboar
and clip the boat to the floating dock.

"Quick, give me your handkerchief. I've left lipstick o
your face." Her task accomplished, she hurried forward an
clipped up the bowlines.

All three of them were in the lower saloon before Harr
explained what all the rush was about. "We've found Rocky."

Jo heaved a sigh of relief. If anything had happened t
Rocky while she was…well, while she and Rowan…it didn
bear thinking… "Thank goodness."

"Where'd you find him?" asked Rowan.

She took her eyes off Harry and turned to him. There wa
none of the relief *she'd* felt in his tone. He sounded serious

Deadly serious.

"Young Ginny found him when she took a shortcut throug
Stanhope Park on her paper route."

Ginny found him. This didn't bode well. She had a sic
feeling the poor kid had seen something no child should eve
lay eyes on. She would go see the child first chance she got

"Come on, Harry," she said roughly. "Get on with it. Sto
dragging it out."

"He was naked with one of those symbols drawn across hi
chest like on the letters. It was centered around a knife woun
The M.E. says the weapon went straight through his heart."

Chapter 13

Jo always felt there was something obscene about gazing on the dead before the undertaker had had time to make them presentable. Like spying on people through a gap in the curtains, catching them at something they'd never do if they knew they were being observed. Rocky definitely had that look of being caught unawares. His eyes were wide open, but she couldn't find any blame in them for her failure to apprehend the fiend responsible.

A full raft of regrets tossed around in Jo's troubled mind. Starting its descent into the pits by spoiling her fabulous two days with Rowan, and ending with Ginny having to witness his lewd presentation of death.

The poor kid would probably have nightmares over it. On Jo's first murder case, the victim had continued to haunt her dreams for weeks.

Between the first and last thought, the knowledge that Rowan's reason for staying had died along with Rocky, almost overshadowed the other casualty, her chance to prove her father's innocence.

Now that Rocky was no longer in the land of the livin
she doubted she'd ever know the truth.

The screen had been erected around the crime scene on
moments before their arrival and the rest of the small suburb;
park had been cordoned off. According to Harry, both Bu
and Jake had gone to interview Molly.

She'd rolled her eyes at this information. It wasn't as if tl
pair of them were joined at the hip. One of them should ha
stayed behind at the scene. Maybe then she wouldn't have fe
like the middle man in a comedy routine, not knowing whic
way to turn. If she followed her instincts would it earn her
rap over the knuckles? Or was Bull hoping she would do ju
that?

Rowan stepped round her, taking a good hard look at tl
way the victim had been staked out. "They didn't make muc
attempt to hide him."

She'd been mulling over that exact thought. "It's like the
were thumbing their nose at the cops. Which shows how muc
they think about our ability to catch them."

"Don't put yourself down. The other two had this case we
chewed over before it came your way."

She let out a sigh and let her gaze wander. "They couldn
have picked a better spot to throw a load of confusion into tl
mix. This is a well-known short cut. It probably saves a coup
of minutes compared to following the path, but it's not goir
to make our job any easier."

She ran her gaze over the grass and dried mud path, chec!
ing it out. "Most of this trash has probably been blowir
around for weeks. Also, it hasn't rained in a while so we ca
discount the footprints."

"Am I included in that *our?*" he asked.

"I doubt it. But it isn't my case, so you should speak 1
Bull. He's *the* man again."

"Don't take it so hard. You're the one with experienc
he'll be a fool if he doesn't utilize it."

"Yeah, right."

"Bull may be old-fashioned when it comes to female cops, but this one time he'll have to get over it."

Behind her, Harry let out a bark straddling the fence between cough and laughter. "See, he doesn't think I have a show, either."

"The Sergeant will back you. Won't you, Harry?"

"On your recommendation, McQuaid?"

"On her reputation." The two of them were thick as thieves, but it pleased her that Rowan didn't trade on it over much.

As Harry nodded, she said, "Thanks, guys, but this never should have happened and that's how it'll read on my record. We all know what happened after my last mistake."

Harry coughed again, but there was no telling if it was in agreement or denial.

"You don't need to go there, Jo."

"It's no secret, is it? I got sent here for almost killing you. Well, this time I've succeeded. Rocky is definitely dead."

Her eyes welled with tears as self-pity got in another strike. "Where do you think they'll send me this time?"

Rowan carried on as if he hadn't heard. The plastic covers on his shoes rustled as he hunkered down beside Rocky and she was glad he wasn't looking her way as she swiped her knuckles across her eyes. Rowan didn't touch the pale flaccid body, but his hand hovered over the area of the wound and pointed with a ballpoint. "Not much blood."

His pen scribed a circle in the air and flicked away a dead leaf that had floated onto the body. "D'you think this was drawn before or after he was killed?"

Jo heaved in a breath. Inside her navy jacket with Police emblazoned in yellow, her breasts quivered on a sigh, but she felt better. Following Rowan's example she bent her knees and crouched down beside Rocky's mortal remains. "After. I'd say."

She turned her attention to the ropes on Rocky's wrists. No bruising. "He wasn't killed here. They tied him up after death. And look at this." She lifted one leg to look underneath. "He wasn't lying in this position till a while after death. Has any one found his clothes?" she asked Harry.

"Not so far. I've put a couple of men onto searching the park. Once they finish here they'll start checking out the Dumpsters and the park's rubbish receptacles. I heard Bul ring Gisborne for reinforcements."

"That's good to know. We're going to need them, thanks Sergeant." Habit took over as she mentally enumerated the tasks ahead of her, unaware of anything else until she lifted her head and her gaze clashed with Rowan's. It was as if Rocky didn't exist, as if they weren't in the middle of a crime scene, but back in the bush, just the two of them. *If only.*

His clear green gaze met hers and her heart squeezed. Oh boy, she was in trouble, deep trouble. Her eyelashes flickered tangling together, camouflaging her emotions, or so she thought. She felt about Ginny's age, fourteen with all the un certainty that comes with burgeoning hormones. Jo licked her lips, but a smile for Rowan still trembled on them. "Did I tell *you* thanks for all you've done?"

"No problem. Anytime," he said without a blink, his eyes wide as if she filled his vision.

A rush of hope welled up inside her and her heart went down for the final count. The future spread itself out before her, beckoning, as if she could have it all, a meaningful re lationship, maybe even marriage and a family, but best of all, the love of an *honest* man.

Rowan thought he was doing a pretty good job of blending in with the furnishings at the back of the squad room. It was small by Auckland standards, but the best the station house had to offer. He'd also discovered something about himself.

The pain he'd expected to experience in this familiar milieu hadn't materialized. Instead, he'd only felt a small pang of nostalgia for the old days. Seemed he'd healed in more ways than one and was ready to move on.

He watched Jo's long dark curls bounce on her shoulders

as she spoke animatedly to Harry. Soon, he determined, he'd make sure Jo was ready to make that move with him.

Bull had the floor. "Okay, anyone not know why we're here?"

The few grunts his audience emitted appeared to satisfy the D.S., and he continued. "At or about one a.m. Saturday morning, Rocky Skelton went out to the Dumpster after he and his wife had cleaned up. Molly, his wife, went off to bed and fell asleep, not realizing he hadn't joined her until she woke next morning."

Turning to the board his finger underlined one of the police photographer's shots of Rocky. "Six-fifteen a.m. the victim was discovered looking like this, by a young girl on a bike. She was in the middle of her paper route so if any of you missed out on the morning's news, you know why."

The obligatory titters sounded forced. Murder wasn't a joke to be laughed at in a town that hadn't seen one in ten or more years. Bull smiled at the response then spoke to Harry. "Sergeant Jackson, er…where are you up to?"

Only one day since Ginny found Skelton's body and already Bull was out of his depth, not that he would admit it. To Rowan's mind it seemed the first two statements were all Bull had rehearsed.

"Most of the guys I pulled off the crime scene, now that we have reinforcements, will be doing a door-to-door for anyone who saw Rocky. I know the hour was pretty late, but someone may have heard something. The others will take the streets bordering the park and radiate out from there."

"Can I butt in here?" said Jo. Bull nodded.

"Although it hasn't been confirmed yet, we ought to keep in mind the victim wasn't killed at the crime scene. That means they had to move the body, so you're also looking for a vehicle that may have wakened one or more of the neighbors. My thoughts are that they probably parked at the top end of the shortcut to save carrying the weight uphill, but don't take that for granted."

"You guys keep that in mind." Bull seemed to find his

second wind as if for once having Jo on his side gave him the confidence he needed. "Jake and I have a list of the regulars at the Hard Luck Inn and we'll check on them today. If you come upon any leads, inform either me or Detective Jellic."

Hmmm, Bull was learning Jo was more than a token female cop.

Bull went to the board. A map with several pins on it, plus notes on everything they'd had so far, were displayed along with crime scene photos and copies of the anonymous notes, both Rocky's and Jo's. "And you, Detective Jellic? Have you had a result on these?" Bull tapped the notes with a pen.

"Forensics say they're snowed under, but I've been promised a full work-down tomorrow at the latest."

"Well, keep on them. If we can't wrap this up in the next few days then we'll have to put up with cops we don't know from Wellington." He looked apologetically in Jo's direction but it didn't stop him from saying, "We don't want them coming here with their big-city ways and looking down on us.

"Jo, before you do anything else, go talk to the widow. Molly wasn't up to saying much yesterday. Maybe you'll be able to get something other than tears out of her today."

Bull rubbed the tip of his nose on the back of his hand and sniffed. "Play up the woman-to-woman angle."

Rowan couldn't see Jo's face, but he watched her squirm in her seat. "I have a few ideas of my own. I'd like to put them into play." She sounded optimistic. Whatever she had in mind, it wasn't something she'd shared with him. By his guess it was to do with her still discounting the satanists. For himself, he wasn't ready to discount anything or anyone, and that was his reason for sitting at the back of the hall.

Without allowing her to feel crowded, he hadn't let Jo out of his sight since their return from Te Kohanga National Park.

While she sat up front, putting forward her take on what they'd discovered so far, the thought that her own life might be in jeopardy appeared to be the farthest thing from her mind, but it was perched right on top of his list. The only way to

ke him walk away from her now was at gunpoint. Dammit,
t even then!

He'd discovered something about himself, he no longer sim-
y wanted Jo, he wanted to make her happy, but despaired
being the right man for the task.

If she'd felt the desperation in his lovemaking last night,
e hadn't mentioned it. She'd simply fallen into a deep slum-
r in his arms, while his own troubles clawed at his gut and
used him sleep, her palm lay against his breastbone as if
e pulse of his heart lulled all her worries. And that was only
e of his problems. Over the last few days, Jo's openness
d competed with his own ambivalence; he had to tell her
e truth about himself.

The night before, he'd discovered a new Jo in the woman
o cried on his chest. "I feel so bad, Rowan. For years...all
ose years I knew only one gift would do for my father, and
blew it. Rocky was the key, and with him dead it's too
e...too late." She'd struggled out of his arms and stared
seeing across the dark sea, fist clenched hammerlike against
r breasts. "Forgive me, Dad. I should have tried harder."

That had been his chance to tell her about his own father,
bert Stanhope, but he'd let the opportunity slip from his
asp. Big mistake. One he had to correct very soon, or he
ight live to regret the omission. It was no longer any use,
ling himself he'd held back, when he realized how readily
shouldered other people's responsibility. The way she had
en he got shot. Now he felt like a cur. Her father at least
d the excuse of being dead, but what was his?

A fluttery sensation made Jo's heart skip when Bull told
r, "Might as well take McQuaid with you, he'll go anyway
d it will give me a man to put somewhere else." Happiness
r her had become the glimpse of a tall silhouette out of the
rner of her eye, a fleeting touch of his hand as they passed,
nple little things that made her feel utterly feminine. Utterly
love.

She could practically guarantee Molly wasn't going to be

as delighted. And here she was at the rear door of the inn v
Rowan at her shoulder, taking comfort from his presence.
should that be his continued presence?

Rowan had been part of the landscape all day. How ma
times had she indulged herself by turning, knowing he wo
be there?

The door opened a reluctant inch at a time. Red-rimm
eyes stared through a veil of smoke. "Oh, it's you. W
d'you want?"

Jo held up her badge as Rowan's knuckles brushed her te
spine, a reminder she wasn't alone. "Sorry to disturb you
such a time. My condolences at your loss, Molly. But I w
dered if you felt better able to talk today. If anything m
had occurred to you about the people who perpetrated t
crime. I know you'll want to find them as much as I do."

"You already know. Those devils took him from m
Loathing seeped out from under her lashes and anger add
color to her pinched face, made brighter by the lank sil
curls framing it.

Molly drew hard on her cigarette, her mouth tighten
pursing around the filter tip until her pale lips seemed to f
at the edges. In a cloud of smoke she turned her ire on Row
"The Stanhopes have a lot to answer, hanging on to mor
that was rightfully ours. My man's dead and no money to b
him."

None of this was Rowan's fault. Jo wished she could f
an excuse for the other woman's bitterness, but she had
own to contend with. Years of living with the lie Rocky p
petuated about her father had seen to that. And dammit
she was only human.

"Recriminations aren't going to bring your husband bac
Rowan replied in a deep voice. Jo felt the rumble vibr
through her rib cage. That was how close he stood. "R
assured Molly, there will be enough money to bury Rocky
style."

The widow rolled her eyes, as if to say, "I'll believe it wh
I see it." Without another word, she opened the door wi

alking ahead of them into the kitchen, shoulders stooped and
ack so brittle a light wind would snap it. Molly's demeanor
as surprising. She and Rocky had been married a long time,
et Jo had never gotten the impression it was a love connec-
on.

A strong odor of bleach and a gleaming kitchen indicated
folly hadn't spent the whole day smoking and crying. As they
ot closer to the table, Jo noted a lonely stub in the ashtray
tting next to a half-drunk cup of coffee. Yeah, the woman
ad been busy. Every surface gleamed; floor, counters, pots
n their hooks and knife handles in rows of three in their
ooden block.

Grasping the back of a wooden chair with a hand that
ooked red and raw, Molly scraped it across the floor, its feet
lattering as she angled it into the position she wanted.

Jo sat opposite, while Rowan settled for hitching one hip
nto the edge of the worktable. She watched his large foot
wing back and forth as she organized her thoughts. "If we
iscount the satanists, was there anyone else holding a grudge
gainst Rocky?"

Molly pounced. "Apart from yourself, you mean?" Her
and fisted on the scrubbed pine counter. There was an intense
tillness about the widow, like a cat gathering itself to pounce.

If it was a knock-down-drag-out fight she wanted, Jo wasn't
bout to oblige. "How about that guy, Smale?"

Molly's face turned surly. She looked at the floor and ig-
ored the question. Jo carried on. "He was sitting at the bar
ear the kitchen door the other night. He and Rocky seemed
o be having a barney over something."

"Credit. He wanted credit. People are always looking for
omething for nothing. It wasn't anything worth killing over."
tubbing out her cigarette, undeterred by the change of direc-
on, Molly went on. "Did you think he didn't know you hated
im for telling the truth about your father?"

"That may be, but my alibi's sound." Jo didn't utter the
vords, "How about yours?" But she knew Molly heard them.
'If you think of anything else keep us informed, meanwhile

I'd like to look through Rocky's personal effects for any cl▪
to his killer there.''

Molly jerked her head toward an open door. "Our roon▪
down there, end of the corridor. Not that you'll find mu▪
we'd very little left. Take a good look. See how you'd like▪
Nice place for a man to spend his last days. It's clean a▪
that's all you can say for it. Not what you'd be used to,▪
course." Again she aimed her malevolence at Rowan.

His hand gripped Jo's shoulder once they were out of sig▪
"Don't let her get to you. I'm not. Skelton's bank accou▪
had stacks of money in them. They didn't have to live he▪
they could have rented a damn nice house, no problem.''

Jo pushed open the only door at the far end. The room w▪
small and cramped, hardly big enough for the double bed a▪
dresser they'd crammed inside.

"Whauh," Rowan showed his disgust or maybe it w▪
claustrophobia. "Obviously she had no idea about the mon▪
There was no reason for them to live this way, unless y▪
count greed."

"Well, she was right about one thing, it's clean. I have▪
feeling that anything of use has already been tossed out.''▪
looked around the room. She'd been hoping Molly had re▪
rected her compulsion for collecting to their sleeping quarte▪
There wasn't enough space, though. Inside the room no▪
particle was out of place, from the hospital corners on the b▪
to the four-squared pile of magazines on top of the dress▪
She wondered how much Rowan would bet on them bei▪
stacked by date?

"We'd better get a move on. By the look of this place c▪
next stop has to be the Dumpster outside."

"Thanks, Jo, you just *had* to make my day."

"Boy, am I glad to be heading home." The last rays▪
sunset elongated their shadows and the lights in the mari▪
hadn't come into their own yet. Rowan's arm was around h▪
holding her tight, pressed against his side and Jo made ▪

bones about stealing some of his warmth to combat her weariness.

Heavens, had she really said that? Her tired brain had taken a moment to register her unthinking comment. Flustered, Jo rushed to correct her mistake. "I meant glad we're finished for the day. I *know* the boat isn't home—"

"Hey, take it easy, peaches. I don't mind." A shimmer of emotion curled inside at the inappropriateness of the endearment to someone her size.

They'd reached the top of the finger where the *Fancy* was tied up and Rowan stopped under the lamp, turning her in his arms until they were facing each other. "Where *do* you call home these days? Here, or is it still Auckland?"

"That's difficult to answer. I can't call Nicks Landing home. It's simply the place where I work. And since Grandma died, even before, my brothers have scattered, one was in SAS, but now I'm not sure what he does. He moves around a lot. So I haven't had a place to call home. At least not physically. But, Auckland has always been my favorite place."

"Auckland, huh? At least that gives us something to work with."

Before Jo could ask him to explain, he bent his head till their lips lined up and covered his mouth with hers. She tasted want and need, tinged with fear for her safety. He pulled her closer, holding her as if he'd never let her go. Like Rowan said, they had something to work with.

She let herself drift into the kiss, into the magic and leaned against his chest with a sigh as he lifted his head. "I'm glad you stayed on."

"Me, too. Tonight we've got to talk. And not about Rocky."

Hope surged through her. Maybe she had been in the wilderness long enough. She could put in for a transfer to Auckland. Central was out, but there were always the suburbs. Browns Bay might be an option. She'd put the idea to Rowan later tonight once they were in bed. After she'd heard what he had to say.

Her stomach growled. She looked up at him, laughing, "Lord, am I hungry."

"Me, too. But to hell with food. I'd rather eat you." He leaned forward, his teeth nibbling her earlobe. "What can say? I can't get enough."

She felt the long hard ridge of his sex pressing into he belly as he pulled her closer. It made her hot all over, and sh laughed, uncertain and suddenly vulnerable. Where was leading? Her and Rowan. Did they really have a chance making this work?

Impatient with the direction of her thoughts she pushed him playfully and took a step back. "Well, I was talking abou food. Energy, fuel. C'mon, let's go, I'm starving."

She pulled him by the hand, laughing all the way along th silvered wooden planks of the finger. There was a long slo swell running and every now and then the deck came up meet their feet, which added to the laughter as they misstep ped. Just to be awkward, Rowan hung back so she had to hat most of his weight, protesting, "You weigh a ton."

He flashed a look fraught with challenge. "And *you* lov it."

They were almost at the berth when he decided to revers tactics, drawing level. They covered the last few feet in a flash Side by side, hearts and minds traveling in unison to the sam rhythm. The same need.

A becoming flush colored her cheeks and her hair was a over the place, but her smile was just for him and made hi heart squeeze. She'd never looked more beautiful.

And he loved her.

Tonight he would tell her. Then, he would explain who h really was. He'd wait till after they'd made love and she wa snuggled up in his arms as they savored the afterglow.

Then he'd tell her.

"Rowan...did you leave a light on?"

"Not that I remember." The galley and lower saloon wer dark, but a pale glow illuminated the windows of the uppe aloon. "I'll go first." He stepped onto the boarding platform nd tried the door. Unlocked.

His first thought was for Jo's safety. "Keep behind me," e whispered and silently swung the door back on its hinges.

"You don't think it's the ones who killed Rocky?"

"Probably not, but we won't take any chances." He put a inger to his lips and she nodded. As he reached the steps he eard a clink of glass and *glug, glug* of liquid pouring from a ottle.

"Damn cheek," he whispered, "they're into the liquor."

He took the last few steps in one, saying, "Put that down nd turn around." The bottle went flying and the glass landed n the floor, soaking the thick carpet pile. His brother turned nd blasted him with a look.

"Dammit, Rowan! See what you made me do."

As Jo appeared, for a second so did his brother's usual olished savoir faire. "Sorry about that, I'm Scott Stanhope, nd you're..." Scott's jaw dropped and all his social niceties vith it. His blue eyes, so like their father's, grew wintry as he ooked her up and down.

Rowan stepped closer, not quite in front of Jo but at her houlder. Too late, he thought, realizing he couldn't shield her r their relationship from the ice storm he knew was on its vay.

Scott negligently flicked off a bead of liquor that had landed n his cuff and proceeded to do the same to Jo.

"You're that bloody woman who almost killed my rother!"

Chapter 14

Liar, liar, pants on fire. The childish retort raced through J[e] mind every time she stopped for breath.

Jeans, jacket and T-shirts came out of the locker in a jang of hangers. *Liar—* She punched them into the soft duffel ba Drawers opened, one, two, three. Fists of underwear hit t[l] pile. *Liar—* Tissue box scrunched and flattened as the z[ ] closed. *Pants on fire.* Two foil-covered missiles explod[e] against the wall. That was it. She was outta here!

But first she had to walk through the saloon she'd left pr[e] cipitately, holding her anger in check. Rowan's story mig[ ] have appeased his brother, but his "later" to her, putting [h] explanation on hold, was never going to happen. Not no[w] Not ever.

And damn Scott Stanhope for the archetypal, self-center[ed] bastard that he was. He'd just ripped her world asunder a[n] what did he say when Rowan asked him what he was doi[n] here?

"I've just bought a million-dollar horse!" Then he laughed when Rowan scowled fiercely.

"Don't worry. I didn't dip into our money. I bought it myself. It was a bargain."

Jo left the stateroom, slamming the door behind her.

Her feet hit the stairs.

Mike Gallagher, a horse trainer, gets into debt and Stanhope helps him out by buying a horse that could win the Melbourne Cup next Tuesday and make him more than his money back, all within a week. Typical! And he was the man Nicks Landing looked up to.

She entered the saloon.

Rowan and his brother were talking together until Rowan spied her duffel and his expression changed.

"Where are you going?"

"Away."

Rowan strode over, reaching for the bag, as she flipped it round behind her. "Don't go."

Two words couldn't mend a broken heart. She'd fallen for a man who was no more than real vision she'd had of their future. And he didn't get it. He just didn't get it.

Such betrayal. She had ended relationships for smaller deceits than the one Rowan perpetrated. "How can I stay? You're a stranger. Someone I only *thought* I knew."

His face might have been carved in stone. She bit back a sob that came up to choke her. *His dear face.* She never wanted to see it again. He'd turned her world upside down and all she had to show for it was a killer of a pain in her heart.

The man she loved had never existed.

She stepped round him, missed, and had to shoulder him aside. Five steps down and she was away. She raced for the exit and could hear them behind her. Rowan's feet pounding the stairs, his brother's lighter ones following.

How could she have been so dumb? She'd seen photos of Scott Stanhope, hosting parties for local dignitaries, with a few actresses and models thrown in to sweeten the mix. Together, their similarities hit her eyes like a poke with a sharp stick.

Why hadn't she realized they were brothers?

The whole of Nicks Landing must have been laughing at her.

Rowan McQuaid!

Rowan Stanhope!

She pulled open the door and turned. Rowan was almost upon her. His eyes narrow and his expression furious. "Thanks for the ride, McQuaid…Stanhope. It was fun while it lasted."

She slid the door across in his face, stepping from the boarding platform to the long finger of decking.

The wind came from offshore and blew her tears away.

They'd been arguing in Jo's office for five minutes and Rowan wasn't getting anywhere. He'd been calling Jo since this morning. She'd left a message with Seth at the reception desk that she wouldn't accept his calls, was too busy to see him. He'd circumvented her instructions by asking for Harry.

She looked like hell—the way he felt. Ever since he'd arrived in her office she'd been masking her true feelings by acting offhand. It hadn't worked.

But she still wasn't ready to listen to his explanation. "Excuses," she called them. She played tough. She played explicit—*liar*—and she countered every argument.

Only the memory of holding her in his arms with him moving inside her, listening to her moans of pleasure, kept him persisting. Jo loved him. He knew it. She knew it.

All he had to do was make her admit it.

Easier said than done.

"This isn't over, not by a long chalk. I love you, Jo."

She blanched, not entirely the response he'd hoped for when he'd played around with the words "I love you" in his head, but neither had he expected her to look as if she might swoon at his feet. If only he knew what she was thinking, but she'd closed her eyes and wouldn't let him in.

He stepped closer. Her throat moved convulsively as his breath stirred the dark curls framing her face. He lifted her hair back from her ear. She tensed. He dipped his head toward er cheek. Jo quivered, fragile as a crystal glass in sync with he note his body played. "Cross my heart and hope to die," he whispered.

The glass shattered. Her eyes flew open, fear expanding her pupils, stark black replacing chocolate brown. "Don't tempt ate, Rowan. You're not indestructible."

Hell, he knew that. Knew it as surely as he knew the pain n his chest was because she'd left him. It had taken that to earn the truth about love. The heart had no defense against it. "Fate has already had its way. I freely admit I didn't want to fall in love with you. I knew the danger, but love isn't that imple." He held her shoulders as if that would force her to ook at him. "I want to learn from my father's mistakes and not repeat them. And I won't stand back and let you, my woman—my life—walk away. If it means fighting for your ove...I'll do whatever it takes. Just listen."

"No! How can love exist where trust is dead? Lies brought us together. Rocky lied about my father. That gave me the incentive to become a cop. Your deception, your *lie*, has torn us apart. When were you going to tell me the truth? You had oads of opportunities, I gave you plenty of openings but you didn't take one of them. Seems *you* didn't really trust *me*."

"Dammit, woman, I do trust you. I'd trust you with my ife."

"What's new? You did that by saving mine, but I gave it back to you. That makes us quits."

He cupped Jo's nape in his hand, tightening his grip as she flinched away from him. "I refuse to give up."

She tried to shrug him off. He forked his fingers through the black silk of her hair, turning her head until she had no place to look but at him.

"Let me go, you oaf. I have a job to do before it turns into another fiasco, and you're in my way." Her dark eyes flashed angry shards of jet.

Just as he thought he was past hurting, past feeling any more pain, his heart clenched on its force. "Resign from your ob...make a fresh start...come work with me."

A harsh laugh that sounded more like a plea for help, e
caped her lips. "Great. Two police castoffs. Who'd take
seriously?"

Anger and frustration ripped at his control. The insults we
getting down and dirty, balancing on the cutting edge of sla
derous. But it couldn't stop him loving her. Theirs was a mat
made in hell, a product of their days working together
Auckland Homicide Division. If you got out of there st
clutching your sanity you were lucky. And he felt lucky.

Lucky enough to push his hand up her skirt and discov
the little swatch of silk hiding her womanhood. He wanted J
Wanted her now! Down on the desk with her legs tight rou
his waist as he hammered into her.

He started with a kiss, swift and hungry, but it got his me
sage across. Her chest heaved as he clamped her tight again
his hip. At last, he found her, cupping her through the sle
barrier. Their gazes fought and he knew he was winning
the first quiver of surrender rippled through her....

"Hrrumph."

The noise came from behind him. He hid Jo from view
he released her and turned to find Harry standing in the offi
doorway. Passion had made him deaf to it opening.

She stepped past him, flinging him a venomous glance. .
was keeping score again, but at least she was thinking of hi

"Come on in, Harry. What can I do for you? Stanhope he
was just leaving." Could she have put it more pointedly? Sl
didn't think so. Yet, a pang of emotion she didn't want
acknowledge smote her as his wide shoulders filled the do
of her office, perhaps for the last time.

After Rowan left, fist clenched round an envelope Har
handed him, she walked over and closed the door, more as
way of stifling regret than anything else. Reluctantly, she r
leased the handle. The click echoed in her mind for a lo
time afterward.

"You ought to give him a chance, Jo."

Her brows rode high on her forehead and the back of h

neck pricked. But she recognized concern in his gaze and stance. Compassion was a rare thing and she accepted it graciously. "Thanks, Harry, but he lied. Couldn't trust me with his name."

"You know what the bard said, 'A rose by any other name…' You knew the real Rowan McQuaid Stanhope."

There had to be a funny side to Harry quoting Shakespeare at her, but her spirits were too low to see it. They'd been scrabbling at the back of her mind since the moment Scott Stanhope turned up, trying not to hit bottom. How ironic that their only moment of relief had been Rowan's kiss.

"Has the whole town been laughing at me?"

Harry's expression was sheepish, "Except for Bull and me no one knew, and we weren't laughing. Though, I have to admit it did raise a smile, seeing McQuaid sickening for love. He hasn't spent a lot of time here since his parents died, and we only wanted what was the best for him. That seemed to be you."

The man was good, but she wasn't falling for any of his tricks. Sure, Rowan had said he loved her, but it wasn't enough, fool that she was, she needed more. She needed everything. Love, trust, the whole nine yards. Hands balled, she doused the excess of emotion, making them tremble as she walked back to her desk and sat down before acknowledging Harry again.

She had murder in mind but it wasn't Rowan's. Oh, she'd thrown out a lot of insults, but he was right, she did love him. Who else could turn her insides to mush with a look, melt her heart with a smile, rescue the tender feelings she'd locked deep inside? Hell, how could she have fallen for a liar?

Jo's stomach clenched so hard she felt sick. It had been years, at least two, since she'd taken out her feelings and examined them so closely. Time to fold them up in a small neat square and bury them again. She had a job to do.

"Anything on the autopsy report?"

"I called the M.E., but he wasn't finished. Said to let you know the blade you're looking for is eight inches long, sharp

tapered point and two inches wide at the handle with a nic
in the blade near the hilt.''

"Sounds like the chef's knife Moira uses. But at least
know where she was on the night of the crime." Harry wa
one of the only cops they'd let in on the secret. On top c
everything else she didn't want to be responsible for spreadin
gossip about her landlady.

Besides, there was the little matter of having lived a
Moira's house for two years without cottoning on.

"Oh yeah, he also said Rocky wasn't laid out like a sacrific
when they stabbed him. He was standing. The knife went i
and up under his ribs with a lot of force behind it.''

"Short-order cook got him, huh?" Uh-uh, no wisecracks
"Sorry, that was uncalled for, I expect you were Rocky'
friend.''

Harry eased a hip onto her desk. "Not so's you'd notice."

Spying the envelope Harry slipped onto the desk, sh
tensed. Stark white, it stood out against the dark wood, lik
another she'd received. Fingers crossed, she asked, "Is tha
for me?" Her voice sounded a note too high and a shade to
feeble. A fine time to become superstitious.

"Don't worry. It's not another anonymous letter. It's th
results of the fingerprint check you ordered done on them.''

"Why didn't you give it to Bull?"

"He and Jake dashed off a while ago. They were up i
arms when they heard the Smale brothers had been bailed b
the youngest of the brood. Besides, when you read the report
I think you'll catch on to the paradox quicker than Bull will.'

Paradox? That was an unusual word coming from Harry
He was full of surprises. "I take it you've read the results?
thought you said you never opened my mail?" She inserted
fingernail under the sticky resealed edge and ran it along it
length.

"This wasn't personal.''

And the other one was? Harry was correct in his assessmen
What else could a threat on her life be considered, but per
sonal?

She pulled out the results and read. As she'd thought, the only prints on the letter to Rocky were his own. And on the one to her? Only one print found. And it was taken off one of the letters cut out and pasted. It matched Rocky's thumb-print.

Her jaw dropped as the meaning sunk in. She closed her mouth quickly as she stared up at Harry.

"I knew you'd find it interesting," he remarked dryly.

Now that was more like the Harry she knew, the one given to understatements.

"Read the footnote."

She read. One of the technicians had noted the unusual font, matching it up with a heavy-metal magazine he subscribed to.

That gave her two options. Either Rocky had sent the letters or someone he knew had cut the letters out of a magazine Rocky had read. Maybe he'd traded magazines? As there was no way his death could count as suicide, she settled for the latter option.

Picking up the envelope, she pushed the sheets inside.

"No one else knows about this?"

"Just you, me and forensics."

She could have hugged him. This might stave off the impending invasion by Wellington cops if Molly would cooperate. "Well, I'm off, Harry. You'll know where to find me."

"That I will. Good night, Detective."

She flipped him a grateful smile and left the office.

At last something was going right.

"Are you still here?" Rowan growled at his brother. He wasn't in the mood for anyone's company, Scott's in particular.

"Don't worry, you've only got me for tonight. I'm flying to Melbourne tomorrow morning to watch the race and to see what I've bought." His brother eased back into the blue-and-tan abstract patterned lounger fitted against the bulkhead. The colors emphasized Scott's eyes and for a moment Rowan imagined his father sitting there with his feet on the coffee

table. His brother wore a scruffy pair of designer jeans, an ol
Aran sweater and he'd paid a million dollars for a horse, sigh
unseen.

It was like seeing him through fresh eyes. No wonder J
had taken one look at him and run. No wonder his mother ha
done the same to his father.

Rowan turned away. "I need a drink, do you want one?"

"No. Tonight I'm teetotal. Have to fly the Hughes up t
Auckland early tomorrow." Although Scott was licensed t
fly a helicopter and a twin-engine plane, it was part of wha
Rowan saw as an affectation, not to fly them himself unles
absolutely necessary.

"What happened to your pilot?"

"I gave him a week's leave. I didn't know about the hors
then."

Rowan poured himself two fingers of Cardhu malt, swal
lowing it down in one gulp, then he poured another.

"Hey, take it steady, brother." Scott's feet hit the floor an
he came over to the cabinet where Rowan stood tipping bacl
the second whiskey. He was shorter by a good four inches
slighter and dark where Rowan took after his mother. "Look
let's face it, Rowan, she wasn't for you. It would have bee
better all round if you'd let it go after the last disaster. I kno
what I'm talking about. Stick to your own kind. They know
the rules."

"I love Jo. And I'm going to have her, so mind your ow
damn business!" His glass hit the top of the cabinet with
clunk.

Scott picked it up and swiped at the damp ring with hi
sleeve. "You think I don't know what you're going through"
Well, my last disaster with a woman happened right here o
the *Fancy*. Would you believe I caught her piercing condom
with a needle! Yeah, I learned my lesson there. Always supply
your own."

Rowan just shook his head and headed for the galley. "Di
you bring anything to eat?"

"I've ordered pizzas."

"Well, I hope you ordered plenty. I could eat a horse. Even million-dollar one."

Scott laughed, sounding relieved.

Jo parked across the street from the inn. It was in darkness ut she'd be sure to find Molly in the kitchen. Apart from etty, she didn't appear to have many friends.

Walking through the alley separating the inn from its nearest eighbor, she approached quietly until a movement in the arkness told her she wasn't alone. "Who's there?"

"It's me, Detective Jo."

Ginny appeared in the light of the old yellowed fluorescent bes glowing through the high-barred kitchen windows. It ersonified what she'd come to believe about Rocky. He'd een all show up front, but weak on the inside where it ounted. Essentially he'd lacked the humanity needed to care r anyone other than himself. No wonder he hadn't been sur-ised someone could want to kill him.

"Hey, Ginny. Why are you hanging around the inn at this me of night? Is your mom working?"

"No, I wanted to speak to Molly. I wanted to say how sorry was about Mr. Skelton. I meant to come before, then I ought maybe Molly wouldn't be too happy about me seeing m naked and all that. It was terrible what they did to him, can't get it out of my head."

"All the more reason for not hanging around in the dark." y rights the kid should have gone for counseling, but the cilities just weren't available. She'd tried to tell Bull he ould bring someone in for Ginny and for Molly. With one ye on his budget, he'd laughed off her suggestions as another f her peculiar Auckland ideas. "Why didn't you go in?"

"Molly has a visitor. He got here just before me and I was ing to wait till he left."

"Well, I haven't got the time to hang around and I don't ink Molly will want to see anyone else after I've had a word ith her. I probably won't be long, so how 'bout I give you lift home? Your mom is probably worried sick."

"That'd be cool. I didn't fancy walking home in the dark

"You go wait by my car. I'll be as quick as I can."

Jo had come here on a hunch. Though it would take Molly collaboration to make it pay off. It would be interesting to s who was visiting her. Most likely the answer would be a pri or funeral director.

For maybe two seconds she had wondered if Molly w involved. A bit of putting two and two together, hoping come up with five. That would make life too easy. Besid she couldn't see someone Molly's size shifting Rocky on h own.

Then there was that business about her and Rocky trying have children. What a rat he'd been. A tweak at her amate psychologist's button suggested Molly's fetish for beauti crystal et al was simply compensation for being childless.

Amateur being the optimum word in that little analysis.

As Ginny's footsteps receded, Jo fished a small flashli out of her purse and swung the beam around as she walke The Dumpster was no more than twelve feet from the do but she could imagine it seeming a lot farther at one in t morning in the dark.

She knocked on the door then rang the bell for good me sure. As she waited she shone the pencil-thin blade of li overhead. The lamp above the door was broken. Trust Rocl His motto should have been, never put off till tomorrow wl you can do today, for tomorrow you might be dead.

She felt sorry for Molly. No wonder she placed such val on perfection. How had she and Rocky gotten together in t first place? They appeared to have very little in common.

Not like you and Rowan. She pushed the notion back whe it belonged in the dark recesses of her mind. Turned out th hadn't had as much in common as she'd thought.

What was Molly doing? Hadn't she heard the bell? She give it another ten seconds and she'd ring again.

"Who is it?" The door never budged and the voice sound far away as if coming from the end of a tunnel.

"Detective Jellic. Sorry to bother you, but I'll only take a minute of your time."

"Hold on then till I unlock the door."

Jo's eyebrows rose. Just who did Molly have in there that she needed to lock the door? A lover...nah, she couldn't see Molly jumping into bed with someone a couple days after Rocky had gotten murdered. Though she'd come across a few like that in the old days, up in Auckland.

The deadlock clicked and the door slid back. Molly had on a navy apron liberally streaked with flour.

Baking. She'd known Molly wasn't the type.

"Shut the door behind you." Molly flung the instruction over her shoulder and padded into the kitchen in a pair of pink slippers with fur trim. Without her heels there was nothing of her from back on. Compared to Jo, she'd always been small. Let's face it, who wasn't, yet tonight Molly appeared to have shrunk.

"You thinking of opening soon?" Jo asked, looking at the mixer tilted back with its dough hook pointing toward the ceiling. Folds of pastry sat in a square and a silver-colored rolling pin sat alongside. She hadn't known they made them in stainless steel, but then she wasn't much of a cook.

"I am, tomorrow as it happens. You know what they say. Needs must when the devil drives," said Molly, thumping the rolling pin down onto the pastry in a way that the nun who'd taught home ec said was sure to make it tough. And sure enough, Jo's attempts had always come out like leather.

Molly might also have picked a more politic saying for a woman whose husband had supposedly been killed by satanists. But then maybe she didn't believe that any more than Jo did.

"So what did you want?" Molly asked, breaking the silence that filled the spaces between the rhythmic thumps and swishes of turning pastry while Jo looked around the room.

Unless she'd hidden the guy under the table, they were the only two in the room. Jo said the first thing to come to her

mind, lowering her eyes to check. "Rowan assures me you
have your check very soon." No one there.

"I'm as likely to fall for a check's-in-the-mail story as I a
to believe in UFOs." The pastry received another few thump
"What do you want now, Sergeant? I have a lot of work ahea
of me. Nothing got done yesterday."

"I wanted to have a look at those magazines that were
the side of your bed."

"You mean you've come to bother me because you've r
out of reading material?"

"No, it's part of my investigation. Did Rocky swap any
his heavy-metal magazines?"

"Not that I know of." Molly wiped her hands on her apro
"Wait here, I'll get them for you. Don't want no strange
seeing my bed unmade."

An unmade bed? Now that she found hard to believe. Th
woman was a neat freak. For a moment she regretted askii
Ginny to wait by the car. She'd like to hang around outsic
to find out who was hiding in the back room. Lover...or a
complice? A shiver of unaccountable fear snaked up her spir
and curled into a tight knot at the base of her skull.

Phew! She huffed out the breath she'd been holding ar
tried to remember if the door had locked automatically behii
her. Damn, she hadn't brought her gun. All she had was th
small flashlight in her pocket. She'd been stupid to come
here alone. Rowan filled her mind in the few strides it took
circle the table on her way to the door. She'd never told hi
she loved him and now...now it might be too late.

All she could see was Rowan's face as he'd left her offi
that afternoon. A few more strides and she'd be out of here

Rowan. She needed to see Rowan.

Jo looked over her shoulder; she was in the clear.

Then she spied the knife block.

"Damned intuition," she cursed, but it didn't stop her fro
turning back.

The whole world stilled, holding its breath as she slid th
knife she wanted out of its slot.

There it was not an inch from the end. A rough nick in the blade where it had hit the mixer while she and Rowan watched Molly. The blade gleamed, catching the light as she eyed its size. Eight inches long, tapered point and two inches at the handle.

Spirits buoyant, she sang out, "Gotcha!"

The word barely sprang from her lips when the air around her thickened and quaked with tension as if its mass surged from Tane's Throat.

Jo stepped back into the dull *thunk* with its pain chaser. A black hole swallowed the cluster of stars exploding in front of her eyes, then she followed them down in a headlong dive with the knife still in her hand.

Chapter 15

Rowan couldn't remember Scott being as enthusiastic about anything as this horse. And that's what kept him in his seat listening, while his brother extolled his horse Winnatexal's virtues ad infinitum. For years all that had made him happy had been business. Racehorses at least had the distinction of being unpredictable—as opposed to money—and when Scott touched it, inevitably, the three of them became richer.

Scott had the Midas touch.

And Taine had the green thumb. His younger brother had always been the one who'd hung around old man Jackson while he worked in the garden and in two years he'd be bottling his first vintage.

So, what was *his* special gift?

Had the good fairies been on strike the day he was born?

He'd like to think they'd given him a loving heart, but maybe that only counted in Jo's favor. As sure as the sun would come up over Nicks Bay tomorrow, he knew he'd never love anyone the way he loved her. The knowledge crowded is chest until he could hardly breathe, thinking he would ever succeed in winning her.

So he listened to Scott's rambles, bloodlines, anything had) be preferable to his own pessimistic wanderings, drinking is fourth—or was it his fifth—scotch. He'd begun to mellow ut.

"You're not really paying attention, are you?"

It took him a few seconds to come out of the place his mind ad been drawn to. Despite his best endeavors to listen to his rother, he had his parents on his mind. "Why did you call iis boat after the first *Fancy*? Don't you feel it was somewhat rass?" The words, "even for you," hung in the air between iem.

"I did it as a memorial to Mom and Dad."

"And it didn't occur to you that Dad might have deliber-tely killed them both by sinking the original boat?"

"Hell, no!" The glass of soda in Scott's hand clattered onto ie table, slopping over onto the polished wood like an old loodstain. "Don't tell me you've been harboring that thought ll these years?"

Rowan nodded.

"God, man, why didn't you tell me? Why did you never ay?" Scott shook his head and chewed at his thumbnail with is elbow balanced on the table. "All this time and you never new how happy they were, but of course you didn't see them eave. Dad was all puffed up and full of himself and Mom lowed. It was as if they'd turned back the clock, in love again or the first time."

Scott seemed so certain, and God, Rowan wanted to be per-uaded, but he wasn't totally convinced. "Then how do you hink it happened out in the middle of nowhere?"

"I figure a foreign merchant ship probably wandered out of he shipping lanes and ran through them, so get any other hought out of your head. I console myself with the thought hat they were happy. That they were together. It's more than iost people get."

Rowan agreed. At least his parents had been togethe
Which brought to mind the night he'd almost died holding J

Darkness filled Jo's vision, filled her soul. She was col
Cold and alone. Damp bleeding from the bare earth seep
into her bones. Lying naked as the day she was born, sl
shivered, dreaming of warm clothes and cursed the inquisiti
wind that sought out every crevice in her body.

They'd tied her up with crime-scene tape. She wondered
whoever found her would see the irony in it.

Anyone with a skerrick of decency would have allowed h
at least one scrap of clothing, preferably her panties, sl
thought facetiously. Deadly laughter bubbled up under tl
duct tape strapping her mouth, nearly choking her. Sl
breathed furiously through her nose to clear her mind.

They said these situations brought out the best and the wor
in people, so she hoped to hell this was her best.

She refused to cry…or beg. Not that she could say mu
with her mouth bound, and she refused to let her eyes ple:
for her.

If anyone was to blame, it was herself. Taken out with
rolling pin. Damn!

What had been Molly's cri de coeur? "Needs must wh
the devil drives." She'd certainly put it to good use on Jo.

The youngest of the Smale brothers, Jeff had refused
meet her eyes as he carried her down the slope, and after
while she'd switched off, suffering the indignity of bei
trussed up like an oven-ready bird in a state of inertia.

The shakes had really begun when he'd dumped her in tl
middle of the crime scene. After that, it hadn't taken mu
figuring to guess Molly's intentions.

Having her skin touch the very ground where Rocky's bo
had lain until yesterday was kind of creepy, but she'd get ov
it. The knife through the heart could take longer to get us
to. The thought made her choke on a snort of laughter.

Was this a type of hysteria? All she had to do was keep
up and Molly would be redundant. She'd die laughing.

Stop it, you idiot!

Closing her eyes, she tried shifting her focus. Concentrate n Jeff. How had Molly tangled him up in a murder?

What drove his actions, apart from Molly's whiney, nagging oice? Guilt or fear? It had to be fear. Or money...oh yeah, at was it. His brother's bail money.

The guessing game made her brain hurt. There was a lo-omotive, all bells and whistles, inside her skull trying to get ut. No wonder her thought processes were stunted.

The site screen that had hid Rocky's body flapped and she rained to see if they'd come back. Too bad someone hadn't ought to remove the screen with the body. It gave them the erfect cover. No one passing by would even know she was ere. A pang of longing broke through the brave front she was igning. Did Rowan miss her?

She hoped so, yet she'd hate him to see her like this. Some-mes love just wasn't enough to wipe out the memories of is sort of abuse. She'd seen it time and time again in her ork...men turning away from their loved ones because that wful image simply wouldn't go away.

Even from her angle she wasn't a pretty sight.

That's why she'd been thankful that the boy's refusal to cknowledge her extended to turning away when Molly had read her out like a starfish, tying her hand and foot to the akes used for Rocky. If only Bull had pulled them up earlier, ke she'd asked, it might have slowed Molly and Jeff down me.

She tugged on her bonds to loosen them for what seemed ke the hundredth time since they'd gone and left her there.

Rowan shifted on the leather lounger, the envelope in his ack pocket rustling annoyingly, the way it had all evening. 'ith barely a glance at the franking mark from Rocky's bank e'd shoved it out of sight. Any information from the victim's ank manager seemed redundant. Let's face it, he'd been too ustrated by Jo flicking him off to be bothered.

As Scott disappeared in the direction of the galley, Row
fished the letter out of his pocket and tore the seal.

What the hell? Rocky had withdrawn fifty thousand dolla
in cash from his account, the day before he died. There w
something about the amount that rang a bell, but all the whi
key he'd drunk was taking its toll and he couldn't retrieve th
information from his dulled memory.

"Hey, you've got a visitor," Scott called up to the saloo
arriving with Ginny in tow.

The kid's face had gone into competition with her ha
Ginny puffed furiously and the infamous pink barrettes da
gled dangerously close to the ends of her curls.

"What's wrong, Ginny? You look done in. Take a seat a
get your breath back."

"I can't, I haven't time," she panted. "I didn't know whe
else to come, but Detective Jo told me you lived here so I r
all the way." She sucked in a breath. "They've got her."

"Who have they got?"

The answer spilled out in a long stream. "Jo. Detective J
She told me to wait and she would take me home but sh
never came back. I was standing in a shop doorway near h
car when this man came out and took it away. At first I thoug
he was stealing it, but he had the keys. Then I thought, I
wait 'cause Jo wouldn't forget me. She told me off for bei
on my own after dark and I was too frightened to go hom
but when they drove away in her car and the lights were o
at Molly's I had to tell someone."

She stopped for breath and Rowan asked, "What man?"

"I don't know. But Molly was in the car and the man w
driving. I couldn't see Jo."

"You should have gone to the police."

"No way. Have you seen that place, it's terrible. I've be
there twice and that Sergeant Bull scares me. But I knew yo
were Jo's babe, so I came to you."

Blinking at the description, Rowan grabbed his jacket fro
the end of the lounger, thrusting his arms into the sleeves.

"Did you see where they went?"

"Yes. They went up the hill heading out of town but they
uld have turned off anyplace. Do you think they've killed
r, too?"

Out of the mouth of babes, and he wasn't thinking of him-
f. Ginny had pushed the right button. "Get your coat on,
ott. You're driving."

"Me?"

"Yeah, I've been drinking, but luckily you haven't, and as
nny here can't drive, it's up to you," he said, keeping the
ne light to avoid scaring the kid any more than necessary.

On his way out, Rowan raked through the jumble of ex-
usted light sticks and ropes he'd dumped in the locker, and
and the flashlight. Seconds later he strode along the marina,
ll phone pressed to his ear, with Ginny and Scott hard on
heels.

"Harry, I need your help, Jo's in trouble. Abducted."

"Hell's bells! I should never have let her go to the inn on
r own. Rocky's fingerprint was on that anonymous letter she
t and the more I thought about it, the more peculiar it
unded."

"Damn you, Harry! If anything happens to her, you'll an-
er to me. But for now, get every man you can lay hands
and start searching for Jo's car. Ginny saw it head west
th Molly in the passenger seat with an unknown man driv-
;."

"What's this all about?" asked Scott.

"Jo received a threatening letter a few days ago and it looks
e they aim to make good on their promises."

"I don't see what I can do."

"You can stop being more of a self-centered ass than usual,
ott. This is the woman I love and if I'm in time, the woman
n going to marry. Got that?"

"Okay. I'll come with you. The mood you're in you could
something stupid...or worse...dangerous!"

The tape rubbed her skin raw. Still, she had to try. Maybe
e wouldn't go as far as chewing her hands off, like an animal

caught in a trap, but old Mother Nature preprogrammed her creatures pretty much the same way.

She gave a few more tugs. Did the stake securing her ri hand seem looser? Or was she imagining things?

What happened now? Were they just going to leave her h to be discovered by Bull or Jake in the morning? Gross!

She'd almost rather die....

No, she wouldn't...life had doubled back on itself a given her another chance with Rowan. Who was she to arg with gifts the gods were throwing her way? Love had sneak under her guard before she'd perfected ducking. And if s got another chance with Rowan, she was going to grab it w both hands.

She hadn't seen or heard either of her captors for a go five minutes. Maybe they had simply left her and made go on their escape in her car. Yet every time the plastic scre bellied out in the wind she tensed, expecting one of them return.

A sudden flash of light dazzled her. It traveled her f length, producing an urge to draw her knees up and hide h self. Humiliation ripped at her soul and frustration tighten the knots round her ankles as Molly laughed at her struggl

"You might as well give up. You won't budge th knots."

Jo clenched her fist, digging her nails into her palm. Insti made her want to thrash around like a snagged salmon, reason and pride told her to stay still.

"Bet you were hoping we'd gone." Her "Well, you w wrong" was almost gleeful. The woman had gone mad.

Why else would she kill her husband?

Why else would she have done this?

"The beauty of it is, we won't need to hide. No one w know it was us who left you here, because you'll dead...like Rocky. It's quite funny really. Rocky setting the scheme for his own murder...although his was really accident. Yours on the other hand..."

Hers had been a foolhardy attempt to get one up on B

nd the others while her mind had been on Rowan and not
e job.

"He only came up with the satanist idea to put you off the
cent. Didn't want you to know the fire was a warning from
e local drug baron for dipping his hand in the till too often.
it up to his elbows in laundered money. Too clever for his
wn good, that was Rocky. But he got you lot good. Sent you
hasing all over the countryside, searching for a gang of devil
vorshipers. And all the time Satan was doing business right
nder your nose."

Jo caught a maniacal note in the laughter that followed. The
erie sound took over where the dampness left off and she
ouldn't hide her shivering any longer.

"And do you know what's really funny?"

A sly malevolence twisted Molly's lips.

"It was you arriving in Nicks Landing that gave him the
lea. The inn wasn't making as much money as he'd hoped.
Molly,' he said, 'if Milo Jellic could make money out of
annabis, so can I.' Of course he went too far. They always
o, criminals. Rocky used to say that's what caught them in
e end. A pity he didn't listen to his own advice."

Jo closed her eyes, wishing she could do the same with her
ars. Her father had never dealt in drugs.

Never!

She refused to believe Molly. To do so, would confirm her
vhole life had been based on a lie.

Molly began pacing, muttering under her breath, until Jeff
male turned up. "Here you are," he said to Molly, handing
omething over. "That's your last from me. Rocky was an
ccident but this is cold-blooded murder and I'm not having
ny more to do with it. You've had your money's worth."

"Yeah, go on then, take the money and run. Who needs
ou?" she called after his retreating figure, the need for silence
pparently forgotten in her madness. "Don't know what
ou're worried about. It'll be a lot easier than that little bull
alf."

The widow started to laugh and the beam from the flashlight

in her hand did a crazy dance among the trees. "I heard y⟨
found the heart, give you a start did it?"

Hope of discovery died as the light hit her from grou⟨
level. Molly set it to shine across Jo's naked breasts.

Tensing, the cold-induced shudders paused as her mind pe⟨
ceived the reason for this new departure. Its conclusio⟨
weren't happiness inducing. As she watched, Molly pulled t⟨
top off the black felt-tip pen Jeff had given her and knelt ⟨
Jo's right-hand side.

The pen pressed into her skin, releasing a sharp inky tan⟨
while Jo continued her gentle, yet persistent assault on t⟨
stake behind the artist's back listening to Molly *tsk* under h⟨
breath as she worked. Knowing Molly's need for perfectio⟨
was it perverse to feel delighted at the difficulty the wido⟨
was experiencing? Drawing a pentagram onto Jo's breasts ⟨
the region of her heart was no easy task, despite the natur⟨
attempt of gravity to flatten them.

Take your time…take your time. The words ran like a litan⟨
in her brain as, with every tug on her bindings, Jo kept up t⟨
rhythm.

Sitting back on her heels Molly sighed, her frown mad⟨
horrific by the cast of the light. "Don't think I take any ple⟨
sure in this work, but you forced me into it."

What? Molly developing a conscience? Funny, that fact ha⟨
escaped Jo. Maybe it was the intent way the widow was goin⟨
about her business. She squinted down the length of her nos⟨
expelling a sharp burst of air. The pentagram still wasn't fin⟨
ished.

"It all started as a way to frighten Rocky, first the calf the⟨
the letters. If I hadn't caught your remark to Rowan in m⟨
kitchen, none of this might have happened. Hell, that rankle⟨
All those fertility tests I suffered. All for nothing. Is it an⟨
wonder I wanted to pay him back?"

Molly began to laugh. "You should have seen his fac⟨
when the letter arrived and then the house…boom! Huh,⟨
wasn't worth saving anyway. But it sure made Rocky thin⟨

here was some sort of cult out to get him. Just for once, the
worm turned.''

Pen poised, Molly bent over Jo's recumbent body once
more. "Hold your breath," she ordered.

You must be joking. Jo started to pant, and kept it up for a
while even though her head spun.

"C'mon, give in gracefully. You're only prolonging the inevitable. And don't think Jeff is likely to arrive with the cav-
alry. For all his belated bout of conscience he hated Rocky as
much as I grew to. The Smales worked with him, growing
cannabis, but when it came to getting his help...well, let's say
he lived up to his name. You can't get blood out a stone.''

Molly burst into another fit of laughter.

A small reprieve. Jo sent up a prayer. Surely someone must
hear Molly's cackling.

"Yet, I managed it. There wasn't that much blood, though.
He just dropped where he stood, in the middle of the kitchen
by Jeff's feet. Huh, Jeff got his money, but I made him work
for it.

"I hadn't intended killing Rocky, but he made me so angry.
Slapped me around and called me a hysterical slut when I
asked him about the vasectomy. In a way he deserved it for
killing all my babies." Wiping her eyes on her apron Molly
released a miniature snow storm of flour. Glistening in the
beam of the flashlight the small white flecks floated onto Jo.

Was there a chance some might remain on her skin? Surely
forensics would pounce on that as a clue. Moira could tell
them she never baked...couldn't bake.

Reaction to the wayward thought set in immediately and
drained the fight out of her. Her optimism had sunk to an all-
time low if she was calculating evidence that might lead to
her killer.

Molly twisted the knife so the moonlight bounced off the
blade. "Like your old man, you were too clever for your own
good. Now I have to kill you...don't worry, I won't make a
hash of it. You've no idea how easily this knife slides through
flesh.''

And I don't want to know!

Jo's stomach churned. She swallowed hard. If she threw up behind this tape, Molly wouldn't need the knife.

"Harry, we've found Jo's car. It's at the top end of the park near the crime scene. Let your people know, but warn them against using the sirens."

"I'll be with you in under five minutes. Don't go in alone."

"I'm not alone, I've got Scott with me, and five minutes might be too late. By the way, Ginny's in my car, let her mother know she's okay, but for God's sake don't frighten the kid when you arrive."

Rowan closed his cell phone and told Ginny, "I want you to promise you'll stay in the car. You remember Sergeant Jackson, he'll get someone to take you home."

"But I have to know if Jo's okay."

"She will be, don't worry, you can see her tomorrow," he said, praying he'd be able to make good on his promise, praying he wasn't too late to save her this time. "Right, Scott. This is how we'll do it." Even as he told Scott what he expected of him, his mind drifted. He'd wondered about this moment. Wondered, knowing how it could end, if real danger awaited could he meet it head-on? Only time would tell and there wasn't much of it left.

"There's two of them up there. Molly's a little woman. You tackle her, and I'll take out the man."

They had to fight their way through a tangle of rhododendrons. Good for keeping cover but hard on the hands and face. Most of the park was planted in English trees. An idea of one of his ancestors who'd still had sentimental ties with the old country and had called England *back home*.

A branch snapped and a curse singed his ears. Scott. "Listen," Rowan hissed. "If you can't keep quiet, go back. You're putting Jo's life in danger."

"No way. I'm not leaving you to do this on your own."

The noise lessened as Scott took more care. "I always won

red why you chose this life, Rowan, but it's exciting in its
'n way. Like watching your stock rise on the trading index.''

Rowan shook his head. God help him, he'd never under-
nd his brother. "C'mon, no more talking.''

He could see a beam of light through the trees farther down
: slope and trod even more carefully, edging closer with
ott rustling lightly at the rear. Then he heard Molly's high-
ched voice as he moved a branch out of his face and caught
: first glimpse of Jo.

Hell!

His heart tumbled over at the sight of his woman spread-
gled naked on the ground in a weird parody of the vision
'd had in the witch's circle. This time it brought no lustful
ughts to mind. Only terror. Molly, knife in hand, knelt be-
e Jo, side on to the slope where he and Scott hid.

Not only would she see him the moment he broke cover,
:'d probably hear him break into the crime scene.

Everything happened at once.

In a crash of limbs, both tree and human, Scott blasted the
llness apart and set everything in motion. A host of impres-
ns rather than clear-sighted action took over.

Scott: "Damn! I've broken my ankle.''

Molly's small face twisted. A grimace etched with anger.
r once-pretty blue eyes burning with animalistic fear, know-
; she was cornered.

Jo's faith in him beaming from her eyes as he burst out of
: shrubbery into an arena, where the game of the day was
: or death.

There was no sighting of the man as Rowan ran, his legs
e lead, dragging, holding him back. Seconds dragged into
urs.

The knife lifted in Molly's hand.

He threw himself across Jo's supine body and caught Molly
ind the middle. She came down over his shoulder, thumping
ainst his ribs, cracking one. The pain a dull heavy ache in
back.

He'd felt worse.

Jo's arm curved in an arc pulling out the stake she was t
to and Molly slumped as the wooden point came down on
head.

A thunder of footsteps announced Harry's arrival. The ot
police couldn't be far behind. Rowan pushed Molly aside a
braced himself on one hand, pushing up so his weight did
crush Jo. Her skin felt icy cold as he turned to reassure
with a smile. "Couldn't wait to even the score, could y
You're one helluva woman, Jo Jellic."

He'd wanted to reassure her, but his words failed to w
the dull bleakness from her eyes. "Somebody find me a bl
ket," he called.

His voice sounded strange to his ears. Was it the shock
another near-death experience? Jo's this time.

He could hear Molly crying as she came round and Ha
wrestled her away from them into the arms of Seth McAllis
The widow deserved all Harry dished out, after what sh
done.

Nothing mattered now except Jo.

Scott's cursing drew a shrug of annoyance that hurt his ri
He wished he'd stop moaning and calling out to him. W
couldn't his brother think of someone other than himself
once? He hated to think that all his brother's money
leached away his humanity.

So what if a sprained ankle meant he missed a horse ra
There was always next year. And all the years that came af

That's what he wanted now, year after year, for himself,
Jo. All the years ahead together.

"We'll have to stop meeting like this," he said and beg
to laugh. Jo didn't seem to see the funny side. Her gaze dar
past his face to somewhere beyond him. He twisted his sho
ders and caught an earful of Scott cursing. "Get this tape
Jo's mouth," he said as his brother gripped his shoulder.

The pain made him feel nauseous. "What the hell are y
doing?" Then he noticed Jo bleeding. A bright red stream
across her breast. "Call an ambulance, quick...Jo's h
Molly must have nicked her with the knife."

Her head lifted as a stream of tortured mumbling boiled up
hind the tape. The world spun out of control as he reached
it to free her. Then he heard Scott say, "I've got it."

An ugly gurgling sound filled his ears, like someone sucking
the dregs in a glass through a straw. The noise took his
eath away as his hand dropped onto Jo's breast, blood spill-
g over his fingers. Someone ought to do something about it.
That was his last thought.

Frustration screamed in Jo's head and with it the word, *"Id-
t!"* But Scott Stanhope couldn't hear her. No one could.
ie'd tried to signal with her eyes. It had made no difference
d her heart had leaped under her ribs as he'd limped up
hind Rowan and pulled the knife from his back.

How could two such different men be brothers?

Rowan's weight was fully on her, his hand heavy on her
east. There was no tenderness in his touch now. No love.
nly the mockery of what might have been. What they might
ve shared.

She wanted to scream, but all she could do was pray. Pray
meone would realize what was wrong with Rowan.

He needed help badly. Scott had done the exact opposite of
e recommended procedure. Puncture wounds should be dealt
ith by a professional. And Lord help him, the fool had col-
psed beside Rowan, moaning about a broken ankle, instead
covering the sucking wound with plastic to seal it.

If it wasn't so damn tragic it would be funny.

She'd never associated Rowan's sophisticated brother with
ipstick, but now she would never see him any other way.

She'd never forget the sight of blood frothing over Rowan's
os while he tried to make light of the situation. It was just
:e him to think of her before himself. She sniffed.

Somebody better get this tape off her mouth soon, or she'd
own in her own tears. Suddenly she had everything to live
r. But only if Rowan survived.

Chapter 16

The pale peach monolith that was Auckland Central survey the city from its bastion of autumn-hued, scoria block work

Jo looked down on the view from the fifth floor, corn window of Detective Inspector Mike Henare's office, sighin She'd come home.

"Well, does it live up to your memories?"

Jo looked over her shoulder as the DI's well-remember rumble filled the space behind her. He was a huge man, barre chested, deep voiced, and his word was law in the homici division. He was the man who'd sent her away from Aucklan and the one who'd brought her back. And for that she cou kiss him, but wouldn't ever dare to attempt turning the thoug into action.

She left the window and folded her long legs into a cha opposite Henare. "I notice a few changes, but all-n-all it's j the same, except for all the colored lights and bunting. Ho estly boss, you shouldn't have bothered."

"Count yourself lucky. If you'd left it another four wee I'd have had to take them down again."

Jo grinned. "Yeah, like you don't enjoy Christmas. My memory isn't that short," she said, remembering Henare's light green eyes twinkling over a white Santa beard.

"Talking about which, according to your last medical you need to give it till after New Year to resume work. Pneumonia is no laughing matter."

"It was only a chill," she protested. So how come her memories of the cold leaching out of the earth and into her bones made her want to shiver?

And the memory of Rowan, shielding her while he bled from a knife wound, made her want to cry?

"That's not what the Doc says."

Jo acknowledged the truth with a slight nod. She knew better than to argue when Henare used that tone.

He stood up, indicating their talk was over, and held out his hand. "Give it until those Christmas lights come down, to return to work. I want you fighting fit."

Taking her dismissal on the chin, Jo shook his hand and said, "Goodbye."

She'd barely reached the office door, before he called out after her. "You seen McQuaid yet?"

The question took her straight to a place she didn't want to be, at least not yet. "No. I wanted to get settled first."

His eyes narrowed and he speared her with a no-nonsense look. "Don't leave it too late."

Dear Lord, what did Henare know that she didn't?

Scott Stanhope had assured her Rowan had made an excellent recovery. McQuaid's elder brother wasn't nearly so bad once she'd gotten to know him, in fact, he'd gone out of his way to help her. One thing she'd learned, Scott would do anything for his brother. He'd had Rowan on his way to Auckland by air ambulance before her icy cold body had slid between the crisp hospital sheets.

And Scott had visited her often, hobbling into her room on crutches to keep her informed of Rowan's progress.

Keeping her eyes on Henare, she nodded, pulling the door closed behind her. "Maybe I'll go see him tonight."

Eight o'clock already. The sun slid down the blue wall of sky, bursting into a blaze of pink as it hit the horizon, long before Jo was ready to face Rowan. She couldn't leave it too much later and then simply turn up at his door.

Yeah, she could have called ahead, but that would have narrowed her options. Right at the moment, she could still turn tail and run.

At least that's what she told herself looking into the foyer from where she stood on the sidewalk outside the golden-beige Quay West serviced apartment block.

Slowly, ever so slowly, she released a thin stream of air between her pursed lips, then moistened them, swallowing quickly, remembering the trouble she'd taken to get her lipstick just right.

To get everything just right.

Jo looked down at her new red suit, wishing she felt as confident inside as she did out. She'd lost a little weight. Would Rowan notice?

He hasn't got a show of noticing unless you go inside.

Ten steps took her into the foyer. She knew because she counted them. It was easier than concentrating on the purpose of her visit, the reason that had brought her here.

The foyer reminded her of the great hall of a manor house she'd seen in some magazine, with wide stairs rising from a sea of marble before branching in two at second floor level. Minus the reception desk, of course. Jo noticed that it didn't take a second for the rail-thin receptionist, hair scraped back tight enough for a face-lift, to home in with her laser-like gaze.

Tossing her freshly shampooed hair, Jo targeted the lifts as if she owned the place, though her normal stride was hampered by the tight cut of her skirt. Pleased to reach her destination without a break in the rhythm of her three-inch heels, she swiped the key card Scott had given her for Rowan's floor and waited.

And waited, conscious of her tapping toes, upping the beat to match her heart rate, taking it faster, beyond impatient and

to nervy. The lift doors yawned open and her stomach turned
ver as she caught her reflection in the mirrored interior.

Too late to back out now.

In hindsight, rehearsing first might have been considered a
iser move, except she didn't have the words, only the feel-
gs. Every time she tried shaping her thoughts into meaning-
l phrases, her emotions overtook logic and threatened to
oke her.

The way they were now.

One floor from the top the lift stopped and she got out. Scott
d given her directions. "Turn left and the door will be fac-
g you." He hadn't told her that the corridor was a mile long
that the lush pile of the carpet would silence each footfall,
aving her alone with her thoughts.

What did you say to a man who had saved your life not
ce, but twice? A man who'd claimed to love her.

A man she'd flicked off because of a silly thing like a name.

She faced the door, acknowledging that in this ambience the
rson living behind the carved door would inevitably be more
tanhope than McQuaid.

When it finally opened she was positive.

Rowan was dressed to go out.

Why else the black tuxedo that fit like a glove over white
irt and black tie? And the toffee streaks of hair she'd twisted
und her fingers were now short and sleekly styled, not
opped. Had he ever looked so handsome, so relaxed, so at
se with his body? So much like a man who hadn't missed
r?

Wearing heels had always brought her eyes level with his,
aking them easier to read. The message tonight read, "Sur-
ise," with more than a dash of hesitation.

Oh, hell, what if he wasn't alone? Her impulsive plan hadn't
ken that into account.

Then Rowan's white smile curled around her senses, turning
r knees to water and her heart to mush. If she needed proof
at she loved him, it was there in the soft, womanly, warm

response he dredged up from her soul. And in the nervo◗
conclusion that she was definitely the wrong woman for hir◗

Yet, she knew with certainty that above all others, Rowa◗
was the one person who deserved the truth.

Rowan took in every detail, from the top of her gleamin◗
hair to the tips of her toes and widened his smile. "Jo, yo◗
look wonderful."

"You, too, Rowan. Scott told me you were well again, b◗
I'd visions of you looking wan, but interesting."

"I heal quick. Scott owns the top floor and I've made u◗
of his roof garden." He stood back as it dawned on him, the◗
were still in the doorway. "C'mon in. Would you like ◗
drink?"

Jo took a step, then hesitated. "But you're going som◗
where."

He looked down at his bow tie, pulling on the end to loose◗
it. "Business. It wasn't important, I was filling in for Sco◗
but I'm a poor substitute for my brother when it comes ◗
social functions."

She moved into the small foyer, her scent reaching out ◗
pull at his senses. He searched his memory to recall if he◗
ever mentioned how much he loved her in red. As if me◗
merized, he gripped the edge of the door as she passed, pra◗
ing she'd worn the suit molding her breasts to awaken men◗
ories of his own journey in that hauntingly familiar territor◗

Praying this visit meant she'd changed her mind about hir◗
forgiven his deception, he joined her on the step down to t◗
living room. Rowan signaled the direction with one hand, u◗
nerved by her silence. "Grab a chair." He brushed the bac◗
of his knuckles against her arm and felt her steely tensio◗
under the fine silky fabric. "Would you like a drink?" ◗
repeated.

She nodded. "Scotch."

Although he'd said "chair," sofa was what he'd had ◗
mind, and disappointment was uppermost in his mind as ◗
returned with the drinks to find she'd chosen a high-back wi◗
chair facing the large, comfortable four-seater.

She looked up as he drew near, her legs crossed and her ankle swinging in front, making a barrier of her pointed-toe toe.

Her mouth pulled back in a one-sided travesty of a smile he stretched out toward her with one of the glasses.

"There's something I have to tell you," she said, forcing ut the words.

"You're pregnant," he barked louder than intended, caught y the surprise at hoping it was true, realizing he'd snatch at y chance to bind her to him. Quickly, he pulled back the ass. "Pregnant women shouldn't drink alcohol."

Jo didn't look up to answer, she was too busy wiping spilled hiskey from her stocking. "I'm not pregnant. How could I e, we always used protection."

Rowan sighed. Too bad.

Of course, Jo hadn't heard the story of Scott's girlfriend uncturing condoms with a needle. It would be just like Scott leave them lying around. He passed over Jo's drink, then lanced at the sofa. It looked a million miles away from where e wanted to be, so he chose the corner of the coffee table istead. "Okay, go ahead, I'm all ears."

"First of all, I want to apologize for blowing up at you ecause of your name. When I was lying in the hospital I alized how—"

"Hell! I never even asked how you were."

"It's no biggie. I feel pretty good. Henare has other ideas, ough. He won't let me work until two weeks after New Year. hat's another thing, they've let me come back to Auckland, ss harmful for our friends in Nicks Landing. Bull seems to ink I attract danger, and I'd be safer in Auckland."

God, that was what he wanted, too, Jo to be safe. Eyes losed, he let memory and emotion overtake him. Jo spread-agled on the dirt and Molly's knife poised to strike. He never vanted to live through another moment like that. If he had his vay, he'd pick her up in his arms and carry her somewhere, nywhere, away from harm. Yet, even as his mind gave voice

to the protective emotion, he knew she wouldn't thank hi
for it.

Loving Jo meant accepting her, gun, handcuffs and all. H
knew what it was to have a life-shaping decision taken out
your hands, and though he was content now...

My God, he was content, all he needed was Jo to make h
life complete. The realization stunned him. The yearning to l
a cop again had disappeared along with his reluctance to con
mit, to love.

For years he'd let Scott take all the responsibility for th
company, staying on the fringes and letting the money pile u
in the bank while he did nothing to earn it. But that ha
changed. He laughed inwardly, imagining Scott saying, "N
before time."

Opening his eyes, he faced Jo and took in the luminou
brown of her irises and her quivering bottom lip as if she fe
vulnerable by being shut out of his thoughts. "You're a goo
cop, Jo, and Henare's lucky to have you. I guess he was caug
between a rock and a hard place after our first little contre
temps."

"Don't you stick up for him. I can't keep up with the ma
One, I almost get you killed and he sends me away. Two,
almost get you killed and he brings me home."

She stopped midbreath and he knew the exact moment th
truth hit her. "You did it. You went and told him what reall
happened that first time. You told him about Max."

"You saved his life."

"I told you I wouldn't make excuses for myself."

He took her untouched drink from her fingers and replace
it with his hand. "You didn't say I couldn't."

She swallowed, hard, and let out a deep breath. "Guess th
puts you ahead of the game."

"Adding up the points again? Haven't I told you there's n
such thing as a score when it comes to you and me, peaches?"

God, he was good. With that one word, "peaches," he g
straight through to her heart, tangling her determination wit
her emotions. With the love she felt for him. It wasn't fai

en she knew she would have to leave once she told him
truth. All she wanted to do was put things right between
m first.

"If you must keep score, how about evening things up by
ing you'll marry me?"

How did he do that? How could he do that?

Rowan had no idea that he was tying her heart in knots.
e lump in her larynx threatened to choke her. Her response
bed her throat raw as she forced her words past the baseball
t had lodged there.

"You might want to reconsider the offer when you hear
at I have to say. I've come here to give you the truth. It's
nething I've prized most of my life, something my father
ght me on his knee. The trouble with that is, on the night
lly abducted me, I found out that the code I've lived
…all that I am, has been based on a lie."

Rowan got down on his knees in front of her chair. Anxiety
itten all over his expression. "Hush now. Nothing you can
√ will change my mind."

Oh Lord, she was going to cry. But first she had to tell him
e truth. "Molly told me my father *really had* been dealing
drugs, and Rocky had gotten the idea for growing cannabis
en he discovered my identity."

Rowan leaned closer, staring deep into her eyes.

His blazed with a declaration of love.

His said they wouldn't take no for an answer, but she
uldn't let him do it. She'd almost ruined his life once, and
e refused to do it again.

"Your explanation doesn't hold water, peaches. I knew all
s before. You told me yourself."

"Dammit, Rowan! You don't get it. You just don't get it."
e gripped him by the shoulder, needing to force him to
lieve. "I didn't know the truth about my father, before. I
lieved it was all lies. And that's why I can't marry you.
ur family is one of the richest in New Zealand and I'm the
ughter of a drug dealer," she finished, then did something

she'd done maybe three times since the day she found out I
father was dead—burst into tears.

Rowan pulled her down off the chair and into his lap, ho
ing her tight in his arms as if he could soak up all her pa
He knew from her sobs that simply holding her wasn't goi
to work. Somehow he had to find the right words.

"As long as I've known you, Jo, you've been hung up abc
truth. I've seen other cops laugh at you for refusing to be
your beliefs, even slightly. And no matter what your fatl
did, or maybe because of it, you became a damn good cc
One of the best I've worked with. Being in love with you ev
two years ago, doesn't mean I was prejudiced in your fav
Well, maybe a little bit. But I wasn't blind. You did a gr
job."

Jo shuddered and he found its echo deep in his chest. S
calmed down to a few hiccups, gulping air in between. H
fingers slid under his coat front and he felt their trembli
warmth through his shirt. Then she whispered, "Did you me
that? Did you really love me way back when?"

He placed soft crooning kisses across her brow and her ey
lids and breathed her in, filling himself with her essence.

"Even then. And now I'm going to tell you a truth abc
love that is indisputable. The heart has no defense against
We didn't choose to fall in love, our hearts did it for us, a
who are we to question what lies in our hearts?"

"I do love you."

"I know. That's why I can't let you go, I'm not that mu
of a fool." *Not any longer.* "If you can love a man who li
to you, albeit by omission, I can love the daughter of the m
we're going to prove was framed by Rocky."

She tightened her grip on him, pulling him close enough
feel her heart race. "Will you accept a heartfelt apology?
first, I kept you in the dark because I was scared Skelton wou
get wind of it."

"You mean, me and my big mouth?" Her tone was w
with self-knowledge. And he knew what it cost her.

"I love what you can do with that mouth," he said, placi

lips over hers for a short demonstration. "Afterwards,
en you were so honest with me I cursed my own ineptitude.
wardice was what held me back. The fear that I'd lose
u..." He didn't have to say, "The way I did."

But Jo had more important matters in mind. He held her
ay slightly, missing her warmth immediately, then looked
wn, as one by one, his dress studs began to disappear from
e front of his shirt. Her palm pressed against his chest above
s heart and set it pounding so hard he felt it might leap
aight into her hands. Right where he wanted it, where he'd
anted to place it for so long.

After a few moments of absolute bliss, Jo tilted her head
to his shoulder. He liked the invitation he read in her eyes
d caught his mouth with hers, widening all the known par-
neters of rapture as she let him finish what she'd started.

A sigh took Jo into a realm of wonder.

Oh...*this* was love...what else could it be?

With his hands forked through her hair, he held her head
ll, just studying her face. His hands slid over her back and
ps, yet he held her with his eyes. "When I think of what
olly tried to do... She was the real devil of the piece."

His body trembled with emotions and the only way to ap-
ase them, was claiming her lips in a swift, harsh kiss filled
th passion's promise.

Chest heaving, he broke away and said, "It never occurred
you that Molly might have told you all that about your
ther simply to hurt you? I've tried to reason it out. In the
d she hated Rocky for what he'd done, depriving her of a
mily. And she hated you for being the messenger, for know-
g how he'd humiliated her."

Leaning forward, he placed a kiss over the spot where her
lm rested, feeling his heart jolt. Loving meant placing your
wer in another's hands, but Rowan's generosity, the way
'd tried to reassure her and give her back her self-
nfidence, proved her trust in him wasn't misplaced.

"You no longer have to worry about me anymore. My fa-
er gave me the first twelve years of my life and I gave him

the next eighteen. Whatever he did or didn't do, the decisic were his, not mine. Now it's time for me…for us.''

She slid her hand up round his neck and caressed his na until he shuddered against her. The physical evidence of I desire burned like a fire against her hip. ''Rowan,'' she wh pered, with a pout of her lips, ''take me to bed.''

The effect was spoiled slightly by her squeals as he ro still holding her in his arms, and carried her down the hall his room, kicking the door aside, too impatient to let her op it for him.

Rowan placed her in the center of the large, soft-gr comforter covering the bed with its carved teak headboa Quickly, he shucked off his shoes and peeled back her jack holding his breath as a matching red teddy came into vie making all his fantasies come to fruition.

His mouth explored the curve of her breasts, tracing the la as he slid her arms out of her jacket and tossed it on the flo

She spread the opening of his shirt apart, baring his che touching him lightly with her fingertips as if she couldn't k lieve he was real…the situation was real.

Then she repeated his grand gesture and slid his tuxe jacket off, slapping it down on top of hers, as if to say ''snap That woman just couldn't stop keeping score, but before t night was over, he intended batting a thousand.

He took care of his shirt himself, reserving the right to x move the rest of Jo's clothing. Working from top to botto he used all the sensual skills at his command.

Every nerve in her body hummed. She felt like a sighir quivering instrument only Rowan knew how to tune, how play.

At last he released her and stripped off the rest of I clothes. Her heart tightened at the knowledge that the ma nificent male specimen before her couldn't hide his need f her. His sex stood to attention, obvious and unrepentant.

Rowan. This man who was going to be hers to have and hold…till death.

Quickly, she made a vow never to get into a situation that
t his life at risk again.

Sliding onto the bed, he reached out for her. Then stilled,
zing upon beauty. Upon the woman in his arms. His hand
mbled as one calloused fingertip knew the velvet softness
her cheek.

This was real.

This was true.

Rowan brushed his lips across the full red pout of hers.

This was it.

He was simply a man holding the woman he loved.

Who loved him right back.

Epilogue

The sun burned into Jo's back as she sat outside a restaura[nt] on the edge of Auckland's Viaduct harbor. It soaked into h[er] bones, making her want to stretch like a lazy cat. A content[ed] cat. A cat who'd gotten the cream.

And no wonder. In the week since she'd moved in wi[th] Rowan, they'd made love endlessly. Exploring each other['s] sensual psyches couldn't be done overnight, at least that w[as] her excuse.

It hadn't prevented Rowan arranging a hurried wedding [for] Christmas Eve, or planning a honeymoon aboard the *Fanc[y]*. Warmth flushed her skin, remembering his reasoning. ''I'[m] taking no chances on you escaping, peaches. This is a li[fe] sentence.'' For both of them. They'd each captured the other['s] heart.

She expected Rowan to arrive any moment. Her skin pric[k]led with anticipation, her smile bordering on sensual. T[oo] caught up in personal romantic flights she didn't notice t[he] interested glances from passing males. There was no two-no[te] whistle from Ginny to alert her today. Besides, she had h[er]

vn one-hundred-percent babe, proof in the sparkling two-
rat diamond he'd given her.

As she lifted her glass of ice water to moisten her parched
oat, a gruff whisper asked, "Starting without me?"

Her pulse stuttered at the sound of his voice but you
uldn't tell from her reply. "I don't like to play alone." She
aned herself. "I'd been thinking of you and needed cooling
wn."

Rowan's chest swelled, molding his white T-shirt to it and
ough his eyes narrowed she could read, "Wanna go home
d make love?" in them. So, she was surprised when he sat
wn opposite her, sliding a thick, sealed envelope in her di-
ction.

She looked at it, puzzled. All the dry legal forms expected
fore a marriage had been signed and delivered. "What's
is?"

"Wedding present. Open it."

A note in his voice indicated this wouldn't be fun. Trying
t to let her anxiety show, she ripped the envelope open with
great show of finesse, then scanned the papers she found.
ames, dates of service, details of trials and sentences given.
ıh?

Returning to the top page, she said, "These men? They
ere cops at the same time as my father." His head moved
ghtly in acknowledgement. "And these." She pushed the
pers under his nose. "These were cases that involved my
ther."

She read on. "I recognize this name, Jurgens, Carl, a scum-
g drug dealer. My father gave evidence at his trial. I re-
ember him being angry because he thought Rocky had
own it for them, but it seems Jurgens ended up in Paremo-
no anyway."

"He got twenty years and did fifteen."

"So, he's out?"

"Three years ago. Guess where he lives now?" Without
uiting for an answer he said, "He's on a farm near Young

Nicks Head. Hell, it's barely fifty kilometers from Nicks La⬛ ing.''

"Molly's drug baron."

"I'd lay odds on it. What's the betting Skelton's swift sl⬛ into anonymity was hastened by your father's death? That ⬛ might even have had a hand in it, after his failure to get J⬛ gens off by bungling his evidence. Skelton's the type w⬛ would have done anything to save his own neck. Look at ⬛ dance he led us.

"Another thing, I checked Jurgens's background. The g⬛ had a sister married to a man named Smale."

"Oh, my Lord. Jeff Smale got away, but the two broth⬛ had their bail rescinded. They're under lock and key at G⬛ borne.''

"Then we start with the Smales." His brows twitched. "⬛ not until after the honeymoon. They'll have to keep awh⬛ longer."

She looked at him with love and reached for his ha⬛ Rowan's strength flowed from him to her. "That's the m⬛ wonderful gift you could have given me. But how did y⬛ manage to get it all?" She looked down at the papers litter⬛ the table. "I tried for years but couldn't get anywhere."

"My name still has some pull."

"What, Stanhope?"

"No. *McQuaid.*"

*   *   *   *   *

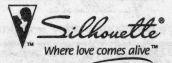

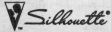

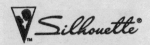
Silhouette®

COMING NEXT MONTH

#1171 THE WAY TO YESTERDAY—Sharon Sala

Mary Faith O'Rourke lost everything when her husband and infant daughter died in a car crash outside their Savannah home. For years Mary felt responsible. She longed for a second chance, and when fate led her to a ring with mysterious powers, she thought she'd found one. But had her dream actually come true, or was the real nightmare just beginning?

#1172 A ROYAL MURDER—Lyn Stone

Romancing the Crown

When Nina Caruso learned that her half brother, Desmond, had been killed, she headed for the kingdom of Montebello to see that justice was done. She expected opposition but not the rugged royal P.I. Ryan McDonough. Nina needed Ryan to discover the troubling truths behind Desmond's death, while Ryan needed Nina for more personal reasons....

#1173 ALL THE WAY—Beverly Bird

Race car driver Hunter Hawk-Cole had always loved life on the edge. He'd never planned on becoming the quiet family man that Olivia Slade was looking for. But when Hunter found out Liv had lied about having his child, his plans changed. Now he was fighting for something he'd never known he wanted—and this time he wasn't going to walk away.

#1174 LAURA AND THE LAWMAN—Shelley Cooper

To nab auction house owner and drug kingpin Joseph Merrill, police officer Laura Langley masqueraded as Ruby O'Toole, a flirtatious art appraiser who soon caught the eye of auctioneer Michael Corsi. But mysterious Michael had secrets of his own. And Laura knew that, in addition to her identity, she had to mask her explosive attraction to him.

#1175 GRAYSON'S SURRENDER—Catherine Mann

Wingman Warriors

Air Force flight surgeon Grayson Clark and social worker Lori Rutledge were destined for heartbreak. She wanted a family, but he wasn't the settling-down type, so when a rescue operation to an overseas orphanage reunited them, Gray had plenty of reasons for them to stay apart. But there was one important reason why they had to be together....

#1176 BEHIND ENEMY LINES—Cindy Dees

Special Forces commander Tom Folly owed his life to Air Force captain Annie O'Donnell, who tended to his injuries and posed as his wife to escape an enemy attack. Living in such close proximity made their sizzling attraction impossible to ignore. But Annie had a secret, and once Tom learned the truth, he would face his toughest battle yet.

SIMCNM08

MY 20–20 PLEDGE TO YOU

In health there are no absolute guarantees. But by following the twenty-plus specific health counsels in these pages, I can assure you that:

- You will be following the best, most scientifically sound attempt you can make at present to stay younger, longer.

- You will find them practical, real, and do-able.

- By following these steps for twenty weeks, you will definitely feel and see a significant change in your appearance, health and vitality.

- You will feel better and have less likelihood of chronic disease.

STUART M. BERGER, M.D.

Other Avon Books by
Stuart M. Berger, M.D.

How To Be Your Own Nutritionist

What Your Doctor Didn't Learn
in Medical School

FOREVER YOUNG

20 Years Younger in 20 Weeks

DR. BERGER'S STEP-BY-STEP REJUVENATING PROGRAM

Stuart M. Berger, M.D.

AVON BOOKS NEW YORK

AVON BOOKS
A division of
The Hearst Corporation
105 Madison Avenue
New York, New York 10016

For Marlaine, my best friend,
whose support is always
invaluable.

I want to express my gratitude to Pat Golbitz, Howard Kaminsky, Larry Hughes, Allen Marchioni, Lori Ames, and Carolyn Reidy, who represent the best in publishing.

To Lorna Darmour, Arthur Klebanoff, David Nimmons, and Marilyn O'Reilly for their knowledge, expertise, and dedication in completing this project.

A special thanks to Sally Jessy Raphael and Karl Soderlund for coming to me with this exciting idea.

And most of all to my parents, Otto and Rachel, who taught me the healing nature of laughter, and who are always there with love and support.

Contents

Looking Forward to Getting Younger

THE SIXTEENTH CENTURY was a dozen years old or so when a Spanish galleon appeared off the coast of the Florida peninsula. On its decks, the famed Spanish explorer Juan Ponce de León sensed that he was within days of completing his sacred mission. As the ship rolled gently beneath his feet, he scanned the horizon. On those shores, he had heard tell, existed a secret fount. Revered by the Indians in the region, its waters had mysterious properties conferring lasting vigor, beauty, and youth to all who drank them. His quest, he knew, was to claim that fountain for Spain's king, Ferdinand II, and to bring that elixir home for the royal families of Europe.

Four centuries later, in a laboratory outside Miami, a white-coated cell biologist straightens up from her computer terminal. On its green phosphor screen, she has been mapping the very secrets that the Spanish explorer had dreamed of. Her quest focuses, not on the flowing waters of a mythical fountain, but on much more intimate ones: the biochemical fluids locked within the human immune cell. It is in these waters, she knows, that the real secrets of aging are to be found, etched in a complex code of DNA.

The book you hold in your hands is the culmination of a journey begun long ago, well before Ponce de

León. It represents a dream that has tempted the human species ever since we lived in caves—the dream of a life without aging, without senescence or decay, where we stay forever young (well, *almost* forever—but then again, who wants to live to be 647 years old, anyway?).

Throughout human history, prolonging youth has been the province of magic and myth. Today, in the final decade of the twentieth century, it has become one of science and certainty. For the first time ever, we have the opportunity to realize that dream.

> Aging, as we have always known it, may no longer be inevitable or irrevocable. Breakthroughs all across the frontier of biomedical science make it increasingly feasible to hope that we may hold back the ravages of senescence—even to abolish many of the degenerative symptoms of the hitherto-universal disease called old age. For nearly every symptom of aging...there are remedies and preventive measures being actively investigated.
>
> —Albert Rosenfeld, in *Prolongevity*

Today, thanks to research developments in the last decade, the deepest secrets of biological aging lie within our grasp. Again and again in these pages, you will find yourself confronting one central truth: *We now know enough to alter significantly the course of how—and how fast—we age.* Ours is the first generation that has a very real, very practical chance of staying younger, longer, than ever before. That is a chance you must be willing to take, or you would not have purchased this book.

A decade ago this book could not have been written, for many of the specific steps we will cover were then unknown. I can sit down to write it today because now we hold hard medical science in hand, promising and fascinating nuggets buried in papers from research labs the world over. Some of these steps may seem familiar, others will be completely new to you. But by combining them all together in one cohesive program, you will realize all of the advantages that medical science can provide. You will have a simple, stepwise program to put these principles to work in your own life—starting this minute.

How realistic is that? Well, according to one eminent specialist on the aging process, writing in the *Proceedings of the National Academy of Sciences,*

> It is not unreasonable to expect on the basis of present data that the healthy life span can be increased by 5–10 or more years....

That is our task in the pages that follow. You and I will bring those discoveries out of cloistered biochemistry laboratories and into your life—so you can begin to benefit from what scientists have pieced together. We will see what is surely the most exciting series of breakthroughs of the age, discoveries that go beyond simply unraveling any one disease or condition. Rather, these scientific advances address the whole spectrum of changes that occur—in our brains and biochemistry, in our cells and synapses—as our bodies age. Correctly and judiciously applied, the specific techniques in these pages are a prescription for remaining vital, healthy, and active until the very end of a long, productive life.

Welcome—to the Longevity Revolution

The prescription you are about to write for yourself draws from a diverse range of topics and disciplines: medicine, nutrition, immunology, cancer prevention, even exercise physiology. For what has happened in the last few years—and the main reason I could write this book—is that a number of scientific disciplines have converged. As that has happened, we have undergone what many call the "Longevity Revolution."

For many years, researchers in these fields had labored in relative isolation. Like so many blind men describing the same elephant, each beheld a small piece: aging as it happened in the cardiovascular system and the immune system, bone and skeletal changes, the chronological development of the brain.

But then, as laboratory scientists and clinical practitioners began to share information across disciplines, they started to find common ground, realizing that in many respects they were working on different pieces of the same vast puzzle. Their work started to coalesce; findings piled upon findings, reinforcing, substantiating, proving and disproving. Piece by painstaking piece, enough information has been assembled from medical science to make possible a book like this, dedicated to putting all of these findings in one place, with one common goal: keeping you younger.

Hardly a month goes by that I do not read of yet another research report, another vital piece of the puzzle about how we can slow—even, in some cases, reverse—the cellular processes of decay. The concrete signs of the pace of research in this area abound:

—The budget of the National Institute on Aging will reach an impressive $194 million this fiscal year, funding some 697 separate research projects.
—America now boasts some dozen scientific institutions devoted solely to anti-aging research and study.
—If you go to the nearest medical research library, you will find more than thirty-four journals devoted to findings on various aspects of aging—and aging prevention.

When I sat down to write this book, my first step was to key into a medical research computer bank the broad topic of "aging research." The answer it gave me testifies to the meteoric growth in this field—it selected more than 45,000 scientific papers for me to review!

All of this points in one very hopeful direction. We are now able to lengthen our lives, prolong our healthy and vital years, and reduce the procession of chronic, debilitating illnesses that have come to define old age. We have inched forward in our understanding of just what aging is, how it works, and—most important of all—what *you* can do about it.

"Youth Preservation": A Science Is Born

It is at this fertile crossroad that the science of "Youth Preservation" has come into being. Or at least, that's the term I use for it. Unfortunately, you will not yet find those exact words listed in the curricula at medical schools or in official proceedings. It remains a hybrid field, a mosaic of cell biology, genetics, biochemistry, oncology, geriatrics, and several other disciplines. But although we don't yet have an agreed-upon name for this science, it is clear that each of these disciplines is a part of the larger picture, and that this larger picture points the way to a younger, more vital you.

A certain part of this revolution is as simple as the fact that we have grown much more skilled at preventing a whole family of specific diseases of old age. It is a biological fact that just a handful of diseases—cancer, coronary artery disease, stroke, diabetes, kidney failure, obstructive lung disease, pneumonia, and the flu account for 85 percent of the debilitating illnesses of old age. Heart disease all by itself accounts for fully one out of every two deaths of older Americans, and high blood pressure directly causes or contributes to 15 percent of all deaths.

Yet amazingly, we can already control many of these diseases. Listen to the expert testimony of former Secretary of Health, Education and Welfare Joseph A. Califano, Jr., before the United States Senate:

"67% of all disease and premature death is preventable."

—Dr. Peter Greenwald, director of Cancer Prevention and Control at the National Cancer Institute, says that 80 percent of cancer cases are linked to how we live our lives—so can be controlled.

—Margaret Heckler, former Secretary of Health and Human Services, says, "Changes in lifestyle and behavior could save 95,000 lives per year by the year 2000."

What these experts are telling us is clear: If you did nothing else but focus on these high-risk diseases—by knowing how to eat, exercise, and live your life so you can lower your risk for them—you would automatically improve your odds for a reprieve from the most common, and obvious, causes of debility, premature aging, and death.

Research shows again and again that many of the problems we have come to expect as part of "just getting old" have more to do with *how* we live than how *long*.

—Coronary artery disease accounts for half of all deaths in those over sixty-five. But there is clear research showing that atherosclerosis—the artery clogging that is the main culprit in premature heart disease—is not a necessary part of aging. In most mammals, and even in some human societies, it doesn't happen. In Chapter 6 I give you six "young-at-heart" guidelines to make sure it won't happen to you either.

—High blood pressure, as any doctor in this country will tell you, rises with age—a rise of about 15 percent is considered "average." But among the inhabitants of Easter Island, these changes in blood pressure don't happen. Clearly, if they can avoid this damaging rise, we can too.

—Bone weakening (osteoporosis) causes 1.2 million hip fractures every year among older women, and some 40,000 deaths. Yet in China and Japan, such fractures are extremely rare—because of factors like diet and exercise. We will review the four crucial bone builder tips in Chapter 8.

In these cases, as in many others, the more we look, the more we see that many of the diseases we associate with age are highly avoidable. As we add more diseases, one by one, to the list of those we can most likely avoid, we tip the balance in our favor to live longer, more active lives.

Family Health History Quiz

To understand what these specific discoveries may mean for you, take a moment to do the following exercise. It is most applicable if you are in your midthirties or above.

If you have lost parents, grandparents, or other older relatives, consider a few simple questions:

What did your father die from? _____

What did your mother die from? _____

What did your grandfather die from? _____

What did your grandmother die from? _____

What have other older relatives died from? _____

Without doubt, your list included such conditions as cancer, heart disease, pneumonia, and infections. Now imagine how your own medical future is changed by striking out those candidates from the list—because you have built them out of your life! By reducing your

chances that those conditions will happen to you, you
have already joined the Longevity Revolution!

Outwitting Mr. Gompertz

How old are you? Older than thirty-five? If so, Ben-
jamin Gompertz has some disturbing news for you.
Gompertz was a British scientist, population expert,
and statistician who lived and wrote in the early years
of the nineteenth century. In a famous formulation,
which has come to be known as Gompertz Constant,
he estimated that the probability of dying increases ex-
ponentially every year after age thirty-five. Scientists
have relied on the Gompertz Constant for years as they
attempt to push back the limits of aging and death.

Just three years ago, Nobel Prize-winning biochemist
Linus Pauling reexamined Gompertz's calculations and

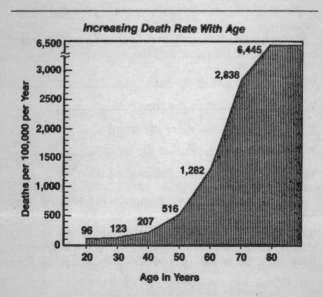

Increasing Death Rate With Age

Life Span According to State

Statistically, your chances for a long and healthy life vary significantly depending on where you live.
Just for your information, you may find it interesting to find the average life span in your state:

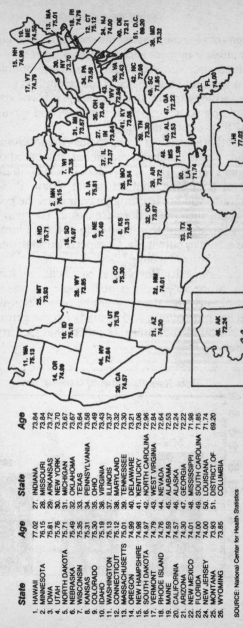

State	Age		State	Age
1. HAWAII	77.02		27. INDIANA	73.84
2. MINNESOTA	76.15		28. MISSOURI	73.84
3. IOWA	75.81		29. ARKANSAS	73.72
4. UTAH	75.76		30. NEW YORK	73.70
5. NORTH DAKOTA	75.71		31. MICHIGAN	73.67
6. NEBRASKA	75.49		32. OKLAHOMA	73.67
7. WISCONSIN	75.35		33. TEXAS	73.64
8. KANSAS	75.31		34. PENNSYLVANIA	73.58
9. COLORADO	75.30		35. OHIO	73.49
10. IDAHO	75.19		36. VIRGINIA	73.43
11. WASHINGTON	75.13		37. ILLINOIS	73.37
12. CONNECTICUT	75.12		38. MARYLAND	73.32
13. MASSACHUSETTS	75.01		39. TENNESSEE	73.30
14. OREGON	74.99		40. DELAWARE	73.21
15. NEW HAMPSHIRE	74.98		41. KENTUCKY	73.06
16. SOUTH DAKOTA	74.97		42. NORTH CAROLINA	72.96
17. VERMONT	74.79		43. WEST VIRGINIA	72.84
18. RHODE ISLAND	74.76		44. NEVADA	72.64
19. MAINE	74.59		45. ALABAMA	72.53
20. CALIFORNIA	74.57		46. ALASKA	72.24
21. ARIZONA	74.30		47. GEORGIA	72.22
22. NEW MEXICO	74.01		48. MISSISSIPPI	71.98
23. FLORIDA	74.00		49. SOUTH CAROLINA	71.85
24. NEW JERSEY	74.00		50. LOUISIANA	71.74
25. MONTANA	73.93		51. DISTRICT OF COLUMBIA	69.20
26. WYOMING	73.85			

SOURCE: National Center for Health Statistics

found that for most of us, the chance of death increases by almost 9 percent *each* year after age thirty-five.

Since your statistical chance of dying doubles every eight years and ten weeks, if you celebrated your thirty-fifth birthday today, that means the odds of your dying double by your forty-third birthday, and quadruple by your fifty-second birthday!

But there is a silver lining to this gloomy Gompertzian cloud. These numbers, remember, are based on an actuarial average. By the very act of picking up this book, and of launching yourself into a Youth Preservation Program, you are leapfrogging ahead of the population on whom such predictions are based. The many specific steps throughout this book help you take strong, positive action to outwit Mr. Gompertz's dismal numbers—and stay forever young.

The Longevity Revolution comes not a moment too soon. More people can benefit from such research than ever before—for the very simple reason that never before has our country had so many people getting older. Look around you. Statistics reflect that fact from every corner:

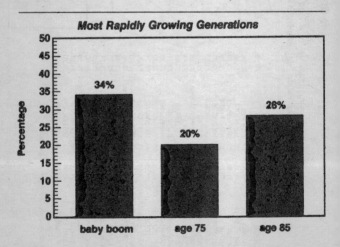

Most Rapidly Growing Generations

—This April, the U.S. Census Bureau reported that the nation's median age is at its highest point since they began tracking it 160 years ago. Today, one American in eight is over sixty-five—some thirty-two million people. That number is greater than the entire population of Australia, Belgium, and Israel combined! By the year 2030, the number will have doubled, to sixty-five million, or one American in five.

—The fastest-growing population segment is the baby boom generation, now aged thirty-five to forty-four. Next come seniors, seventy-five and older.

Still not convinced? Then just look at the shape of things to come, according to the National Institute on Aging:

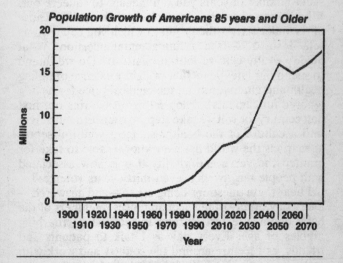

Population Growth of Americans 85 years and Older

Such clear pictures are worth thousands of erudite words. The trend to an entire society living longer is unprecedented in our history—or, for that matter, in the history of the human race.

Not Just How Long, How Well

"A major objective now and in the future should be maximizing health and well-being ... so as to make life worth living for as long as possible. This will require a more careful application of preventive medicine."
—Dr. Denham Harman, biochemical gerontologist

"Adding life to years, not just years to life, is the goal of aging research."
—Dr. Edward Schneider, Dean,Gerontology Center,
University of Southern California

Of course, there's more to longevity than just the sheer number of years you can manage to squeeze out. What counts as much—or more—is their quality. Those of us under sixty—the group in which you count yourself, I suspect—face a fundamental question: What quality of life can we look forward to? Do we intend to spend our later years in a twilight existence of failing health and vitality, paying the medical price for having ignored fundamental biological verities during our first half century, or will we take steps to transform ourselves into a culture of the healthiest, most youthful septuagenarians the world has ever known, able to take for granted the verve and vitality that is now associated with people ten, twenty, even thirty years younger?

I hear these questions being asked—and answered—every day. Many of my acquaintances, members of the baby boom, are just starting to feel the encroaching nibbles of age. Every day as I talk to patients and friends, as I lecture around the country and work with colleagues from New York to Hawaii, I become more convinced that the issue of what can be done to lengthen life and improve its quality is of unparalleled importance to the overwhelming majority of Americans.

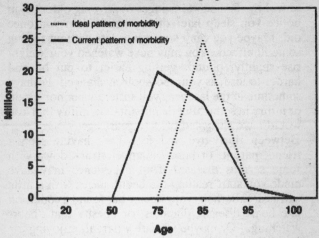

Two Views of Aging

What all of those people share—and this is true whether you are thirty-six or sixty-three—is a fervent desire to slow the rate at which their bodies are aging. Not just to live longer, but to live better. They seek a way to avoid the chronic diseases, encroaching fatigue, and degrading changes that seem to characterize old age. As a nation, we are looking to find what we can do to make our lives better, extend our most healthy, vibrant, active years, and shorten the time of weakness and failing health. We are a people ripe and ready to join the Longevity Revolution.

The goal is to put you on the dotted curve above—to compress the time you spend ailing and frail, and extend the time you spend in full, robust, and energetic health.

For each of us, the realization of aging surfaces in different ways. Are you:

—Between twenty-five and thirty-five, just beginning to feel the first subtle twinges of growing older? You notice you sleep later on weekends than you once did. Maybe you can't stay out as late without feeling some ill effects. You may have watched your weight rise slightly, pounds getting easier to put on and harder to lose, as your metabolism changed. Perhaps sometime in the last year you suffered a minor sprain or injury in some athletic pursuit—an injury that you would have shrugged off five years ago.

—Between thirty-five and forty-five, having seen a friend, parent, or family member struck down with some serious disease? That experience may have made you start reading the health pages with a little extra care. Perhaps your doctor has found a condition like heart disease, diabetes, or obesity that "bears watching." Or maybe you are a parent, enjoying the new life you have brought into the world, but being reminded that you have a finite amount of time left in your own life.

—Between fifty-five and sixty-five? You may feel in good shape, but have started to take a certain amount of impairment for granted? You tire more easily, and have grown used to living with the arthritis, or gout, or heart condition your doctor diagnosed. You cannot help but hope that you will avoid the seriously deteriorating health that seems to have overtaken many of your contemporaries. You want to make sure you spend your next years enjoying what you have worked for instead of fighting discomfort, decay, and disease.

If you see yourself described here, or if you have simply wondered if there isn't something you ought to be doing to increase your health and longevity, I think you will find much to interest you in the pages that follow.

Among the important breakthroughs you will discover in these chapters:

—Your own health and life-style test to help you design an anti-aging program that is just right for you (Chapter 4)
—How you can best use the newest anti-aging skin-care treatments (Chapter 5)
—The nutritional keys you can use *now* to decrease the aging of your skin (Chapter 5)
—The just-discovered nutrient that promises a bone-rejuvenation breakthrough (Chapter 8)
—A specific nutritional plan to take you off the danger list for cardiac problems (Chapter 6)
—The effect that one simple change may have on reversing skeletal aging (Chapter 8)
—The "Antiviral Cocktail," first developed for AIDS, that can help increase your immune strength (Chapter 9)
—The safe vitamin treatment your doctor can give you to help restore your immune system to its youthful vigor (Chapter 9)
—The simple principles you can use to keep your brain younger, longer (Chapter 10)
—The dietary key to reducing the cellular changes leading to old age, and an eating plan to help you use it (Chapter 11)
—The new findings about the difference between exercise and activity—and how they affect your longevity (Chapter 11)
—The one single change some of you can make that is *100 percent guaranteed* to extend your healthy lives (Chapter 7)
—A step-by-step plan to reprogram the internal computer that may be aging you prematurely (Chapter 13)

My 20-20 Pledge to You

In health there are no absolute guarantees. But by following the twenty-plus specific health counsels in these pages, I can assure you that:

1. You will be following the best, most scientifically sound attempt you can make at present to stay younger, longer.
2. You will find them practical, real, do-able with inexpensive tools you have at your disposal.
3. By following these steps for twenty weeks, you will already feel and see a significant change in your appearance, health, and vitality.
4. The steps in these chapters will definitely help you feel better, with more energy and less likelihood of chronic disease.
5. By *not* heeding these principles, you will certainly shorten your healthy, productive life span.

I hope you take the 20-20 pledge: *That by following the twenty-plus guidelines throughout this book, you feel better in twenty weeks—and could add up to twenty years of productive, healthy, vigorous life.*

In return, I have to ask for one promise: that you will do your best to start thinking differently. Like Ponce de León, you need to become something of an explorer. But unlike his fantastic quest, yours has a sure chance of success, for it is based on science, not on speculation.

Being an explorer means you will have to get used to a whole new way of thinking. Perhaps the most significant changes of aging happen, not in your arteries, muscles, and bones, but in that marvelous organ nestled between your ears. When it comes to Youth Preservation, it is clear that the biggest differences lie in the

choices we make many times each day: decisions about
what we will eat, how we move, how we treat ourselves,
even what inner tapes we play as we drift to sleep at
night. Being around enjoying life in thirty, forty, or fifty
years means having a strong inner commitment to longevity, starting right now.

You may find that hard at first because we are all so
conditioned to see our lives in terms of the allotted
threescore years and ten. Society has accustomed us to
expect to live that length of time and no more, and I
believe that at a very profound level we actually "program" ourselves to make it come true. I'll get to the
specifics in Chapter 13, but the main point to keep in
mind as you read this book is that you may be called
upon to make a radical shift in that "programming," in
how you see your life now, where you are headed, and
what your future will look like.

If you've thought of retirement, of dropping out and
taking it easy, of "coasting out" your last golden decade
and a half, you may find yourself wanting to reconsider.
I hope you will come to see retirement as just one of
your options, along with other scenarios that have you
working productively and energetically, physically and
mentally active for more years than you had ever dared
hope.

That's the kind of thinking I hope you'll do a lot of
throughout this book. Because if you conscientiously
apply the principles in it, you'd better have a good plan
for how you want to spend all that extra time you'll be
building into your life!

More on this subject later, but for now I just ask you
to keep your heart and mind open to changing the way
you see yourself and your life path, and to consider that
a work in progress as you read the pages ahead.

So if I have that promise from you, and you have
these pledges from me, let us not waste another minute
that you could be using to grow younger. Come along,

and together we'll take up where Ponce de León left off and finish that noble quest begun so many centuries ago. I hope you *are* looking forward—to growing younger!

2

Fables, Fountains, and Facts

All the days of Methuselah were nine hundred sixty and nine years: and he died.
—Genesis 5:27

Do not try to live forever; you will not succeed.
—George Bernard Shaw

GEORGE BERNARD SHAW was right. Obviously, I can't promise you that after you read this book, you can look forward to an added nine centuries of life. (Even back in Methuselah's time, when miracles like burning bushes and parting seas were everyday occurrences, living to his ripe age of 969 was considered pretty out of the ordinary.) More common, according to the very next chapter of Genesis, was that Man's "days shall be an hundred and twenty years"—the very age, by co-incidence, that Moses died.

It turns out that those biblical "biologists" were pretty accurate—even today, the biological maximum life of *Homo sapiens* is generally agreed by most aging experts to be in the range of 115 to 120 years. That may seem strange, at first. After all, how many people do you know who live to be 115? Well, the factor to keep in mind is that such a figure represents, not the average, but the likely utmost top limit. That number has not changed appreciably since ancient Rome, when Pliny the Elder wrote that centenarians were, if not common, not unknown either. He even described a popular actress who was then one hundred years old. Today, the oldest documented living person is 114 years old; the oldest person ever authenticated lived to the age of 120. And while biomedical science may succeed in pushing back that limit, extending the hypothetical upper limit is not the main focus of this book.

I hold a much more practical—and, I believe, more easily achieved—goal. Obviously, most of us don't live anywhere near our 115-year limit. What the biblical scholars estimated as threescore and ten has been refined by latter-day biostatisticians as 74.7 years—the average life expectancy today in America. But the real question is: What happens in that gap between 74.7 years and 115?

Closing the gap is what this book is all about. Together, we can give you the edge so that you can more fully achieve your inbred biological maximum. It is the same goal that Wilder Penfield, the famed American neurosurgeon, envisioned when he wrote that he foresaw a day when "more men and women reach life's true goal, fulfilling the cycle set for us, bypassing the plagues, disease and famine."

We want to take his advice, to *take maximum biological advantage* of the preset limit built into our body's aging time clock—and to do it in such a way that what time we do have will be the healthiest, happiest possible. We first need to know what aging really is—and that, in turn, means debunking a few fables about what it most certainly is not.

First, the Fables...

Through the centuries, mankind's preoccupation with the subject of aging has been matched only by its collective imagination in devising ways to deal with it. The history of Youth Preservation spans several millennia of wild expectations, dashed hopes, and failed promises.

Five thousand years ago, in the oldest tale of Western civilization, the Babylonians told of the king Gilgamesh, who wanted to live forever. To do so, he was told by a sage, he must eat a certain plant growing under water, whose powers "restore lost youth to a man. . . . By its virtue a man may win back all his former strength. Its name shall be 'The-Old-Men-Are-Young-Again.' " Gilgamesh vowed to eat it and "return to what I was in my youth."

While that may have been the first time this idea arose, it was certainly not the last. For thousands of years, across many of the world's great cultures, the quest continued. The Chinese, the ancient Hebrews, Greeks, and Romans, medieval monks and twentieth-century Swiss doctors, each offered their own unique contributions to the pursuit of elusive immortality. Several thousand years ago, Chinese apothecaries whipped up an anti-aging cocktail called "tan," compounded from gold and the mercury-containing ore cinnabar (given the proven toxic effects of both metals, it is likely this "youth-preserving" formula hastened the deaths of those who swallowed it).

The Taoist religion held as a central goal the prolonging of life through nutrition, meditation, sports, and even sex. In biblical times many Middle Eastern societies believed that living to a ripe old age was God's reward for right-living and faith. For them, the key to remaining youthful—or at least alive—was not an elixir, but one's behavior. Those fortunate few who lived long enough to show the effects of age—no scant feat in an era when most people died by age forty— were considered models of appropriate living, deserving honor and reverence by virtue of their longevity. The

Arabs spoke of a Well of Life that, like Ponce de León's fountain two millennia later, would confer glorious youth on those who enjoyed its waters.

In Europe during the Middle Ages, the practice of alchemy held as a goal, not to turn lead into gold—as is popularly believed—but to create nostrums that would forestall aging. The topic continued to fascinate Europeans for several hundred years. One scholarly work, written in the sixteenth century, explained that aging was the result of the loss of "vital particles" that we exhale with each breath. The way to stay young, it suggested, had been discovered by the occupant of an ancient Egyptian tomb who had lived an impressive 115 years. According to the inscription on the burial vault, he owed his longevity to "the Breath of Young Women." A colorful prescription, to be sure (and one that more than a few of my male patients would gladly accept!), but hardly accurate.

In our own century, the quest has taken a more scientific turn. In the 1920s, it was believed that the secret to prolonging vigor in men at least was to transplant into them the testicles of virile apes. Needless to say, this fanciful treatment did not yield any positive results (but I can't help wondering if the elderly male patients showed any increased craving for bananas!).

During the next decade, longevity again captured the popular imagination, in the form of the immensely popular book *Lost Horizon*. The tale told of Shangri-La, a city high up in the mountains, where the secret to infinite youth was to be found.

Not long thereafter, this time in the mountains of Central Europe, a researcher named Ana Aslan discovered what she thought was the cure to aging. In the early 1950s, this Rumanian biochemist created a drug called Gerovital-H3, which she claimed would reduce the changes of aging. It set off a flurry of research, and scores of eager patients flocked from the world over to her clinic at the Geriatric Institute in Bucharest. Today, some thirty-five years later, research has shown that the initial hopes for the drug were over-optimistic, and that the drug does not have any significant anti-aging effects.

Not far away, in Switzerland, you can still check into one of the most renowned (and expensive) clinics and be injected in the rump with a puree made from the cells of lamb fetuses. These cells are claimed to inspire your old decrepit cells to be younger—a dramatic notion, to be sure, but there is no evidence in any credible scientific journal to suggest it works.

In recent years the anti-aging doctors have trotted out an alphabet soup of different chemical compounds—BHT, SOD, L-DOPA, NDGA, to name a few—to chemically forestall the cellular damage of aging and so keep us younger. While several of these compounds initially appeared to show promise, none has given us the magic key to aging that their inventors hoped.

And Now, the Facts

After many long centuries of fanciful theorizing, it is only in the last few years that we have advanced to the point of pinning down the true causes and mechanisms of aging—and with them, the clues to staying young.

The rest of this chapter is dedicated to bringing you up to date on some of the most current thinking. I hope you'll read it because it will help you understand the rationale for the steps we will undertake together in later chapters—the self-help core of this book.

However, I understand that you may be a doer, not a student, and may be impatient to get started on your twenty-week plan for improving your health and extending your life. You may be less interested in the theory than in beginning your own specific anti-aging steps *now*. If that is you, you are welcome to skip the rest of this chapter and go directly to the next chapter, which begins the interactive self-assessment for your own Youth Preservation Program. But if you do that, promise me one more thing—you will come back and read this chapter later . . . please?

A key event happened in 1964 when a premier microbiologist named Leonard Hayflick made a basic but crucial discovery. The human cells he was looking at would divide only about fifty times, then die—and little could be done to change that pattern. Hayflick's discovery took us a major step forward because it focused the debate on aging away from the larger organ systems to the innermost workings of the body's trillions of cells. It became a cornerstone in the whole new scientific discipline of biogerontology, the biological study of aging.

Today it is a scientific truism that we will not understand aging until we understand the astoundingly complex mechanics that happen within our cells. However, if everybody agrees that the cell is the "scene of the crime," there is less accord about exactly what happens inside it when we grow older.

There is no shortage of theories. Look at a recent list compiled by the National Institute on Aging:

Wear-and-tear theory
Rate-of-living theory
Metabolic theory
Endocrine theory
Free-radical theory
Collagen theory
Somatic mutation theory
Programmed senescence theory
Error catastrophe theory
Cross-linking theory
Immunological theory
Redundant message theory
Codon restriction theory
Transcriptional event theory

Behind each of these intriguing names are learned scientists, thoughtful adherents, and detractors. To give you an idea of all those theories would require several volumes and a graduate course, and that is hardly our goal here. But it is useful to get a basic familiarity with a few of the most common theories, because it is on this work that much of this book is based.

Most of the backers of the prime theories fall into one of two broad camps: those I call the "Entropists" and those I term the "Genetic Fatalists."

The Entropy of Age

Newton's Second Law of Thermodynamics, known to physicists as "entropy," states that things cool off over time. Scientists tell us that means that any organized system tends to move from order to chaos. (Anyone who has ever seen my workdesk at home—or, for that matter, any parent who has tried to keep a child-filled household tidy—knows exactly what I'm talking about!)

The same principle of entropy holds true, too, at a biological level. Every living organism is engaged in a constant struggle with the forces of entropy and disorder. That struggle is what aging is. Not only do our cells, and organs, and functioning become more disorderly with every passing year, the fact is, we literally "cool off"—our body temperature will have dropped by an average of two degrees by age seventy! In a very real sense, being alive means being engaged in a constant struggle against disorder, and our final capitulation to chaos comes only when we expire.

There is a whole school of thought that relies on entropy as the most likely explanation of aging. The Entropists say that it is wear and tear, the accumulating clutter of living that does us in. They postulate that the aging of the body's cells is much like the decay of, say, an old barn. Little by little, different things break down, damaged by the ravages of time. A hinge may fail there, a coat of paint peel here, a window sag somewhere else, and *voilà*—soon we are experiencing the creaky, slow, throbbing decrepitude of old age.

Although experts agree that such a gradual process occurs, they do not all agree about where to place most of the blame. Some say the "scene of the crime" is DNA, the genetic code that lies at the heart of human cells. Because of exposure to toxins, chemicals and ultraviolet light filtering through the skin, these complex chains of information-carrying chemicals may break, twist, become transposed, or otherwise get out of order. When they do, goes the theory, the cells are not able to pass along their genetic blueprints accurately, and key chemical reactions within the body's cells begin to go haywire. When enough of these cells break down, the scientists hypothesize, the changes accumulate into serious deficits that weaken whole organs. It is an intriguing proof for this theory that those animals whose cells repair DNA damage quickly and efficiently are also those who live the longest.

Another theory focuses more on the enzymes our cells produce. Sometimes they become faulty, and instead of the well-ordered cellular chemical production lines that Nature designed, our cells start to look like a crazed, disorderly factory floor, turning out too much of some things and not enough of others.

Another popular theory that researchers have focused on has been termed the "error catastrophe" theory. It suggests that defective proteins in the body's cells accumulate into an intracellular chemical soup that interferes with the cells' proper biochemical tasks and thus weakens them. Others suggest it is not that the chemicals are made wrong, but that they never get broken down and recycled properly. The image these biologists paint is one in which the cells' "work space" grows increasingly chaotic because its "janitors" are out on strike.

A "Radical" Theory of Aging

The most compelling of the many aging theories advanced by cell biologists is called the "free-radical" theory. It is this theory that underlies many of the nutritional counsels throughout this book—and it plays a role in many of the twenty-four rejuvenation steps we will explore.

This dramatic-sounding name, with its overtones of terrorists and saboteurs, may remind you of something from political theory instead of biology. Indeed, from your cells' point of view, that is almost exactly right. *Free radicals* are very reactive chemical by-products that are created as oxygen is burned as fuel in our cells. (For that reason, chemists also know them as "oxidation products.") Chemically, they are molecules out of electrical balance. Unfortunately, the only way they know to rebalance themselves is to steal an electron belonging to another molecule, thereby unbalancing it. And so the chain reaction goes, unleashing all sorts of havoc.

Free radicals can interact with fatty molecules, lipids, in your cells. Then, they create a pollutant, a sort of intracellular sludge called "lipofuscin," a pigment that can change the color of skin. However, their damage is far more than cosmetic. As they react explosively with many of your cells' natural chemicals, these free-radical reactions can inflict severe damage on the fragile equilibrium of the cells. (In fact, the damage they do is the same that occurs when you are exposed to radiation—except it is happening all the time, from the inside, instead of from an external radiation source.)

Free radicals destroy key cell enzymes, fats, and proteins. If they borrow electrons from fat molecules in the critical membrane wall of a cell, they can actually destroy the integrity of the cell. Too, they can interfere with the elegant intermeshing ballet of DNA and RNA that is responsible for cell division. As these miscreants do their dirty work, trouble begins to spread far and wide. They can trigger inflammation, damage lung cells and blood vessels, and lead to mutations, cell destruction, degenerative diseases, and even cancer. In terms of the destruction they cause, free radicals are the biological equivalent of a terrorist bomber gone berserk in the control room of a nuclear reactor. As enough of the cells' vital mechanisms are damaged, the cell can become less efficient, malfunction, or even die.

And when enough of *that* happens, there is a cascade of biological damage. The cumulative levels of oxidation radicals put millions, even billions, of cells out of commission. As you read this sentence, free radicals are slowly building up and being destroyed in your body. But as you age, their numbers certainly increase, and as they do, the chances also increase that these cellular saboteurs can do greater and greater harm to the "works" of your cells.

One school of thought, based on the breakthrough research of the eminent biologist Dr. Denham Harman, believes that the cumulative effect of free-radical damage is the root of cell aging—and all the debilitating, difficult diseases that often come with increasing years. The researchers are quite unequivocal: "Chances are 99% that free radicals are the basis for aging," says biochemist Harman, the father of free-radical theory. "Aging is the ever-increasing accumulation of changes caused or contributed to by free radicals." These scientists blame free radicals for many common degenerative diseases: arthritis, diabetes, hardening of the arteries, heart and kidney ailments, Parkinson's disease, even cataracts. As I was writing this chapter, the largest group of free-radical scientists in history met in an international colloquium to review the newest findings about these agents—and how to disable them. You will find some of their findings—particularly those about antioxidant nutritional defenses—in the chapters to come.

HOW NOT TO BE NATURE'S GUINEA PIG

Why on earth would Mother Nature have evolved us to have such potentially damaging chemical reactions? Denham Harman suggests two reasons: First, the same free radicals that cause aging and cancer also make it possible for all of the biological mutations that Nature has used over billions of years to make you the terrific, nearly perfect person you are. You can thank free radicals for the fact that you no longer swing from trees and walk on all fours! In that respect, free radicals are biological wild cards, thrown in to keep the evolutionary game interesting and moving along.

Second, the fact that free-radical oxidation plays a part in aging and cancer "may play a useful role, possibly a necessary one... by aiding in the disposal of old organisms after they have provided new 'experiments' for evaluation against the environment." Gulp. We are, of course, the "old organisms" Harman is talking about. But just in case you don't like the idea of being one of Nature's guinea pigs as your free radicals run wild, you will find suggestions for a potent antioxidant plan in the twenty-two steps throughout this book.

Although scientists may disagree whether the aging culprit is DNA, free radicals, defective cell enzymes, or some combination of these and other factors, what links all of them is a belief that losing our youthful vigor is a process of entropy, the result of the wear and tear of existence. They tell us it is when our cells grow increasingly snarled, jumbled, and generally muddled with chemical clutter that we start to look, act, and feel old.

> Old age is like a plane flying through a storm. Once
> you are aboard, there is nothing you can do.
>   —Golda Meir

The second major school of theorists says there is
more to aging than mere entropy. These scientists are
the Genetic Fatalists, whose credo, as voiced by one of
their proponents, runs: "Life is a terminal disease."
Their idea is simple. The human body is programmed
to self-destruct, and the code to do so is written in our
genes.

A concise view of this theory was written by the eminent immunobiologist Lewis Thomas in his *Medusa and
the Snail:* "This is . . . what happens when a healthy old
creature, old man or old mayfly, dies. The dying is built
into the system so that it can occur at once, at the end
of a genetically pre-determined allotment of living."

The possibility of genetic programming certainly goes
a long way to explaining why the human species seems
to have a fixed upper age of about 115 years. That
presumably represents the maximum age our genes are
"set" to. The adherents of such a theory cite the evidence of evolution: In order to continue the species,
humans need survive only about thirty years—just
enough time to have children. From an evolutionary
perspective, the following seventy years are just so
much window dressing, which confers little survival advantage for the species. They cite, too, the fact that the
way our bodies change as we age—even down to such
physical changes as our ears lengthening and our noses
widening—as evidence for cellular programming to dis-
tribute fat, connective tissue, and even bone mass differently. Why then, they ask, could we not also be
programmed to expire?

Some experts postulate that certain organs or organ
systems control the body's internal clock. Noting that

the immune system loses 90 percent of its power between the ages of fourteen and seventy, many biogerontologists have suggested that this complex system of cells, organs, and chemical messengers may be the body's "longevity timer." Others point to one part of the immune system, the thymus gland, as our biological pacemaker. Whether the cause is to be found in the whole or the part, what seems clear is that when our immune system weakens past a certain point, we succumb to the cancer or infections which a younger person would fight off.

The pathologist Roy Walford, a preeminent researcher at the University of California at Los Angeles, believes that immune system decline is probably controlled by a group of genes with the tongue-twisting name of major histocompatibility complex—MHC, for short. The MHC may affect breakage and repair of DNA, the levels of free radicals, even the pace at which our tissues develop and regenerate.

I have even heard other researchers point out that what may seem like built-in immune programming to grow older may in fact be due to the foods we eat throughout our lifetime. They believe that our immune system can be overtaxed by creating antibodies to deal with the many foreign proteins in the foods we consume. In the long haul, they argue, a steady barrage of foreign substances exhausts our B cells, T cells, and the natural killer cells of our immune defenses so that eventually they become depleted and cannot rise to the challenge when we need them—to fight off infections and cancers.

Tower of Biological Babel?

By now, you may feel that you are listening to the tower of scientific babel—or do I mean babble?—and can't distinguish a word that seems helpful. When the truth is finally sorted out, it may turn out that both sides are right. Our species' upper age limit of 115 years may be set by genetic limits locked into our genes, but we may rarely reach it because of the daily wear and tear that damages our cells long before then.

For you, who just want to live better and longer, this is something of an abstract discussion. When the experts seem so far apart, postulating such disparate mechanisms as genetic programming, DNA damage, accumulated cell toxins, even the food we eat, how can you make sense of it all? After all, if we don't know just what causes aging, how can we slow the process down?

Although I would be the first to admit that we do not yet have the final theoretical answer, I hope you aren't feeling dismayed. There is a relatively easy answer here: What you need to keep in mind is that there are several quite clear things that are helpful to focus on.

If you can increase your life expectancy from the seventy-four years that the statisticians tell us is now the norm even *halfway* up to the theoretical current maximum of 115 years, you would lengthen your life by 27 percent—more than one quarter. This may sound like an ambitious goal—indeed it is. But it doesn't mean it is not practical. Linus Pauling, three-time Nobel Prize-winning biochemist, estimates in *How to Live Longer and Feel Better* that using health measures presently available, we can increase our life expectancy from twenty-five to thirty-five years. Gerontologists Denham Harman and Roy Walford have estimated the potential additional time as five to ten years, which gives us a life span of about eighty-five years. Even the august National Institute on Aging, a mainline institution if there ever was one, published a paper saying that certain interventions "can improve heart and lung function, staving off normal age-related decrements by as much as 10 years."

People in developed countries have already added an

astounding twenty-eight years to their average life span since the beginning of the twentieth century. *There is no reason whatsoever for not continuing that progress,* extending your life span even further.

The major point to keep in mind is that such an increase requires no fundamental change in scientific understanding, no major conceptual breakthroughs of the sort that researchers work and worry over. It doesn't necessarily matter, in fact, *which* of the many theories ultimately prove right.

All that it requires is following the steps detailed throughout these chapters. As you do so, you will build risk factors and unnecessary toxins out of your life; you will give your cells a chance to rebuild themselves. Your goal is to eliminate the factors that could prematurely truncate your life long before its true biological deadline. By doing so, you will let your body take advantage of the wonderful longevity that Nature originally designed into it.

74—THE MAGIC NUMBER?

If you live to the age of a hundred, you have it made, because very few people die past the age of a hundred.
—George Burns

There is a grain of truth to the venerable comedian's counsel. If you are about to celebrate your seventy-fourth birthday, don't dust off your will just yet. Yes, seventy-four may be the average age, but that is a statistical confusion. It really reflects the large numbers of people who die prematurely from diseases and accidents. The thing to keep in mind is that, if you are healthy enough to live to a healthy, vital seventy, the chances are you will live another decade longer!

The System Is the Secret

What has become increasingly clear is that the answer to staying young will be found, not in one magic bullet, but in a connected web of behavior—how we eat, sleep, work, exercise, even think. That understanding is the basis of the more than twenty longevity steps you will find throughout this book, and that together make up a "systems approach" to keep you young.

It was the famed British physician Sir James Crichton-Browne who wrote: "There is no short-cut to longevity. To win it is the work of a lifetime, and the promotion of it a branch of preventive medicine." I couldn't agree more, and it is that principle that underlies the changes I will be asking you to make in your life over the next twenty weeks.

I hope you don't see those twenty weeks as a shortcut to longevity—they are not. Instead, you should think of them as a training period, a time for you to explore, acquire, and learn the new habits that you will incorporate into your life and carry for a lifetime. If you do that, you will reap a handsome dividend in terms of the length, the quality, and the pure enjoyment of your years ahead.

The Changes of Aging

To me, old age is always fifteen years older than I am.
—Bernard Baruch

EVERY ONE OF your body's systems, from your hair to your toenails, will undergo predictable changes as you age.

To stay young and vital for as long as possible, you need some idea of what really happens as a body grows older (keep in mind this isn't just *any*body we're talking about—it's *your* body!). So put on your physician's white coat and let's look at the physiological changes that lie ahead for you. Only by understanding what Nature has in store for us can we hope to control the aging process.

"An adult is a person who has ceased to grow vertically, but not horizontally."

This change is called the "Great Metabolism Shift," and it starts somewhere around the beginning of your fourth decade. Your energy furnaces start to burn differently, and Nature begins to swaddle you with an extra layer of fat. As fat increases, you also lose lean muscle mass; so your fat-to-muscle ratio increases significantly over the years, as shown on the charts on page 36.

Body Fat Changes With Age—Women

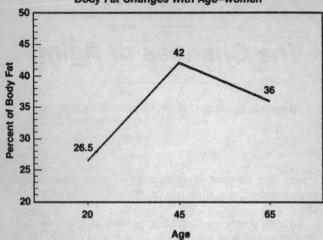

Body Fat Changes With Age—Men

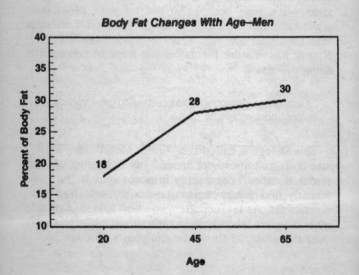

The Incredible Shrinking Woman

In recent years, no disease has gotten more notice than osteoporosis. Few people realize that this is not just a disease of bones that break, but also of *bones that actually shrink.*

By the time you are sixty-five, your body is only about half as efficient as it once was in absorbing mineral nutrients from foods. Instead of your body taking minerals like calcium, magnesium and potassium from your food, it borrows them from your bones. The bones weaken, losing, on average, 25 percent of their density.

This bone loss can take a significant toll on your height. For most people, the average length of the vertebral column is relatively constant—about 24 inches for women and 27 inches for men. That means, if you subtract the height of the leg bones, we are rather similar in height.

TALLNESS TEST

The next time you find yourself in a group of people of different height, observe carefully what happens as you sit down. When you sit, you are all more or less eye to eye, even though you may have to look up or down at them when you stand up. The differences in people's height are due mostly to the length of the leg bones.

As your body borrows minerals stored in the spinal vertebrae, those bones actually begin to collapse and compact, falling in on themselves. As your spinal column shrinks, you gradually lose the 24 inches or 27 inches of spine length you once had, and you become a "little old lady" or a "little old man."

The average American man can expect to lose up to 2¾ inches in height between the ages of 25 and 70; women, a less drastic 1⅞ inches. Sometimes, the loss is not so gradual: The collapse of just one of the vertebrae in the middle of the back can remove as much as 1⅛ inches of height.

Over the years, you can expect something like this:

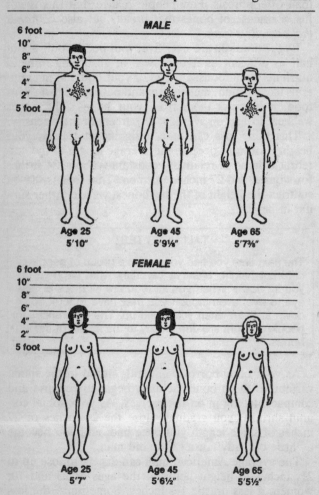

MALE

6 foot
10"
8"
6"
4"
2"
5 foot

Age 25
5'10"

Age 45
5'9½"

Age 65
5'7⅜"

FEMALE

6 foot
10"
8"
6"
4"
2"
5 foot

Age 25
5'7"

Age 45
5'6½"

Age 65
5'5½"

OUT OF ARM'S WAY...

Even your arms shrink as you age. Your arm span, measured from fingertip to fingertip with your arms outstretched, will be one-half less at age sixty-five than it is today. But through an interesting biological optical illusion, they appear to lengthen with age. The reason? Your arms shrink far less than your spine, so that as they hang next to your body, they will appear relatively longer.

The changes go all the way to your fingertips. Right now, if you are twenty years old, your nails take an average of one third less time to grow out than they will at age sixty. After another decade of getting older, by age seventy, they will grow less than half as fast as they do now.

But if you're worried that every part of you will shrink with age, don't—your feet, at least, actually become longer and enlarge as you age.

Face to Face with Age

At age 50, every man has the face he deserves.
—George Orwell

Orwell was talking about the obvious, outward changes that are most noticeable in the face. Rather than reading all the biological details, in this case, you'll see the picture on page 40 is worth a thousand words.

Hair Today, Gone Tomorrow?

Not necessarily. It is true that hair undergoes major changes with age because it is one of the fastest-replicating tissues of the body. There are three primary changes you can expect:

Facial Changes With Age

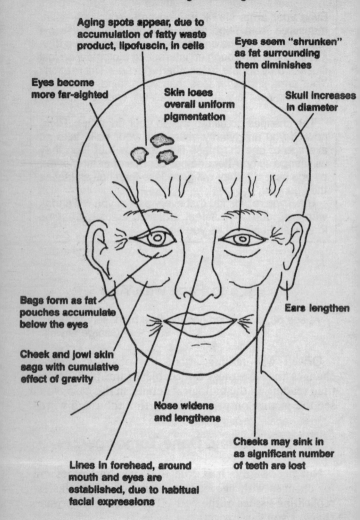

Aging spots appear, due to accumulation of fatty waste product, lipofuscin, in cells

Eyes seem "shrunken" as fat surrounding them diminishes

Eyes become more far-sighted

Skin loses overall uniform pigmentation

Skull increases in diameter

Bags form as fat pouches accumulate below the eyes

Ears lengthen

Cheek and jowl skin sags with cumulative effect of gravity

Nose widens and lengthens

Cheeks may sink in as significant number of teeth are lost

Lines in forehead, around mouth and eyes are established, due to habitual facial expressions

—For both men and women, the hair becomes much finer. Each strand loses about one fifth of its thickness.

—Hair color comes from the pigment contained in each hair shaft. As you age, the coarse, pigmented hair is replaced by nonpigmented strands—and when you look in the mirror, you find more (gasp!) gray hairs.

—The density of individual hair follicles—how thickly your head is "forested"—drops from a high of six hundred follicles per square centimeter on your thirtieth birthday to half that number by age fifty.

—If you are a *man*, your hair will probably change its pattern of distribution, even if you do not go bald. You can expect to lose hair around your temples, the result of your male hormones. Whether you will also manifest the creeping hair loss of a receding hairline and a widening bald area on the crown of your pate, well, that depends on your genes.

—If you are a *woman*, there is a one-in-six chance that you will have lost most of your body and pubic hair by age sixty (unless you come from Japanese stock, in which case it is virtually 100 percent likely).

Hear Today, Gone Tomorrow?

...One man in his time plays many parts,
His acts being seven ages.
The sixth age...his big manly voice,
turning again toward childish treble, pipes
And whistles in his sound.
                    —*As You Like It*, Act II, scene vii

We now understand medically what the Bard meant. As your vocal cords pull taut with age, they resonate higher. The result:

"HUM" TEST

Hum softly the first notes of "Greensleeves" ("The Sounds of Silence" will do for the younger generation). The difference between the first and second notes is the difference between your speaking voice now and at age seventy. Or, to put it another way, if at seventy you start to hum the tune you will naturally begin on the same pitch that the second note falls on today.

Your speaking voice—in both men and women—rises about twenty-five cycles per second. To get an idea of how your speaking voice will rise, try the "hum" test.

More Than Skin Deep...

Perhaps the most profound changes happen where you can't see or hear them, deep within your cellular and organ systems. In virtually every niche and cranny of your body, aging means the power and strength of your organs and cells are gradual waning.

Losing Our Immunity?

Aging is the progressive accumulation of changes with time... associated with or responsible for the ever-increasing susceptibility to disease and death which accompanies old age.
    —Dr. Denham Harman, "The Aging Process,"
Proceedings of the National Academy of Science,
                            November 1978.

The vulnerability he speaks of is intimately linked to the immune system. During your twenties and thirties, and particularly after age forty or so, your immune system begins to wane in several ways:

—Certain types of immune sentries—T cells, B cells, and neutrophils—become less efficient at protecting you from bacteria, viruses, and cancer.

—By age seventy, your immune system has lost 80 percent to 90 percent of the vigor and germ-fighting reserve it had when you were fifteen.

—Your body becomes less vigilant about fighting off threats to your health, leaving you more vulnerable to infections and cancer.

—Your immune troops become careless and imprecise, failing to distinguish adequately between enemy targets and friendly targets they should leave alone. When this happens, in what doctors call an "autoimmune response" ("auto" means "self"), your body starts to fight itself, even your most vital organs. When the armies that Nature gave you to defend your body turn mutinous, you pay a steep price.

When immune cells attack . . .	You get . . .
Joint linings	Rheumatoid arthritis
Pancreas cells	Diabetes
Nerve fibers	Multiple sclerosis
Stomach lining	Pernicious anemia
Liver	Chronic active hepatitis
Thyroid gland	Graves' disease

An aging immune system, then, is one that has grown both weak and careless.

Plumbing Problems

You can expect your urinary system to lose fully one half its efficiency between age thirty and age eighty. That means your kidneys filter only half as much blood waste per hour. At the same time, the walls of your bladder change, and its capacity diminishes. The result? Rest-room stops become more and more frequent—and urgent.

Neuro-muscular Changes With Age

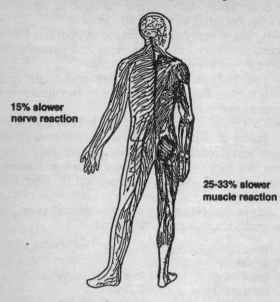

15% slower
nerve reaction

25-33% slower
muscle reaction

The body's electrical system, the nerves, also show signs of wear. Your overall muscle coordination and reflexes drop by one third to one quarter. Some of that is due to the speed of electrical nerve signals along the body, which slows down a few percent each decade. By your midsixties, those signals are traveling about 15 percent slower than they used to.

Are You All Wet?

Even your body's cells themselves change. For instance, do you believe that the body's cells become more or less moist with age? The answer may seem obvious: They actually lose moisture with each passing year, dropping from 42 percent to 33 percent of your body's composition from age twenty-five to seventy-five. This dryness may be part of what accounts for the general sensation of losing the suppleness and silkiness of youth.

There is a very important practical consideration you should know about. As you age, you need to take smaller drug doses to get the same effect. Partly that is due to the fact that your liver and kidneys perform less efficiently. But we know now that part is also due to the greater concentration of drugs in your cells, which in older adults are less diluted by cellular fluids.

Oxygen Changes

One of the most profound changes comes in how your body processes oxygen. Oxygen, of course, is the fuel that stokes your cellular energy furnaces. As the years pass, the oxygen processing mechanism changes in two main ways:

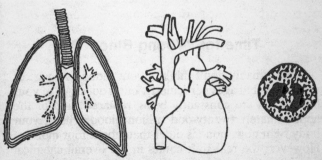

Oxygen Processing Losses With Age

—50% loss of lung capacity + —33% loss of heart pumping action = 50% less oxygen delivered to cells

—Your lung capacity drops from six to three quarts of air with each breath. Right there, less oxygen is available to your bloodstream.

—Then, the average American heart loses up to a third of its pumping capacity, due to the damage caused by disease processes that appear with increasing age. The pumping rate may drop from a high of almost four quarts a minute at age twenty-five to only two and a half quarts at age sixty-five.

This adds up to a significant double whammy: By retirement age, your cells may be getting just half the oxygen they were getting when you graduated college. Small wonder every set of stairs seems to get steeper!

Lowering the Energy Throttle

The common perception of "losing energy" with age reflects a profound biologic truth. Your *basal metabolism*—the rate at which your body burns fuel—drops almost 3 percent every decade. By age seventy, it has tapered off by about one fifth from its peak when you were young. In effect, your body's engines throttle themselves down, bit by inevitable bit.

Time for "Young Blood"?

You probably don't think of your blood as a part of your body that ages particularly, but it does. All of your blood cells are constantly being replaced, and of the approximately twenty-odd trillion blood cells in your body right now, none is older than about four months. However, the real shift comes in the overall chemical profile of the four quarts (men, make that six) of red stuff in your arteries.

Reading Your Own "Blood Age Print"

As you age, the combination of chemicals in your blood changes significantly. If you are a healthy thirty-four-year-old, how your blood profile looks today has little in common with how it will look at age sixty. That means the blood system carries its own rough "age print" which a blood expert (hematologist) can "read" to get a rough idea of how far along you are in the aging process. To cite just four vital measures:

—Blood chemicals, like the hormone renin aldosterone and the blood component albumin, drop as we age. Others, like glucose, uric acid, and the abnormal protein called rheumatoid factor, rise.

—Your blood pressure creeps up over the years, so that what would be a worrisome elevation in a twenty-five-year-old is just about average for his or her mother. Most of us can expect our overall blood pressure to increase about 15 percent between the ages of thirty and sixty-five.

—Likewise, you can expect your cholesterol to rise—for a while. A level of 220 would be of some concern in a twenty-five-year-old, but just about normal at age fifty. But then, after about age fifty-five, it starts inching its way back down again.

—Your blood level of abnormal proteins increases. One of these proteins, rheumatoid factor, is implicated in arthritic inflammation of the joints.

Come to Your Senses...

[The] last scene of all...
Sans teeth, sans eyes, sans taste, sans everything.
                    —*As You Like It,* Act II, scene vii

It is a common view that our older years should be a time to "stop and smell the roses," but unfortunately Nature has built in an obstacle. Experiments suggest that the sense of smell declines significantly with age, particularly for men.

Happily, though, Nature does not rob you of all senses equally. Shakespeare notwithstanding, the sense of taste is very little affected directly by age.

TAKE THE TONGUE TEST

Look at your tongue in the mirror, you will see that it is covered with small bumps, or *papillae*. If you looked at these bumps under a microscope, you would see that each contains a total of between two thousand and nine thousand taste buds—the nerve endings that register sweet, sour, salt, and bitter, and tell you the difference between lime sherbet, fresh peaches, and chopped liver.

Starting at age fifty, the taste buds become less able to regenerate. Within about twenty years, perhaps 70 percent have died off, leaving a scanty seventy-five taste buds on each papilla.

We become less sensitive to the four basic tastes after age fifty. Happily, this loss doesn't lead to a corresponding two-thirds drop in your tasting enjoyment, because Nature has built in redundancy to the human body. If you do lose some sense of taste with age, it is most likely due to some other reason—drugs, sickness, even changes in nerve-transmitter chemicals in the brain.

Ah yes, the brain. Most of us think of the brain as one of the most vulnerable organs to the ravages of age. From a biological perspective, that is accurate: Your brain shrinks, losing about 10 percent of its sixteen billion nerve cells by age seventy, and about 40 percent of its weight.

Loss of Taste Buds With Age

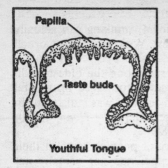

Youthful Tongue

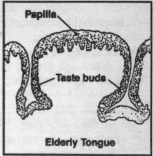

Elderly Tongue

It is a rough-and-ready rule of thumb that if aging is left to its own course you can count on it robbing your body of about 1 percent of its overall functional capacity each year after about age 35. Notice that I said "left to its own course"—after all, you wouldn't be reading this book if you were planning to leave aging to its own course!

Your Body's Functional Capacity

There is a wicked inclination in most people to suppose an old man decayed in his intellects. If a young or middle-aged man, when leaving a company, does not recollect where he laid his hat, it is nothing; but let the same inattention be discovered in an old man and people shrug and say, "His memory is going."

—Samuel Johnson

Samuel Johnson's wise observation is echoed by the newest brain research. Despite physical losses, it just isn't true that we face an inevitable loss of our thinking and brainpower as we age, and it most certainly doesn't have to happen to you. Consider recent research findings:

—"Despite the common belief, thinking can actually improve with age."—New York Hospital–Cornell Medical Center.
—"In every age group, even among the oldest, individuals were found whose performance on mental tasks did not decline with age, but was indistinguishable from that of younger adults."—*Handbook of the Biology of Aging*, 1985.
—"At all ages the majority of people maintain their levels of intellectual competence—or actually improve—as they grow older."—National Institute on Aging.

ADD IT ALL UP AND WHAT DO YOU GET?

Brain weight	decreases 40% by age 70
Number of nerve trunk fibers	decreases 37% by age 70
Blood flow to brain	decreases 20% by age 70
Speed of blood equilibrium mechanism	decreases 83% by age 70
Basal metabolic rate	decreases 20% by age 70
Kidney filtration rate	decreases 50% by age 70
Body water content	decreases 15% by age 70
Resting heart output	decreases 30% by age 70
Handgrip strength	decreases 45% by age 70
Oxygen uptake while exercising	decreases 60% by age 70
Lung volume during exercise	decreases 47% by age 70

Aging Overview

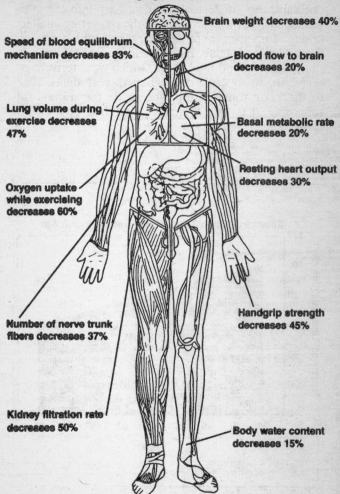

Brain weight decreases 40%

Speed of blood equilibrium mechanism decreases 83%

Blood flow to brain decreases 20%

Lung volume during exercise decreases 47%

Basal metabolic rate decreases 20%

Resting heart output decreases 30%

Oxygen uptake while exercising decreases 60%

Number of nerve trunk fibers decreases 37%

Handgrip strength decreases 45%

Kidney filtration rate decreases 50%

Body water content decreases 15%

By Age 70

My medical training showed me firsthand just how one can keep intellectual abilities sharp into the most advanced age. I will never forget the staggering intellect of one of my medical professors, a man who is now on the near side of eighty. He was held in awe for his razor-sharp intellect and total recall, which were terribly intimidating to my cadre of green medical students. Woe to the poor young intern who made the mistake of supposing that Dr. Weinstein had lost any of his faculties!

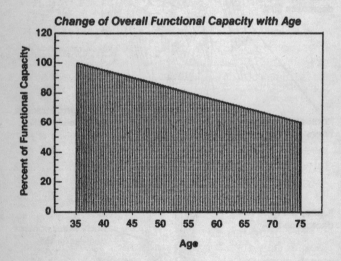

Sex and the Seventy-Year-Old

One other bit of good news: Obviously, a woman's hormonal profile changes dramatically with menopause, and it has long been thought that men's hormones showed a similar waning in their later years. Happily, current research indicates that the levels of the male sex hormones testosterone and androgen in older men remain equal to those of their sons, even grandsons.

The best part of this prescription is that the levels of sex hormones stay highest among those men who have the highest level of sexual activity.

The Anti-aging Motto: Use It or Lose It

We now understand that to a great extent the body operates on a "use it or lose it" principle. That is true of heart, mind, and muscles. That means that there are ways to make sure you will be as sharp, vital, and alive in thirty years as you are right now.

If there is one youth secret that runs through all the research on growth and aging, and throughout this book, it is summed up in those five words—use it or lose it. You possess the keys to staying young and vital—if you choose to use them.

Let's Get Personal

Let's bring this down to a very personal level and look at how these changes will touch *your* life (how much more personal can you get than inside your own body?). You will dust off your crystal ball and peer into the decades ahead.

Using some basic medical tools, you can in effect project your medical future with some educated guesses about what your body will look, act, and feel like as you age.

Dear Old Mom and Dad—
Your Aging Blueprint

You already own the simplest tool to give you a hint about your medical future—the family photo album. Take a look at a picture of your parents or grandparents when they were your age. Look at their hairlines, their body shape, their weight distribution, their faces—then and now. Do you see something of yourself in them (or, more accurately, vice-versa)?

Now compare earlier photographs of them with later ones. In a very real way, the differences your parents have manifested over two decades are a blueprint for the changes you can reasonably expect to experience as you grow older.

—Did your mother develop the bent-over "dowager's hump" that signals osteoporosis?
—Did your father's joints swell with rheumatoid arthritis?
—Did they lose their looks and vitality, or stay hale and hearty until relatively late in life?

There is a solid scientific reason for this exercise. Your parents, after all, are practically your closest genetic match—they just have a twenty- or thirty-year jump on you in how long they've aged, and are the best living examples of how your basic gene set is likely to age.

Aging Forecaster

The second method is more scientific, based on data gathered in examining thousands of people. It takes into account certain average changes that come with age.

These data are based on a statistical golden mean, and there is no guarantee that you will age exactly the same way, but it certainly gives you a general idea about what the decades ahead may hold for you.

Fill in as many of the answers in the lefthand column as you can. Then follow the instructions in the middle column, and behold! the righthand column will give you a reasonable extrapolation of where you might be yourself a few years from now.

Certain aspects affecting your health are such important variables that they merit a more in-depth, and more precise, prediction.

Your Personal Aging Forecaster

Your current:	Factor in these biological changes:	Personal prediction at age 70:
Weight	Men: Subtract 7% Women: Add 4%	
Height	Men: subtract 2½" Women: subtract 1¾"	
Number of teeth: _____ (32, if none are lost yet)	Subtract 1 tooth per decade	
Blood pressure	Men: add 20/10 Women: add 30/10	
Overall functional capacity, start with 100% at age 25	Subtract 10% for each decade	
Body temperature	Subtract 1.5 degrees	
Cholesterol	Men add 40 points Women add 50 points	

Blood Pressure Predictor

Biostatistics let us create a more accurate model to predict possible changes in your blood pressure over the coming years. To predict your possible blood pressure at a given age, use the charts on page 57.

1. Find that age along the line at the bottom of the first chart.
2. Looking at the correct line for your gender, read straight across to the vertical line to find a number. That number represents the top number (systolic) of your blood pressure reading.
3. Do the same on the second chart. That number represents the bottom number (diastolic) of your blood pressure reading.
4. Now for your final result:

Number from
top chart

At age ____ my blood pressure may be: _____

Number from
bottom chart

You can customize this for yourself even more accurately if you know your current blood pressure.
5. If you know your current blood pressure, write numbers here: _____
6. Next, find the average blood pressure for your age category in the table on page 58.
7. Subtract the blood pressure number shown in the table from your current blood pressure and write the difference here: _____
(Don't worry if it's negative—it just means you have a lower-than-average blood pressure profile.)

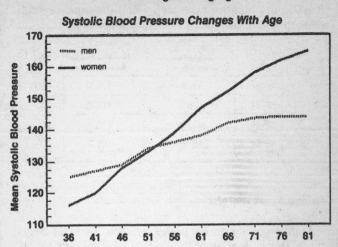

Systolic Blood Pressure Changes With Age

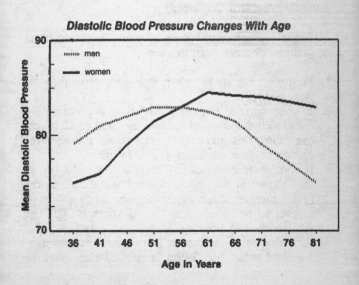

Diastolic Blood Pressure Changes With Age

8. Add the number from step 7 and the number from step 4 here for your personalized prediction: _____

Age	Average Male Blood Pressure	Average Female Blood Pressure
18–24	124/76	111/70
25–34	125/79	112/73
35–44	126/82	119/78
45–54	131/85	129/82

Guess Your Weight

Unlike getting on the scales down at the local drugstore, this is done with the help of medical epidemiology. Use the chart on page 60.

Your Cholesterol Computer

If your doctor has told you what your cholesterol level is, you can proceed with this test.

1. Find your age on the chart opposite, depending on your gender.
2. If your current cholesterol level is approximately equal to that indicated for your age and gender, you can follow this curve up to get a rough average prediction of your cholesterol later in life.
3. If your current cholesterol level differs widely from that shown in the chart, determine the difference. (For example, a thirty-year-old woman should have a level of no more than 190. If yours is 205, the difference is 15 points.)
4. Add the point difference from step 3 to the age-adjusted value you found in step 2. This gives an

Cholesterol Changes With Age

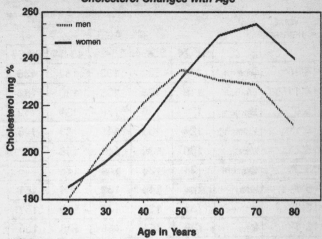

approximate range that you might hit at that age—providing you don't make changes in your diet, exercise, or medications.

You may want to copy down these predictive results and file them away. Twenty weeks from now, when you have had a chance to incorporate many of the basic longevity steps outlined in this book into your life, you might want to consult these results. If you do, I think you may find a pleasant surprise: Thanks to this book, and the changes you have made in your life, you will have improved your score on these variables. But more important than your test score is how you feel, look, and act. Because in those twenty weeks you will have started making yourself biologically younger than your present chronological age.

So next time you hear someone say, "You're not getting any younger," remember your twenty-two longevity steps and smile—because you'll know better.

FOREVER YOUNG

Ideal Weight Chart

YOUR HEIGHT		AGE				
		18-24	25-34	35-44	45-54	55-64
4'10"	Women	114	123	133	132	135
4'11"	Women	118	126	136	136	138
5'0"	Women	121	130	139	139	142
5'1"	Women	124	133	141	143	145
5'2"	Men	130	139	146	148	147
5'2"	Women	128	136	144	146	148
5'3"	Men	135	145	149	154	151
5'3"	Women	131	139	146	150	151
5'4"	Men	139	151	155	158	156
5'4"	Women	134	142	149	153	154
5'5"	Men	143	155	159	163	160
5'5"	Women	137	146	151	157	157
5'6"	Men	148	159	164	167	165
5'6"	Women	141	149	154	160	161
5'7"	Men	152	164	169	171	170
5'7"	Women	144	152	156	164	164
5'8"	Men	157	168	174	176	174
5'8"	Women	147	155	159	168	167
5'9"	Men	162	173	178	180	178
5'10"	Men	166	177	183	185	183
5'11"	Men	171	182	188	190	187
6'0"	Men	175	186	192	194	192
6'1"	Men	180	191	197	198	197
6'2"	Men	185	196	202	204	201

Calculated from: U.S. Center for Health Statistics, North American Association Study of Obesity.

4

How Old Are You, Really?

"This is it. This is what fifty looks like."
—Gloria Steinem, on being told how
young she looked on her fiftieth birthday.

IF YOU ARE to commit to making yourself younger, you have to know where to start—to know how old your body systems are right now. That seems easy—you know how old you are, right? Medically speaking, that isn't necessarily accurate.

A range of biological factors makes the body's real biological age—where its physical systems fall along the continuum from birth to death—only loosely related to the number of years since birth. From your body's perspective, your age is an absolutely relative, approximate measure. You have surely heard a "youthful" seventy-year-old say of a young person that he is "old beyond his years," or have watched a friend age quickly in a few months' time. In each of those instances, you have picked up on a series of subtle—and not-so-subtle—clues about the energy, vitality, mental acuity, general fitness, and sharpness of these people's senses and reflexes, as well as a broad range of different elements about their biological, social, and psychological functioning.

Too, not all parts of your body age at the same rate. You may have a heart that functions at a level "younger" than the age shown on your driver's license, thanks to careful diet and exercise. Yet your skin, liver, or other organs may function like the organs of someone much older because of genetic weakness or stresses they have endured.

Reckoning how the body's systems work is what I do with my patients, and what your own family doctor does during your physical. As your physician checks out your heart and lungs, bones and mobility, blood pressure and lab results, she or he is in effect assessing how you are doing relative to others of the same approximate age. It is when you fall outside the range of age-adjusted values that you are diagnosed with some problem.

In this chapter, you will do much the same thing, assessing your body's relative biological age—what I call your "Youth Quotient."

YOUR PERSONAL "YOUTH QUOTIENT" ASSESSMENT

YOUR PHYSIOLOGY

1. Is your blood pressure: ____
   A. In the range of 120/80–140/90 (1)
   B. Above 140/90 (10)
   C. Above 95/60 but below 120/80 (−10)
   D. Less than 95/60 (10)

2. Is your blood cholesterol level: ____
   A. More than 260 (15)
   B. Between 230 and 260 (10)
   C. Between 180 and 220 (1)
   D. Between 140 and 180 (−10)
   E. Below 140 (−5)

3. Is your resting pulse: ____
   A. Less than 60 beats per minute (−10)
   B. 60–70 beats per minute (1)
   C. 70–90 beats per minute (10)
   D. More than 90 beats per minute (15)

4. Has your doctor ever told you that you are anemic? ____
   A. Yes (10)
   B. No (1)

5. Are you: ____
   A. 20% or more above desired weight (10)
   B. 5%–20% overweight (5)
   C. About right for your height (1)
   D. 5%–20% underweight (5)
   E. 20% or more under (8)

6. Compared to this time last year, your weight: ____
   A. Is pretty much the same (1)
   B. Has risen or fallen, but you can control it with diet and exercise (5)
   C. Is rising or falling now, and is very hard to maintain (10)

FAMILY HISTORY

7. Do any family members have diabetes, hypertension, or heart disease? ____
   A. No (1)
   B. Yes (10)

8. Has anyone in your family ever been diagnosed with cancer? ____
   A. No (1)
   B. Yes (5)

9. Do others in your family have severe allergies? ____
   A. No, not that I know of (1)
   B. Yes, mostly hay fever (3)
   C. Yes, significant allergies to foods or environment (5)

10. Do you have trouble breathing, shortness of breath?　　　___
   A. No (1)
   B. Sometimes, but infrequently (5)
   C. This is a regular or common feeling (10)

11. Do you cough when you wake up in the morning?　　　___
   A. Almost never, except when I have flu or a cold (1)
   B. Sometimes, but it passes quickly (5)
   C. This happens regularly (10)

IMMUNE FUNCTION

12. Do you frequently catch cold, flu, or other illnesses?　　　___
   A. Never—or very rarely (1)
   B. 2–4 times a year (5)
   C. More than 4 times a year (10)

13. When you get sick, how long does it usually take to recover fully?　　　___
   A. 3–4 days (1)
   B. About 10 days (5)
   C. I haven't felt really well for a very long time (10)
   D. Can't remember the last time I was sick (−10)

14. Do you have a history of chronic illness?　　　___
   A. No (−10)
   B. Yes, but for less than 5 years (5)
   C. Yes, for 5 or more years (10)

15. When you get a cut or bruise, does it heal quickly? ___
    A. Yes, it usually heals completely in a few days (1)
    B. I have noticed that I heal more slowly than I used to (5)
    C. Bruises stay a long time; cuts leave a visible mark (10)

16. Your overall health is: ___
    A. Excellent—I am very satisfied (1)
    B. Usually all right, but could be better (5)
    C. Fair to poor—I wish it were better (10)

SPECIFIC SYMPTOMS

17. Have you noticed any problems with walking, balance, or coordination? ___
    A. No (1)
    B. Yes, ongoing minor problems (5)
    C. Yes, they significantly impair my movement (10)

18. How is your skin? ___
    A. Smooth and supple, not scaly or irritated (1)
    B. Rough, cracked, dry in some months. Occasional problem patches (5)
    C. Chronically dry, itchy, flaky, or irritated (10)

19. Do you have headaches? ___
    A. A few times a year, or less (1)
    B Often, but they go away quickly (5)
    C. Often, and they are painful and debilitating (10)

20. Do you experience leg or arm muscle cramps?　　　___
    A. No, almost never (1)
    B. Occasionally—sometimes when I am sleeping (5)
    C. Yes, frequently, especially when I walk or exercise (10)

21. Do you have arthritis, joint pain, or pain in your feet and hands?　　　___
    A. Only rarely (1)
    B. My joints sometimes seem stiff; I notice pain in my hands and feet more (5)
    C. Pain in joints and extremities has really limited my mobility or actions (10)

22. Do you have pain in your back, especially down low?　　　___
    A. Only rarely, and it goes away (1)
    B Twinges, but not debilitating (5)
    C. It is a constant feeling, and affects my mobility, actions, or mood (10)

23. Do your extremities ever feel cold, numb, or tingly?　　　___
    A. No, I do not experience those feelings (1)
    B. They happen sometimes, but not regularly (5)
    C. Yes, I have noticed those sensations regularly (10)

24. Do you get diarrhea, constipation, or digestion problems?　　　___
    A. No, or only when I am ill or have eaten the wrong foods (1)
    B. Yes, but the problems are more irritating than serious (5)

C. These are frequent problems; I watch carefully what I eat (10)

EXERCISE

25. When was the last time you did any strenuous exercise? ___
    A. Within the last 5 days (− 10)
    B. Only within the last month (1)
    C. Longer than a month (10)

26. Do you get out of breath? ___
    A. When I do strenuous aerobic exercise for more than a few minutes (− 10)
    B. Whenever I exercise or have a short exertion like running for a bus or playing with a child for a little while (5)
    C. When I climb stairs or carry parcels (10)

27. Do your legs cramp when you walk more than a few minutes? ___
    A. As a regular occurrence (10)
    B. Sometimes, but rarely (5)
    C. No (1)

28. Have you had any broken bones in the last year? ___
    A. No (1)
    B. Yes, one incident (5)
    C. Two or more separate times (10)

29. Your general energy level is: ___
    A. Variable—some days I feel fine, but mostly I could use more energy (5)
    B. Great—I have lots of energy (1)
    C. Constantly sluggish. I often want to sleep. When I do, I often don't awake refreshed (10)

NUTRITION AND DIET

30. When it comes to fiber in your food, you: _____
    A. Consciously eat raw vegetables and
       fruits, grains, and legumes (−10)
    B. Usually eat at least a salad once a day,
       whole grains or equivalent (1)
    C. Eat mostly frozen or canned vegetables
       (5)
    D. I don't like vegetables or grains (10)

31. Does *most* of your protein come from: _____
    A. Veal, white-meat chicken (5)
    B. Vegetable sources (nuts, grains, or
       legumes) or fish (−5)
    C. Red meat (10)

32. How often do you eat fried foods, butter,
    or other cholesterol-containing foods? _____
    A. More than once a day (10)
    B. About once a day (5)
    C. Less than once a day (−5)

33. Do you eat cruciferous vegetables
    (cauliflower, broccoli, Brussels sprouts)? _____
    A. At least once a week, fresh (−5)
    B. No more than occasionally (5)
    C. Hardly ever or never (10)

34. What about calcium? _____
    A. I know the calcium content of foods and
       make an effort to eat calcium-rich foods
       (−5)
    B. I take calcium supplements (1)
    C. I don't make any special effort (10)

35. Do you eat more: ____
    A. Simple carbohydrates (candy, sweets, jelly, desserts) (10)
    B. Complex carbohydrates (pasta, bread, grains) (−5)

36. Do you salt your food: ____
    A. Heavily (10)
    B. Lightly (5)
    C. Not at all (1)

37. Have you noticed allergies to any food or drink?   ____
    A. No, nothing obvious (1)
    B. Yes, to 1 or 2 specific items (5)
    C. Yes, to 3 or more food or drink items (10)

LIFE-STYLE AND HABITS

38. Do you drink alcohol?   ____
    A. More than 2 drinks per day (10)
    B. 2 drinks per day (3)
    C. Occasionally, less than 2 drinks daily (−5)
    D. No (−10)

39. Do you always wear seat belts?   ____
    A. Yes (1)
    B. No (10)

40. Do you smoke cigars, pipes, or cigarettes?   ____
    A. Yes (10)
    B. No (−10)

41. Do you breathe others' smoke at home or at work?   ____
    A. Yes (10)
    B. No (1)

42. If you are light-skinned, do you take
    measures to protect your skin from the sun? ____
    A. Yes, I stay out of the sun or remain
       thoroughly covered (1)
    B. Yes, I wear sunscreen (5)
    C. No, I like looking tanned and healthy
       (10)

43. Which best describes your sleeping habits? ____
    A. I usually get 6–8 hours of sleep a night;
       I awaken refreshed (1)
    B. I don't always get enough sleep, but
       catch up on weekends (5)
    C. I have problems falling asleep, wake
       through the night, have trouble waking
       in the morning, or don't feel rested (10)

44. When it comes to worrying: ____
    A. Once I make up my mind, I don't look
       back. Fretting is not my style. I leave
       problems at work (1)
    B. Like most people, I have a lot on my
       mind sometimes, but not usually (5)
    C. I often worry about things that haven't
       happened yet. I replay what I should
       have said or done in situations (10)

45. How many prescription drugs do you take? ____
    A. None, have never taken them regularly
       (1)
    B. 1–3 types of drugs now or in the last
       year (5)
    C. At least 4 types now or in the last year
       (10)

EMOTIONAL STATUS

46. About your work life and career choice: ___
    A. I really enjoy my job and the challenge it brings me (1)
    B. I am generally satisfied, but sometimes it gives me real problems (5)
    C. My job is a chore, I wish I were somewhere else (10)

47. Is there someone in your life you trust absolutely and can tell your deepest secrets to?   ___
    A. Yes, my mate or best friend (−10)
    B. Usually, but I don't often bother people with my problems (5)
    C. There is no one in my life I can confide in right now, I tend to be a loner (10)

48. In life: ___
    A. I am quite independent in making decisions that affect me (1)
    B. Much of what I do depends on my mate, boss, family, or others. Sometimes I don't feel in control (5)
    C My life is very constrained by others (10)

49. Does your life allow you to really enjoy your friends and hobbies?   ___
    A. Yes, I am pretty happy with my balanced life-style (−5)
    B. My time is mostly dedicated to obligations and duties (5)
    C. I can't remember the last time I really had great fun (10)

50. Right now, you would describe your
    emotional state as: ____
    A. Pretty upbeat and stable, all things
       considered (1)
    B. It varies, but I don't get too down or
       stay that way (5)
    C. My life feels pretty bleak and out of
       control (10)

51. Your sexual relations are: ____
    A. Satisfying and positive (1)
    B. Some areas definitely need help (5)
    C. A significant issue—I have no satisfying
       sexual outlet (10)

52. Choose the phrase that best describes you: ____
    A. Calm, even-tempered and generally
       happy. Friends comment on it (1)
    B. A "hard worker" with high standards at
       work, school, in relationships. Trying to
       keep everything under control, I don't
       always succeed (5)
    C. I am under heavy stress. I am quick to
       anger (10)

53. Your relations with others tend to be: ____
    A. Satisfying, with clear lines of
       communication (1)
    B. A strain. I often feel like I can't
       connect (5)
    C Often short-lived and marked by
       disputes (10)

54. When you look in a mirror, you feel: ____
    A. I look good for someone my age, as
       well as I feel (−5)

B. I could look better with some work on
    diet, exercise, etc. (1)
C. To look good is a major, difficult effort
    (10)

SCORING:

Total score for your biological age: ___

1. Write your chronological age here: ___
2. Look up your total score to find your
    biological age and your Youth Preservation
    Level: ___

Pay Special Attention to Your Youth Preservation Level

That letter is your key to the Youth Preservation steps
you will be making in every chapter from now on. If
you are in Level A, you will have a different regime
than if you are in Level D throughout this book. You
need to know your Youth Preservation Level in order
to tailor the Youth Preservation steps to you.

If you don't like what you see right now, as you add
up the grand total, remember: The farther behind you

Score	Your Biological Age	Youth Preservation Level
−82 to 43	Subtract 5 Years from Chronological Age	A
43 to 170	Subtract 2 years from Chronological Age	B
170 to 296	Keep Chronological Age Unchanged	C
296 to 423	Add 2 Years to Chronological Age	D
423 to 550	Add 5 Years to Chronological Age	E

Grand total for Your Biological Age: ___

are, the greater your potential to make tremendous, positive changes in your health and life expectancy. You may want to take this quiz again after you have made the life-style changes in the chapters that follow. I guarantee that you will score "younger"—because biologically your body's processes will actually *be* younger.

Keeping the Outer You Looking Young

THE FIRST PLACE to start making yourself younger is where it is most obvious—with the body that greets you in the mirror and which everybody sees. This chapter focuses on that outer you, your skin and face. It gives you six easy steps that you can do, right now, to make yourself look younger and regain the glow of youthful, radiant skin. Follow these steps, and in ten weeks from now you will start to see results. By the time you are twenty weeks into the program, I expect you will see a significant improvement in your skin's health and appearance.

But first, let's settle one thing once and for all. Many of my patients, when they first consult me for ways to make themselves look more youthful, confide this to me as though it were a dirty little secret. They think the idea of taking care of themselves is vain somehow. I disagree. Our society places an obsessive value on youth and vitality. Much of our power as individuals, and our self-worth, is intimately related to how youthful we, and others, feel we look. Appearance is the face you present to the world and, as such, it is very important. Outward appearances are far more than empty vanity.

Happily, mainstream medicine is now coming to agree. Note this editorial in the *Journal of the American Medical Association*:

It is increasingly apparent that appearance, certainly including cutaneous appearance, contributes to society's evaluation of an individual's competence and to that individual's sense of self-worth and well-being. . . . The prospect of [an] effective anti-aging product for the skin may have direct medical benefit beyond its effect on premalignant lesions.

—*Journal of the American Medical Association,*
1/22/88, Vol. 259, No. 4, p. 569

Translation: Experts realize that *looking as young as you feel is a vital part of being a vital person.*

The public has understood this fact longer than the doctors have. In the time it takes you to read this page, Americans will have spent $19,000 on skin preparations—a rate that adds up to a whopping $27 million every day! It's not just women; men, too, are finally starting to understand that looking their best makes them feel their best.

At the same time, scientists have found a fascinating relation between how old somebody looks to an observer and their scores on a battery of laboratory tests that measure aging throughout the body's systems. It seems that youthful-looking people have bodies that function biologically below their chronological age, and the reverse is true of people who look prematurely aged—independent of their chronological age. Clearly, inside and out, looking young is part of what it is to *be* young.

What's in Store for Your Skin?

Consider the difference between old and young skin. As your skin ages, here's what happens biologically:

—You lose elasticity.
—You lose 10% to 20% of your skin's pigment cells each decade (that's why very old people seem to have such light, almost translucent skin).

—You lose 50 percent of the Langerhans cells, immune cells that protect against skin cancer.

—Your skin gets rougher and less evenly pigmented (age spots).

—Your skin turns from a rosy color to a more yellowish hue.

Just a Pinch...

The Pinch Test is an approximate way to test your skin's age. Put your hand flat on a table, back side up. Pinch a fingerful of loose skin on the back of your hand between thumb and forefinger of your other hand, then let it go. Note how long it takes until the area you pinched has flattened out completely. That time suggests a reading of your skin's relative age.

That's a picture of what happens if Nature takes its course. Now let's see what you can do about it—the good news here. Today, there is an array of quite effective ways to keep your skin young and supple. Best of all, they are ways that work! Let's look at the six skin-care principles, combining nutrition, several new developments in skin products, and a few commonsense changes. With them, you can not only dramatically slow

Time for Pinch to Return to Normal

Women	Men	Skin Age
0 sec	0 sec	10–19
0 sec	0 sec	20–29
1 sec	<.5 sec	30–39
3 sec	1 sec	40–49
12 sec	4 sec	50–59
21 sec	20 sec	60–69
1 min	43 sec	Over 70

the rate of your skin's aging, but actually *reverse* some
of the ravages that time has wrought.

Step One: The Tretinoin "Miracle"

You have probably heard of last year's dermatologic
superstar, topical tretinoin, or Retin-A. Just last year,
the *Journal of the American Medical Association* caused
an immense public stir when it published a study showing that this vitamin A-derived cream actually seems to
reverse some of the changes caused by aging, renewing
and rebuilding skin cells so the skin is less rough, mot-
tled, and wrinkled. Where most creams merely hydrate
your skin—that is, restore lost water and puff it up—
Retin-A goes deeper into the dermal layers and actually
stimulates new cell growth. The result? Your skin gains
a new lease on life, actually filling in small creases and
wrinkles, smoothing out rough spots. Since this discovery, Retin-A has been flying off pharmacists' shelves,
and dermatologists have hardly been able to keep up
with the demand.

The excitement is because Retin-A is the first product
that can demonstrably, dependably make skin look
younger. It smoothes out fine wrinkles, sun spots, and
skin blemishes. It clearly promotes the growth of new,
healthy skin, lifts the top surface of the skin away from
deeper layers, and increases the rate of formation of
new skin cells. The result is that Retin-A–treated skin
is rejuvenated; creating not just new skin but more
healthy, rosy, and fresh-looking skin. It is no miracle
cure, surely, but one of the best tools to soften and
lighten the patina of age that starts taking its toll on
our faces after age thirty. I have seen Retin-A make
positive changes in many patients after just several
months.

You can expect it to:

—Help minor wrinkles, such as those around the nose and eyes
—Reduce blemishes, discoloration, or sun spots
—Help give your skin a better tone
—Make your skin somewhat softer and smoother
—Restore a more rosy glow to your skin

But don't expect a complete face-lift in a tube. Deep wrinkles and furrows will remain unchanged. And do be patient. After all, what Nature did in decades you can't expect to undo in weeks. You will probably require six months of daily applications to begin to appreciate fully the noticeable improvement in your skin's texture and luster.

Are You a Retin-A Candidate?

Some people are ideal Retin-A candidates because of their skin type. Are you:

—Of Celtic origin (Irish, Scottish, English)?
—With blond or red hair?
—With fair skin?
—With blue eyes?
—One who spends any time in the sun?

If your answer to several of these questions is yes, congratulations: You are the ideal candidate to reverse the damages of skin aging by Retin-A. That doesn't mean other people won't be helped, too. It's just that they are most sensitive to the kind of sunlight damage that Retin-A works best on. But since almost all of us have some degree of photoaging, we, too, can be candidates for "saving face" with Retin-A.

Putting It to Work in Your Own Life

If you are interested in Retin-A for you, the first step is to discuss it with a knowledgeable dermatologist. He or she will probably start you off with the 0.1 percent dosage concentration that is most widely used. Nine out of ten people have a reaction when they first use the cream—discomfort, peeling, or irritation. Don't worry—that is an expected and customary phase of your body's adaptation to the biological power of Retin-A.

Then, as you get used to the treatment, many doctors including Dr. Albert Kligman, professor emeritus of dermatology at the University of Pennsylvania, who discovered Retin-A's anti-aging properties, recommend increasing the dosage concentration to 0.2 percent or 0.5 percent after a period of time, if your skin can tolerate it.

To help make Retin-A available to everybody who could benefit from it, the makers of Retin-A have just announced that they will manufacture a special quarter-strength .025 percent version. This formulation should be available in your pharmacy by the time you read this. This means that many people with sensitive skin, who might have problems tolerating the full-strength 0.1 percent-formulation Retin-A, can still take advantage of its real wrinkle-smoothing benefits.

Retin-A is almost as easy to use as cold cream. Just spread a pea-sized dab of it each night on your face and neck. I usually start patients on an every-other-day regimen, to let their skin get used to the cream. If you tolerate it well, you can then slowly increase the frequency to once a day. If your skin gets irritated, ask your doctor for a lower concentration or use the cream every third day, until the redness goes away, then try returning to a more frequent schedule.

The latest research suggests that you should get the most significant cosmetic results in the first year and a half that you use Retin-A. At that point, the improvement seems to level off, and you can go on a less frequent maintenance regime that keeps the positive changes you have gained so far.

Retin-A Hints

You can dramatically improve the chance of Retin-A working for you by following a few simple guidelines:

—I recommend you apply Retin-A at night, before bed; then wash or shower it off in the morning.

—A few minutes before applying Retin-A, wash your face with a mild, nonastringent cleanser.

—Because Retin-A makes your skin effectively younger, and promotes the growth of new skin cells, your face also becomes that much more sensitive to sunlight. That means it is *essential* that you protect your new, tender (and youthful!) skin. *Always* wear an SPF (sun protection factor) 15 sunblock when you go out in the sun—even for a quick shopping trip. I tell my patients to get in the habit of putting on a sunblock each morning before they go out.

—It may also help to use a moisturizer each morning after you have removed the Retin-A. If you do, make sure it is a hypoallergenic product, to avoid irritating the tender new skin.

—If you are pregnant or nursing, do not use Retin-A.

—One consumers' advisory: Make sure you use the real thing. With the avalanche of press attention to tretinoin, several companies have jumped into the market to get their share of the pie, offering confusingly named products that are a far cry from what the doctor ordered. One such ersatz product calls itself Retinol-A, another Retinyl-A, and several others may have sprouted up by the time you read this. The truth is, there is no generic Retin-A, and the name of the only real product, made by Ortho Pharmaceutical Corporation, is Retin-A.

Retin-A has not yet been carefully tested in controlled experiments on large numbers of people, so we are still learning about its long-term effects. But it is already clear that Retin-A represents a quantum step in anti-aging skin care. It is an exciting step, and one which can make a difference in your own life and in the face that you see in the mirror! But keep three cardinal rules in mind:

—DON'T expect miraculous changes to happen overnight.
—DO expect an irritation reaction, particularly in the beginning.
—DO make Retin-A part of an overall skin-care team—not the only player.

What's Next?

Retin-A is only the first of what promises to be a new generation of skin-care creams. These products, the "cosmaceuticals," actually have proven medical effects and are more than simple moisturizers. Several other promising possibilities are now coming through the research pipeline, and will be appearing in the coming years.

Now that you have made Retin-A the first step of your young-skin program, let's look at what else you can do right now to keep your skin youthful.

Step Two: Moisturizers

When it comes to moisturizers, there is good news and bad news. First, the bad: None of the $10 billion worth of commercial cosmetics we buy each year really reverse the damages of age at the cellular level. Now the good news: They may make you look as if they do.

Moisturizers work on a simple principle. They keep

water next to your skin, and as the moistened skin swells, it masks small wrinkles, blemishes, and imperfections. Wrinkles don't really go away, of course, because no real repair has been done. When you rinse off the cream, or the moisture evaporates, they are still there. Still, for simple cosmetic value, these products may deliver a lot of illusory bang for the buck. For that reason, there is no reason not to continue using them, if you like the way you look.

You should know, however, that none of the "high-priced spreads" containing exotic oils and ingredients necessarily do a much better job than such old-fashioned stand-bys as basic cold cream and petroleum jelly. Nivea and Vaseline are hardly romantic, but these heavy oils do as good a job as any to keep the skin moist.

Summary Moisturizers have a place in your young-skin regime, but none of them, neither the basics nor the most elegant and expensive concoctions, actually do anything to repair the underlying problem.

Step Three: C Is for Collagen

There is, however, one kind of cream that may be an exception to this rule because laboratory science suggests it gets to the root of the problem. A prime component of skin is the connective protein collagen. It now appears that vitamin C may actually strengthen and rejuvenate the collagen in your skin in several ways.

For ten years, laboratory researchers at Duke University have been working with vitamin C and skin cells. Their work suggests that in the test tube a topical application of vitamin C cream works to help skin synthesize vital new collagen, the essential component that is damaged by aging. While we do not yet have absolute proof that vitamin C works in the body, at least one cosmetic manufacturer, Avon, has created a vitamin C-based skin cream that delivers the ascorbic acid (vitamin C) where it does the most good: right on the aging skin cells. Similarly, vitamin C has been shown to inhibit certain skin cancers.

Summary Vitamin C cream can't hurt, and may be a valuable addition to your young-skin regimen.

Step Four: Youth-Preserving Skin Nutrition

In addition to vitamin C, there are two other vitamins that play an important role in making your skin young from the inside out. To understand why, it's necessary to understand the phenomenon called "cross-linking." When you are young and your skin is at its most supple, the strings of collagen protein it contains are relatively well formed and neat. But as you age, the accumulated damage of sun, chemicals, wind, smoke, and biological toxins tangle those protein strings. In cross-linking, the proteins can grab on to each other, linking molecules where they should not and generally getting very tangled. When that happens, your skin loses its elasticity and becomes rigid.

> A good way to visualize cross-linking is imagine hanging twenty strips of sticky adhesive tape from your hand, and vigorously moving them around. As the tape strips touch, they stick and become tangled, until soon they bear very little resemblance to the twenty neat rows you started with. With this happening throughout your skin's connective tissue, no wonder it loses its youthful suppleness!

Scientists now believe that the antioxidant vitamins C, A, and E can help prevent and undo the cellular damage of cross-linking. They work, not just in your skin, but in all the body's tissues where cross-linking can occur: connective tissues, tendons, blood vessels, cornea, bones, and many organs. These vitamins can also help promote skin healing, reduce the formation of scar tissue, and give your skin and mucosal tissues the elements they need to grow healthily and smoothly.

THEY FORM THE CORE OF YOUR YOUTH PRESERVATION PROGRAM, and are essential for your skin's youthful appearance and long-term health. *Your vitamin-supplement program is based on your score from the personal "Youth Quotient" Assessment quiz you took in Chapter 4.* Turn to page 73, at the end of Chapter 4, to find your Youth Preservation Category. That category determines the level of nutritional help your skin needs.

Youth Preservation Category	Vitamin C	Vitamin E	Beta-carotene*
A	2 grams	400 I.U.	12,000 I.U.
B	3 grams	400 I.U.	15,000 I.U.
C	4 grams	600 I.U.	17,500 I.U.
D	4 grams	600 I.U.	18,000 I.U.
E	5 grams	600 I.U.	20,000 I.U.

* An entirely safe form of vitamin A

Vitamin A vs. Beta-carotene

You may wonder if there is something missing from this picture. Why don't I prescribe vitamin A? After all, A is important for keeping your skin, eyes, and the mucosal linings of your body healthy. Even your nails, glands, hair, and teeth need enough A to stay healthy and attractive. Studies show that four out of ten Americans—especially blacks and Hispanics—do not consume the RDA (Recommended Daily Allowance) for vitamin A.

However, vitamin A can also be toxic. Because this fat-soluble vitamin is stored in your fat and liver, it can build up to dangerously high levels. Too much vitamin A can create severe complications, like gout, anemia, and worse. Happily, there is a safer way to make sure you get enough.

"Better Than A": Beta-carotene

The truth is, not all vitamin A is created equal. Ready-made vitamin A, called retinol, comes from animal sources. Another form, the carotenoids, is present also in plants. The most important of carotenoids is beta-carotene. This orange chemical is a first-stage form of vitamin A, called a "precursor." Your body converts beta-carotene into the vitamin A it needs. That means you can make beta-carotene into the vitamin A, enjoy its vital youth benefits, yet avoid the possible toxicity of regular vitamin A. (One study, at Harvard University, had 11,000 physicians taking as much as 30 milligrams of beta-carotene each day. I don't recommend such huge doses—but when it comes to safety, 11,000 Harvard doctors can't be too wrong!)

The point is, your body will convert just how much beta-carotene it needs into usable vitamin A, while naturally protecting you against a toxic overdose. This makes beta-carotene an "A-Plus" nutrient—all the benefits of vitamin A PLUS complete safety. That's why you should get used to taking the harmless, beta-carotene form of vitamin A.

Beta-carotene, like the other skin nutrients vitamins E and C, is a powerful antioxidant. It fights the free radicals that cause aging in your skin and throughout your body. At Harvard researchers have shown that beta-carotene may prevent or slow the development of skin cancer. Not only does beta-carotene fight biological damage to our cells as we age, it has even been shown to extend life expectancy in animals, from mice to men. That's why you must make sure to get enough of it.

You can boost your beta-carotene by eating foods like those shown below:

BETA-CAROTENE-RICH FOODS

Greens:
Chicory
Watercress
Dandelion
Mustard
Radish
Collard

Beets
Broccoli
Butternut squash
Carrots
Kale
Parsnips
Pumpkins
Spinach
Sweet potatoes
Tomatoes

Others:
Cantaloupe
Papaya
Vegetable soups
Milk
Fresh tomato sauce

If you follow the plan and eat at least one 3-ounce serving of green, red, or yellow vegetables a day, you'll be giving yourself enough beta-carotene to make your skin and your whole body look younger. Because beta-carotene helps protect against cancer and aging, it is one of the easiest and most delicious parts of your Youth Preservation prescription.

Summary Get sufficient vitamins C and E and beta-carotene from food and from the supplement regime I suggest, based on your Youth Preservation Category.

Step Five: The Sin of Sun

Mad dogs and Englishmen
go out in the midday sun.

—Noel Coward

This step has little to do with research breakthroughs or exotic treatments. It's news you've surely heard before. Yet it is *your single best and most effective way to keep your skin young.* The tip? Stay out of the sun. Period.

Sunlight—that seemingly promotes a "healthy" tan—works like a destructive time machine, giving you the skin of a person many decades older. When rays of light enter the skin cells, they react with oxygen, creating the free radicals we discussed earlier. These unstable oxygen molecules, in turn, damage virtually every aspect of your cells: membranes, fats, the proteins the cells need to operate, and the DNA and RNA they need to replicate. This process, called "photoaging," damages your skin in ways that normal aging does not:

—Changing its color from rosy red to yellowish
—Toughening, roughening, and wrinkling extensively
—Spotting with brown patches, red spidery veins, and warty growths
—Accelerates by many times the normal loss of elasticity

Of course, this is just the damage you can see. At the same time, overexposure to the sun increases your risk for three kinds of skin cancer, one of which, malignant melanoma, is especially deadly. If you think you've heard most of this before, stay tuned anyway because you probably haven't heard about two new wrinkles under the sun—more reasons that scientists have found that sunlight is bad news for those who want young skin.

TRY THE "CHEEK-TO-CHEEK TEST"

Many of what we usually think of as the inevitable changes of aging are, in truth, the results of photoaging. You can see the dramatic proof of that through what I call the "cheek-to-cheek test." Compare the skin on your buttocks (that is, if you're not a habitual sunbather *au naturel*) with the skin on your face, arms, and hands. The skin that was covered shows what the "inevitable" and normal skin-aging process looks like. The difference between that and the more exposed skin areas is the price of indiscriminate photoaging— a price that is avoidable.

Ozone and Aging

The ozone layer, ten to twenty miles above the planet's surface, may not seem very relevant to your life. But we now know it directly affects your chances of ending up with cancer and prematurely aged skin. The ozone layer works like a layer of sunscreen over the whole planet. This chemical blanket absorbs large amounts of ultraviolet radiation, preventing our sensitive skin from being bombarded by it.

Unfortunately, planet Earth's sunscreen is dissolving even as you read this. The protective ozone layer has decreased 3 percent in recent years, bringing a 15 percent rise in skin cancer cases. That means, 78,000 more people will get skin cancer, and more than 1,000 will die. It is because of the decrease in the ozone layer that the rate of skin cancer has never been higher. If the trend continues, as experts predict, we will see tens of thousands of new skin cancer cases, and thousands of needless, avoidable deaths.

Also, a Cornell Medical School study shows that too much sun can deplete your body's stores of the very beta-carotene that protects it. Another reason (if you needed one) to make sure you take adequate beta-carotene supplements.

Clearly, it is more important than ever to control the amount of sun your skin gets. However, that is probably not news to you. The real news is how to do it most effectively.

Summary Stay out of the sun as much as possible.

Step Six: Sunscreen, the Skin Savior

Most sunscreens do a good job of absorbing certain kinds of light rays—called "ultraviolet B (UVB)." That is the type of sunlight that gives you a burn. The UVB rays only penetrate your skin's top layers, and with most protective sunscreens, much of this radiation can be blocked. How much is blocked is what is meant by the sun protection factor (SPF) on the label of the bottle or tube.

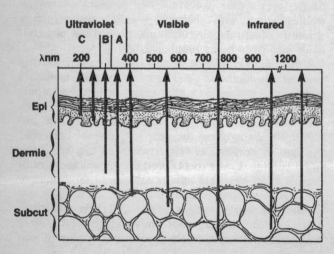

Skin Penetration of Light Rays

Paba vs. Natural Melanin Ultraviolet Protection

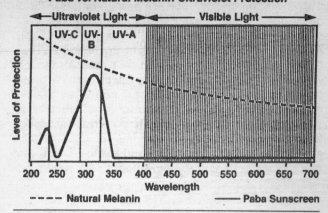

◄——— Ultraviolet Light ———►◄——— Visible Light ———►

UV-C | UV-B | UV-A

Level of Protection

Wavelength

200 250 300 350 400 450 500 550 600 650 700

- - - - Natural Melanin   ——— Paba Sunscreen

But that's only half the story. Experts have recently come to understand that there is another villain responsible for sun aging, ultraviolet A (UVA) light. Where the UVB rays penetrate only the top layers of the skin, the more powerful UVA rays penetrate even deeper, damaging the deepest layers of the skin and the supporting collagen tissues.

Unfortunately, many of the commercial sunscreens use PABA (para-aminobenzoic acid), which stops UVB but still lets most of the dangerous UVA penetrate to your skin's deepest levels. These creams prevent visible burning, so can lull you into a false sense of security: You stay out longer, exposed to harmful UVA rays. These rays not only increase the risk of skin cancer, but accelerate the aging of the deepest layers of the skin.

The only moderately effective sunscreens that work against UVA and UVB rays are those containing both PABA and a chemical called oxybenzone (by the time you read this, these preparations will be the majority on the market). Such "wide-spectrum" preparations represent the state-of-the-art in sun protection.

However, there is one thing you need to know about

wide-spectrum creams. *The sun protection factor listed on the bottle or tube applies only to their UVB (sunburn) protection.* When it comes to the damaging UVA rays, their protection value is equivalent to about a 2. That means you have to use them with great care, for though they keep you from burning up to fifteen to thirty times longer, they only give you minimal protection against invisible aging damage, no matter what number is shown on the label. So, until more powerful wide-spectrum blockers are available, limiting sun exposure mechanically—with clothes, hats, and shade—is still the way to keep your skin supple, smooth, and young.

A NOTE ABOUT ALLERGIES...

You may have tried sunscreens with PABA or oxybenzone, found that you had a severe inflammation, or a burning or itching sensation when you went out into the sun, and concluded that you were allergic to PABA. You're probably half right—you may have an allergy but most likely, it's not to these ingredients. Laboratory tests show that fewer than one person in a thousand have documented allergic reactions to PABA.

But if you feel you are that one person, or you have especially sensitive skin that does have problems, you can shop around for products without PABA. It doesn't matter which other UVB sunscreen they contain: So long as you choose a suitable SPF, you'll be protected. I recommend that you try Sundown Broad Spectrum, because it uses titanium, which blocks UVA rays, and is free of PABA. However, if you have problems with one brand, always experiment with another until you find one you tolerate better.

Summary If you must be in the sun, use wide-spectrum sunscreens containing PABA and oxybenzone. If the PABA bothers your skin, switch to another sunscreen with an equal SPF number, and preferably one that contains oxybenzone for UVA protection.

Looking Ahead to Tomorrow's Breakthroughs...

Part of the task of this book is to alert you to research developments that, if they are not here yet, may be available soon. In the burgeoning field of anti-aging skin products, Retin-A represents only the first generation of true anti-aging treatments that actually reverse the process. The science of skin rejuvenation is exploding with even more exciting developments. As this book goes to press, a ferocious war is going on in research laboratories the world over to develop other, more powerful ways to rejuvenate the skin. Let me share with you some of the research breakthroughs that will change your life (or at least your skin's life) in the next few years. Remember—you heard it here first!

Factor X

From biomedical researchers in Denmark comes word of what may be the most promising new substance on the research horizon. Developed by the British biotechnology laboratory Senetek, it has a name that conjures images of secret laboratories and mysterious ingredients: Factor X. If early reports prove out, it may indeed be a stunning breakthrough in anti-aging treatment. Factor X may be nothing less than the biochemical fountain of youth that can prevent the changes that age causes in skin cell structure.

Normally, as the body's cells live longer, they change shape and their volume increases, so fewer of them can fit in the same space. The result is that the body's tissues become less compact—and biochemically less efficient. At the same time, older cells in the skin dramatically slow their production of critical cell proteins, such as elastin, that your skin needs to stay flexible, supple, and healthy.

Enter Factor X. When this extract is added to the cells and they are observed under a microscope, the changes that normally happen in older cells seem not to happen. They remain compact looking and, acting like younger cells, continue to churn out the critical proteins that help the skin stay young.

Clearly, such a product, if it proved viable, would represent a stunning breakthrough in the chemical treatment of aging—not just for the skin, but for cells throughout the body. Thus far, it is very hard to get much information about the project, and key details remain shrouded in secrecy. Dr. Nick Coppard, one of the biochemists in charge of the project, says only that they hope to begin human trials with an anti-aging skin lotion within the next year. They may have even begun by the time this book goes to press. Keep your eyes open for late-breaking news about how you can use Factor X to keep your skin looking younger, longer.

Looking ahead to future developments, there are several new products that could revolutionize how our skin ages.

Full-spectrum sunscreens that block the full range of skin-damaging ultraviolet light will be available. Versions of these that are already on the market are relatively crude; as we learn more about the UVA skin aging, we can expect to see safer and more effective sunscreens that will afford you high-range protection for the entire spectrum of ultraviolet radiation.

Genetically engineered sunscreen is being developed by a California laboratory called Advanced Polymer Systems. Utilizing a remarkable fusion of high-tech and natural approaches, this sunscreen contains the strongest natural sun protection known, the skin pigment melanin.

Melanin is the perfect sunscreen you would come up with if you were as smart as Mother Nature and had tens of millions of years to work in. This pigment shields you from wavelengths of ultraviolet light in direct proportion to their damaging effect on your skin. Studies show that black Africans, who have very high levels of natural melanin in their skin, have a "built-in" sun protection factor of 15. Soon, you may be able to benefit from the same protection.

Unfortunately, melanin has been too scarce to use—until now. California researchers have found a way to produce large quantities of natural, safe melanin using genetic engineering. However, melanin doesn't work effectively if you just slather it on, so other researchers have come up with an astonishing way to apply it where it does the most good.

They encapsulate it in tiny microscopic sponges, so infinitesimal that a single one measures about $\frac{1}{1000}$th of an inch and weighs about $\frac{1}{4}$ *billionth* of an ounce! These "microsponges" trap the genetically engineered melanin next to the skin, creating an effective, safe layer of the natural pigment that Nature meant you to have.

This radical approach promises a safer, more effective, natural sunscreen. Though the project is still on the drawing board, look for the first melanin products in the early 1990s.

Sun protection in a pill. What would have sounded like science fiction just a few years ago is being investigated and developed in research centers around the country. The goal: sunscreen products you swallow instead of applying.

Researchers at the University of Arizona Medical Center are working on a way to boost your body's own sun-protection mechanism: a tanning hormone that increases the natural melanin. They have created a superactive analog of a natural hormone called "melanocyte stimulating hormone" (MSH), which "instructs" the body to manufacture more pigment cells in the skin. Biochemically, it is the same reaction that occurs when a chameleon changes color—or when you get a natural tan. This hormone would make your skin look as if you had been at the beach all summer—but with none of the serious aging effects that would create. The goal is not just to make you look naturally healthy and fit (though you would), but to block sunlight so it doesn't penetrate to damage and age the deeper skin tissues. Early tests suggest that the hormone product is nontoxic and could be swallowed like a pill.

The protective tan MSH creates may last as long as several months—guarding you against the sun, reducing your risk of skin cancer, and giving you a glowing, appealing tan. The research is only in its earliest phase in animals, so don't expect to see these products on the market for at least six or seven years. But if MSH works, it will be among the hottest news on the scientific horizon.

Scientists at Harvard Medical School are trying a very different approach. Instead of blocking the sun from striking the skin cells, as with lotions, or filtering it with the skin's own pigment, they are trying to help the body repair the damage that light can cause within the skin itself. A photobiologist in Boston reports early laboratory research based on the theory of anti-oxidants, which are thought to be key to many of the body's aging processes. The goal is to neutralize the deadly oxygen by-products—the free radicals—which are created in your cells by exposure to ultraviolet light. Because free radicals cause skin aging, cross-linking, and skin cancer, researchers hope that by chemically inactivating these destructive oxygen molecules, tissue damage can be prevented before it happens. They envision using this kind of pill not as a replacement for the bottle of sunscreen at the beach, but as protection against limited short-duration exposures to sun.

"Sun protection in a pill" is one of the most exciting and creative ideas on the anti-aging horizon. Laboratories are trying to perfect the first generation of oral sun protectors. The medical evidence all points to one inescapable conclusion: *Within the next few years, we will have a stunning new array of tools that not only control, but reverse disfiguring skin aging.*

The Six-Step Skin-Care Program

However, in order to take full advantage of these new developments, you must do all you can now to keep your skin young, using every tool at your disposal today. Your prescription is to heed the six vital steps to skin rejuvenation . . . starting right now! Include these six crucial steps in your younger-skin regimen:

1. Ask your doctor if you are a candidate for Retin-A cream.
2. If you use a basic moisturizer, do it only for cosmetic, not therapeutic, results.
3. Consider using a nutrient-enriched (vitamin C) skin cream.
4. Take an appropriate Youth Preservation nutrient regime (as determined by your personal Youth Preservation Quotient), and keep your diet high in beta-carotene.
5. Keep out of the sun as much as possible. Period.
6. If you use a sunblock, use one that contains a wide-spectrum PABA-oxybenzone agent.

Young at Heart: Building Yourself a State-of-the-Art Heart

Heart disease before eighty is our own fault, not God's or Nature's will.

—Harvard University cardiac specialist
Paul Dudley White, M.D.

ENERGY. FITNESS. VIGOR. They are synonymous with all it means to be youthful. For true biological youth has little to do with how many birthdays you have chalked up. What counts is your vitality, how you can bound up a flight of stairs or enjoy playing with a child or grandchild with energy and full enjoyment. It means waking to each day brimming with vigor and enthusiasm, knowing you can count on your body to perform what you demand of it, knowing it will deliver the energy, vitality, and stamina you need to lead an active life.

All of that depends on one muscle—the one beating in your chest right now. You are only as youthful as your heart is, and this essential muscle determines your vitality, how young you feel, and whether you will have the breath, energy, and stamina to meet life on your terms. It is an essential component not just of longevity, but of a truly healthy, vital existence.

A too-old heart makes you too old to enjoy the wonderful bounty that life holds for those who have the vitality to seize it. Premature heart aging robs more than five million Americans of this vitality, makes them sluggish and sedentary, and steals years from their productive, active lives. They weaken or die too young with a heart that is too old; the victims of 100 percent preventable, 100 percent unnecessary cardiovascular aging.

But this unnecessary killer disease doesn't happen so much to people in other societies, and it won't happen to you if you follow the guidelines I recommend. Below are the six easy steps you need to keep your heart strong and sound, pumping forcefully and faithfully, assuring you of decades of active, positive life. They are the state-of-the-medical art in preventive cardiology, geared to add several years to the life of your heart. Follow them and I promise you: One year from today, your heart will be "younger" than it is today. You will have a 100 percent state-of-the-art heart!

1. STOP SMOKING NOW, TO REJUVENATE YOUR HEART.
2. EAT A "HEART-SMART" DIET THAT REDUCES SATURATED FATS.
3. CONSUME FISH AS A MAIN MEAL AT LEAST TWICE WEEKLY. AVOID FRIED FISH.
4. EAT FIBER TO REDUCE FATS AND CHOLESTEROL.
5. TAKE TIME EACH DAY TO RELAX AND REDUCE STRESS.
6. GET MODERATE EXERCISE AND ACTIVITY SEVERAL TIMES A WEEK.

With these steps you can do *more* than just prevent your heart from aging. You can actually *reverse* destructive heart and artery changes that may have already occurred.

Much of this may sound familiar. That's fine. Our goal is to help you incorporate these cardio-fitness rules into a life-prolonging, health-prolonging plan—to make you 100 percent "young at heart."

A Heart Choice

It has been said that the average American's heart loses up to one third of its pumping capacity by age seventy. *But new research shows that such a cardiac decline is neither inevitable nor necessarily built in.* Maintain your heart right, and it will work about as well at age eighty as it did at twenty. Heart decay occurs, not because of normal aging, but because of a lifetime of cardiac ignorance, mistreatment, or abuse. It's up to you: Which lifeline do *you* want to be on?

Summary The loss of heart function with age is not "natural." It *is* preventable. Staying young at heart is up to you.

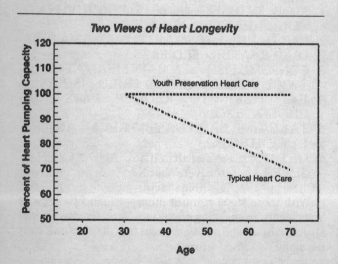

Two Views of Heart Longevity

Test Yourself: How Old Is Your Heart?

The greater your present risk for cardiac disease, the older the effective age of your heart and cardiovascular system. Are you:

GROUP A:

From a family with a history of heart disease? _____
A smoker? _____
With cholesterol above 230? _____
With blood pressure above 140/90? (If so, see special note on page 111.) _____

GROUP B:

A diabetic? _____
More than 15% overweight? _____
A survivor of one or more heart attacks? _____
Ever diagnosed with angina? _____
Suffering occasional sharp chest pains? _____
A competitive, hard-driving personality? _____
Sedentary and inactive? _____

For each Yes answer in Group A, add two years to your cardiac age.
For each Yes answer in Group B, add one year to your cardiac age.

If you have any of the factors in Group A, your risk for having heart disease, and perhaps a heart attack, is two to four times higher than if you don't. The factors in Group B are less severe, but also increase your risk for heart disease. Combine factors in both groups, and the risk increases that much more. A person with high blood pressure and high cholesterol who smokes is *eight times* more likely to have a heart attack than one who has none of these factors.

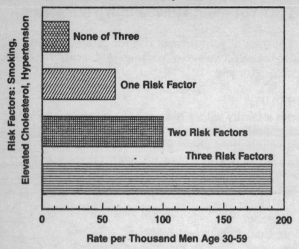

Risk Factors for Coronary Heart Disease

Risk Factors: Smoking, Elevated Cholesterol, Hypertension

None of Three

One Risk Factor

Two Risk Factors

Three Risk Factors

0   50   100   150   200

Rate per Thousand Men Age 30-59

The good news is that *you can change most of these factors.* You have the chance to reap the wonderful rewards of being youthful, energetic, and strong at heart for many years to come!

Young-at-Heart Step One: Where There's Smoke, There's Danger

Do you know the *single most effective* way to reduce your heart's age? Stop smoking. Right now. There is no better way to dramatically and significantly lower the effective age of your entire cardiovascular system. Consider:

—The heart disease rate is twice as high in smokers than in nonsmokers—four times as high for heavy smokers.

—Smokers are at higher risk for sudden death, heart attack, artery disease, and aneurysm, and are twice as likely to have a stroke as nonsmokers.
—Smoking ages virtually every part of the cardiovascular system prematurely and unnecessarily.

Happily, just as soon as you stop smoking, your risk begins dropping sharply; so that after five years, you are at no higher risk for stroke than a nonsmoker. After ten years, if you smoked less than a pack a day, your heart risk would be virtually identical to that of someone who never smoked. *Every day you don't smoke, your heart heals itself and gets younger!* Stopping smoking *now* is the single most dramatic step you can take to make your cardiovascular system effectively younger. Period.

Summary The sooner you stop smoking, the sooner your body will rebuild your heart.

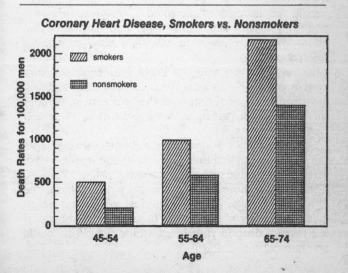

Coronary Heart Disease, Smokers vs. Nonsmokers

Young-at-Heart Step Two: Clean out Those Pipes

Diet can influence your long-term health prospects more than any other action. Of greatest concern is our intake of dietary fat for chronic diseases such as coronary artery disease...and strokes. —U.S. Surgeon General's Report on Nutrition and Health, 1988

The Surgeon General, our highest health authority, has finally said what many have known for some time: Diet is the most important tool against heart aging. National health authorities have now made "less fat" America's number-one diet priority.

Yet the National Institutes of Health reports that most Americans' cholesterol levels are still too high. That means that, although the basic goal is clear, people are confused about how to put dietary recommendations into practice. They hear "high-density lipoproteins" and "low-density lipoproteins"; "triglycerides" versus "cholesterol"; "saturated," "polyunsaturated," and "monosaturated" fats—and end up befuddled about what they ought to eat, *right now*, to make a difference.

Enough. If you want to keep your cardiovascular system young, if you want to enjoy the health and longevity advantages of a state-of-the-art heart, remember this one simple principle: *Keep your pipes clear and clean.*

A young circulatory system is one whose arterial pipelines are smooth and unblocked, with the least possible arterial thickening and blood-blocking plaque deposits. The cleaner, more fat-free you keep your blood, the more you reverse aging in arteries, veins, and heart. Every percent you lower your blood cholesterol means a 2 percent drop in your heart-attack risk. What could be simpler?

Below are nine basic diet principles, based on recommendations of the National Institutes of Health, the American Heart Association, and virtually every responsible cardio-health authority. Follow these rules, and every bite you take will help you strip away years from the biological age of your cardiovascular system.

This plan has helped thousands of my patients give themselves a cardiac "retread." It has given them state-of-the-art hearts to make them feel more buoyant and energetic, more alive and vigorous. They feel more alive, can exercise (some for the first time in years!) and have more energy for work, hobbies, and family. With these nine diet rules you can turn back the clock on aging, remove previously deposited fats from your artery walls, give your cardiovascular system a "retread"—and ensure a longer, more vigorous life. You can see why I want *you* to start experiencing such terrific benefits!

NINE DIET RULES FOR A STATE-OF-THE-ART HEART

1. Increase your intake of complex carbohydrates (starches).
2. Greatly reduce red meats and animal fats and trim off all visible fat.
3. Eat fewer eggs or eggs without the yolks.
4. Eat more fish. Try for three times each week.
5. When you do eat fats, make sure they are monosaturated, not saturated or polyunsaturated (see Appendix A, "Cardiac Longevity Foods").
6. Increase your fiber intake—whole grains, fresh fruits, and vegetables. You should eat fiber with every meal.
7. Reduce consumption of highly refined foods, including refined sugar.

8. Instead of fried foods, eat broiled, baked or boiled foods.
9. Reduce your intake of coffee.

Summary Reduce saturated fats and cholesterol in your diet.

Turning Back the Clock

By themselves, these tips aren't radical. What is radical is how they can actually reverse heart and arterial damage that may have already occurred, and effectively drop your cardiac age.

Cholesterol Transport in the Body

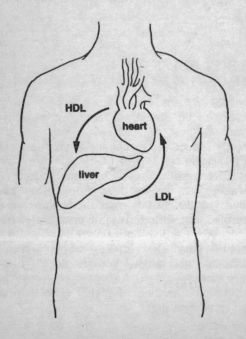

Let me explain. Cholesterol circulates in your body by piggy-backing on one of two one-way messengers: LDL (low-density lipoprotein) moves cholesterol from your liver to your tissues and organs (like your cardiac vessels); HDL (high-density lipoprotein) transports it back. By changing the ratio of those elements, with more HDL carrying cholesterol back to the liver and less LDL carrying it out to the blood vessels, you can halt the process that ages the heart and arteries. The single best way to do that is through the ratio of saturated fat and cholesterol you eat.

Research shows that if you lower your LDL level to below 100, your body can actually start pulling deposited fats and cholesterol out of your blood vessel walls, so they can heal themselves and return to a smoother, "younger" state. That means heart rejuvenation, pure and simple, allowing your heart and arteries to function as long and well as Nature designed them to.

By lowering your total cholesterol and reducing your LDL, *you can actually reverse the damage accumulated before you ever picked up this book*! In six months your blood vessels will actually look smoother, more open and elastic—*younger* in every biochemical sense—than they are right now.

New Surprise: Coffee and Cholesterol?

Brand-new research in the *American Journal of Epidemiology* suggests that coffee drinking may raise your cholesterol. Interestingly, no such link has been found for tea, colas, or other caffeine-containing drinks, or even for decaffeinated coffee. However, something in coffee seems to cause this problem. Until we know just what it is, it appears that drinking less java means a younger heart.

Young-at-Heart Step Three: Make Your Diet More E-Fish-Ent

Next comes an easy way to balance the fats in your blood. *Starting today, with this evening's dinner, eat fish at least two times each week.* Doctor's orders.

Fish contains the best fats, the Omega-3 fatty acids, among them EPA (eicosapentaenoic acid) and DHA (docosahexaenoic acid). Among their many positive effects, they:

—Make your blood platelets less sticky
—Reduce several chemical steps that lead to arterial lesions
—Reduce LDL levels
—Reduce overall cholesterol
—Reduce blood pressure
—Minimize inflammation

They are your key to achieving a clean, smooth, youthful heart and blood system. You will greatly reduce your risk of early death from coronary disease. Fish oils have also been shown to help people who have had their arteries opened surgically to keep them clear, and young. Obviously, you should have your fish dishes broiled, baked, poached, or boiled—not fried.

Fish oil works best when it is eaten as fish rather than as pills. There is less risk of side effects or overdosing; you have one less pill to take, and using fish as your protein source means you will be eating less meat, whose saturated fats boost cholesterol. And fish is so much more delicious!

Summary Eat fish as a main meal at least twice weekly. Avoid fried fish.

Young-at-Heart Step Four:
Fiber for Your Heart

You may think fiber helps with bowel regularity, or weight loss, or even as cancer protection—and it does. But it also reduces excess blood fats and cholesterol.

Fiber helps prevent your body from absorbing the wrong fats from foods. Its chemical and mechanical action sweeps unhealthy fats out of your intestines, reducing cholesterol that would otherwise gum up your blood, blood vessels, and heart.

People in societies that consume high levels of fiber have significantly younger hearts and low rates of cardiovascular aging. The Japanese, who eat more fiber per capita than any other nation, lose one seventh as many people to heart attacks as we do in the United States, which has one of the world's lowest rates of fiber consumption. In America vegetarians who eat a lot of fiber have less fat in their blood, and lower average blood pressures, than people with low-fiber intake. A high-fiber diet can lower triglycerides and cholesterol by one fifth to one third, slowing down the aging of your entire cardiac system.

When it comes to clearing out fat, not all fiber is created equal. I especially recommend:

—Soybean fiber, which has been shown to significantly decrease cholesterol in people with moderately high levels.
—Oat bran, which is also highly effective. Get in the habit of starting your day with a bowl of regular (not instant) oatmeal.
—Corn fiber, which is one of the newest food supplements, and has been shown to reduce cholesterol by an average of 20 percent, and other blood fats by

more than 30 percent. Even better, this insoluble fiber has very few calories.

—Guar gum is another terrific blood fat-fighter. A Stanford University study shows that guar-gum supplements reduce both the overall cholesterol level and the specific type of cholesterol (LDL) most implicated in aging your heart and blood vessels. I have given many of my patients these supplements to reduce high cholesterol, blood fats, and with them, the age of their cardiovascular system.

—A natural fiber preparation called "psyllium hydrophilic mucilloid," available at your local pharmacy, is also effective in lowering cholesterol.

Other fiber sources that can extend the life of your heart are:

	Fiber Sources to Fight Cardio-aging	
Fiber class	Found in these foods	Absorbs fats & cholesterol
Pectin	Apples, grapes, potatoes, squash, oranges, lemons, grapefruit	Yes
Gum	Oats, oat bran, barley, lentils, chick-peas, black-eyed peas, pinto beans, navy beans, split peas	Yes
Mucilage	Seeds	Yes

In addition, many fiber foods are good sources of vitamins, such as vitamin C and the B vitamin inositol, which your body needs to fight fats and cholesterol.

Diet Before Drugs

Eating the proper food is always your first and best line of defense against early heart aging. Only if you cannot achieve results with diet alone should your doctor prescribe drugs to help lower your cholesterol. Some of these drugs (called "bile-sequestrants," such as cholestyramine or colestipol) prevent the cholesterol from being absorbed from your digestive tract in the first place, and some of them (such as lovastatin) work in the bloodstream itself.

You should ask your doctor for the first kind. According to the National Heart, Lung, and Blood Institute, bile-sequestrant drugs should be the first treatment after diet; they are preferable to drugs that work in the bloodstream. If you must use medication, discuss the different options with your doctor.

But remember: By following the guidelines in this chapter, you should need no drugs at all. To get you started, I have included a special appendix section at the end of this book, with a specific state-of-the-art heart diet, and extensive information on heart-preservative fiber-rich foods.

Summary Use fiber and diet—not drugs—to reduce fats and cholesterol.

Special Note for Hypertensives . . .

We can't talk about keeping your heart young without a word about blood pressure. If you answered yes to the question about blood pressure in the self-test on page 101, you may be the one in six Americans who has hypertension. That puts you at higher risk for several diseases, including heart attack and stroke. In addition, your cardiovascular system is aging faster than it should.

Usually you can do something about high blood pressure. With your doctor's help, you can probably remove yourself from this risk group completely. But to start, here are three heart-helping hints to lower your blood pressure, your risk for stroke and heart attack—and your biological age.

BLOOD PRESSURE MYTH

Many people seem to think you can tell persons with high blood pressure because they are nervous, jittery, or tense. That is more myth than medicine. Hypertension and personality bear no relation to each other. People with high blood pressure can be tense and anxious or placid and laid-back.

First—Reduce the alcohol you drink. If it's two drinks a day, make it one. Try some nonalcoholic beverages, or dilute the alcohol you do drink with mixers. This is an absolutely necessary step to reducing the excess blood pressure that is prematurely aging your circulatory system.

Second—Stop using salt on your food, and start paying careful attention to the salt content of the prepared, frozen, and canned foods you eat. Make sodium-free salt substitutes a part of your diet. Expand your taste in seasoning to include garlic, onions, and herbs in place of salt in every dish. You've probably heard those two tips before (from your own physician, I hope!), but you may not have heard this final recommendation.

Third—Eat more fiber, the natural way to control blood pressure. It has been shown that when low-fiber eaters include more of it in their diet for one month, their blood pressure drops significantly. Many natural forms of fiber—vegetables and grains—also include minerals like magnesium, calcium, and potassium, which also help stabilize blood pressure.

All three of these heart-helping hints are essential to controlling this insidious and common factor responsible for aging your body before its time. After following these tips for a month, check yourself against the chart at right.

If your blood pressure is still too high, talk with your doctor to see if you are a candidate for blood-pressure-lowering medicine. Remember: You *can* eliminate high blood pressure, and by removing this premature aging factor from your life, you take a large step toward extending your most healthy and vigorous years.

Age	Average Male Blood Pressure	Average Female Blood Pressure
25	124/76 E	
30	125/76 E	
35	125/80 E	115/75 F
40	128/82 F 129/81 E	119/75 F
45	130/83 F	125/78 F
50	134/83	130/81 F
55	134/83 F	139/83 F
60	136/82 F 140/83 E	148/84 F

Young-at-Heart Step Five: A Calm Heart Is a Young Heart

The next step is both simple and very difficult. Relax. We have long known that too much stress puts you at risk for heart attack. Who can't recall being under stress and feeling their heart thumping or racing? Unfortunately, that is just the visible sign of the serious long-term effects stress puts on your heart:

—Men with what doctors term the "Type A" personality—hard-driving, impatient, achieving, competitive—are twice as likely to develop heart disease as their calmer, "Type B" fellows.
—Those who have lost a spouse to death are much more at risk for heart attack than are their same-age friends who have not experienced emotional trauma.

—Residents near major airports, living with the steady stress of aircraft noise, have high rates of heart disease and hypertension.

—From the *New England Journal of Medicine,* research shows that everyday stresses—acts as simple as talking about an emotional subject, doing math problems, or speaking in public—could trigger episodes of oxygen deprivation and erratic heartbeat. Though silent and painless, these episodes are nonetheless damaging.

—As this chapter went to press, a report in the *American Heart Journal* showed that psychological stress can lead to heart-rhythm abnormalities, and even fatal heart malfunction.

The evidence is clear: Stress weakens your heart, aging it before its time. Heart youth means reducing stress, to rejuvenate your heart.

What's Your "Stress Load"?

Stress is very individual. What may seem a killing amount for one person might seem just about average for a second, and not bother a third person at all. We even require a certain amount of stress in our lives to feel motivated and stimulated. It is not the absolute level of stress that counts, but how you experience it— your "stress load." This following quiz was designed for the U.S. Department of Health and Human Services to help you assess your stress load:

1. Do you have a supportive family?   Yes ___ (10)   No ___ (0)
2. Do you belong to a nonfamily social activity group, meeting at least once each month?   Yes ___ (10)   No ___ (0)
3. In a week, do you do something you really enjoy that is just for you?   Yes ___ (5)   No ___ (0)
4. At home, do you have a place to relax or be by yourself?   Yes ___ (10)   No ___ (0)

5. How often do you bring work home at night? ___(multiply by −5)

6. Do you actively pursue a hobby? Yes ___ (10)   No ___ (0)

7. Do you engage in deep relaxation (meditation, yoga, etc.) at least three times each week? Yes ___ (15)   No ___ (0)

8. How many packs of cigarettes do you smoke each day? (multiply by 10)

None	___
One	___
Two	___
Three or more	___

9. How many evenings each week do you use a drug or a drink to help fall asleep? ___(multiply by −5)

10. Do you use a drug or drinks to help calm down during the day? ___(multiply by −10)

11. How many times do you exercise 30 minutes or longer in a given week?

I don't	___	(0)
One	___	(5)
Two	___	(10)
Three	___	(15)
Four or more	___	(20)

12. How many nutritionally balanced and wholesome meals do you eat each day?

None	___	(0)
One	___	(5)
Two	___	(10)
Three	___	(15)

13. Are you within five pounds of your "ideal" body weight for your age and bone type? Yes ___ (15)   No ___ (0)

14. Do you practice time management techniques in your daily life? Yes ___ (10)   No ___ (0)

TOTAL SCORE: _____

SCORING:

100–120	Congratulations! You take care of your stress load well enough that you are not a candidate for stress-related heart aging.
60–100	You deal with stress adequately, but you have room to improve. Your heart could be having stress damage.
Below 60	Your stress levels are unhealthy. You risk aging your heart prematurely.

Now, let's improve things. Go back and look at the test questions. Each suggests a way you can build stress out of your life and give yourself a younger heart! You might:

1. Take up a hobby you enjoy.
2. Join a group that lets you get out with friends regularly.
3. Work to bring yourself within five pounds of your "ideal" weight.
4. Do some form of deep relaxation (meditation, yoga, biofeedback, etc.)
5. Make sure you get exercise every few days.
6. Learn to eat nutritionally balanced and wholesome meals.
7. Take time each week to do something special just for yourself.
8. Create a place to relax or be by yourself at home or nearby.
9. Learn and use time management techniques in your daily life.
10. Stop smoking (but you knew that!).
11. Learn to use relaxation exercises instead of alcohol or drugs to unwind before sleep.
12. Don't bring work home at night.

Do such measures work? Yes, says an intriguing study released from the Medical School of Athens. Epidemiologists, ruling out other known risk factors, found that men who took a half-hour nap daily to control stress were 30 percent less likely to suffer from coronary disease than men who didn't! Studies at Harvard show that relaxation exercises can help regulate irregular heartbeats in people with heart damage. Obviously, you don't have to take a siesta each day religiously, but some form of stress control will help take years off your heart.

Summary Taking time each day to relax and reduce stress keeps your heart young.

Young-at-Heart Step Six: Exercise

This last is a very simple, and very essential, point. *Every hour that you sit or lie around instead of being active shortens your life.* Period. While almost every part of your body benefits from exercise, by far the most good comes in your heart and circulatory system. Exercise can:

—Reduce bad LDL fats and increase good HDL fats.
—Reduce blood pressure in sedentary people.
—Help vanquish angina (heart pain due to lack of oxygen).
—Lower the risk of heart attack by more than half.
—Decrease excess body fat, which otherwise weakens your heart and shortens your life.
—Help you live longer.

Workers in high-activity jobs have less coronary artery disease than their low-activity colleagues. In the words of one textbook: "When people remain active, their body . . . tends to resemble that of younger people." The research message is clear—need I say more?

Well, yes. There are two myths about exercise that may be preventing you from taking advantage of its full heart-rejuvenating potential. Let's put them to rest.

Exercise Myth #1: "You have to do serious aerobic workouts, marathons, and the like to benefit. I'm no athlete."

You don't have to be. The fact is, any exercise is better than none. Among the kinds of exercise that have been shown effective are:

Playing with children
Walking to errands
Cleaning windows
Vacuuming or mopping the floor
Bowling
Golf
Cleaning out the attic or cellar
Pruning trees
Body surfing
Gardening
Raking leaves
Dancing
Taking a hike
Playing
Climbing stairs
Mowing the lawn
Walking the dog
Swimming

This list proves the point: Any time spent being active is better than time spent not being active. If you expend even 1,000 calories each week above your daily needs, you begin to derive clear health benefits. You don't have to be a Greg Louganis or Carl Lewis, you just have to *not* be a couch potato. To be sure, if you are a more avid athlete, your potential benefit is that much greater. But just because you can't run a marathon is no reason to give up on the solid benefits of moderate activity to keep your heart young.

Exercise Myth #2: "I'm too old to exercise. I can't make up for a life of not exercising."

Banish another myth. In truth, a reasonable program of activity and exercise will make you younger at any age. Researchers from the Palo Alto (California) Clinic measured age against one common laboratory standard of aging, the maximum oxygen uptake (VO_2Max), and found:

> If an inactive 70-year old were to begin an exercise
> program of "moderate activity," the result would be a
> gain of 15 years. ... If the subject were to achieve the
> "athlete" level of conditioning, there would be a poten-
> tial improvement of *40 years* [emphasis in original].
>   *—Journal of American Geriatrics*

If that can work for seventy-year olds, think what it
can do for you! As I sat down to write this chapter, a
study was just published from the famed Honolulu
Heart Program at Kauakini Medical Center. They
found that even among people forty-five to sixty-four
years old, those who led active lives had almost one
third less coronary heart disease than their inactive
counterparts. Those men have functionally younger
hearts, and can expect to live longer and better. Tennis,
anyone?

Summary Moderate exercise and activity are crucial
to giving yourself a state-of-the-art heart.

Looking Ahead: Tomorrow's State-of-the-Art Heart

—One of the most innovative and exciting weapons in
our fight against high cholesterol came recently when
the FDA approved a new "cholesterol card" test.
You simply prick your finger and squeeze a drop of
blood on the card, which changes color to signal if
your cholesterol levels are in the low/safe, medium/
normal, or high/danger range. As of this writing, the
card is available only to doctors. But there are plans
to license it for home use as well, and I hope it will
be available by the time you read this. It is a quick,
almost painless, and inexpensive means of assessing
your own cholesterol risk.

—From Boston University and Harvard medical
schools, a new discovery uses the natural vegetable

compound beta-carotene to boost the most advanced laser-surgery techniques for clogged arteries. Powerful laser scalpels have proven difficult to use to open clogged arteries because they can also damage the surrounding blood vessel walls. But by treating patients with beta-carotene before surgery, doctors can alter the fatty deposits in the heart arteries, making them more vulnerable to laser light. Combining this natural vitamin and high-tech lasers, surgeons can vaporize dangerous fat deposits more easily without harming adjacent blood vessel walls.

—Some 500,000 Americans have an inherited defect in their cholesterol regulation system that predisposes them to heart attack. At the University of California at San Diego, researchers are working on a gene transplant that would replace those defective genes with biologically correct ones. If the experiment works, they will be able to inject these "corrected" genes, to be incorporated into a person's own genetic code. The hope is that as these new genes grow to replace an individual's own faulty genes, they will help clear excess cholesterol from the body.

—Scientists at Johns Hopkins University are working to develop a new breed of diagnostic tool, a miniaturized electronic capsule that can be swallowed. Like a tiny internal satellite, once inside the body it sends radio signals that trace the heartbeat from the inside out. Such capsules may just be a first step: One day, electronics that you swallow may give you and your physician a more accurate, in-depth look at cardiac functioning than is now possible. The earliest prototypes may undergo testing in three years.

—Promising new drug research may hold good news for the sixty million Americans with high blood pressure. Radically different kinds of drugs, called "renin blockers," are now being perfected in Upjohn's research laboratories. They work on a new principle: They bind a million times more strongly to blood pressure enzymes than the body's own natural chemicals do, so they interfere with the runaway hypertension syndrome—before it turns dangerous. This drug may be generally available approximately five years from now.

Young-at-Heart Review

Remember the basic building blocks of a state-of-the-art heart:

1. THE LOSS OF HEART FUNCTION WITH AGE IS NOT "NATURAL." IT *IS* LARGELY PREVENTABLE.
2. STOP SMOKING NOW, TO REJUVENATE YOUR HEART.
3. REDUCE SATURATED FATS IN YOUR DIET.
4. EAT FISH AS A MAIN MEAL AT LEAST TWICE WEEKLY. AVOID FRIED FISH.
5. USE FIBER TO REDUCE FATS AND CHOLESTEROL.
6. TAKE TIME EACH DAY TO RELAX AND REDUCE STRESS.
7. GET MODERATE EXERCISE AND ACTIVITY SEVERAL TIMES A WEEK.

Where There's Smoke...
There's Aging

Cigarettes are the most important individual health risk
in this country, responsible for more premature deaths
and disability than any other known agent.

—C. Everett Koop, M.D.
U.S. Surgeon General

WELCOME TO THE briefest chapter of this book. If you
are one of the fifty-four million Americans who still
smoke, I wrote it just for you. If you're not, you can
read it if you wish or skip ahead to the next chapter.

You may not be surprised that the message of this
short chapter can be reduced to two short words: Stop
Now. Simply put, smoking is one of the most effective
ways to age your body prematurely and cause you to
die too young. *This means that to stop smoking is one
of the most effective steps you can take to slow the aging
process throughout your body.*

Smoking works against every single principle of this
book, and defeats your goal of living longer and more
healthily. If you have a two-pack-a-day habit, you have
a 70 percent greater chance of dying of disease than
your friends who don't smoke, and you can expect to
shorten your life by eight to nine years. In this case,
the charts on the next page are worth a thousand words.

I expect you already know all of this. But what you
may not know is that there is a real silver lining for you

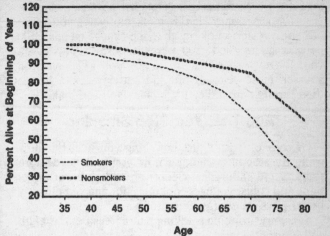

Longevity of Male Smokers and Nonsmokers, from Age 35

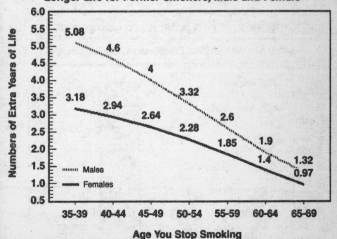

Longer Life for Former Smokers, Male and Female

behind these grim statistics. *As a smoker, you are in a unique position to make an immense positive change in your life expectancy.* If this book motivates you to do nothing but stop smoking, that one change means a 100 percent guaranteed, 100 percent positive impact on your longevity. By that single act, you will have won yourself more years of life and better years of health than through any other life change you can make.

Age That You Stop Smoking

Of course, it isn't just how long you live, but how well. By stopping smoking now you will have more stamina and endurance, clearer breathing, fewer infections and colds, younger-looking skin, and significantly better physical energy and vitality.

Summary Stopping smoking guarantees better health and longevity.

I don't want to dwell on what you've already heard about the dangers of smoking. Instead, I want to give you some information that you may not have heard—and a specific four-part program to help you stop.

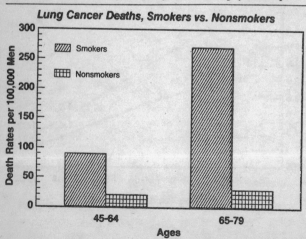

Lung Cancer Deaths, Smokers vs. Nonsmokers

Part One: Just the Facts

Research shows that accurate information is a big part of helping you stop smoking. So, your first step to enjoying a healthy, long, smoke-free life is to get the most well-rounded picture of what smoking does to your health. *This information is the first step in your commitment to stopping smoking.*

You know that quitting now will give you a younger heart and cardiovascular system. You probably know, too, that the same is true of your lungs. Because smoking increases your risk for lung cancer between ten and

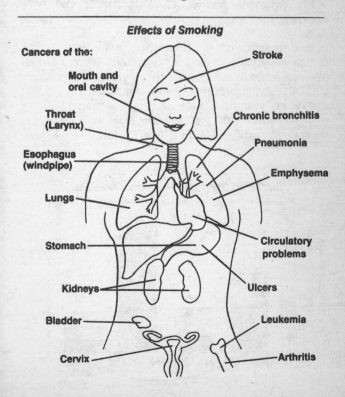

Effects of Smoking

Cancers of the:
- Mouth and oral cavity
- Throat (Larynx)
- Esophagus (windpipe)
- Lungs
- Stomach
- Kidneys
- Bladder
- Cervix

- Stroke
- Chronic bronchitis
- Pneumonia
- Emphysema
- Circulatory problems
- Ulcers
- Leukemia
- Arthritis

twenty-five times, stopping now removes you from these risk groups—increasing your longevity potential still further.

While stopping smoking rejuvenates your heart and lungs, and increases your life span, it also decreases the risks shown on page 125.

What better way to rejuvenate and protect so many areas of the body—Just Say No to Tobacco!

For Mothers Only

For pregnant women, smoking has special risks (below).

Add these factors up, then figure in the severe aging effects smoking has on your heart and blood vessels, and you begin to see why it is the single most pernicious cause of early mortality we know, one that takes 315,000 lives every year. But more important, it points the way to *the obvious step you can take right now* to easily, simply, give yourself years of extra-quality life. Know-

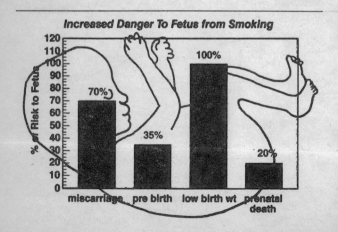

Increased Danger To Fetus from Smoking

ing the whole health story, you know that *you can choose to build these problems out of your life.* So what are you waiting for?

Summary Knowing all the facts is the first part to quitting.

Part Two: Addiction

So now you are convinced you should stop smoking. You're in good company—so have the thirty-seven million people who actually have dropped the habit in the last twenty years. However, what keeps one in three Americans smoking today is a question of addiction, pure and simple.

You don't need lectures about an addiction you can't help. What you need are some useful tools to help you break that addictive pattern, and give the single biggest boost to your longevity, vitality, and health. That means understanding your physiological relation to smoking— what it does to your body's biochemistry. This quiz was developed by the Public Health Service of the National Institutes of Health to help you gauge your nicotine tolerance.

NICOTINE TOLERANCE QUIZ

1. How soon after wakening do you first light a cigarette?
   A. Within 30 minutes
   B. After 30 minutes
2. Is it hard for you to obey the "no smoking" rules in areas like the doctor's office, theaters, or restaurants?
   A. No
   B. Yes

3. Which is the most satisfying cigarette you smoke all day?
   A. The first one of the day
   B. Some one other than the first

4. How many cigarettes do you smoke in a typical day?
   A. 1–15
   B. 16–25
   C. More than 25

5. Do you smoke more before noon than during the rest of the day?
   A. No
   B. Yes

6. Do you smoke when you are ill and staying in bed most of the day?
   A. Yes
   B. No

7. Is your cigarette brand's content of nicotine and tar:
   A. High (1.3 mg or more)
   B. Medium (1.0–1.2 mg)
   C. Low (0.9 mg or less?)

8. Do you inhale:
   A. Never
   B. Sometimes
   C. Always

SCORING:

1 A = 1 point, B = 0 point
2 A = 0 point, B = 1 point
3 A = 1 point, B = 0 point
4 A = 0 point, B = 1 point, C = 2 points
5 A = 0 point, B = 1 point
6 A = 1 point, B = 0 point
7 A = 2 points, B = 1 point, C = 0 point
8 A = 0 point, B = 1 point, C = 2 points

Total: _____

If you score 6 points or more, consider yourself as tolerant to nicotine. For you, quitting may involve some degree of physical discomfort as your body adjusts.

If you score below 6 points, you are not likely to be physically addicted yet, so quitting should be easier.

Summary Knowing your physical tolerance is a necessary step so you know what to expect when you quit.

Part Three: What's in it for You?

Good—you have taken yet another step on your road to a smoke-free, youthful body. But as any smoker knows, physical needs are only a part of the picture. Now that you have assessed your physiological tolerance, this section will help you understand the psychological benefits you get out of smoking. The following is another test developed by the National Institutes of Health to help you do that. It is your next step. Make sure you answer every question by circling the number in the column that applies.

For each category below, a score of 11 or more is high, 8 to 10 is medium, and 7 or less is low.

Stimulation Category: Total your answers to A, G, and M. If the total is more than 9, you rely on cigarettes to stimulate and enliven you, to help you work, organize, or be creative. You are a good candidate for a substitute of another kind of "high": five minutes of exercise in your office, a brisk walk.

Tactile Category: Total your answers to B, H, and N. If the total is 9 or above, an important aspect of your smoking is the feel of it. Try substituting a pen or pencil, doodling, or occupying yourself with a small toy. You may want to squeeze a tennis ball or handgrip exerciser, or even hold a plastic cigarette.

Pleasure Category: Total your answers to C, I, and O. A high score suggests that you are one of the people for whom cigarettes provide some real pleasure. If this

	Always	Usually	Sometimes	Seldom	Never
A. I smoke cigarettes to keep myself from slowing down.	5	4	3	2	1
B. Handling and touching a cigarette is part of enjoying smoking.	5	4	3	2	1
C. I feel pleasant and relaxed when I smoke.	5	4	3	2	1
D. I light up when I feel tense or mad about something.	5	4	3	2	1
E. When I run out of cigarettes, I can hardly stand it until I get more.	5	4	3	2	1
F. I smoke automatically, I am not always aware when I am smoking.	5	4	3	2	1
G. Smoking helps me feel stimulated, turned on, creative.	5	4	3	2	1
H. Part of my enjoyment comes in the steps I take to light up.	5	4	3	2	1
I. For me, cigarettes are simply pleasurable.	5	4	3	2	1
J. I light up when I feel upset or uncomfortable about something.	5	4	3	2	1
K. I am quite aware of it when I am not smoking a cigarette.	5	4	3	2	1

	Always	Usually	Sometimes	Seldom	Never
L. I may light up not realizing that I still have a cigarette burning in the ash-tray.	5	4	3	2	1
M. I smoke because cigarettes give me a "lift."	5	4	3	2	1
N. Part of the plea-sure of smoking is watching the smoke as I exhale.	5	4	3	2	1
O. I want a cigarette most when I am relaxed and com-fortable.	5	4	3	2	1
P. I smoke when I am blue or want to take my mind off my worries.	5	4	3	2	1
Q. I get "hungry" for a cigarette when I have not smoked for a while.	5	4	3	2	1
R. I often find a ciga-rette in my mouth and don't remem-ber putting it there.	5	4	3	2	1

is you, you are a particularly good candidate to stop because you can substitute other pleasurable outlets—reasonable eating, or social, sports, or physical activities—for smoking.

Tension Category: Total your answers to D, J, and P. Those who score high here use tobacco as a crutch, to reduce negative feelings, relieve problems, much like a tranquilizer. You are likely to find it easy to quit when things are going well, but staying off is harder in bad times. For you, the key is to find other activities that also work to reduce negative feelings; dancing, meditation, yoga, sports or exercise, meals, or social activities work for many such smokers.

Addiction Category: Total your answers to E, K, and Q. Quitting is hard for those who score high in this group because you are probably psychologically addicted and crave cigarettes. You aren't likely to succeed by tapering off gradually. Instead, try smoking more than usual for a day or two, until the craving dulls, then drop it cold turkey, and *isolate yourself* from cigarettes for a long period. There is good news, though: Once your craving is broken, you are less likely to relapse because you won't want to go through that distress again.

Habit Category: Total your answers to F, L, and R. High scores indicate that you are a "reflex" smoker. For you, quitting may be relatively easy. Your goal is to break the link between smoking and your own triggering events—food, a cup of coffee, sitting down to work. Think of tapering off gradually. Each time you reach for a cigarette, stop and ask yourself *out loud:* "Do I really want this cigarette?" If you answer no, then skip it.

The higher your score in each category, the more that factor plays a role in your smoking. If you score low in all the categories, you probably aren't a long-term smoker. Congratulations—you have the best chance of getting off and staying off.

Combined high scores across several categories suggest that you get several kinds of rewards from smoking. For you, stopping may mean you need to try several different tactics. Being a high scorer in both TENSION and ADDICTION is a particularly tough combination. You *can* quit—many such people have—but it may be more difficult for you than for others. If you score high in STIMULATION and ADDICTION, however, you may benefit from changing your patterns of smoking as you cut down. Smoke less often, or only smoke each cigarette partway, inhale less, use tapering filters or low-tar/nicotine brands.

Summary Knowing why you smoke will help you know how best to stop.

Part Four: How Best to Quit

Just as people smoke for different reasons, they also stop for different reasons and in different ways. Today, the field of smoking cessation has become a whole new topic of study among behavioral psychologists, psychiatrists, and practicing physicians. The range of possible interventions is both broad and effective, so that virtually every person who is motivated can find a way to stop.

For instance, you may not have fully appreciated the staggering range of techniques and approaches that have been tried. All are available to help you stop smoking:

Nicotine chewing gum*
Graduated smoke filters
Hypnosis (group or individual)*
Education/motivation lectures*
Aversive conditioning
Doctor's intervention
Physician and psychologist intervention*
Medication
Educational
Self-help books
Audio and videotapes
Acupuncture
Individual therapy
Rapid smoking
Relaxation therapy
Electric shock therapy
Satiation smoking*

Group counseling
Stress management
Biofeedback
No-smoking clinics
No-smoking contracts

Hundreds of test studies have shown that most of these methods help between one third and one half of their subjects to stop smoking. Only a handful of methods, those I have marked with an asterisk, seem to show greater-than-average effectiveness. Through all this research, several principles have become clear:

1. Different ways work for different people.
2. The best ways tend to combine several approaches.
3. Groups can be helpful.
4. If you can stay off cigarettes for a year, you probably won't relapse.
5. If you are sufficiently motivated to stop, you will.

Summary You can find an effective method to stop smoking.

Doing It Your Way...

Despite all these available avenues, research shows that most smokers simply prefer to kick the habit on their own, and that many millions have been successful doing so.

Here are the addresses of some of the best no-smoking programs and kits available, and those which you can usually obtain free of charge:

—The American Cancer Society—
   7 Day Quitter's Guide
   3340 Peachtree N.E.
   Atlanta, GA 30326

—Information Resources Branch
Office of Cancer Communications
National Cancer Institute
Building 31, Room 10A
Bethesda, MD 20892
or call: 1 800-4-CANCER

—Your local chapter of The American Lung Associ-
ation (listed in the White Pages)
or:
The American Lung Association
P.O. Box 596DN
New York, NY 10001

You now possess everything that I can give you in a
book to help you stop smoking. You have the basic
information, data about your nicotine tolerance, a psychological smoking profile, and information about what
means are available to help you stop. The next move
is up to you. Take the single biggest step you can to
promote your health, extend your life, and make sure
the years you add to that life will be more worth living.
Keep in mind all you stand to gain:

—Better wind, stamina, and endurance
—Increased capacity for exercise
—Better and more restful sleep
—Fewer colds and infections
—Reduced respiratory symptoms (coughing, mucus,
asthma)
—Stronger heart and circulatory system
—Reduced unsightly aging of the skin
—Lower risk of cancer and debilitating disease
—More energy and vitality
—Extra years of life

I hope you will do yourself the biggest health- and
youth-preserving favor you can. Make today the first

day of your wonderfully long, wonderfully healthy, *smoke-free* life.

In review, the key points of this chapter are:

1. STOPPING SMOKING GUARANTEES BETTER HEALTH AND LONGEVITY.
2. KNOWING ALL THE FACTS IS THE FIRST STEP TO QUITTING.
3. KNOWING YOUR PHYSICAL TOLERANCE HELPS YOU KNOW WHAT TO EXPECT WHEN YOU QUIT.
4. KNOWING WHY YOU SMOKE WILL HELP YOU KNOW HOW BEST TO STOP.
5. YOU CAN FIND AN EFFECTIVE METHOD TO STOP SMOKING.

Keeping Your Bones Young

CAN YOU RECALL how it felt to move when you were young? Think back to a time when your every movement seemed free, fluid, easy. Your gait had a buoyant energy, your walk was steady and vigorous. You stood erect and alert, yet relaxed. It felt natural to bend, reach, and flex with easy grace. You took for granted an energetic strength. In all of your motions, from the smallest gesture to the most athletic jump, you felt a wonderful, free confidence, knowing that your body would do what you asked without complaint.

One of the joys of youth is that we enjoy every ounce of the natural physical grace that Nature designed into our bodies. Yet too often, we see that grace and flexibility diminish as we age. It may start with creaks and stiffness in the joints, or the twinges of an ailing back. Gradually you feel your joints become stiffer and less pliant. Maybe you cut down on sports or any activity that requires significant movement. No more can you count on bursts of speed, for you have lost confidence in how your body will react. With the passing of each year, you may watch the person in the mirror become more stooped; your walk becomes stiffer and more halting. As this continues, bit by inevitable bit, you will eventually take on the cramped movements, unsteady gait, and stooped posture of an old person.

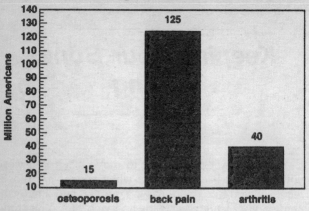

People With Degenerative Bone Problems

It is a rare adult indeed in this country who does not suffer from one or more common skeletal problems, including the stiffness and swollen joints of arthritis, the debilitating agony of lower back pain, or the bone-wasting syndrome of osteoporosis.

But that doesn't have to be your future. And it won't be because this chapter includes the four key "bone-builder" steps you need to keep your bones healthy, hard, and young for decades to come. These steps will help you prevent or forestall common degenerative problems that weaken your body's bony frame. These bone builders are your key to maintaining strength and youthful fitness, increasing your ease of movement, and generally keeping your frame young and supple. More than that, they are your assurance that you will retain the lively walk, grace of movement, and general vigor that spells YOUTH.

Modern laboratory research on nutrients and cell chemistry suggests that most skeletal aging that occurs is not only preventable but reversible. Scientists are learning how to keep our musculoskeletal system strong and supple far longer than we ever thought possible. With the right care and attention, you can expect to stay spry and active into your sixth, seventh, and eighth decades of life. However, to enjoy that kind of health twenty years from now means you have to take simple steps today.

The Basics on Bones

You may think of your bones as the rock-hard, permanent supports for your muscles and organs. That is only partly true. Biologically your bones are more like bank accounts in a constant state of shifting deposits and withdrawals. But instead of money, they bank the minerals your body needs: calcium, magnesium, phosphorus, silicon, fluoride, and copper.

If you are in your midtwenties, those accounts are currently the strongest, and most mineral-rich, they will ever be. But by age forty, both men and women become

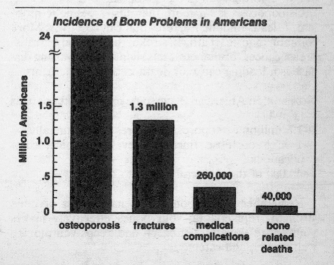

Incidence of Bone Problems in Americans

less efficient at absorbing mineral nutrients from food. By age sixty-five, your body is only half as efficient as it once was. So, if it can't get minerals like calcium, magnesium, and potassium from the food you eat, it borrows them from your bones. As this borrowing syndrome continues, your bones become depleted, porous, and brittle, and you develop *osteoporosis*. Over a lifetime, this process can rob an average of 25 percent of your bones' density. *Bone aging is almost entirely due to the gradual loss of vital skeletal minerals.*

Porous bones age prematurely, collapsing and compacting. It becomes a particular problem in the spine; postmenopausal women lose up to 5 percent of spinal bone mass every year! Soon this aging actually shrinks the spinal column. By age seventy, the average American man can expect to lose as much as 2¾ inches in height; women, a less drastic 1⅞ inches. The change can be sudden: The collapse of one cervical vertebra can cost you an inch in height in a week! As the spinal vertebrae collapse, you start to show the dowager's hump, so often seen in older women.

Osteoporosis is far more than just a cosmetic problem. It leads to bone fractures that can cost lives. More common than heart attack, stroke, rheumatoid arthritis, breast cancer, or diabetes, this silent, bone-wasting disease is a leading cause of death in older Americans.

—24 million Americans have some form of osteoporosis (1 in 11).
—1.3 million osteoporosis fractures occur annually.
—1 in 5 of those fractures develop medical complications.
—40,000 of those fractures lead to death.

Remember: Since bone aging means loss of bone strength, rejuvenating your bones effectively makes your entire skeleton younger—and keeps you moving well, easily, and safely.

Are You at Risk?

In order to keep your skeletal frame as young and strong as possible, your first step is to find out if you are a likely candidate for premature bone aging and weakening. Do you fit into any of these risk groups:

1. Are you a woman?
2. Do you have small bones and a slight build?
3. Are you of Asian or Latin American heritage?
4. Do you smoke?
5. Did you have menopause before forty-five?
6. Do you have light (blond or reddish) coloring or hair?
7. Are your eyes any color other than brown?
8. Did you ever take oral steroids (such as prednisone) for more than six months?
9. Did your mother or sister break a wrist, hip, or vertebra other than in a serious accident?
10. Do you drink a lot of coffee or cola?
11. Do you get almost no exercise at all?
12. Do you get highly strenuous and prolonged exercise or have you ever exercised so much that you stopped menstruating?
13. Have you ever suffered from anorexia or dieted so much that you stopped menstruating?
14. Have you ever suffered from alcoholism?
15. Do you have a visible spinal curvature (dowager's hump)?
16. Do you now take, or have you routinely taken, diuretics, insulin, steroids, antiulcer, anticoagulant, or anticonvulsant medicines?

A yes answer to one of the above questions suggests you could be at risk for osteoporosis, but if you answered yes to two, three, or more of them, you should definitely begin incorporating the bone builder hints as soon as possible.

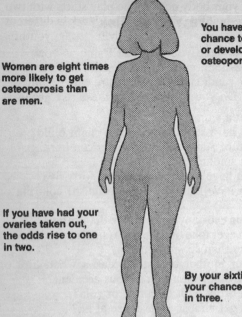

You have a one-in-four chance to have, or develop, osteoporosis.

Women are eight times more likely to get osteoporosis than are men.

If you have had your ovaries taken out, the odds rise to one in two.

By your sixtieth birthday, your chances become one in three.

AS A WOMAN:

—Women are eight times more likely to get osteoporosis than are men.

—You have a one-in-four chance to have, or develop, osteoporosis.

—By your sixtieth birthday, your chances become one in three.

—If you have had your ovaries taken out, the odds rise to one in two.

Bone Builder Step One: Micronutrients

The first step to rejuvenating your bones is a micronutrient plan to make sure you get all the minerals and vitamins your body needs. The plan starts with two essential bone-building vitamins. They work in different ways to help your bones maintain their strong, youthful mineral balance.

Daily Bone-Building Micronutrient Mix

Vitamin C	1 gram
Vitamin D	400 I.U.
Vitamin B_{12}	100 mcg
Manganese	1 mg

Next comes *calcium*. I recommend:

If You Are...	You Should Take:
Male:	1,000 mg
Female:	
Teens	1,200 mg
Premenopausal/taking estrogen	1,000 mg
Postmenopausal or over 60	1,500 mg
In a risk group:	
Fair-skinned Caucasian	1,500 mg
Asian	
Small-boned	
Smoker	
Drinks much alcohol	
Pregnant or nursing, 19 and older	1,400 mg
Pregnant or nursing, younger than 19	2,000 mg

Remember: Just taking calcium alone is not enough to reverse bone aging. But it is an essential component of any bone-building plan.

Bone Builder Step Two: Eat the Right Minerals

The next step is to make certain that you get enough of certain bone-building minerals in the food you eat.

That means eating a variety of whole foods that contain the following minerals to promote skeletal longevity.

Magnesium is a key bone builder. Unfortunately, most refined American diets are low in good sources of this vital mineral. Ironically, the diet your great-grandparents ate a century ago was two or three times richer in magnesium than diets today, thanks to all the magnesium-laden fresh vegetables and whole grains they ate. You should do the same.

Manganese also fights premature bone aging. I have listed some of the best manganese-rich foods below.

Boron. It is rare that we discover a wholly new nutrient, but that is what this bone-building mineral seems to be. The news on boron is by far the most exciting to appear on the bone-rejuvenation horizon recently. And recent it is—the pivotal findings about boron, its role in bone strengthening hitherto unsuspected, came just as I was assembling the research for this book!

A recent landmark study from the Grand Forks Human Nutrition Laboratory of the U.S. Department of Agriculture (USDA) shows that the mineral element boron, long overlooked, can play a key role in promoting and maintaining bone health—and in protecting our bones against aging and weakness.

This new bone builder is doubly powerful because it does double duty. First, it works as a team player, helping the body absorb other crucial bone-building nutrients from the food we eat. Research suggests that women who get enough boron in their food—3 milligrams per day, the amount you would get by eating moderate amounts of fresh fruits and vegetables—showed *significant improvement* in how their bodies absorbed calcium and magnesium. That means it works a bit like a catalyst—enough boron in your diet helps assure that your body will properly metabolize the other bone nutrients you need.

Boron also seems to work on another level, too. It can play a role in raising the levels of your hormones.

This is helpful because these hormones, including estrogen and testosterone, are *directly related* to your bones' strength and resiliency. They are chemicals Nature uses to keep your bones healthy and young. That's why bone loss usually occurs after menopause, and why the most commonly accepted treatment for postmenopausal bone weakening is to prescribe female hormones. The hope is that boron may work to boost these hormone levels naturally, conferring the same kind of protection that hormone treatments would.

Because this news about boron is so recent, there is still much we have to learn about it. Laboratory scientists at USDA and elsewhere must determine optimal and safe boron-supplement levels. It may be that we can get enough boron from our diet, or that special supplements are recommended for people at risk for premature bone weakening. I expect that there will be a lot more news about this bone-longevity breakthrough appearing in research journals soon. I expect that boron will take its place in the bone-strengthening nutritional armamentarium within five years.

But you don't have to wait. You can start taking advantage of boron now—by including it in your diet, today. *The single best way to get enough boron is* to eat plenty of fresh fruits and fresh vegetables. They are Nature's prime, safe sources of this key bone builder. By eating a balanced diet of boron-rich foods, you can give yourself the same dose of boron that was used in the pioneering studies.

Below is a list of the best bone-building foods for an optimal balance of nutrients—including boron.

GOOD SOURCES OF:

Calcium: dairy products, low-fat yogurt, sardines (with bones), salmon, tofu, broccoli, spinach, collard greens, sesame seeds, seaweeds (used in Japanese cooking)

Magnesium: Dark green vegetables, broccoli, Brussels sprouts, spinach, dark-green lettuce

Manganese: Legumes, sunflower seeds, meat, dark-green lettuce, cloves, spinach, wheat germ, and black beans

Boron: Tofu, plums, peaches, grapes, raisins, apples, wine, prunes, almonds, pears, peanuts, dates, green leafy vegetables.

With all these minerals, the rule is "diet before drugs." Studies show that vegetarians suffer from osteoporosis much less than nonvegetarians. By including a good balance of fresh fruits and vegetables in your diet (which, of course, you are doing after having read the young-at-heart chapter) you will automatically— and deliciously!—help your bones get enough of the vital minerals they need to stay youthful and strong.

Bone Builder Step Three: Nutritional Tips

In addition to eating the right foods, here are some special dietary tips to help prevent destructive bone aging.

—Eat a lot of fiber, but in natural, not supplemented, forms: whole grains, brown rice, oatmeal, and bulgur are better than refined wheat bran.

—Limit the amount of concentrated animal protein you eat. A very high-protein diet causes minerals to be flushed from the body—among them bone minerals. A more balanced, lower-protein diet helps guard against mineral depletion.

—Drink fewer carbonated drinks. They are acidic, which can upset your mineral balance.

—Both rhubarb and spinach contain oxalic acid, which can block mineral absorption.

—Reduce alcohol consumption to avoid flushing out minerals.

—Cigarettes have been shown to reduce estrogen levels and hasten menopause—another great reason to stop smoking.

—Avoid special very low-calorie diets, especially those with incomplete nutrients (weight-loss powders, drinks, or one-item diet programs).

Bone Builder Step Four: Exercise

Exercise is the vital fourth component to adding years to the life of your bones. It is now generally accepted that certain kinds of weight-bearing exercise are Nature's way of keeping your bones strong, healthy, and young. Check the guide below.

Weight-Bearing Exercise	Nonweight-Bearing Exercise
Impact aerobics	Biking
Basketball	No-impact aerobics
Dancing	Swimming
Football	Yoga
Gymnastics	
Hiking	
Lacrosse	
Running	
Skiing	
Squash	
Tennis	
Volleyball	
Walking	
Weight lifting	

If you are not now exercising, you should start gradually. Your goal should be to exercise for an hour or so, three to four times each week. Whether that means a session at the spa, a brisk after-dinner walk, or a racquetball game with a friend, you will be making an important contribution to your body's longevity.

But remember: Exercise by itself won't dramatically reduce the effective age of your bones. However, taken along with supplements and dietary bone builders, it is of vital importance to prolonging the life of your skeleton.

Your Doctor Can Help

The four bone-building steps outlined above will almost certainly help you rejuvenate your bones, lower the effective age of your skeletal frame, and protect against bone aging. But the key is to start the steps early enough in life so that your bones have not already started to weaken. However, since you may have already suffered significant bone aging, and so may need even more help, your doctor has a large array of treatments to reverse this age-related weakening. Treatment options include:

Time-release sodium fluoride
Fluoride calcium therapy
Estrogen replacement
Low-dose estrogen and calcium
Parathyroid hormone
Calcitonin
Growth hormone

If you follow the bone-building steps I've described, especially if you start now, the odds are you will never need any medical treatment because you will have effectively reduced the age of your entire skeletal system.

Good-bye, Creaky Joints!

Scientists have described some 110 forms of arthritis, all of which can contribute to premature aging, loss of mobility, and to a general feeling of being old before your time. Arthritis is the most common chronic disease in men, and the single leading cause of disability in old age. So, if you want to ensure yourself a more mobile, more active, more youthful life, there are some tips that can help keep arthritis at bay.

Keeping your joints young and pain-free requires two kinds of attention: physical and dietary. First, let's get physical.

It is the large, weight-bearing joints—knees, hips, and spine—that are most vulnerable to arthritis. That means you need to take special care during activities that use those joints, and this should be a focus of your arthritis-prevention efforts:

—*Sitting* places more stress and strain on the back than any other position. The basic law is: Don't sit longer than thirty minutes without getting up and stretching your back and legs. If your work involves sitting for long periods, make sure your chair supports your lower back, has armrests, and keeps your knees raised to a level slightly above your hips. If necessary, you may want to raise your feet on a small wooden box so that your knees are slightly higher than your hips.

—*Standing* can create joint stress as well. To relieve stress from standing, lift one leg so that hip and knee bend, and place one foot up on a short step or stool. After a few minutes, put that foot down and raise the other foot.

—*Lifting* often ignites serious lower-back pain. Always lift by bending your knees and keep your back as straight as possible. Try to lift and carry objects close to your body.

—*Sleeping* can be the most restful position for various joints if it is done correctly. Lie on your back with one to two pillows under your knees so that your hips and knees are bent, or on your side with hips bent so that your knees are pulled up toward your chest (fetal position), and with a pillow placed between your knees.

—*Muscles, ligaments, and tendons lose fibers with age,* which restricts the movement of your joints. One way to avoid damaging those joints is always to begin any strenuous exercise with a warm-up period of slow, easy, gradual stretches.

Diet also plays a key role in the joint pain that makes you old and creaky before your time. Your diet can help keep your joints young and supple in the following ways:

—Fish oils work as anti-inflammatory agents, helping alleviate the pain and premature aging of arthritis. Fish oils don't actually lubricate the joints themselves, but they chemically change the blood and reduce the body's own chemicals that lead to painful joint tenderness, swelling, and inflammation. Thus they break the chain of pain and inflammation that leads to arthritis. As we saw in the chapter on heart youth, you don't have to take fish oils in pill form; you will derive more overall benefit by eating fish. Certain varieties of fish have higher levels of the essential fatty acids that help protect your joints. Among the richest sources are: tuna, salmon, sardines, mackerel, sable, whitefish, bluefish, swordfish, rainbow trout, eels, herring, and squid.

—When it comes to keeping your joints young and agile, what you don't eat can be as important as what you do eat. It is clear that diet plays a role in preventing and relieving crippling arthritis pain. British researchers conducted a study on fifty-three patients with serious, crippling rheumatoid arthritis. When specific foods were eliminated from the diets of these patients, they reported "significant improvement" in joint symptoms. They had less morning stiffness, joint pain, and walked better. In other words— their joints and movement got effectively "younger."

I read about a mother of three children who suffered from progressive, crippling rheumatoid arthritis for some ten years. Then, her doctors asked her to abstain from eating dairy products, especially milk and cheese. Within three weeks her symptoms abated dramatically. For the first time in years, she was able to walk without pain, felt herself regaining strength in her hands, and could stop taking anti-inflammatory drugs. When, as a test, she started eating dairy products again, her severe arthritic symptoms returned within twelve hours. She has now been living symptom-free for several months.

You can put your diet to work in the same way to forestall the premature aging of joint pain. If arthritis is a problem, I suggest you avoid eating large quantities of foods in the nightshade family, since these are known to trigger or exacerbate joint inflammation. These foods include: zucchini, eggplants, tomatoes, bell peppers, white onions, potatoes, squash, and paprika.

—Incorporate this anti-arthritis formula into your daily plan:

Vitamin B_3 (niacinamide)	100 mg
Vitamin B_{12}	150 mcg
Vitamin B_5 (pantothenic acid)	250 mg
Vitamin B_6	100 mg
Vitamin C	3 grams
Zinc	75 mg
Evening primrose oil or linseed oil	Use in cooking and on salads

For a Better Back

You can't feel young with a crippled back. Today, 195 million Americans have had some back problems, and fully three in ten have a severe, chronic back ailment. These people know only too well that the ago-

Back Longevity Exercises

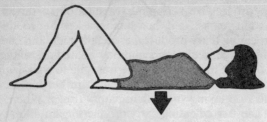

PELVIC TILT

Lie on your back, knees bent, feet on the floor. Tighten the muscles in your stomach and squeeze your buttocks together, pushing your back into the floor.

Objective: *to strengthen the lower abdominal muscles.*

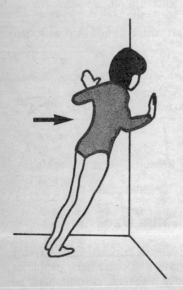

PECTORAL STRETCH

Stand facing a corner. Extend your arms and place your palms against the wall. With your body straight, lean toward the wall, keeping your legs straight and your heels firmly on the floor. Repeat, gradually increasing your distance from the wall.

Objective: *to stretch the chest and calf muscles.*

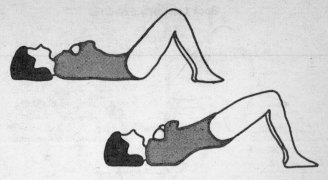

ARCH AND CURVE

Assume an all-four's position with your head in neutral position. Allow your back to arch. Then, curve your back upwards at the waist level, tightening your stomach muscles.

Objective: to stretch and strengthen the back and abdominal muscles.

BACK STRENGTHENING EXERCISE

Assume all-four's position. Lift one arm and one leg on the opposite sides, hold and relax. Alternate sides.

Objective: improve coordination balance and strength of the back and supportive muscles.

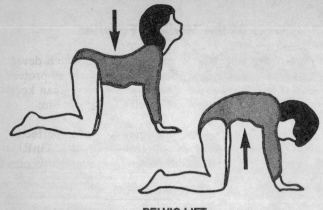

PELVIC LIFT

**Lie on your back. Bend both knees so feet are flat
on the floor. Squeeze your buttocks together and
lift your hips off the floor.**

Objective: *to strengthen the buttock muscles.*

nizing pain of spinal or disk degeneration robs you of
the freedom and movement of youth, casts a pall over
your life, can even debilitate you.

To continue to enjoy the free and easy movement of
youth during your whole lifetime, you have to avoid
this most common crippling malady. Beginning on page
152 is a series of exercises and tips that you may want
to incorporate into your daily regimen. These are used
at the New York Hospital for Joint Diseases Orthopedic
Institute, and were designed by Neil Kahanovitz, M.D.,
and Kathleen Viola, RPT. These exercises are your
single best insurance against forfeiting youthful mobility
to an aching back.

At the Medical Frontier

Here are some of the most exciting research developments that will be available soon to help us protect and rejuvenate our bones and joints, so we can keep our body moving easily and well throughout life:

—*Screening tests for bone aging* are being perfected at Columbia University. A test, called a "GnRH-agonist test," has been developed that can reliably predict if a woman is likely to develop age-related bone wasting after menopause. The hope is that you could eventually get the test as part of a routine physical. A positive result would alert you and your doctor that special treatment is necessary to keep your bones young and strong.

—A tantalizing *bone-rejuvenation breakthrough* may depend on something as simple as the time of day, according to studies done by Dr. David Simmons, an orthopedic researcher at the University of Texas Medical Branch. There, doctors are exploiting the fluctuations of the body's own internal clock—what are called "circadian rhythms"—to keep bones at their strongest.

The researchers suspect that the peak time when the human body builds bone may be in the evening, before midnight. That's when the levels of crucial bone-forming hormones, such as parathyroid and growth hormones, are at their highest. (As parents and pediatricians know, nighttime is also when children suffer most from the growing pains that are linked to bone growth.)

This suggests that drugs that help to increase bone growth, like testosterone and estrogen, or to inhibit bone shrinkage, like calcitonin, may work more powerfully during prime time than during the wee hours of the morning or during the workday.

These discoveries suggest that one common medication used to reverse bone aging builds more bone when it is administered in the morning, has little effect when taken at noon, and may actually decrease bone strength when taken late in the day.

The idea is so new that researchers are testing it only in lab animals, comparing a medication schedule of 8:00 A.M., high noon, and 4:00 P.M. If the animals show a difference in bone growth, the findings could be applied to humans, who could take a pill or even an inhalable spray of bone-strengthening drugs at the most propitious hours.

This simple discovery could prove to be one of those buried nuggets of medical lore that need only a perceptive medical mind to unearth them. If it proves out, it will be significant news on the anti-aging front. Simply watching the clock might give us a new, entirely cost-free way to avoid, and treat, bone aging. The sophisticated notion of cooperating, not competing, with the body's own internal hormonal rhythms may suggest that we should eat certain bone-strengthening foods at certain meals, to ensure that their nutrients are available when our body needs them most to build strong bones.

—A *new radiation drug,* dysprosium-165, promises relief to many of the six million sufferers of rheumatoid arthritis. Created by physicians in Boston, this short-lived, safe radioactive drug can be injected into damaged joints. It does with radiation what a surgeon would do with a scalpel, eliminating the damaged and inflamed tissue that creates crippling arthritis pain. Used in the knee joints, the procedure has relieved pain and restored free movement to more than three hundred patients so far, with virtually no side effects, for a fraction of the cost of surgery. It is now in clinical trials only in Boston and New York, but is hoped to become available to arthritis sufferers in fourteen major cities throughout the United States within the next year.

—In Israel an *electronic therapy,* called "transcutaneous electrical nerve stimulation," is being studied to relieve arthritis pain. It appears that the electrical fields diminish the body's inflammatory process in arthritic joints, and so reduce joint pain.

But remember: Rather than use such futuristic developments to remedy joint and skeletal pain, you can use the tips in this chapter to keep your bones and muscles young, supple, and strong—and avoid problems altogether!

9

Make Yourself Immune to Age

IF YOU WANT to assure that you live a long, healthy life, nothing is more crucial than your immune system. This network of blood cells, antibodies, and chemicals is your body's protection against the diseases that age us all. It fights germs, from common bacteria to exotic parasites to the deadliest viruses. It is also your sole guardian against the malignant, often deadly, growth of cancer. Your immune system is all that stands between you and diseases that can sap your energy, threaten your life, and make your body weak and infirm many years too soon.

Unaided, your immune system will lose almost 90 percent of its strength between the ages of twenty and seventy. As the years pass and those losses accumulate, your dulled immune defenses allow you to catch infections more easily. The body's energy is sapped in a chronic low-level fight against illness. As it weakens further, you may be one of the approximately seventy-five million Americans who will develop cancer in their lifetime.

Immune Rejuvenation means turning that process around. And you can. *There is no reason you can't have a superpotent immune system your whole life long.* By keeping your immune defenders intact and well armed, working at peak strength, you help make yourself "immune to age."

The steps in this chapter are drawn from several areas of research to help you do that. Some are based on the most complete findings about immune nutrients and anticancer diets published by the National Cancer Institute. Other suggestions in this chapter come from research being done, here and abroad, on how to strengthen the immune system of people suffering from the devastating disease AIDS. The "Antiviral Cocktail," which I will describe in this chapter, is based on findings from clinics and laboratories that show promise in helping strengthen the immune system. The intravenous vitamin C treatments are the ones that I am currently most excited about. Having used these with many, many patients, I have seen quite astounding results.

Together, these steps make up a solid prescription for immune longevity. That adds up to fewer infections, less debilitating illness, and less time wasted feeling sub-par. Immune Rejuvenation is your biological insurance policy that you will fight off disease, stay strong against cancer, and always enjoy the high energy and radiant health that Nature gave you.

That is 100 percent achievable if you follow the basic steps outlined below. Remember: You can give your body's disease-fighting troops a big advantage in their effort to keep you healthy and youthful, free of diseases and full of vitality.

The three steps to keeping your immune system young are:

1. Build *out* cancer from your life.
2. Build *up* your immune system to keep it young and healthy.
3. Build *in* added protection against disease-causing viruses.

Step One: Eat to Conquer Cancer

Believe it or not, you can conquer cancer in your life. Right now, statistics show that you have a three-in-ten chance of getting cancer during your lifetime, and that someone in your family has a three-in-four chance of being touched by cancer. With odds like that, you could well be among the almost one million Americans who will be diagnosed with some form of cancer this year. But if you could *remove* yourself from the list of "cancer candidates," this would give a tremendous boost to both your longevity and the quality of your life.

You can avoid being a "cancer candidate." The National Cancer Institute estimates that 80 percent of all cancers come from how we live. We know an *enormous* amount about how to build cancer risk out of our lives. According to the *New England Journal of Medicine,* diet is "second only to cigarette smoking as a determinant of cancer in this country." So, *just by eliminating cancer-risk habits, you can give yourself an 80 percent chance of avoiding cancer entirely.* This one step alone potentially offers you several extra decades of productive, healthy life. Yet despite all we know, only one American in seven has ever discussed with a doctor about putting these principles to work in his/her own life. In 1988 a survey showed that while 68 percent of Americans believe there is a link between diet and cancer, the great majority don't know what to do about it.

Fortunately, you don't have to count yourself among them. That's because many of the same health tips we have already discussed—your keys to rejuvenating your skin, heart, and bones—dramatically lower your cancer risk. If you are:

—Eating more fiber . . .
—Eating less fat . . .

—Eating more mineral- and vitamin-rich fresh vegetables...
—Stopping smoking...
—Moderating alcohol consumption to a reasonable
level...

... then congratulations! You have already taken the
most significant and positive steps to put cancer out of
your life!

Of these health tips, reducing fat is particularly crucial. It has been shown that lowering cholesterol levels
help the phagocytes, a vital type of immune cell, and
that a generally low-fat diet not only reduces the free
radicals that cause cancer, but actually helps the immune system work better.

You should know about one other important anticancer counsel. Make sure that you eat some of the
following vegetables at least once each week:

Broccoli	Kale
Brussels sprouts	Kohlrabi
Cabbage	Mustard greens
Cauliflower	Rutabaga
Chinese cabbage	Turnips
Collards	

New research shows that these vegetables, which belong to the cruciferous family, contain chemical compounds called indoles, which are thought to help reduce
cancer, particularly colon cancer.

By making these changes in your living habits, you
will be doing exactly what the nation's foremost cancer
experts, from the National Cancer Institute to the National Research Council to the Surgeon General himself, recommend. Before long, you will begin to reap
the benefits: a younger heart, cleaner arteries, and
stronger bones. But the best benefit is to your long-

term health and peace of mind, for you will have cut your vulnerability to deadly cancer by a factor of eight or more, and made a major improvement in the quality and length of your life! Amazing, isn't it, how changing a few health habits can do so much good to so much of your body?

Step Two: Your Personal Nutrition Plan for Immune Youth

A change of diet is half the cancer battle. The other half involves a pro-active, balanced supplement plan to make sure that your cellular defense system has all the micronutrients it needs to fight off cancer and keep part of your immune armies strong. One way to do that is with a balanced program of antioxidant nutrients, to fight the biological changes that damage your immune system. Clearly, a finely tuned immune system is essential to radiant health and long life. Which may be why women, who tend to have stronger immune systems than men, usually live longer.

Scientists at Memorial Sloan-Kettering Cancer Center in New York City have shown that nutritional deficiencies, especially of key immune-health nutrients, weaken the immune system. To keep your immune health at its youthful peak, your body's trillion or so immune cells need the right balance of vitamins, minerals, and amino acids. Yet study after study show that many millions of Americans are low on at least one key immune-boosting vitamin or mineral, like vitamin A, vitamin C, or zinc. It is no accident that the group with the lowest immune function—the elderly—is also the most likely to lack key immune nutrients. To avoid the premature aging that cripples so many people, here are the ingredients you need:

Vitamin A. Known to broadly strengthen the immune system, boost immune cells' reactions, and aid the body's fight against cancer, especially lung cancer. People who get more vitamin A have a lower incidence of cancer, and A specifically works as an antioxidant and anticarcinogen in the body. Instead of taking the pure form of A, which you can overdose on, I recommend beta-carotene, a harmless substance that your body converts into usable vitamin A.

Vitamin B$_{12}$ (cobalamine). One of the most important of the B-vitamin family when taken for immune health. It helps immune cells directly, and low levels are known to impair immunity.

Vitamin C (ascorbic acid). The number-one immune-boosting vitamin, C is known to increase several different kinds of immune-cell components, strengthen the cellular arm of the immune defenses, and increase production of the body's natural germ-fighting chemical interferon.

Vitamin E (alpha tocopherol). Plays a crucial role in preventing cancer directly, neutralizing cancer-causing chemicals, and generally boosting the immune system, according to research from Harvard Medical School, Tufts Medical School, the U.S. Department of Agriculture, and many other laboratories. It strengthens both arms of the immune system, protects against infection, and soaks up dangerous cancer-causing chemicals in your cells. High levels of E can reverse the age-related decline in immune strength, and low levels are associated with increased cancer risk.

Selenium. One of the two key mineral protectors against cancer, according to research being conducted at the University of California and the National Cancer Institute. Like vitamin E, selenium has been found to increase immune response, and people living in areas with sufficient selenium in their diets show a lower cancer incidence.

Zinc. The other primary immune mineral. The *American Journal of Clinical Nutrition* and researchers at M.I.T. have reported that zinc is necessary for the body's overall immune strength and that it seems to enhance the vital immune cells lymphocytes. In particular, zinc helps the anticancer activity of the body's immune T cells.

Organic germanium. A powerful immune stimulant long used by the Japanese, which has only recently been introduced into this country. It boosts the body's levels of interferon, increases several kinds of immune cells, including the body's natural killer and macrophage cells, and acts as an antiviral. It also has been found to fight tumors in both humans and animals.

Now, let's put that general information to work so you can *greatly extend your young and healthy years.*

Youth-Preservation Immune Dose:	Your Correct Category:	
A	Beta-carotene	20,000 I.U.
	B_{12}	200 mcg
	Vitamin C	2,000 mg
	Vitamin E	400 I.U.
	Zinc	50 mg
	Selenium	100 mcg
	Organic germanium	150 mg
B	Beta-carotene	20,000 I.U.
	B_{12}	250 mcg
	Vitamin C	3,000 mg
	Vitamin E	400 I.U.
	Zinc	50 mg
	Selenium	150 mcg
	Organic germanium	200 mg
C*	Beta-carotene	25,000 I.U.
	B_{12}	300 mcg
	Vitamin C	4,000 mg
	Vitamin E	600 I.U.
	Zinc	75 mg
	Selenium	200 mcg
	Copper	0.1 mg
	Organic germanium	300 mg

Youth-Preservation Immune Dose:	Your Correct Category:	
D*	Beta-carotene	25,000 I.U.
	B$_{12}$	400 mcg
	Vitamin C	5,000 mg
	Vitamin E	600 I.U.
	Zinc	75 mg
	Selenium	200 mcg
	Copper	0.1 mg
	Organic germanium	300 mg
E*	Beta-carotene	30,000 I.U.
	B$_{12}$	500 mcg
	Vitamin C	6,000 mg
	Vitamin E	800 I.U.
	Zinc	100 mg
	Selenium	200 mcg
	Copper	0.2 mg
	Organic germanium	300 mg

*Important: For categories C, D, and E, take the dose for only three weeks, then go to category B for three weeks, then use category A levels for your maintenance dose.

Each of the steps I have discussed includes a basic combination of key immune micronutrients—vitamins, minerals, and amino acids. In Chapter 4 you established your Youth Preservation Category (see page 73). Use the level you achieved there to determine your correct immune-supplement regime.

"DRIP" Your Way to Immune Youth

Although most of this book is geared to things that you can do yourself at home, there is one powerful immune booster that you should know about, and that requires working with a physician. It is one I frequently use with my patients for its spectacular results in boosting immune function and effectively lowering immune age.

It involves many of the same immunonutrients listed in the table, but it is given in intravenous ("drip injection") form. The treatment has made a dramatic difference in a wide range of significant immune-related problems: the chronic, virally induced fatigue syndrome; the nearly ubiquitous infection of cytomegalovirus, which afflicts several million Americans; and long-term Epstein-Barr infection. These diseases can impair the absorption of vitamins, so that you are unable to take in the very nutrients you most need to fight off debilitating viruses.

To break this vicious viral cycle, a treatment was developed by Dr. Robert Cathcart, a pioneering orthopedic surgeon in California, who made his reputation as a premier orthopedic specialist at Stanford Medical Center. The treatment uses an injectable immune "cocktail" consisting of several key immune nutrients. I have found the best results by including vitamins C, B_5, and B_{12}, and zinc and manganese in the "cocktail." The elements must be carefully measured in appropriate proportions, and balanced and adjusted carefully to match the body's acid-alkaline chemistry. Then the mixture is gradually dripped into a vein in the arm. The treatment is painless, safe, and lasts only an hour or ninety minutes.

Similar intravenous immune-nutrient regimes are now being used internationally. Because these treatments can produce truly impressive changes in people's immune health, freeing them from chronic infections and illness, more and more doctors in the United States are using vitamin C intravenously in the fight against the immune-weakening diseases, including chronic viral infections, environmental and chemical allergies, AIDS, and cancer.

With my own patients, I have seen truly astounding improvements in overall vigor and health. They become seemingly younger and healthier in a matter of days with intravenous treatments. The results have brought about many complete cures among people who had tried numerous other approaches with no success. After a course of immune-boosting infusions, these patients

have left my office, not only free of the viral disease
that had plagued them for years, but with an immune
system that is, in every functional way, stronger and
dramatically rejuvenated.

I have taken drip injections to boost and strengthen
my own immune system, and I urge you to think seriously about trying such treatments. If you are interested, look for a nutritionally aware physician in your
area who can offer this nutrient-based intravenous
approach.

Step Three: To Stay Young, Vanquish Viruses!

You have already seen how to conquer cancer and
boost your overall immune power. You have come to
the final frontier of true Immune Rejuvenation: van-
quishing the viruses that age you too soon and too fast.

Viruses play a large part in how and why we lose
function and age too soon. Each time a virus makes us
sick, it ages our body. In part, at least, the reason that
we lose function with age has to do with an accumulation of years of viral insults. I can't count how often
I have heard patients say, "I haven't quite been the
same ever since I was sick last winter." You may have
said it yourself, feeling that some part of your vitality
has disappeared in the wake of an infection, mononu-
cleosis, or even a bad season of the winter flu. You may
have witnessed how a particularly serious illness can
age a person shockingly fast.

We are learning, too, that viruses play a much larger
role than we ever suspected in a wide range of diseases,
including:

—Chronic-fatigue syndrome
—Leukemia
—Epstein-Barr syndrome

—Cervical cancer
—Uterine cancer
—Burkitt's lymphoma
—Liver cancer
—Lymphoma
—Meningitis
—Herpes
—Encephalitis

Each illness takes a little extra toll on our overall health, and makes us look, act, and feel older. That, in turn, leaves us more vulnerable to the next viral attack.

With viruses at the root of so many illnesses, it follows that *the best way to break that cycle is to protect ourselves against them, so that they don't make us sick and old before our time.*

The best hope to do that comes from research on a new treatment for the deadly viral disease AIDS, and it involves a substance called "egg lecithin lipids" (you may also have heard it called AL-721). Developed in Israel, this food product—derived from three ingredients found in egg yolks—seems to work like a natural antiviral agent, helping to reverse the immune-system damage done by the AIDS virus. Some patients taking daily doses of the lecithin lipid paste report dramatic

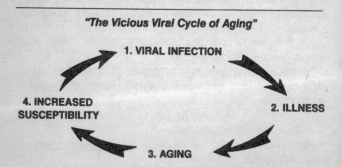

"The Vicious Viral Cycle of Aging"

1. VIRAL INFECTION

2. ILLNESS

3. AGING

4. INCREASED SUSCEPTIBILITY

improvements in their immune system. It may work, in part, because it restores certain characteristics of young cell membranes and makes the cells' metabolism run more efficiently. There is much we still have to learn about the antiviral potential of lecithin lipids, and research is ongoing as I write this.

You don't have to have AIDS to put the antiviral power of this wonderful new treatment to work for you. Just as the "Antiviral Cocktail" shown below may work against the AIDS virus, it is believed to help control several other kinds of viruses—herpes, the ubiquitous cytomegalovirus, and the Epstein-Barr virus implicated in chronic-fatigue syndrome. Because all these viruses can damage your organs, sap your energy, and age you prematurely, it makes sense that an antiviral mixture can provide a good safeguard against their ravages.

Since the "Antiviral Cocktail" is made entirely from natural food products, it is very safe, and you can make your own "home brew" formula. For the lecithin, this version uses a soy product instead of cholesterol-laden eggs, and it doesn't carry a pharmaceutical brand name, but biologically it can be used as a generic, home-brew equivalent of the promising Israeli antiviral treatment.

Many of my patients have used this home-brew formula to derive many of the same beneficial antiviral effects of lecithin lipids. You should find that it can make a real difference in arming your body to fight the viruses that would otherwise accelerate your aging process.

"ANTIVIRAL COCKTAIL"

1. At a health-food store, purchase PC-55 lecithin, a high-strength soy-lecithin concentrate.
2. Add 1 tablespoon of PC-55 to 1 cup of orange or other fruit juice.
3. Let mixture sit 5 minutes, then blend until well mixed.

4. Add 1 generous tablespoon of olive oil or peanut oil, and blend thoroughly for several minutes.
5. The cocktail is best taken in the morning on an empty stomach. IT SHOULD NOT BE EATEN AS PART OF A BREAKFAST CONTAINING ANY FATS (eggs, whole milk, butter, margarine, cheese, or yogurt). You can drink it with fat-free cereals and 100 percent skim milk, or fresh fruit.
6. I recommend that you drink this mixture every third day. The vegetable oil should be kept in a refrigerator between uses. CAUTION: IF YOU HAVE CANCER AND ARE UNDERGOING TREATMENT FOR IT, OR HAVE HIGH CHOLESTEROL, YOU SHOULD NOT DRINK THIS COCKTAIL.

Tomorrow's Immune Health

By following the three-step process in this chapter—anticancer nutrition, immune boosters, and the "Antiviral Cocktail"—you will be doing everything now known about how to make your body's immune system younger, and your health more vital. Believe me, you will feel, and show, the results.

There is no other field where the changes are coming so quickly and dramatically as in immune health and rejuvenation. Among the developments that hold the most promise for the next five years:

—At Harvard University Medical School, scientists have created what they call "antibody bridges," molecules that work like tiny guided missiles, attaching one end of themselves to cancerous cells that the immune system may miss. These molecules then attach their other end to killer immune cells, forming a bridge between the immune cell and the cancer cell. Then the killer immune cells activate and destroy the cancer cells before they can grow into a deadly tumor.

—A major step in understanding the immune system occurred the week I sat down to write this chapter, when researchers at the University of California discovered a brand-new, unsuspected kind of immune helper cell. This fundamental biological discovery deepens our understanding about how the body fights bacteria and viruses, and will help us design more effective treatments against them and promote wound healing.

—One of the best immune boosters now under investigation may be entirely natural, cost-free, and wonderfully enjoyable: that old standby, the belly laugh. For years, there have been anecdotes and books suggesting that laughter helps boost the immune system. Two new experiments have helped lend scientific proof to that assertion. In one, researchers measured the levels of immune proteins in the saliva of people before they watched a film of a hilarious stand-up comedian. The researchers found that the immune factors, essential components in the body's first-line defense against viruses, rose dramatically after the subjects viewed funny videos, and stayed stable after they viewed more serious videos.

This finding coincides with other research showing that students who scored highly on questionnaires designed to measure humor have higher levels of virus-fighting antibodies in their saliva than do their more sober friends, and tend to react to a funny film with pronounced changes in antibody levels.

—One of the most intriguing avenues of research involves borrowing from Nature to restore youthful vigor and power to the immune system. The idea is simply to restore certain of the body's own chemicals, which are in abundance when the immune system is at its peak—in youth and adolescence—but which decline with age. Researchers at Veterans Administration hospitals in Wisconsin have found that the failing immune systems of elderly veterans are not fully capable of mounting a strong response when they are given seasonal influenza shots. However, their immunity was improved when the flu shots were "boosted" with a synthetic immune substance called "thymic hormone." This is based on a natural immune-boosting substance that a healthy body produces at high levels when young, but tapers off with age. Tests are under way to learn whether resupplying the body with this pro-immune hormone can effectively rejuvenate the age-weakened immune system.

Another hormone, called DHA, may also play a role as a potential immune regulator. At the University of Southwestern Texas Medical School, a researcher has already used it to extend the life spans of laboratory animals. This scientist took a breed of mouse with the inborn immune disease systemic lupus erythematosus, which usually begins to die after six months of life, and injected the mice with DHA hormone. About half the mice survived as long as ordinary, disease-free mice— *and even longer*. Other reports suggest that the same hormone also extends the life span of immunodeficient animals. The next step is to test DHA in animals with an AIDS-like immune condition. These studies offer hope that the answer to revitalizing the age-weakened immune system may be largely a matter of putting back hormones that age has taken away.

—Scientists have long argued that the blueprints for how we age are written in our DNA. They suggest that a genetic self-destruct mechanism built into our cells affects crucial bodily processes, creating aging and even death. If that is true, researchers hope, then we can isolate those genes and actually manipulate the aging centers that right now are ticking away in our body's cells. Researchers in Irvine, California, have taken a major step to doing just that. They have studied the genetic code of a simple creature, a roundworm, and have determined a single, crucial gene, labeled "Age-1 (hx 546)." When researchers changed that one gene and reimplanted it into a generation of worms, those worms lived two thirds longer than their ordinary siblings. That's the equivalent of a human being able to live 125 years! The research is a terrifically exciting first step, as it suggests where we can look to find similar genes in humans. One of the researchers predicts "a huge payoff twenty years down the road." The next step to be taken by the National Institute on Aging is to apply this same finding to other, more complex animals. If that experiment succeeds, it will bring us one step closer to being able to do it for the most complex animal of all—*you.*

Smart Beyond Your Years: Making Your Brain Younger

ANY ADULT WHO has spent time with teenagers can't help but feel a certain envy of their sheer, clear brainpower. At such a young age, before the predations of age, disease, and chemicals have set in, their minds seem to function at a biological peak. They work like natural learning machines, effortlessly absorbing facts and impressions instantly. Unlike adults, they rarely grope for a name or recollection. Their brains are razor-sharp and retentive; new intellectual challenges, whether learning a language or memorizing information for an exam, come with ease.

Few of us keep that keen mental edge. As the years pass, our mental faculties seem to lose their original power, clarity, and speed. Subtle errors creep in; a stealthy forgetfulness, a creeping inattention appear in our third decade. Names, facts, and ideas take longer to recall, and we cannot absorb, retain, and remember things in the same effortless way we once did. To ease the load on our mind and memory, we surround ourselves with various devices like Rolodexes, calendars, calculators.

But it doesn't have to be this way. By using the newest brain-youth tools you can do much to retain sharp, youthful brain and mental functions. A host of research

174

teams has shown that you can bring your brain to its biological maximum, stimulate greater alertness, heightened concentration, and a surer, more confident recall. With no pain and no expensive treatments, you can give yourself a functionally younger brain, regain the mental powers you once took for granted, and enjoy the benefits longer than you ever thought possible. That is, you can be smart beyond your years.

The real excitement comes when the experts show that it is possible to retain our intellectual faculties until a very advanced age, and even to reverse certain intellectual declines that have already started. Keeping your brain young is essential to reaping the rewards of an alert, enjoyable life. That is the life you deserve, brimming with interest, opportunity, and spice. The Youth Preservation tools that follow will help you keep your brain finely tuned, retentive, and sharp.

Young Between the Ears

You need to know something of the physical changes that occur in that gray globe between your ears as you age. Over the next few decades, your brain will shrink constantly. It will lose neurons, those connections between brain cells that allow you to think, feel, reason, even to understand the words on this page. By age seventy, most people have lost more than one billion of their ten billion nerve cells. By age ninety, some parts of your brain may have lost up to 40 percent of their nerve-cell connections!

Happily, though, we don't lose 40 percent of our brainpower. If we did, we'd be in real trouble. Nature has cleverly designed it so that as some brain cells die, the remaining ones actually expand, filling in and making new nerve connections to fill the gaps. The medical name for this process is "reactive synaptogenesis," or "resprouting," but you can think of it as just like a forest—as one tree falls, its neighbors expand, their branches taking over, enlarging to fill the vacant space. In the amazingly complex forest of your brain, that same process is occurring right now as new cells expand to make new connections and take over functions that are lost when old cells die.

New research has even indicated that the devastating changes of Alzheimer's disease may simply be an acceleration of the normal aging process that happens to us all—only the thinning out of the nerve synapses is magnified and speeded up to a tragic degree.

This means that the first step to keeping your brain strong and youthful must occur at a physical level. You must use diet and nutritional tools to slow the rate of the cellular changes in your brain, reduce brain-cell loss, and encourage regrowth of cells.

Step One: Food for Thought

It has been proven that nutritional status affects brain function. Therefore, the first step to keeping your brain working at full, youthful efficiency is to get adequate nutritional support. Here are certain nutritional basics to give your brain the maximum chance to stay young:

—High levels of dietary fat have been shown to lower brain function in animals—yet more evidence that it is a good idea to keep dietary-fat levels low.
—Antioxidants seem to play a clear role in keeping your brain at its peak. The brain has many fat-containing cells, which are particularly vulnerable to the oxidation damage caused by free radicals, which increase with age in the brain and cause certain brain-aging changes. A solid regime of antioxidants—beta-carotene, vitamins C and E, zinc, and selenium—can

inactivate those destructive chemicals and prevent the premature aging of brain cells.

—Zinc is essential to the growth, development, and functioning of the brain. Levels of the mineral affect neurotransmitters, brain wave patterns, the brain's physical structures, even the thinking process. As brain cells are lost with age, they need to be rejuvenated, so adequate zinc is essential for lasting brain health.

—Lecithin is a food product containing choline, which has been shown repeatedly to improve mental-test results, help memory, and maximize brain function. In experiments, doses of choline made animals actually perform like much younger animals on mental tests! Lecithin seems to work by increasing one of the brain's key neurotransmitters, acetylcholine.

Of course, all these nutritional basics share one thing in common: You should already be following them. Zinc, lecithin, antioxidants, less fat in the diet—each of these counsels also appeared in the chapters on immune youth and cardiac rejuvenation. So, by following the programs already outlined, you will also be helping to keep your brain young—all with no extra work!

There are three other brain-boosting tips you should know about:

—The B vitamins—especially B_3, B_5, B_6, B_{12}, thiamine, and folacin—are critical to healthy brain functioning. They have been found to protect against mental slowness, memory defects, and mood disorders. Studies are now showing that deficiencies of B vitamins may impair recent memory, produce depression, create apprehension, hyperirritability, and emotional instability. These deficiencies appear to be much more common among older Americans than we have ever recognized. It may be more than a coincidence that this is exactly the group with the most serious problems in mental functioning. For that reason, I prescribe a solid B-complex vitamin supplement to many of my patients of all ages.

—Copper, iodine, and manganese are critical brainnutrient minerals. They can affect brain functioning and mood, boost mental alertness and sharpness, improve memory, reduce nervous anxiety, and generally keep the mental status stable. Accordingly, make sure your diet includes foods that are a good source of these minerals, including dried beans, peas, shrimp, oysters and most seafood, seaweed, onions, whole grains (including the bran), green leafy vegetables, prunes, dark chocolate, seeds, nuts, fruits, and many other unprocessed foods.

Metals and Memory

Of course, not all minerals help the brain. The "heavy metals"—among them aluminum, mercury, lead, and cadmium—can be very toxic to the brain. Lead poisoning can cause mental sluggishness and even retardation. Cadmium can lead to significant memory loss and diminished mental function. Both aluminum and cadmium are thought to be factors in the tragic brainwasting of Alzheimer's disease. Memory problems can be a symptom of heavy-metal poisoning, which you may be exposed to in many ways. Do you:

—Live in an area with a lot of environmental pollution, including smog or smoke?
—Live next to a major roadway or airport? German researchers have found that people living next to roadways have dangerously high levels of lead.

—Cook or eat food from aluminum pots or use aluminum foil? Certain acidic foods—tomato juice, lemonade, vinegar, orange juice—can draw the aluminum into them.

—Use ceramic bowls and dishes? Glazes used in some pottery can leach lead into certain foods.

—Have silver fillings in your mouth? Scientists in The Netherlands show that tooth fillings can release toxic metals into the body.

—Regularly take over-the-counter antacid remedies? If so, look on the label: One of the main ingredients is aluminum. If you've been taking them for a long time, you can be getting too much aluminum.

—Use an aluminum-containing antiperspirant? If so, you may be chronically absorbing excess aluminum through your skin.

If you fit into several of these categories, I recommend that you go on a special detoxifying regimen, in addition to the supplements we discussed earlier, to help keep your brain young and clear. This once-a-day, four-week program will help clear out heavy-metal residues before they can create a toxic buildup in your brain. Take

50 milligrams of glutathione
500 milligrams of cysteine

These amino acids bind heavy metals to help your body flush them out. The vitamin C and selenium that you are already taking will also help remove lead from your brain, and help your body eliminate heavy metals.

Step Two: Train Your Brain

The nutritional counsels above are only half the solution. With them, you have started to make your brain more physically youthful. Now comes the next step: to keep your brain young and to realize its maximum biological potential. That requires mental exercises and imagery to constantly train, expand, and hone the brain.

Modern research suggests that we need to exercise our brain to stay youthful and strong. We know that such training has a profound impact on how much, and how fast, our brain ages—or, better, on how young it stays. This process—termed "cognitive training"—is the best way to maximize our biological potential and keep our brain strong and sharp far longer than otherwise. The most exciting studies show that you can even *reverse* the brain's physical deterioration that may have already started!

—A score of research papers have shown that continual brain training and learning can offset and even reverse brain aging. Older animals that live in rich and varied environments, with the opportunity for constant learning, actually show organic changes in their brains. The nerve connections grow more complex, with more synapses, and more closely resemble the brains of healthy younger animals.

—A study of four thousand older volunteers showed that many of them could greatly improve two kinds of brain skills that had declined with age, simply by using brain-training techniques. Two out of five subjects made so much progress that they actually regained the performance levels they had shown fourteen years earlier, in effect turning back the clock a decade and a half in their brain's functional age!

—A report by a National Institute on Aging task force showed that one in five older people with intellectual impairment may be able to reverse the downward slide.

—Cognitive training was found to increase older people's accuracy on standard mental-function tests, so they scored as though they were "younger."

The picture is clear: You don't have to lose brain-power as you age, and some of what you may have lost already can be retrieved and retrained. Rather, our intellectual skills, like muscles, seem to atrophy with disuse. Just as we need a physical workout, we need a mental one as well. With sufficient practice and stimulation, you can do much to reverse the "inevitable" mental declines of old age.

Putting It to Work for You

How can you take advantage of these new findings, and give your brain the mental workout it needs to stay younger, stronger, and more alert? One good way is by taking tests designed to sharpen specific skills of spatial orientation and inductive reasoning. Research suggests that practicing on such tests can help you sharpen those skills, and effectively lower the functional age of your brain.

Just doing these tests one time won't, of course, take years off the age of your brain. The key is consistency. You need to build into your life these kind of challenging mental exercises on a regular basis. There are several ways I tell my patients to do that:

—Get in the habit of doing games, tests, quizzes, puzzles, or brain twisters. You can pick up a collection at your local bookstore. Scrabble, word jumbles, acrostics, even crossword puzzles give the brain necessary exercise. Card games are particularly helpful for training reasoning and retention.

—Take a course at a local college or adult-education center. The practice you get in memorization, inductive or deductive reasoning, spatial orientation, or calculation will help give you the mental exercise you need.

—Pick up any one of the scores of preparation books for the SAT or other standardized scholastic tests. They are treasure troves of exactly the kind of varied, stimulating mental exercises that can help your brain stay young.

—If there is a university near you, its psychology department may have a specialist in psychometric testing. He or she may be able to help you obtain hundreds of brain-expanding tests and test instruments.

—Look in the "psychometrics" section of your local library for test instruments you can use as brain-training tools.

Step Three: "Memory Magnifiers"

There is no more important way to keep your brain young and powerful than to boost the power of your memory. Loss of memory is the first sign we associate with failing faculties, and a good memory is one of the most impressive aspects of clear mental functioning as we grow older. Happily, it is also one of the mental processes on which you can have the most significant, and dramatic, impact.

To boost memory requires no specialized tests at all. Here are four "memory magnifier" techniques that you can do on your own, as you go about your everyday life, with no tools or expense. Practice them and apply them diligently, and you can expect to see a dramatic rise in your retention and recollection abilities.

—*Mnemonics and acronyms* are the techniques of creating a word or sentence, each letter of which stands for one of the words you want to recall. Every Good Boy Does Fine has enabled countless music students to remember the letters of the treble clef musical staff E, G, B, D, F. This technique is used by every doctor to survive medical school. To retain the overwhelming crush of information physicians required—such as the names of the myriad nerves serving one part of the face—you make up a word whose letters are associated with each item. This technique works well with a shopping list, the names of your spouses or extended relatives, the signs of the zodiac, your boss's children.

—*Rhyme association.* Who can forget the first-grade spelling rule "I before E except after C"? And who hasn't reckoned the length of months by repeating "Thirty days hath September..."? The trick still works: Match an item you want to recall with a rhyming word, and you won't forget it. For best results, make up your own personal rhyme: ["Mish, mash, take out the trash."]

—*Visual association.* Pairing each item you want to recall with an associated visual cue is a powerful memory builder. You'll remember Mrs. Greenbottom, Mr. Brooks, and Ms. Burns much better if you turn their names into images. The more outrageous and improbable the images, the more firmly they will lodge in your memory banks. That's why I'll bet you remember Mrs. Greenbottom longest of the three! This technique also helps experienced card players recall the flow of cards. They create a visual image of which number cards in which suits have been played, then they recall, say, a gap in the lower middle of the spades, or a solid run in the face cards in hearts. With each new play, they adjust their internal picture accordingly. That way, they only have to remember four groups of one suit each, rather than fifty-two separate cards.

—*Loci association* is a well-proven memory-enhancing technique. To recall a list of things, you envision an area you know well. It may be your bedroom, your office, or your street. Then you mentally "place" each item on the list at a different spot in the familiar landscape. To recollect the items, you simply take a tour through that area, picking up each item as you see it.

The technique works to organize any serial list: one's thoughts for a speech, Saturday's planned errands, or what you want to take on an upcoming trip.

The key in all of these techniques is the process of association itself. Memory is nothing more than associating the item we want to remember with a cue. Studies show that the more effort that we put into the act of perceiving or remembering something, the better we recall it. Your goal is to make that process conscious, pairing every item with a tangible and unexpected cue. Whether it is a rhyme, a word, a place, or an object doesn't matter. What counts is the effort you put into it. That's why devices you make up yourself work better than those you copy from others, and also why the best memory joggers are often the most outrageous ones.

At first, you may find this association process awkward, but it soon becomes second nature. As it does, you will notice a marked improvement in your memory. You will begin to make the physical changes in your brain's neuronal structure that strengthen memory. But most of all, you will give yourself a younger, more retentive mind, and reduce your effective mental age, making your brain younger in every sense of the word.

Looking Ahead—Super Brains?

Tomorrow's brain clinics may offer pills, shots, or treatments that greatly increase your brainpower, or at least help give the brain a chemical overhaul, restoring retention, alertness, and analytic capacity seemingly lost years before. Neurobiochemists are pursuing several promising avenues of research, including:

—The hormone DHEA may strengthen the brain as well, according to current research. Scientists surmise that DHEA is such a powerful bioregulator because the body can use it to synthesize more than a dozen distinct steroid hormones. In the brain, it seems to help cells grow in a more organized, interconnected fashion. Injected into test animals, it created dramatic improvements in their performance on laboratory mazes—in some cases allowing old mice, who had previously performed poorly, to run the mazes as well as young mice. It appears to work by helping the animals retain what they have learned from previous attempts.

—Test animals are getting smarter at the University of Rochester too, according to a paper published in the journal *Brain Research*. Neurochemists took rats with seriously failing memories and infused their brains with a chemical, norepinephrine, found in a normal, healthy brain. Immediately the rats began performing almost like much younger rats. To test the idea, the researchers then implanted into the rats' brains, cells that release the chemical. In several months, when the cellular transplants "took," there was a marked improvement in the rats' memories.

There is a feeling of great excitement in neurobiology laboratories around the country. There is a clear sense that we are closer than ever before to unlocking the chemical keys that will allow us to stay more alert, more retentive—just plain smarter—longer. We may even be able to reverse the most common degradations in brainpower, keep a razor-sharp intellect and memory ten, twenty, or thirty years longer than we can today.

Until then, is there any way you can prepare yourself for these new findings? Absolutely. By giving your brain adequate nutritional support, in terms of micronutrients, vitamins, minerals, and amino acids, protecting it against accumulated toxins like heavy metals, and giving it the exercise it needs to stay young—in other words, by following the three brain-longevity steps in this chapter!

Can't Live Without It: Activity and Aging

Teach us to live that we may dread
Unnecessary time in bed
Get people up and we may save
Our patients from an early grave.
—British Medical Journal, 1947

A physically active life may allow us to approach our true biogenetic potential for longevity.
—Journal of the American Medical Association, 1980

SUPPOSE I TOLD you that you have available *today* a powerful, proven method to stay young and vigorous longer. This single measure could ensure that for many more years you will meet life on your own terms, unencumbered by ill health or fading energy. It would help you greet each day with renewed energy and vitality, and give you the strength and vigor to do and be all you can. Even better, this technique is:

—Cost-free
—Enjoyable
—Free of special diets, treatments, or medication
—Easily incorporated into your life
—Guaranteed to have a positive impact on your health
  and longevity

The "secret" ingredient that makes this all possible? It is as simple as *regular physical activity*.

But you knew that, right? After all, we've already seen in other chapters how activity and exercise help the heart, circulatory system, and bones. But before you dismiss it as too simple, let's look at what you may *not* have known—because the news is just now breaking in scientific journals. Among the surprising and hopeful findings:

—There is a direct activity-longevity link.
—Your physical activity will determine your freedom from illness.
—There is new evidence on how much activity, and what kind, gives you the "longevity effect."
—You may need *less* exercise than you think to live better and longer.

Make no mistake: There is real news here. Most exciting of all, these findings represent a real advance from what we thought just a few years ago. I recall a recent newswire about a new medical advisory publication from the Canadian government. "If people are to live as long as possible without serious health problems," it said, doctors should prescribe exercise for patients. "The use of activity rather than bed rest in medical treatment is a real revolution in the 80's, . . . but doctors don't routinely prescribe exercise . . . because they just don't know." It may be years before this revolution trickles down to the average doctor's office, but there is every reason for you to put it to work *now* to feel, act, and look younger, longer.

All of this research boils down to a simple principle: Increasing your physical activity will add years to your life and life to your years, *even without strenuous exercise.* This short chapter reviews our state-of-the-art understanding of the activity-longevity link, and shows how you can use this knowledge in your own life.

The Activity-Longevity Link

For a long time, physicians have known that activity and exercise help specific parts of our body—the heart, the bones, etc. Now they have extended this research to show conclusively that *activity and exercise may be your single biggest defense against the changes of age.* To cite just a few voices from respected medical journals:

"Many of the changes commonly attributed to aging can be retarded by an active exercise program. . . . A high degree of physical fitness should offset age changes."—*Journal of the American Geriatric Association.*

"A portion of the changes commonly attributed to aging is in reality caused by disuse and . . . is subject to correction."—*Journal of the American Medical Association.*

"When people remain active, their body composition tends to resemble that of younger people."—*Handbook of the Biology of Aging.*

"Physical activity discourages disease, the absence of exercise invites disease."—*Predictive Medicine, A Study in Strategy.*

"Increased activity is associated with increased life expectancy. There is no doubt whatsoever that inactivity will shorten your life."—*The Physician and Sports Medicine.*

"Exercise results in improved survival . . . countering deleterious effects of a sedentary life."—*Society of Experimental Biology Journal.*

"By age 80 . . . additional life attributable to adequate exercise . . . was more than two years . . ." *New England Journal of Medicine.*

The latest research has proven beyond a trace of doubt what generations of mothers and gym teachers have long suspected: ACTIVITY IS LONGEVITY.

Not Just Longer ... Better

Increased longevity is only half the battle. What counts as much as how long you live is how *well*. None of us wants to live for many years being feeble and doddering, our energy and faculties sapped. Our goal, rather, is to realize the longest possible "well-span"— years of being fully alert, energetic, and radiantly alive. I know your goal is to extend this period of life as long as possible, to keep the sparkle in your eyes, the spring in your step, and the joy in your heart for many decades to come. Plain and simple, it is your level of physical activity that will let you do that. If you want ...

—Less chance of heart attack, chest pain, and artery disease
—Less likelihood of broken bones due to osteoporosis
—More muscle strength
—Less fat and more lean body mass
—More stable blood sugar
—More energy and better breathing
—Less joint pain
—More flexibility
—Less depression
—Better mental functioning, better memory, improved reasoning and confidence
—Better, more restful sleep

... then activity and exercise are the keys. A dramatic demonstration of how exercise makes you biologically younger was reported in the *Journal of American Geriatrics*. Doctors measured biological age through a common laboratory standard of the level of oxygen uptake of the lungs. They compared the scores of seventy-year-olds and younger subjects, who did and did not exercise, and found that when inactive seventy-year-olds started "moderate activity," their physiological profiles showed up to fifteen years younger. Those who continued to the "athlete" level of conditioning had a potential reduction of *forty years* in their age. It may be that the mythical Fountain of Youth is as close as the nearest health club!

If exercise rejuvenates the body, you'd expect inactivity to age it—which is just what studies show. When healthy people are forced to take bed rest or be confined, their biochemical profile starts to resemble that of someone much older. On certain physiological tests, people aged ten years during only thirty-six weeks of bed rest! Research with hospital patients, prisoners, and astronauts shows that inactivity takes a measurable toll on the immune system, the blood, cholesterol, heart function, bones, nerves, body composition, even brain waves. The moral is clear: Exercising is your best bet to stay supple, energetic, and alert, to keep your mood high, your muscles strong, and your mind clear. It is the best way to take years off your body's age, and to make sure that the years ahead will be the most enjoyable, vigorous, and healthy ever.

Be an Activist, Not an Athlete

By now, you know *why* you should be more active. For your life span, and your enjoyment of it, the benefits of increasing activity levels are beyond dispute. But wait just one minute, I hear you say. "Even if I have resolved that my days as a couch potato are numbered, I am also a far cry from being an athlete." Perhaps even the thought of running shoes makes you tired, and the idea of heavy, gasping, sweaty workouts makes you want to just curl up with a good book. You may be one of the millions who have tried exercising, only to give up in frustration after being unable to stick to a rigorous program. Does that mean you should turn to the next chapter and write off your chances for Youth Preservation through exercise?

Once upon a time, medical science might have said yes. But now I have good news—just for people like you. The latest research tells a very different, and much more hopeful, story. You may notice that throughout this chapter, I have referred to "exercise" together with "activity." Not long ago, the conventional wisdom held that one had to be a marathoner or a serious athlete, or at least a health-club habitué to gain longevity benefit from exercise. Exercise was thought to be an "all or nothing" proposition.

But the newest findings suggest that you can benefit, not just from grueling exercise, but also from more moderate levels of regular activity in your weekly routine. Just by increasing your basic levels of weekly activity, you increase your life expectancy. Conversely, says a Harvard Medical School researcher, "There's no doubt whatever that insufficient activity will shorten your life."

The key here—the real news you should know from the most recent findings—is that what counts is activity, not just athletics. Studies have shown that regardless of the strenuous exercise they do or do not get, men whose jobs require them to walk more, lift more, and generally be more active have fewer health problems and live longer.

These tidings mean that it's worth acquiring some new habits: Walk those extra few blocks to the store, take the stairs instead of the elevator, and do whatever you can to build-in occasions to be active rather than sedentary as you go about your daily life. Moderate activity will do. If you expend more than about 1,000 calories each week beyond your basic needs, you will cross the threshold to achieving better health and longevity. Best of all, think of all the pleasant ways to do that:

Gardening   Going for a swim
Dancing   Bowling
Playing with children   Chopping wood
Riding a bike   Walking the dog
Taking a Saturday hike

Even washing windows, scrubbing floors, and cutting the lawn—while not perhaps high on your "recreation" list—burn up calories and count toward your activity levels. Just think, this coming week you could make the house look terrific, treat yourself to an hour's walk afterward, play with the kids—and feel virtuous while doing it, knowing you are adding years—healthy ones—to your life!

This "activity revolution" provides real hope for a lot of us who may have sat out the "fitness revolution." *We who cannot dedicate ourselves to strenuous athletics can still reap many health and life-span benefits—just by staying moderately active.*

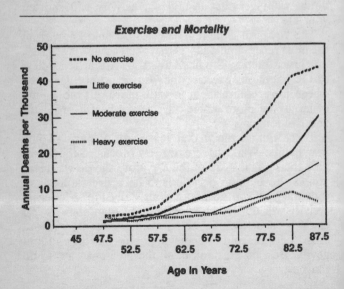

Exercise and Mortality

A few years ago, the Secretary of Health and Human Services issued a report showing that less than 20 percent of Americans exercise strenuously and often enough to meet popular aerobic fitness standards. Now we know that there is some hope for the 200 million-plus who haven't achieved star-athlete level of fitness training: For all the rest of us, then, these new findings offer great promise for longer, healthier lives.

Summary Regular activity, not just strenuous exercise, is the key to health and longevity.

Feel Free to Exercise...

Although activity does more than we once supposed, I do not mean to discourage you from more intense exercise. It can extend your health and longevity benefits still further. The chart opposite, based on epidemiological research, tells the whole story.

Certainly, those who get more exercise show the most dramatic improvements in longevity. But the real story is the one told by the rest of the curve. *The greatest benefits come when you change from no activity to moderate activity, rather than from moderate activity to high activity.*

Confucius said, "Every journey begins with a single step," and so it is with the activity-exercise continuum. If you are like most of my patients, you may find that by an easy increase in your general activity level, the next step gets easier and more pleasant. You may never end up a decathlon champion—but you will end up healthier and biologically younger.

That is really the moral of this chapter, and what I hope you take away with you. The more activity and exercise you get, the better (so long as you do not have physical limitations that make exercise unwise). But because you can't bench-press three hundred pounds doesn't mean you can't start increasing your levels of basic daily activity. Keep in mind that regular activity is just as important as hard exercise—and for many of us, much more realistic. So remember: Activity *is* longevity. To ensure yourself a long and healthy life, you really *can't* live without it.

Less Is More: The VLC Plan for Long Life

IF YOU ARE a seriously dedicated, die-hard Youth Preservationist, this chapter is for you. It is something of a "graduate course" in the ways you can preserve your youth and lengthen your life. The information it contains may not be something that everybody wants to use, but I do want you to know about it.

So far, we have emphasized those elements you need to *add* to your diet or life-style to live longer and feel much better. But if you were to ask virtually any reputable longevity biologist in any of the world's premier laboratories, you would soon learn that the greatest impact on your life may come, not from what you *add* to your diet, but from what you *subtract*.

All those eminent scientists know that there exists one undisputable, sure-fire route to preserving youth and vitality. It is one you can follow starting right now, and it is *virtually guaranteed* to add years, perhaps even decades, of healthy time to your life. Best of all, they would tell you, it is amazingly simple and costs you nothing.

You may be thinking that such a powerful technique must be a closely guarded secret, right? Not at all. It has been proven and reproven over more than fifty years of laboratory studies, published in hundreds of papers, proven and replicated around the world.

Does this sound too good to be true? It's not. Allow me to let you in on the "secret" the experts know. The single surest way to guaranteeing yourself a longer, healthier life span boils down to three letters: VLC, and they stand for Very Low Calories.

It is a scientific truism that *animals live significantly longer by dramatically reducing the number of calories they eat.* And the animal to whom that means the most is . . . *you.*

The experimental evidence for the VLC phenomenon is rock solid and beyond dispute. Among its astounding, proven benefits, such a diet:

—Extends life spans in lab experiments
—Lowers blood pressure
—Reduces destructive antibodies that attack the brain
—Reduces the loss of certain brain cells
—Strengthens the immune system
—Slows the aging process
—Lowers cholesterol and heart-disease risk
—Reduces muscle oxygen loss, and improves muscle function
—Reduces free-radical damage to the body's tissues
—Helps stabilize the blood sugar imbalance in diabetes
—Helps the body run at peak metabolic efficiency

Most dramatic of all, scores of studies show that animals on VLC diets live dramatically longer, without disease, with longevity increases of 50 percent, 65 percent, even 83 percent! In the words of one expert in the life-prolonging science of VLC diets: "Food restriction is unique in . . . the extent to which life is extended."

We do not yet understand just why and how a VLC diet prolongs life so dramatically. In part, it may work because it reduces body fat, which in turn diminishes toxic free radicals, and lowers cancer and heart-disease risk. But the longevity payoff of a VLC program goes beyond just these differences. Whatever the precise mechanism involved in VLC turns out to be, many generations of ancient, healthy laboratory mice are (long) living proof that it works!

VLC is not just a matter of eating "lite" foods, a few low-cal snacks, and skipping the occasional lunch. Not by a long shot. VLC diets that have been tested have involved a reduction in daily calorie intake down to about 60 percent of normal. In a typical group of test animals, this meant getting fed only every other day. It also meant they ate in such a way that vital nutrients were concentrated, and every single bit of food energy was used where it did the most good. As their reward for eating less and eating more efficiently, these particular animals lived 83 percent longer than their normal-feeding companions. In human terms, this would translate into living to the ripe old age of 137!

Of Mice and Man

Now you, of course, are not a laboratory mouse. But you don't need to be. If there is one thing all the experts agree on, it is the view expressed in one major paper, which reviewed a number of scientific studies on VLC diets: "The basic aging processes of all mammals are similar . . . nutritional manipulations that slow the aging process in rats will do the same in humans."

In other words, there is every genetic and biological reason to think that what works for laboratory animals works for the human animal. There is enough learned consensus that it will work for humans that several prominent gerontological scientists are enthusiastic about proposing VLC diets for humans. One eminent physician, a member of the medical school faculty at the University of California, Los Angeles, has been on such a very low-calorie longevity regimen for years—he is still going strong today and fully expects to enjoy buoyant energy and health for many decades to come.

Although the odds are that such a program works for the human animal, for most of us the problem is one of motivation. Few of us are eager to cut our diet so deeply. (I can hardly imagine anyone eager to go on an every-other-day eating program!) In order to get the maximum longevity benefit, and match the dramatic results of those studies, you would eventually need to cut back to a level of about 60 percent of the calories you now take in. For women, who normally need 2,000 calories per day, that would mean gradually dropping to 1,300; for men, it would mean a reduction from 2,700 to 1,650 calories. Gulp!

But when it comes to a VLC program, there is a much *easier* way. I don't really recommend such a drastic calorie reduction, because I find it is simply too hard for people to stay on such a restricted diet. In addition, trying to keep track of actual calories can be a tedious and painstaking process. But since the calories you eat usually translate directly into weight, let your pounds be your guide. Find yourself on the VLC Target Weight Table on the opposite page.

Normally, you probably weigh approximately 20 percent more than the value shown on the chart. For example, a woman who is 5 feet 7 inches tall, between age 55 and age 64, might weigh 155 pounds—or 20 percent more than the values in the VLC Target Weight Table. In any safe and appropriate VLC program, your goal is to reduce your weight to 20 percent below what you usually think of as normal for your age and height—that is what the values in the chart represent. Obviously weight is not the only thing that counts—it is also important that you eat the right foods to give your body the longevity nutrients it needs.

VLC Target Weight Table

YOUR HEIGHT		AGE				
		18–24	25–34	35–44	45–54	55–64
4' 10"	Women	92	99	107	106	108
4' 11"	Women	95	101	109	109	110
5' 0"	Women	97	104	111	111	114
5' 1"	Women	99	106	113	114	116
5' 2"	Men	104	111	117	118	117
	Women	102	109	115	117	118
5' 3"	Men	108	116	119	123	121
	Women	105	111	117	120	121
5' 4"	Men	111	121	124	126	124
	Women	107	114	119	122	123
5' 5"	Men	114	124	127	130	128
	Women	110	117	121	126	126
5' 6"	Men	118	127	131	134	132
	Women	113	119	123	128	129
5' 7"	Men	122	131	135	137	136
	Women	115	122	125	131	131
5' 8"	Men	126	134	139	141	139
	Women	118	124	127	134	134
5' 9"	Men	130	138	142	144	142
5' 10"	Men	133	142	146	148	146
5' 11"	Men	137	146	150	152	150
6' 0"	Men	140	149	154	155	154
6' 1"	Men	144	153	158	158	158
6' 2"	Men	148	157	162	163	161

Calculated from: U.S. Center for Health Statistics, North American Association Study of Obesity

Do You Have to Go "All the Way"?

Many of my patients want to know if there is some way to gain some of the longevity benefits without such a severe diet—and without being a mealtime maniac. They ask: "Is there any reasonable way I can benefit from the VLC effect that has helped those Methuselah mice?"

My answer is: "Absolutely." Even if you don't want to go "all the way" to a strict VLC diet, you can still use its sound biological principles to extend your life and improve your health.

The VLC diet is simply the logical conclusion of many of the ideas in this book. The basic anticancer, heart-smart, pro-longevity steps we have discussed so far—less fat, less meat, more fish and filling fibers, less refined sugar and alcohol, appropriate vitamin and mineral supplements, and regular activity—are all 100 percent compatible with reducing the body's excess calories. You may decide to shoot for a personal weight reduction goal of 5 percent, 10 percent, or 12 percent below your current weight—but whatever your goal, you cannot help but gain—in health and in longevity.

The VLC High-Efficiency Diet

If you are interested in trying a VLC regime, there are three principles to remember:

1. In general, the fewer calories you eat, the more years you add to your life.
2. The less you eat, the more *efficient* your diet must be.
3. You must undertake such a plan gradually and correctly or you can do yourself more harm than good.

In other words, the best way to use VLC is with a little TLC—the Tender Loving Care you must have to give your body what it needs, while removing what it doesn't.

Six VLC Tips

If you are interested in trying a VLC diet, here are six primary principles to keep in mind:

1. *Make every calorie count!* EFFICIENCY is the name of the game in a VLC diet. With so many fewer allowable calories, those you do eat must give you the most possible nutritive "bang for your buck." Your goal is to assure that you get enough energy and protein to stay vigorous, and nothing extra. That means:

—NO refined or highly processed foods. Simple carbohydrates and sugars must be cut to an absolute low.
—Eat about 80 grams of protein daily, and make sure your protein and carbohydrate sources are as "pure" and fat-free as possible.
—Keep fat to a bare-bones minimum—*no more than 20 percent of total calories*.
—Eat no more than 300 grams of dietary cholesterol daily.

2. *Go for bulk.* It is easy to cut down on food if you eat things that help you feel full. You will want to balance your diet to include a lot of fiber and bulky foods—ideally those that pass through your system undigested, yet give you a feeling of having eaten. As a goal, aim to eat at least 50 grams of fiber each day.

3. *Use a fullness enhancer.* Another way to give you the feeling of fullness you need to stay on a VLC plan is to use a substance like guar gum. Guar gum is non-

digestible, nonnutritive, and comes in liquid form. Once in your stomach, it expands to help you feel full. I have put hundreds of patients on guar-gum supplements to lose weight—it is a crucial component in any VLC diet.

4. *Don't spare those nutritional supplements.* Because you are eating so little food, you could short-change yourself on essential vitamins, minerals, and amino acids. On any VLC plan, you must take a strong, wide-spectrum micronutrient supplement to make sure your body gets all it needs to stay healthy on a reduced calorie diet. Micronutrient supplements won't add to your calorie intake, but they will give your body the necessary nutritional support. You will find an example of such a supplement plan in Appendix B, to give you an idea of the optimal levels to use if you are on a VLC diet.

5. *Ease into a VLC program very gradually.* If you try to drop to 80 percent of your weight immediately, you will be ravenous for a few days, and then fall off the VLC wagon with a resounding thump. It is far better to reduce your weight in gradual steps. You may want to establish a goal of a pound of weight loss every two weeks for the first five pounds, then a pound a month until you get down to the proper VLC maintenance level. It may take some time to achieve your target, true—but it is the best way to ensure you will stay with the program. *A drastic and transient weight loss WILL NOT enhance your longevity or health, and it WILL make it harder to achieve your VLC target.*

6. *Prepare yourself for a change in your appearance.* Your VLC efficiency diet will cause a real change in your body. You will lose excess fat—in places you didn't even know you had it. As you become lean, your body's metabolism will adapt to your new dietary levels, becoming ever more efficient. Your body's engines will run more cleanly and efficiently, extracting maximum energy from every bit you eat. You should be prepared for the new, lean person that emerges.

For those of you who are sincerely interested in going on a VLC diet, I have included my own sample diet in Appendix C. It brings you to a level of 1,600 calories for women and slightly higher for men, a significant reduction of calories—AND A SIGNIFICANT STEP ON YOUR WAY TO A LIFE-PROLONGING DIET!

One Final Note

Let's talk frankly. I understand that you may not want to undertake a difficult regimen like a full-fledged VLC diet. That's fine. After all, by reading this book, you have already taken steps to give yourself not just many more years of life, but *better* years of life. I can guarantee that you will enjoy increased benefits—in health, vigor, energy, and well-being—regardless of whether you go all the way and adopt a rigorous VLC program.

My goal in this chapter, like my goal in this entire book, is to tell you about what tools exist right now that allow you to make a real, significant difference in the quantity and quality of your life. In that spirit, I want at least to make sure that you know about the proven life-improving promise of VLC high-efficiency diets. But beyond that, the choice is up to you. Different tools work differently for different people, and I am not saying you have to put yourself on a severe VLC diet. You can take advantage of many of these benefits by going part way—that is, by setting your own personal VLC target. You may choose a weight goal different from the value in the VLC Target Weight Table, maybe halfway between the number on the table and your normal weight. What I do want you to understand is that *whatever weight reduction you make is a change for the better*. You will still derive real benefits from the program because every step toward your VLC target gives you greater longevity and health benefits.

That's what this book is all about: feeling better, looking better, living longer. These benefits can all be yours if you decide to make the "secret" of the high-efficiency, extra-longevity VLC diet a part of your life.

Reprogramming Your Aging Computer

YOU HAVE OFTEN heard it said that "you are only as old as you think you are." I prefer to phrase it slightly differently: We are as *young* as we think we are. When it comes to staying young and leading a full exuberant life, it is not just your brain that counts, but your mind. That may be the single most important element, and it is the focus of this short final chapter.

According to a new field of research that has opened up in the last few years, your mind may be both the simplest, and the most powerful, weapon in your fight against premature aging. This new discipline is called "psychoneuroimmunology," or PNI for short. It charts the links between what goes on in our mind—our emotions, attitudes, and beliefs—and the health and vitality of our organs and physiological systems. The goal of PNI scientists is to unravel the mind-body connection that has perplexed and tantalized humans for millennia. Over the next two decades, I believe, this discipline will hold the most exciting and promising keys to longevity and long-term health.

However, far more important is what it means for you right now. It offers you nothing less than the keys to reprogramming the master computer that is ultimately responsible for aging—your mind.

The last five years have brought a torrent of fascinating and exciting findings from PNI researchers worldwide. They have shown that:

—In both men and women, mental programming for hope, hopelessness, or depression affects one's chances of getting, and surviving, many kinds of cancer, including lung, breast, cervical, and skin cancers.
—The personality programming you received as a child can affect your likelihood of developing cancer later in life.
—Animals given control over their environment fight off tumors better and live longer than animals with no control.
—Institutionalized people who have more control over their lives show dramatic improvements in overall health, even reversing bodily changes due to aging.
—Personality type may play a role in a person's susceptibility to diseases like asthma, peptic ulcers, arthritis, diabetes, multiple sclerosis, even heart disease and cancer.
—Brain chemicals that regulate happiness, sex drive, mental functioning, sleep, depression, aggression, and all of our other brain functions, have been found to activate specific immune fighters such as scavenger cells, T killer cells, antibody-producing cells, and immune boosters like interferon and interleukin-2.
—Our immune system's strength reflects our emotional and mental coping mechanisms. Life-style and psychological stresses can weaken our immune defenses, increase the likelihood of catching infections, and raise our risk for many kinds of diseases.
—People with strong psychological coping skills have been found to have more powerful immune systems, and higher levels of killer immune cells, than people with poor coping skills.
—Grieving, stress, and depression have all been proven to lower your body's immunological fighter cells dramatically.

—Research at Vanderbilt University Medical Center shows that patients who are programmed to expect a slow recovery after surgery exhibit more physical problems, and those who expect to leave the hospital quickly are much more likely to.

—By programming themselves with mental-relaxation tools, people can lower blood pressure and reduce the frequency of heart-rhythm abnormalities.

—George Washington University physicians found that patients can use mental imagery to change the levels of certain immune cells necessary to fight cancer.

—It has been discovered that people with multiple personalities have dramatically different physical reactions with their different personas. The changes include tolerance to medications, eyesight and sensory acuity, allergies, right- or lefthandedness, and neurological characteristics. Mental programming for each personality transforms the same individual into many measurably different biological "beings."

The list of discoveries is long and varied, touching on virtually every aspect of our body's functioning. This information avalanche points to one inescapable conclusion. From our hearts and blood pressure to our immune system, from our resistance to the common cold or to the deadliest cancer, every bodily process responds to some conscious mental and emotional control.

Your mind is the computer that controls the biological processes that age you. Even more astounding, we have learned that each of us holds the tools to *reprogram that computer* so we can retard the aging process and extend our young, healthy years. This represents a mind-boggling scientific awakening. We are just learning to harness the mind's awesome potential. I have no doubt that this is the medicine that will be practiced in the twenty-first century—but you can start using it now.

Who's Running This Computer, Anyway?

Your body's master aging computer already lies within you, and it is running even as you read this. In fact, it is already executing a complex and detailed "program" that will control your rates of aging, of fitness, and health. Your longevity program is the sum total of your expectations about what the next half century holds for you. It includes how you envision what your state of health will be, what you anticipate doing and being able to do, how you expect to feel, what physical limitations you see lying ahead for you, even when you expect to die.

Unfortunately, if you are like most people, *right now, you are running a longevity program that is fatally flawed*. It's not your fault. One cannot grow up in our culture without "programming in" some very negative expectations about aging. We are surrounded by a national conspiracy to sell ourselves short when it comes to growing older. For example, you probably see yourself on a slow downward curve after the age of fifty. You expect to lose your faculties, feel less energetic, move more slowly and with less ease, get sick more often. Perhaps you've seen older relatives grow infirm and frail for the last decade of their lives, so you may anticipate that course for yourself. You probably plan to retire, have some leisure time, and then find yourself on a slippery slope where you sicken, weaken, and eventually die. I expect that you see each change in your bodily state as a part of a diminishing, inevitable pattern of decay. Such negative images surround us, reinforced by experiencing how people used to age in previous generations, and by the national media and a culture that disseminates much nonsense about what it is like to be on the far side of sixty.

The mind-body scientists have demonstrated that your mental aging computer commands many powerful ways to *make those expectations come true*—slowly, gradually, and inevitably—through its control over your bodily processes. And it will do it, unless you rewrite the program. Now, for the first time, you have a chance to take conscious control of this extraordinarily powerful anti-aging tool and put it on your side.

PNI has shown us that we have the ability to create a "longevity conspiracy," linking our mind and our body's physiological systems for better health, more vigorous years, longer youth. Science has given us the tools, and it is up to each of us to believe in them, stop selling our future short, and put them to work right now.

Four Steps to a New Longevity Program

Fortunately, there are some simple and easy ways to reprogram your aging computer. Because, sophisticated as it is, it only operates on what you tell it. If you repeatedly remind your computer that you plan to live a long and healthy life, and that frailty and decrepitude have no place in your life, it will react accordingly. Here is a set of positive visualization exercises to help you do that.

Longevity Visualization Exercises

I. Relaxation Imagery

1. *Relax* two or three times each day, sitting calmly for ten minutes in a comfortable chair, with your feet flat on the ground. Imagine yourself at ninety, being active, energetic, full of life.

2. *Create* your own internal "movie" of how you want to feel. Picture yourself among friends, enjoying yourself, feeling strong and wise. Imagine being sur-

rounded by many people who love you and value your long lifetime of experience.

3. *Repeat* twenty times in succession, twice daily, an affirmation like: "I feel myself getting stronger, healthier every day. I will live to be a healthy, vigorous ninety-eight-year-old."

II. Life Goals

At least once each week, I hope you can take some time out to ponder the following topics:

—Give some serious thought to the most major life change you plan to make after age seventy. Will you continue to work? Will you volunteer to help people? Perhaps you will branch out completely and start something you have always wanted to do. Will your goal be to make money, to serve people, to have a very creative or helpful career? At what age do you expect to change? What do you have to do now to prepare for it?

—Draw a timeline of your life, numbering each decade. Put a short label on each decade, describing its main feature or accomplishment. Now place yourself along the line. Notice at what age you ended the line. Now extend it another twenty years, and fill in the extra decades with what you want them to hold.

—Sit down and write up exactly what you want to do to celebrate your ninety-fifth birthday. Where will you be? Who will you be with? What will be the most special thing about it? Figure out what kind of physical exercise you will enjoy most in the next twenty years, and in the twenty years after that. Make a list of something special you want to do in each five-year period for the next thirty years.

—Contemplate which friends you expect to be closest to in your eighties. Sit down with them now and share with them your thoughts and hopes about what you will be doing together.

—Discuss with your family, spouse, or lover what you are looking forward to most about living another forty years. As ideas occur to you, describe in detail what you will be doing in the year 2025.

—Think about the young people now in your life. Imagine what wisdom you will want to share with them when you are ninety.

—Spend a moment thinking about the aspects of your life that will be better, more fulfilled, or more interesting thirty years from now.

—Think about where you expect to be living in your late eighties. Is there a part of the country or of the world where you have always wanted to live? At what age do you plan to move there?

—If you see a negative image about aging, say to yourself, "That doesn't apply to me, because I am going to be a healthy ninety-year-old."

—Contemplate the most exciting project you want to have accomplished by the time you are one hundred.

—Take a moment to sit quietly and relax, and decide what age—at least ninety—you expect to live until. Get used to that age and remember it every time you hear, read, talk, or think about the future.

These are just a few ideas to inspire your own creative efforts. Your goal is to replace every one of your current negative images about what the future holds with positive, health-affirming, longevity-boosting scenarios, in which you are active, energetic, and healthy. This may seem awkward or strange at first, but it will soon become automatic. What you want to do is reshape your expectations so that you continuously desire, believe, and expect the image of yourself to come true. Your mental computer will help make sure that it does.

III. Physiological Changes

These changes are designed to give you specific, concrete images to help specific physiological systems in your body.

1. For two minutes, visualize a positive change taking place in your own skin, arteries, spine and bones, and brain.
2. Visualize that image as many times as you can each day.
3. After a week, change to another image of another part of your body.

IV. Longevity Role Models

To remind you what your future could hold, I suggest you copy out this list and post it someplace where you will see it often:

Sophocles wrote *Oedipus at Colonus* at age 92.
Frank Lloyd Wright designed award-winning buildings into his nineties.
Bob Hope, age 86, entertains and travels around the world.
George Burns, age 93, appears in films and on television.
Martha Graham, age 95, continues her work as a choreographer.
Louis Nizer, age 87, continues to win cases in his law practice in New York City.

These are the best reminders that we all can be candidates for this list in our nineties!

Remember: Your longevity program can only keep you as young as the expectations you feed into it.

Putting It All Together

> A major objective now and in the future should be to maximize health and well-being during our essentially fixed span of life.
> —Dr. Denham Harman, gerontological researcher

WE HAVE COME a long way together since we began our journey long ago on the deck of Ponce de León's ship. You now possess Youth Preservation techniques and formulas to extend the benefits of youth in many of your body's vital biological systems. You have improved your skin and appearance, your bones, muscles, blood, heart, and brain. You have reviewed the benefits of exercise and activity, learned the principles of a VLC diet plan, and gotten the tools to reprogram your mind's longevity computer. That is a lot of learning, and a lot to be proud of!

We have covered a lot of ground, so it might be useful to review the basic longevity steps, the key components in your twenty-two-point plan to better health, longer life, and increased well-being.

FOR A YOUNG OUTER YOU:
1. ASK YOUR DOCTOR ABOUT RETIN-A CREAM.
2. TAKE THE YOUTH PRESERVATION NUTRIENTS BETA-CAROTENE, VITAMIN C, and VITAMIN E.

3. KEEP OUT OF THE SUN AS MUCH AS POSSIBLE.
4. USE A WIDE-SPECTRUM, PABA-OXY-BENZONE SUNSCREEN.

TO STAY "YOUNG AT HEART" (CARDIAC LONGEVITY)

5. STOP SMOKING NOW TO REJUVENATE YOUR HEART AND LUNGS.
6. CUT SATURATED FATS TO A BARE MINIMUM IN YOUR DIET.
7. EAT FISH AS A MAIN MEAL AT LEAST TWICE WEEKLY.
8. EAT FIBER TO REDUCE FATS AND CHOLESTEROL.
9. TAKE TIME EACH DAY TO RELAX AND REDUCE STRESS.
10. DO MODERATE EXERCISE OR A BASIC DAILY ACTIVITY, SEVERAL TIMES EACH WEEK.

FOR YOUNG BONES (SKELETAL LONGEVITY)

11. USE THE DAILY BONE-BUILDING MICRONUTRIENT FORMULA.
12. INCLUDE THE NEWEST BONE BUILDER BORON IN YOUR DIET.
13. REDUCE ALCOHOL CONSUMPTION TO AVOID FLUSHING OUT MINERALS.
14. DO EXERCISES TO STRENGTHEN JOINTS AND BACK.
15. USE THE ANTI-ARTHRITIS NUTRITIONAL SUPPLEMENT PLAN.

STAYING "IMMUNE TO AGE" (IMMUNE LONGEVITY)

16. OBSERVE THE ANTICANCER EATING GUIDELINES.
17. CONSIDER INTRAVENOUS VITAMIN C TREATMENTS.
18. USE THE "ANTIVIRAL COCKTAIL" TO REDUCE VIRAL ILLNESS.

YOUNG BETWEEN THE EARS (BRAIN LONGEVITY)

19. FOLLOW THE FOOD-FOR-THOUGHT EATING GUIDELINES, INCLUDING ANTIOXIDANTS.
20. KEEP MENTALLY ACTIVE AND USE MEMORY MAGNIFIERS TO TRAIN YOUR BRAIN FOR LONG-TERM HEALTH.
21. CONSIDER GOING ON THE LONGEVITY-PROMOTING VLC DIET.
22. USE MENTAL IMAGES TO REPROGRAM YOUR INTERNAL AGING COMPUTER.

These twenty-two steps represent the most comprehensive, hopeful prescription available today for longevity. If you incorporate them diligently into your life, I am 100 percent certain that in twenty weeks, you will feel better, look better, think more clearly, and enjoy more energy and vitality. Best of all, you will have put yourself on the road to a significant longevity boost. Twenty-two steps, twenty weeks, can give you twenty months (or years!) of extra, *healthy* life.

Putting It All Together

Throughout this book, we have explored very concrete, very specific steps necessary to add years to your life. However, I don't want to leave you with the notion that your key to long and healthy life is twenty-two distinct, disjointed fragments. We are now at the point where we can put it all together—because you are, after all, more than simply the sum of your biological parts.

Keeping yourself young, beautiful, and vital longer is not a matter of checking items off a list, but of creating one healthy, unified whole.

We have examined various branches of health—immune, cardiac, skin, neurological, skeletal, and mental. It is true that each of those branches must be healthy for the whole tree to flourish. But as any gardener knows, the roots are as important as the individual branches.

In your case, the root of true, healthy longevity lies deep within your cells. All of the changes we have talked about, in one way or another, go back to that fundamental cause of aging.

At the beginning of this book, we discussed several theories of aging. The most compelling, the free-radical theory, suggests very clearly that the losses of age are due to accumulated damage to trillions of your body's cells. That accumulated damage is the real cause of aging—and the real source of potential longevity.

If you look back at the twenty-two steps outlined above, as well as reviewing many of the other counsels given throughout this book, most of them share one thing in common: *They help fight the basic aging processes in your cells.* They give your body the antioxidant nutrients it needs, and minimize your exposure to damaging fats, toxins, and ultraviolet light. They create an environment where your cells work cleanly, without interference, as Nature designed them. Taken together, they focus longevity changes where they do the most good: at the root of aging, in the innermost machinery of your cells.

It is no biological coincidence that several basic steps in your twenty-two-point plan work synergistically in several different parts of the body. Eating fiber has benefits for your heart, your blood vessels, and your bones; antioxidants help your immunity, your skin, and bones; exercise helps your heart and bones and brain; and so forth. When you bear in mind that each of these steps is aimed at having an effect at the basic level of your cells, it makes sense that they will improve many different aspects of your well-being.

It should be clear by now that there is no thirty-words-or-less formula for resetting your cells' innermost biological clock. As we have seen again and again, such a formula can never be just one simple answer, nor one magic bullet. If you could ask virtually any responsible thinker in this exciting field about what each of us can do *right now* to stay young, you would hear that it involves a combination of different interventions, programs, and practices. That advice is at the core of the twenty-two steps you have been given. These steps let you do everything possible *now* to rejuvenate and re-energize the systems that keep you young and alive—from the deepest cells of your long bones to the most hidden folds of your brain, to the outermost surfaces of your skin. Taken together, these twenty-two steps could quite possibly add twenty years to your life—years of healthy, energetic living.

Prepare Yourself for Tomorrow's Breakthroughs

There is one last thing to think about. Throughout this book, I have tried to keep you informed about the terrifically exciting news that is waiting just on the medical horizon. In the course of writing this book, several new major findings have been announced. Others, I'm sure, will have been announced by the time you read this. Such is the breakneck pace of change in the field of rejuvenation.

Does that make this book obsolete? Just the reverse. The twenty-two steps in this book will keep you in tiptop shape to benefit from new research breakthroughs. It will do you little good to pick up the morning paper on, say, March 4, 2003, and find out there is a new magic youth pill if you are already wasted from cancer, bedridden with heart disease, stooped over with arthritis and osteoporosis, addled with Alzheimer's disease, or debilitated by any of a host of other chronic and crippling maladies! The twenty-two points we've discussed are changes you can make *today* so you can keep in the youngest shape possible for what science learns *tomorrow*.

On a More Personal Note

I hope you will congratulate yourself on the changes you have made in coming this far. Give yourself credit for being smart enough to see that you *can* fight your own war against the decay of aging, and assure yourself of youthful energy and health. You already know you can make a real difference in your well-being and longevity by simply putting the knowledge you already have to work. That is the realization we started with in the first chapter, and it seems a fitting place to close this part of our adventure.

In truth, an adventure like this is never ended. Our only solid guarantee is that the Youth Revolution will continue, that discoveries will broaden, and that more and more people will wake up and start to follow the kinds of changes we have discussed. Until they do, you are in the vanguard of those making changes now to ensure dramatically more, and dramatically *better*, years of vigorous life.

My very personal thanks for coming this far on this exciting journey. Through these pages, you have joined the growing club of far-sighted visionaries who are smart enough to start putting these state-of-the-art ideas to work now. Together, we will finish the quest that our ancestors started so long ago.

I have no doubt that we will see wonderful research developments in the next five, ten, or twenty years. Best of all, you will have the satisfaction of being in the best possible shape to take advantage of them because of the changes you have already made.

I wish you luck, and I know you will not be sorry, for you now have the potential to live a better, more vigorous and healthy life than ever before.

To help you realize that potential, I want to extend you the special invitation below. I am planning to host a wonderful free party—a reunion for readers of this book—on New Year's Day in the year 2045 (that's a Sunday). So, put the date in your calendar now, stay in touch...and I expect to see you there, ready to dance.

Until then, be well, and be youthful.

Your healthy presence is cordially requested at a gala celebration of long life, strong health, and extended youth.

To be given by Dr. Stuart M. Berger, MD.

Sunday, January 1, 2045 12:00 noon Place to be announced

Appendix A

Sample Cardiac Longevity Menu

HERE IS A VERY specific five-day diet for a state-of-the-
art heart. The low levels of fat in this menu are first
steps to reducing the toll that age takes on your heart
and blood vessels. If you wish to pursue this subject in
greater detail, I refer you to my book *How to Be Your
Own Nutritionist.*

DAY 1:
Breakfast:
Low-sodium tomato juice
Whole-wheat toast with unsweetened jam
Low-fat yogurt with berries

Lunch:
Vegetarian chili topped with low-fat yogurt
Tossed green salad
Banana

Dinner:
Poached salmon
Brown rice and herbs
Salad of romaine lettuce, green peppers, tomato,
alfalfa sprouts, or: broccoli in garlic sauce
Pineapple spears and strawberries

DAY 2:

Breakfast:
Bowl unsalted, unsweetened oatmeal
Skim milk
1 sliced banana or other fruit
2 slices whole-wheat toast or bran muffin
Herbal tea

Lunch:
Carrot and celery sticks
Sardines in tomato sauce
Whole-grain crackers
Peach
Skim or low-fat milk

Dinner:
Lean veal chops
Barley pilaf
Chicory and chopped celery salad
Steamed baby carrots
Broiled grapefruit

DAY 3:

Breakfast:
Carrot juice
Whole-wheat cereal with skim milk
Blueberries

Lunch:
Low-fat cottage cheese with vegetables and kidney beans
Rice cakes
Nectarine

Dinner:
Vegetable sticks
Broiled brook trout
Parsleyed wild rice
Fresh spinach and garlic
Fresh fruit sorbet

DAY 4:

Breakfast:
Low-fat cottage cheese
Grapefruit slices
Whole-wheat bagel

Lunch:
Hearty minestrone soup
Whole-grain roll
Skim or low-fat milk
Plums

Dinner:
Pasta primavera
Salad of tomato, cucumber, red onion
Poached pear

DAY 5:

Breakfast:
Low-sodium tomato or vegetable juice
Oatmeal with cinnamon and apple
Skim or low-fat milk

Lunch:
Tuna-vegetable salad on whole-wheat toast
Lettuce and tomato
Pear

Dinner:
Broiled chicken
Baked potato with yogurt and chives
Salad of spinach, onions, carrots, mushrooms
String beans amandine
Kiwi fruit and berries
1 piece low-fat, low sodium cheese

For Dressings and Seasonings Use:

Vegetable oils	Lemon juice
Low-fat yogurt	Garlic
Low-fat cottage cheese	Onion
Vinegar	Herbs

Cardiac Longevity Foods

Foods That Preserve Your Heart	Foods That Age Your Heart
Fish high in essential oils:	
Salmon	Deep-fried fish
Mackerel	Fish in cream or butter
Tuna	sauces
Trout	
Haddock	
Cod	
Other fish:	
Sole	
Snapper	
Lean meats:	*Fatty meats:*
White-meat poultry without	Dark-meat poultry
skin	Fried chicken
Veal	Duck
Lean beef	Ham
	Pork
	Fatty beef
	Luncheon meats
	Hot dogs
	Bacon
	Spare ribs
	Lamb
	Sausage
	Liver
	Kidneys

Cardiac Longevity Foods

Foods That Preserve Your Heart	Foods That Age Your Heart

Low-fat or skim dairy products:

High-fat dairy products:

Skim milk, or 1% or low-fat milk	Cream, regular milk
	Half-and-half
Farmer cheese	Nondairy creamers
Low-fat yogurt and cottage cheese	
Low-fat low-sodium cheeses	Regular yogurt
	Regular cottage cheese
Part-skim ricotta	Hard and semisoft cheeses
Part-skim mozzarella	Ice cream, sour cream
Ice milk	Eggs
Skim-milk buttermilk	

Fruits and vegetables:

Leafy green vegetables	Canned vegetables
Fresh vegetables	Canned fruits in syrup
Fresh fruits	Coconut

Grains:

Whole grains	Processed grains
Brown rice	White rice
Whole-wheat flour	Refined flour
Kasha	
Couscous	
Millet	
Bulgur	

Beans:

Pinto	Pork and beans
Navy	
Kidney	

Cardiac Longevity Foods

Foods That Preserve Your Heart	Foods That Age Your Heart
Polyunsaturated oils:	
Safflower oil	Saturated fats
Sunflower oil	Animal fats
Corn oil	Hydrogenated fats
	Coconut oil
	Palm oil
Monosaturated oils:	*Salts:*
Peanut oil	Soy sauce
Olive oil	Mayonnaise
	Pickled foods
	Snack foods:
	Chips
	Candy
	Cake
	Pastry

Fiber Content of Common Foods

Food	Serving Size	Fiber Content (in grams)
Grains		
· Wheat bran	· ⅓ cup	· 6.5
· Oat bran	· ⅓ cup	· 4
· Popcorn	· 2 cups	· 3
Vegetables		
· Spinach	· ½ cup	· 6
· Sweet potato	· "	· 4
· Brussels sprouts	· "	· 4

Fiber Content of Common Foods

Food	Serving Size	Fiber Content (in grams)
· Corn	· ½ cup	· 4
· Baked potato (med.)	· "	· 3.5
· Turnips/ rutabagas	· " (cooked)	· 3

Legumes

· Lentils	· ½ cup uncooked	· 11
· Kidney beans	· ½ cup cooked	· 6
· Pinto beans	· "	· 5
· Split peas	· "	· 5
· White beans	· "	· 5
· Lima beans	· "	· 5
· Peas (green)	· ½ cup cooked	· 4

Fruits and Nuts

· Apricots (dried)	· ½ cup	· 15
· Prunes (stewed)	· ½ cup	· 15
· Almonds	· ½ cup	· 10
· Peanuts	· ½ cup	· 6
· Blackberries	· ½ cup	· 4.5
· Raspberries	· ½ cup	· 4.5
· Prunes	· 4	· 4

Cereals

· All-Bran (with extra fiber)	· 1 ounce	· 13
· Fiber One	· "	· 12
· 100% Bran	· "	· 9
· All-Bran	· "	· 9
· Bran Buds	· "	· 8
· Corn Bran	· "	· 6
· Bran Chex	· "	· 5
· Natural Bran Flakes	· "	· 5

Fiber Content of Common Foods

Food	Serving Size	Fiber Content (in grams)
40% Bran Flakes	1 ounce	4
Cracklin' Oat Bran	"	4
Fruit 'n' Fiber	"	4
Fruitful Bran	"	4
Shredded Wheat & Bran	"	4
Wheatena	"	4

Appendix B

Sample Supplementation Plan for VLC Diet

ON A VLC DIET, it is essential to include a strong, balanced micronutrient-supplement plan. This ensures that your reduced level of calories will not lead to a deficiency of the vital micronutrient elements you need.

Vitamins:

Vitamin A	20,000 I.U.
Beta-carotene	20,000 I.U.
Vitamin B_1 (thiamine)	100 mg
Vitamin B_2 (riboflavin)	100 mg
Vitamin B_3 (niacin)	100 mg
Vitamin B_5 (pantothenic acid)	200 mg
Vitamin B_6 (pyridoxine)	50 mg
Vitamin B_{12}	200 mcg
Folic acid	400 mcg
Choline	200 mg
Inositol	200 mg
Biotin	100 mcg
Vitamin C	2,000 mg
Vitamin D	400 I.U.
Vitamin E	200 I.U.
Bioflavinoids:	
Rutin	400 mg
Hesperidin	400 mg

Minerals:

Calcium	400 mg
Magnesium	200 mg
Iron	10 mg
Zinc	50 mg
Selenium	100 mcg

Appendix C

Sample VLC Diet Plan

HERE IS YOUR sample menu plan for twenty-one days of a prolongevity VLC regimen. This plan is exactly balanced to give you the optimal mix of nutrients you need to take advantage of the strong life–span- and health-promoting benefits of VLC eating.

Be a bit generous with your servings of vegetables and salads, but be very stingy in using oil or fat in cooking or serving. If you do both those things, this plan provides approximately 60 percent carbohydrate, 20 percent protein, 20 percent fat—and for women, 1,600 calories each day. Men following the plan should eat the same foods, except they can increase their servings of salads and carbohydrates within reason, to allow for the extra calories the male body needs.

DAY 1:
Breakfast:
2 large buckwheat pancakes, topped with berries and wheat bran
1 cup skim milk

Lunch:
Tuna salad made with:
water-packed tuna, celery, onion, low-fat yogurt on
2 slices whole-wheat bread
1 peach

231

Dinner:
Mixed salad with oil, vinegar, and herbs
1 large baked potato with low-fat yogurt and chives
3-oz chicken cutlet sautéed with peppers, tomatoes, and onion in very little oil

Snack:
4 rye crackers
Carrot sticks
Large apple

DAY 2:
Breakfast:
½ grapefruit
1 poached egg
2 slices whole-wheat toast with unsweetened preserves

Lunch:
Vegetarian chef salad made with:
½ cup kidney beans,
½ cup chick-peas, oil, vinegar, and herbs
1 cup skim milk
½ grapefruit

Dinner:
Endive salad with oil, vinegar, and herbs
1 cup herbed brown rice
1 cup broccoli
5 oz poached salmon

Snack:
4 rice cakes
1 cup low-fat yogurt with strawberries

DAY 3:
Breakfast:
1 cup cooked oatmeal
1 banana
1 cup skim milk

Lunch:
Tofu with bean sprouts, lettuce, and tomato on
2 slices whole-wheat bread
1 apple

Dinner:
Spinach salad with low-fat yogurt-based dressing
with dill
Small butternut squash
1 cup French-cut green beans
4 oz lamb chop
1 whole-wheat roll with 1 tsp butter

Snack:
2 whole-wheat matzohs
A few almonds
1 orange

DAY 4:
Breakfast:
Canteloupe wedge
Whole-wheat bagel with
1 oz melted low-fat cheese

Lunch:
Taco shell, stuffed with lettuce and tomato
½ cup beans
½ cup grapes

Dinner:
Mixed salad with oil, vinegar, and herbs
1 cup mashed potatoes
1 cup baby carrots
5 oz broiled sole

Snack:
4 Wasa crackers
½ cup low-fat cottage cheese
1 tangerine

DAY 5:

Breakfast:
1 cup puffed rice with blueberries
1 cup skim milk

Lunch:
1½ cups minestrone soup
1 slice whole-wheat toast with
1 oz melted low-fat cheese
1 apple

Dinner:
Arugula salad with oil, vinegar, and herbs
1 large sweet potato with 1 tsp butter
1 cup Brussels sprouts
4 oz sliced baked turkey breast

Snack:
2 rice cakes with
2 tbs natural peanut butter
1 banana

DAY 6:

Breakfast:
1 large bran muffin
½ cup low-fat cottage cheese
10 orange slices

Lunch:
Tomato stuffed with chicken salad
1 whole-wheat bagel
Mixed fruit with low-fat yogurt

Dinner:
Spinach salad with oil, vinegar, and herbs
1 acorn squash
1 cup cauliflower
5 oz broiled brook trout
1 whole-wheat roll

Snack:
2 cups air-popped corn
1 pear

DAY 7:
Breakfast:
1 cup bran flakes
1 banana
1 cup skim milk

Lunch:
1 cup black-bean soup
1 oz low-fat cheese
2 slices 7-grain bread
1 tsp butter

Dinner:
Arugula salad with oil, vinegar, and herbs
1 cup rice
5 oz lean steak, with peppers, onions, tomatoes
1 whole-wheat roll

Snack:
Carrot sticks
A few cashews
1 small papaya

DAY 8:
Breakfast:
1 cup cooked Wheatena
3–4 dried apricots
1 cup skim milk

Lunch:
Cucumber salad with low-fat yogurt and chives
2 pieces whole-wheat pita bread with
Hummus
Sprouts

Dinner:
Mixed green salad with oil, vinegar, and herbs
1 cup minestrone soup
Escarole
2 cups whole-wheat pasta and
Red clam sauce

Snack:
A few hazelnuts
1 banana

DAY 9:

Breakfast:
Citrus salad
1 soft-boiled egg
2 slices whole-wheat toast with
1 tsp butter

Lunch:
1½ cups whole-wheat pasta salad with vegetables
1 cup cabbage slaw
2 rye crackers

Dinner:
Endive salad with oil, vinegar, and herbs
1 cup boiled new potatoes with 1 tsp butter and herbs
1 cup cooked spinach
4 oz grilled salmon

Snack:
4 rice cakes
2 oz low-fat cheese
3 dried figs

DAY 10:

Breakfast:
1 cup puffed corn with blueberries
1 cup skim milk

Lunch:
½ grapefruit
½ cup low-fat cottage cheese with chopped
vegetables
1 whole-wheat biscuit

Dinner:
Chinese vegetable soup
1½ cups rice
5 oz chicken cutlet, stir-fried with
Chinese vegetables

Snack:
2 whole-wheat matzohs
A few almonds
1 mango

DAY 11:
 Breakfast:
 1 large oat-bran muffin with unsweetened preserves
 1 cup skim milk
 1 apple

 Lunch:
 1½ cups 3-bean salad on
 Bed of lettuce
 1 cup chilled steamed broccoli
 2 rice cakes

 Dinner:
 Spinach salad with
 Low-fat yogurt-based dressing with dry mustard
 1 cup whole-wheat pasta marinara
 1 cup green beans
 5 oz veal cutlet with mushroom wine sauce

 Snack:
 1 cup low-fat yogurt with
 Mixed fruit topped with
 Wheat germ

DAY 12:

Breakfast:
1 cup shredded wheat
1 banana
1 cup skim milk

Lunch:
2 slices 7-grain bread with
1 oz melted low-fat cheese
Lettuce and tomato

Dinner:
Arugula salad with oil, vinegar, and herbs
1 cup herbed barley and peapods
5 oz broiled mackerel

Snack:
4 Wasa crackers
Small amount of nut butter
1 apple

DAY 13:

Breakfast:
1 cup cream of rye with
1 tsp butter
½ cup low-fat cottage cheese with herbs
1 orange

Lunch:
Tuna salad in whole-wheat
Pita with chopped vegetables

Dinner:
Mixed green salad with oil, vinegar, and herbs
1 cup lentil soup
1½ cups whole-wheat pasta primavera
2 pieces whole-wheat Italian bread

Snack:
½ cup low-fat cottage cheese with
Mixed citrus fruit
A few cashews

DAY 14:
 Breakfast:
 2 whole-wheat waffles topped with
 Low-fat yogurt and strawberries

 Lunch:
 Mixed green salad with oil, vinegar, and herbs
 1 cup tabouli salad with a few pine nuts
 1 apple

 Dinner:
 Endive salad with oil, vinegar, and herbs
 1 cup zucchini and tomato
 9 shrimp sautéed in olive oil and garlic over 1 cup
 rice

 Snack:
 4 rice cakes
 1 oz low-fat cottage cheese
 1 orange

DAY 15:
 Breakfast:
 1 cup puffed wheat
 1 peach
 1 cup skim milk

 Lunch:
 Spinach salad with oil, vinegar, and herbs
 1 cup rice with chopped vegetables
 1 pear

 Dinner:
 Mixed salad with oil, vinegar, and herbs
 1 large baked potato
 1 cup wax beans
 5 oz liver and onions

Snack:
1 cup low-fat yogurt with
Dried fruit and wheat bran
1 slice whole-wheat bread with small amount of nut
butter
Unsweetened preserves

DAY 16:
Breakfast:
1 melon wedge
1 egg yolk, 2 egg whites, as omelet or scrambled
2 whole-wheat biscuits with
1 tsp butter

Lunch:
1½ cups minestrone soup
2 pieces 7-grain bread with
1 oz melted low-fat cheese

Dinner:
Spinach salad with
Low-fat yogurt-based dressing with dry mustard
1 cup Italian green beans
2 cups whole-wheat pasta with mussels marinara

Snack:
2 Wasa crackers
Small amount of nut butter
1 banana

DAY 17:
Breakfast:
1 cup Nutri-Grain
1 banana
1 cup skim milk

Lunch:
1½ cups vegetarian chili
1 oz low-fat cheese

Dinner:
Arugula salad with oil, vinegar, and herbs
1 cup buckwheat pilaf and corn
1 cup Brussels sprouts
5 oz red snapper

Snack:
2 cups air-popped corn
Celery sticks
A few cashews
3 dried figs

DAY 18:
Breakfast:
1 cup cooked oat bran
1 apple
1 cup skim milk

Lunch:
1½ cups rice and beans with
Chopped vegetables

Dinner:
Mixed green salad with oil, vinegar, and herbs
1 large sweet potato
1 cup cauliflower
5 oz sliced baked turkey breast
Fresh cranberry sauce

Snack:
4 rice cakes
1 oz low-fat cheese
A few hazelnuts
1 pear

DAY 19:
Breakfast:
1 large corn muffin
1 oz low-fat cheese
1 pear

Lunch:
4 oz sardines in water or tomato sauce
2 slices whole-wheat bread
Lettuce and tomato
1 orange

Dinner:
Endive salad with oil, vinegar, and herbs
1 cup broccoli
2 cups vegetable lasagna with low-fat ricotta
1 piece whole-wheat Italian bread

Snack:
½ cup unsweetened granola with
Dates and nuts

DAY 20:
Breakfast:
1 cup puffed millet
1 nectarine
1 cup skim milk

Lunch:
Mixed salad with oil, vinegar, and herbs
1½ cups whole-wheat pasta salad with vegetables
and
Grated low-fat cheese

Dinner:
Arugula salad with oil, vinegar, and herbs
1 cup rice and herbs
1 zucchini, steamed
5 oz broiled lobster tail

Snack:
4 rye crackers
Small amount of nut butter
1 apple

DAY 21:
　Breakfast:
　1 cup cream of rice
　3 prunes
　1 cup skim milk

　Lunch:
　Large spinach salad with lemon and herbs
　1 hard-boiled egg
　2 slices whole-wheat bread
　1 apple

　Dinner:
　Vegetable soup
　1½ cups oven-baked french fries
　3 oz lean hamburger
　Whole-wheat roll
　Lettuce and tomato

　Snack:
　3 rice cakes
　1 cup low-fat yogurt
　Mixed fruit

Index